OBSESSION
An American Love Story

Also by the author
The Garden

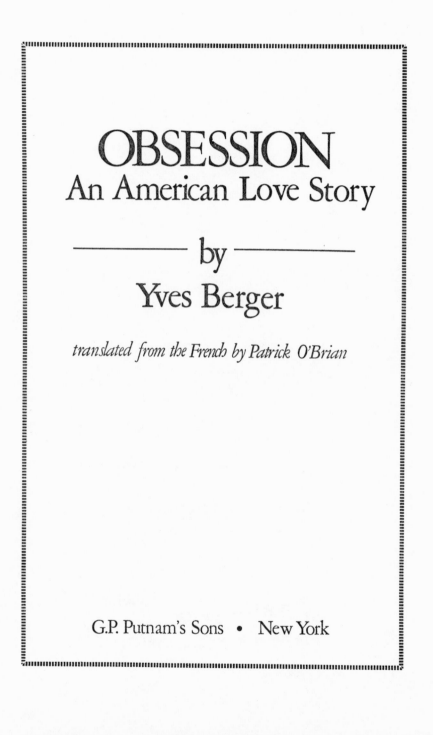

OBSESSION
An American Love Story

———— by ————

Yves Berger

translated from the French by Patrick O'Brian

G.P. Putnam's Sons • New York

First American Edition 1978 Grasset & Fasquelle
French edition copyright © 1976 by Editions

English translation copyright © 1978 by G. P. Putnam's Sons
All rights reserved. This book, or parts thereof, may not be reproduced in any
form without permission.

Published simultaneously in Canada by Longman Canada Limited, Toronto
SBN: 399-12049-1

Library of Congress Cataloging in Publication Data

Berger, Yves.
Obsession.

Translation of Le fou d'Amérique.
I. Title.
PZ4.B4972Ob   1978   [PQ2662.E67]   843'.9'14
77-21666

PRINTED IN THE UNITED STATES OF AMERICA
The author expresses his thanks
to Lilian Allard for her assistance
in the preparation of this American Edition.

Pour Marthe,
de Rivière du Loup

The Indians possess the secret, not of metaphysics, but of a more intense vitality in which one longs to be cast away.

—ELÉMIR ZOLLA

When I grow up, I want to be an Indian.

—CHILDREN

In 1945 I was just turning ten and there was nothing to show that I was different from other children, nothing to make anyone suppose that I would live a life far out of the ordinary run, when all at once I was seized with the malady of love. Love at ten years of age! At first they hardly believed it. But then they had to acknowledge that they were wrong: mine was a genuine, thoroughgoing passion, and from that moment on nothing else counted for me at all. Such very early ripeness could not but cause anxiety, and the anxiety was certainly there. "Come now, go out-of-doors," they said when I hid myself away, sitting alone in a corner to brood over my passion, gazing at pictures of my beloved. I did not hear. I no longer heard anything. It was only later that I knew what they were saying about me.

And what they were saying did not always make a great deal of sense. . . . Some of them, neighbors or people who just happened to be at hand, thought the fact that I had stopped behaving like a child made the fury of my passion the more comprehensible. But they did not yet know that what they looked

7

upon as some kind of a symptom was in reality the clean break itself: from one day to the next I had done with games, done with the road—we lived by the side of a road—done with company, done with friends, and in their place there was this need for being alone. It was like an uneasiness of my whole being, an inaptitude for life, with fits of anger and suddenly changing moods and an urgent reaching out for something else, for another reality, another geography; whereas I suppose that a child happy in the lovingly restricted world formed for him by his family, his town, his village . . .

To go back to what people were saying. The description was sound, the analysis false: as a child I broke with childhood *because* I fell in love, and that was the direct opposite of a love brought into being by the rejection of childhood. But let us leave that to one side. As other, more farseeing speakers saw it, there was France, and until very recently there had been the German occupation: so was it not on the verge of possibility, was it not almost comprehensible that a rather odd boy there in that same France who was, as it were, *undergoing* his country should fall in love with a stranger? For it was indeed with a stranger that I had fallen in love. And to be sure I had always felt that France was a little country, one in which, like a fly trapped in a single room, I banged against the walls of the Alps and the Pyrenees. Later I shall speak of my taking off from these shores of ours and my flight beyond the seas. And I left that small, closed-in France, a France shut out from all the wilder flights of the imagination, deprived of exotic delights and poor in charm—I left all the more easily because at the time of which I am speaking the helpless France I knew was enduring an army of occupation, looking abroad for aid just as I was looking abroad for love. If by some strange chance the German foreignness had attracted me, even that would have grown thin in my commonplace, everyday France; but in fact I experienced the presence of the enemy with fear and disgust— he was a phony stranger, because as I saw it there could only be one: my own. And so, early in life and exulting in my discovery, I found that my passion contained something that passions usually lack: wholesomeness, principles, and an ethic; and it kept me from finding glamour in strength and righteousness in death.

Now here again (as though I could not do without them) I come back to my family, friends, connections, acquaintances, to all those who either sincerely or just idly pitied me for having come so young to the knowledge of a loving heart and its wild ups and downs. The worthy souls . . . If only they had known . . . For a long while I could never talk about my childhood. If I even tried to tell brief snatches of it my voice would die in my throat. Then one day there was no difficulty anymore. And when I discovered that, I knew I had grown up.

My father was a self-employed haulage contractor. He had a truck, and when a customer gave him an order, he would set out on the road. At the outbreak of the war in 1939 the French army requisitioned it, paying no more than a trifle and being in no sort of a hurry over producing that, either. He bought another secondhand one that needed little gasoline; this made sense, because the government issued fuel tickets to the owners, and once they were used up there was no question of filling the tank; and that meant that his work was strictly limited. Then in 1944 the German army, like the French five years before, seized the truck. My father, deprived of his means of livelihood and thus of the power of feeding his family, was given top priority, and when the Liberation came he received the first truck to come out of the Panhard works. But as fate would have it, the Panhard workers had not been able to gauge the moment of liberation to within one truck, nor could they tell who their customer was to be, so what they gave my father was a machine that with the clearest possible conscience they had meant for the Germans—a means of weakening the enemy. I suppose that for the works it must have been a kind of a joke of a truck and one that they soon replaced; for us it was a catastrophic vehicle and one that we had to put up with to the very edge of disaster. I could swear that, in the art of sabotage, willful blunders, and

9

the use of misbegotten metals, the Panhard workers had
reached an unparalleled degree of skill, because the thing that
fell to us turned out to be a real masterpiece of its kind, and we
never had the slightest doubt that if there had been a competi-
tion for the most horrible truck ours would have won hands
down. My father never set out for Paris, Lyons, or Nice with a
load of groceries, early vegetables, citrus fruits, or cement
without coming back or rather not coming back, while the
truck stood in a garage by the side of the road either on the way
out or on the way back, with him sitting in a nearby hotel, furious and anxious as you may well imagine, and waiting for the
mechanic to tell him what was wrong and how long it would
take to make repairs. To say nothing of the most important
point: what it would cost. And every time, every trip, there was
some breakdown: a part broken or ground away or pitted or
worn out before its time, a leak here or a gumming up there;
and for years and years I retained a humiliating memory of the
time a garage near home discovered that our water tank was
made of common sheet iron, whereas all other trucks had theirs
of good sound steel, a revelation that made me blush even
when I was alone. The vile brute of a truck.

Between journeys, between bouts with mechanics, the telephone rarely rang; it never rang often enough, and Dad went
through long stretches when he had no work, since it appeared
that nobody needed a truck driver or his truck. And when he
was on the road, traveling or waiting until he could travel, if
the telephone rang there was every dismal likelihood that the
caller would be himself, phoning from somewhere in the
neighborhood of Vesoul or Saint-Galmier to roar out the news
of some fresh disaster and to say he could not tell how long he
would be away, since the mechanic had not yet given his ver-
dict. I spent my childhood—the earliest part, those which are
called one's tender years—with a naturally irascible father rendered uncontrollably furious by the unhappy course of events,
and a pathetic mother whom nothing had prepared for this obstinately repeated poverty and wretchedness: a mother a little

more bent every day, a little more resigned; and when all hope vanished and when she was living between despair at the telephone's not ringing and dread when she heard its bell, all she looked forward to was some miracle or the death that came so soon. And now for the last time I should like to speak of my mother: to tell of the way she followed my father, suspecting what he was about, going after him along the road, dodging behind every tree; for he had set out secretly in the dark of the night with rage in his heart, and he meant to fling stones at the windows of the Panhard works in the town. Day after day I saw sadness, dejection, quarrels, shouting, and cold anger, all of them great black birds for a child, come and make their nests in our home; and I saw bitterness, continually dripping, seeping into our memories and forestalling our hopes. So I ask you, good people, whether you do not feel that all this was enough to throw me toward her, she being a stranger and my beloved, enough to carry me, bear me away to that place where she was, away out of the tragedy, out of France, and perhaps out of time?

I cannot, indeed I cannot, tear myself away from that childhood; but fortunately it was also the childhood of the love that grew up with me, and the wonder that I am just going to tell about certainly had its birth in the sequence of my days. My days. My life. Here I am, coming up against those days once more, I who should so like to tell you, my beloved, that I was happy when I was young, a happy child, happiness itself; for if that had been so I should have loved you for yourself alone, for what you are—I should have loved with a pure, springing impulse, with a kind of gratitude, yes, with a total understanding of you, a grateful understanding. How I'd like to tell you that no wound, no frustration, no longing to get my own back, no griping hunger had anything to do with this love. . . . But I should be lying, shouldn't I? I loved you because I needed you. Because without seeming to do so, without touching them, you breathed gently on my wounds. Because you let me come to you, to you, so lavish with the loveliest of images. And

11

then surely the heart of the matter was that you had scarcely any notion of me, or even none at all. . . . It was enough for me to imagine you. I never asked you to love me; all I asked was that you should let yourself be loved. Without saying anything. Not without doing anything, to be sure. Only too often your doings are what my friends hold against you. On occasion you can be mean and cowardly. Murderous and unfeeling. Like them I am far from approving of everything you do. But this is not the time for blame. It is the time for loving, and now you see I'm going to love you; I'm going to say that I love you and why.

We are agreed that I'm having nothing to do with lies of any kind. From now on let's leave childhood, the German occupation, and trucks right out of this . . . if we come across them again let it be without their being named. Here we are, both of us, and it's not by mere chance that I fell in love with you: you are rich—the richest in the world?—and your wealth counted all right. We don't have to blush about it and we don't have to let it crush me, either. Fabulously rich. And I love you for that: I love you for being the first, for having more than anyone else, more gold, more silver, more grain, more minerals, everything that slakes thirst and satisfies hunger, everything that comforts and reassures in this very obviously rotten, bankrupt world; you are everything that I did not have and that I suffered from not having—suffered for years and years, beloved, until I reached manhood. I went too long without bread not to rave about your wheat, you see, too long without money not to dream about the maze of your banks, places made to your measure, for worshipping you. Oh, my golden woman of dollar bills! I admit there are times when I should like not to be what I am but another man, when I should like to base my self-esteem upon destitution. (Yet if that were the case, should I love you?) Sometimes a great wave takes me, a wave whose foam is made of tears, and between weariness and regret I should like to find that I was made for poverty, for total indigence; but then the wave that carried me away brings me back

12

to the surface of things, back to head height, within reach of pictures and images, here in the world of reality; and I clearly perceive that I do not possess the strength for that choice, a choice that did not choose me. Let's go on.

No, don't let's go on. After all, it would be unbearable if in fact your wealth had triggered off my love and I did not say so.

"You did say it."

I did say it. Now I unsay it. Let's try to get a clear view of this. Don't forget that when I began to love my stranger I was ten years old. And at that age, I ask you, what did I really know about gold or silver or power? Nothing. That's the gospel truth: I loved you because I longed for you, with a love that came from my depths; then later, much later, another feeling appeared in the current of the first, and it is that feeling which speaks when I say I love your wealth. And what it means, don't you see, is wealth itself, with all its colors and its solid weight—an artless picture of gold ingots, gold coins, gold dust, heaps of gold rising to the sky, the music of tumbling gold? Then again, I do find it hard to look away from the dazzling vision of power. But my mind remains clear enough to distinguish between good power and bad. As I said before, the statement of my beloved's serious defects will come later. Here I just want to mention her pride—no, more than that, her arrogance. Her way of reducing her neighbors to silence. Sometimes. Often. The way she threatens. The way she thunders. When she does that she reaches her full size. Her full height— that's the word I was looking for. For my stranger-love is tall. I knew that when she inspired me with this passion I am trying to describe. Yet I had never seen her. She was doubly a stranger: I mean I had never seen her in the flesh. Only in photographs.

Or rather in pictures. From the moment her thunderbolt struck me I carried out my retreat from the world by means of books. Did I turn to them in the first place without any preconceived ideas and then fall in love as my reading showed her to me, or did I read because I already loved her? There is no telling. Not that she was in all of them: far from it. Indeed, during the war and after it, when the fighting had stopped, I must say that books which spoke about her were hard to find. I had to look through the old ones and reread the passages that described her, told about her, praised her, those that went minutely into your beauty, my beloved, celebrating your wealth, your liberality, your splendid strength. . . . At one time I was obliged to feed my love on a steady diet of the same texts and illustrations, going over them again and again. I remember the time I opened the first book that spoke about her, the very first book that she was in. A child's book, of course. Straightaway I was afflicted with the extreme tension of love—can I call it an actual lover's tension when in fact I waited for so long before pressing, crushing, and possessing her? No. All I underwent was the tension of a lonely, loving creature, all the more lonely since the war and then the long armistice made a journey impossible—a journey that I could not have carried out in any case, for want of money. So I fed my flame with books alone, and for me the books blazed high. I explored the bookshops in the town to find them and I bought or stole them and for me every single one that spoke her name turned into a work about my beloved. My golden girl! My book-borne bride! The piles of books, hardback, paperback, new or dog-eared and battered, brought disorder into my neat, plain room, and those who beheld my love might judge its strength by the vast body of information about my beloved that I tirelessly amassed. "One day I shall know her," I used to say, quite calmly, though with Germans walking about in our streets this meeting seemed the most remote of contingencies or, to put it bluntly, a childish dream. Yet they did not harass me with disapproval: no doubt my people, convinced that I was crazy, found comfort in the thought that a passion that filters through books—even if it meant hundreds and hundreds of books rising in pyramids—was less disturbing than one that, in a boy of ten, would insist upon a flesh-and-blood woman. . . .

Then I grew up. And the older I became the more I was in

14

love. It was as though I had never found her—as though I had
to seek her everywhere. Where? Still in books. Only less and
less in children's books. Soon not at all. At this stage the idea of
the journey did not yet possess my mind to any great degree,
but I was more and more certain that presently I should go and
see her. It was enough that she should wait for me, and I had
no doubt that as far as I was concerned she would never
change. I never feared for her during the war: I knew she was
so rich, so strong . . . And as the world in general knows she
came out of it all right. I often used to tell myself that when I
did see her, I should know her very well. It would happen like
this: I should go to her; I should be in her, and I should talk to
her. About herself. She would be absolutely astonished by my
knowledge. And then she would give herself to me with such
an eager, glowing spring that I should die of it. She would never disappoint me. I should tell her of her defects at length. I
should offer to put them right for her—help her to put herself
right, I mean. "With me, you'll be faultless," I'd tell her with
all the arrogance of passion. She would always be the woman
of the very first book, of that child's album in which I first saw
my woman as an adult.

Then I grew still more. I became the owner of more and
more books and from them I learned to know her even better.
At moments it seemed to me that I was aging in words as others
age in time, growing from childhood to manhood through
books, volume after volume, and naturally through books that
became harder and harder. I did not presume to write to her.
Nor about her. When the Jesuit missionaries set off for their
Canadian adventure, they had the notion of entrusting certain
young men to the care of Indian chiefs, and these young men,
spending some years among the tribes, would learn their language: for inability to speak it would make preaching ineffec-
tual. *Truchements:* that is what these interpreters-to-be were
called. Soon I had *truchements* of my own—GIs whom I met in
the south of France after they had landed and when they were
moving northward up through Avignon. I made friends with

some of them. I knew a little of their language. They improved my knowledge for me. When I met her, she and I would understand each other perfectly, thanks to them.

The first GIs moved on and others took their place. They came in waves of ten or twenty and I got to know the best, the pleasantest, and probably those who in their own way were most in love with her, and I said to them, "Tell me about her." And they told me about her various beauties, her surprises, her violence, and her tenderness; and almost all of them were homesick for that tenderness. At times, particularly among the older men, I sensed a regret. I listened as they told me a thousand tidings, all of which I knew very well, having read them over and over again; and every time it was as though I had never heard them at all.

Then the inexhaustible movies broke out, bursting among us, and I dreamed of a supernatural ear that would record all the vast proliferation that the hissing, whispering reels poured out, and two or even three times a day and every day when I could, I went to see her in her different phases—the stars, the Westerns. Bouts of fever stirred the surface of my waiting mind and with a prickling skin I built up the plan of setting off without delay. Some half-wits will suppose that the reason I let both the fever and the plan die away was that I was afraid of being disappointed—that I anticipated disappointment. That fear never occurred to me at all.

Then once more I grew, and for the last time. I became a man. And with my age increasing I remained the same in relation to her. I was unfaithful to her in a way. But what would it have amounted to, not being faithful to her? In monologues, in voluptuous pleasures of heart and mind, in great spreading joy just before night's sleeping point, in wild raptures and ecstasies, no one has ever given me what she gave me so lavishly, nor what she allowed. No, I was not unfaithful to her. Besides, she did not hold it against me. I should have felt guilty if she had been hurt, but both for ordinary and for extraordinary occasions all I had to do was to open a book to find her once

again, the same as she had always been with me in books—
lovely, available, endlessly talking about herself or listening to
endless talk describing her; and she would display wholly
unexpected attitudes, those infinitely rare postures and aspects
that bring people running by tens and hundreds of thousands
to see her, gazing, peering, contemplating, wondering, and, as
I know from my own wild, outrageous passion, loving her.

Oh, America . . . I was a child who had lost all patience
with Europe, with Africa, with Asia, and since I am saying everything, with Oceania too. And then a youth, and then a man.
Hemmed in, confined, away from you. The countries of the
world, those outgrown shirts, were too tight over my shoulders; they pinched my elbows. So I looked for you in newspa-
pers and in atlases. I heard and I interpreted that thunderous
roar, the roar as of a waterfall, that you perpetually feed—a roar
whose echo sometimes booms louder and deeper than the
sound which gave it birth.

There were some who tried to put me off, saying that it was
too late and that I had waited too long, that there was nothing
to be said about her anymore, nothing to be written, and that
into the bargain she had turned whore, frantically giving herself to the first comer: or, very knowing, they imagined they
had caught the spirit of the present age and that they detected a
fundamental lack of any moral sense whatsoever in my beloved. But nothing could shake my resolution. I cherished no
illusions about her profligacy abed, in which I had sometimes
recognized her particular approach, which is magnificent. And
I should like to know why, for the sake of what principle, she
ought to have resisted her often brilliant suitors when they
came begging for the boon of inspiration? I have read some
thousands of letters that people from every corner of the world
have meant for her. Here I shall mention only one, a letter from
Sergio Leone, and of that letter no more than two sentences,
which very rightly say: "We Europeans grew up in a fabulous
mythology. For people like me, America was a positive religion."

17

Oh, America . . . In the maps I saw you as a woman—vast
areas of midriff and belly, the hollows of your deep valleys and
streams, the folds that are the dimples in your skin, and toward
the northern basin the legs of your rivers with the playful wind
moving upstream like the five fingers of a hand, the rounds of
your breasts and then at the end of your body, quite unexpected and incongruous, the little tail of Florida, put there maybe
to remind us that the division between the sexes is ambiguous.
For, do you see, I should have loved you if you had been a boy
instead of a woman, just as I love you now.

As I grew up I embarked upon my education. I married. I became a physician. Solange and I married, and between us we
had two children. Then one day when I was just thirty a certain
letter reached me in provincial Allier, where I was practicing: I
was invited to take part in a medical congress in America, in
her country, far over there. Solange was pleased for my sake
and I was only to be gone three weeks.

Sometimes in my dreams I cannot seize the Arkansas where
it falls into the Mississippi; cannot seize it either with my
hands or my birchbark canoe, and this nightmare comes to me
straight from Father Marquette and Joliet: they were the first to
have sailed so far and for so long on the great river, and that
was the point where they brought their downriver exploration
to an end. And sometimes I am going ahead of Tecumseh, traveling from wigwam to wigwam to help him assemble his army,
the Indian's last chance; and as I do so I am hurried and feverish and presently the anxiety robs me of my dream. In this way
my evening, late night or morning or afternoon reading and
what I have learned prints itself on me as on a plate and it
makes its way into my sleep, and when I wake up I am bitter at
being unable to choose my life, my time, my country. . . . Yet
dreaming keeps me balanced and my lives are manifold, often
running parallel with that America which the French once
called *l'Amerique septentrionale.* By day I recharge my picture
batteries and by night, when I am asleep, something that I

clumsily, gropingly call regret for passing time depletes my energy.

And the machine spins on. That first night in New York I could not sleep at all. The hostesses who looked after our group had warned us and everybody had provided himself with sleeping pills, but I did not take mine. As I discovered later, New York is an easy city, one that you should accost without mythology. But for God's sake! Me above all! With my head full of mythology—with mythology that kept battling away when all I wanted to do was to go out, plunge into the streets and walk and listen and feel and then die at first dawn in one last wave of sounds, lights, colors, smells—like an orgy. My dogged, obstinate mind kept saying, "Where? Go where? Start where? And what if you waste your time?"

My mind kept on at me for a solid hour in that hotel room on the forty-second floor where the silence was so deep that I might have forgotten the world below if it had not reminded me of its existence by police-car or fire-engine sirens—perhaps the first thing you notice in New York. They shatter the silence or rip it apart, slashing it with lightning strokes and straining, tautening your nerves. It was between two such shrieks that an idea made its appearance, one that was immediately agreed to by both the parties concerned, my mind and I—Brooklyn.

Perfectly simple. According to my mind, which knew everything about North America, Brooklyn had once been an Indian trail. Myself: "What, an avenue laid out to follow all the meanderings of a trail like one in Fenimore Cooper?" My mind: "Yes, yes," and it went on to list the towns in the United States that the pioneers had built on the lines of an Indian trail.

Now that the two parts of my being had been brought together again, I looked at a map to find the way and then set off in the direction of Brooklyn. It was two in the morning: that is to say seven o'clock in waking Europe. In France at this time my dreaming mechanism would have shut down; it would have been resting from its nighttime discharge. Now it was upset; it was being asked to work in abnormal conditions, and by

19

fits and starts it produced images and memories and a whole mass of information. But all this must have tired, worried, and no doubt angered the machine. It wore me out. Wiser, more stolid beings will say that there was no need to pace about Brooklyn to know that there was nothing left of that Indian trail of four hundred years ago: as far as the trail or its remains were concerned, all I had was the mere words that evoked it, words that someone had uttered in the distant past and that had been repeated after him so that my feverish mind should see visions. My mind was exhausted with fatigue; it was wandering; and when my watch told me it was five in the morning, I summoned the strength to hail a taxi, which took us back, dead tired.

The people who had organized the congress were anxious that we should recover, so they allowed us a little time off; the serious matters, with meetings, speeches, seminars, talks, and lectures, were to start only after our first full day in New York. Concealed behind a column in the vast hotel lobby I let the herd of my colleagues pass by, and I pondered. It seemed to me that if I decided to spend the daytime in a museum—the Museum of the American Indian, of course—it would mean surrendering myself heart and soul to my mind, if I may so put it. I swore I should make better use of these daylight hours than I had of those of the night. Thumbing through a leaflet I found that there was a tour of Manhattan by boat. Taking this, I thought, would amount to a perfectly fair compromise between my mind and me. On the one hand Peter Minuit and his Dutchmen had bought Manhattan from the Indians—at this my mind, quite charmed, instantly gave the details: from the Delawares in 1622 in exchange for a bale of red cloth, some glass beads, brass buttons, and fishhooks, to a total value of sixty guilders or twenty-four dollars. . . . Besides, I was joyously anticipating seeing from the water the skyscrapers resting on Manhattan's base of solid rock, quite exposed to view from the cruise boat, according to the brochure. So I set off for the Circle Line.

The Circle Line is a company that possesses, among other things, the monopoly of tours of the island. Speaking of a boat trip around Manhattan amounts to speaking of the Circle Line, and the two expressions are so wholly synonymous that either of them, addressed to a cabdriver, will bring the traveler to the same place, a pier that is also a number: 83.

I went aboard one of those substantial affairs with an upper deck, a saloon deck, and a hold which the Parisians call a *bateau-mouche* and the magniloquent New Yorkers a cruise yacht. Although I had come early, there were already a great many people on the boat, including some Frenchmen just ahead of me. I took care not to speak to them, trying out that blank look of a foreigner who hears but who does not understand a word, even if he is being insulted; but no doubt my inward remark about the number of people waiting had reached them through some inexplicable contact, for scarcely had I uttered the words to myself than one of them said aloud, "What a crowd." Following them, I reached the upper deck, which was strewn with chairs, and here I installed myself, waiting until the powerful, rumbling vessel should move away from the dock.

I had provided myself with a booklet to follow the trip: very precise people might also have used it in the event of disagreement, to decide which was right, the text or the record—a record played on board gives an account of the trip. Just as I was sitting down, my seat was literally wrenched from under me by a short, fat, camera-carrying Japanese; and as though I did not exist he squatted against the chair back and began photographing the shore. Although I could not see it, there must have been something amusing about him, because the moment I looked angrily away from the squat lump at my feet, my eye fell on another Japanese, tall and thin this time, in the act of photographing his photographing countryman: one half of his face

21

showed as a shut eye while the other was hidden behind the black wart of the camera, and I could sense that he was pressing the button, click-click. . . .

We were moving off. And at once nothing mattered anymore except the roar of the engines below, down by the waterline. For the first time since I had arrived the night before, I said to myself, "You're making a journey." I uttered the wonderful word journey, and there it was, the journey was present, existing in the very opposite of silence or music, in the midst of this chattering species of being that could not, I thought, contain more than one individual who was really interested in seeing and discovering and applauding Manhattan—you only had to look at those Saturday children and, through them, at their parents to perceive that they had just come to find something different, to pass the time, to be bored differently and to bore others in a fresh, unexpected manner, and I was deep in these glum reflections when suddenly, as though they had rehearsed it, they were all standing, one eye fixed and the other clamped to their clicking, whirring cameras, and I too had to get up to see the sight the others were not seeing but which they would display, the sight of the receding shore.

As soon as the moorings were cast off the record began: without a scratch, without a jerk, it too set out on a long journey— two and a half hours of monologue and who can tell which was to blame, the wind that had got up or the noise emanating from the three hundred people crowding the boat from stem to stern and trying to drown the record's voice; though perhaps it was the fault of the children, who were already making a din, or of the inadequate loudspeakers, but in any case within a minute of the first words, which were mere noises, I knew that throughout the whole trip I should hear nothing but that raucous voice, a graveyard of stillborn, bumbling syllables, grinding away on deck much as the engines throbbed and rumbled down below. Shortly before we left, some passengers had gone down to the saloon and come up again with bars and wafers of chocolate, bags of popcorn and bottles of soda pop, and everywhere there were young people, gathered in bands of six or eight, talking and drinking beer, already indifferent, obviously indifferent, to the sights that were beginning to glide by.

I have acquaintances—not that they admit it, because they would feel guilty, but I have maneuvered the conversation so as to get a clear idea of their malady—who are incapable of looking up. And if you do not look up, then New York is just a town like any other. You have to learn to raise your eyes, because the spectacle is in the heavens; and the way of finding out whether you have really seen New York is to calculate the number of pedestrians you bumped into or only just avoided as you walked about the city. This occurred to me as I was watching the procession of masses, shapes, cubes, and spires which here form giants of an unknown, unseen species, as well as dwarfs that are dwarfs only because of their neighbors' magnitude; and quite as much as I wondered at the giants, I also wondered at those squat, thickset compositions beside them far over there on the dry land, in a distance that lessened as the boat moved farther from the shore; for they seemed to have been struck by some morbid arrest of growth. The people had sat down again with a great shuffling of chairs that drowned both the flagging record and the gasping engines, and I was able to see the last fringes of the land, the part I like least, because the land thrusts quays, jetties, piers out into the sea like so many everlasting, greedy, grubby fingers; and leaning over the rail I let my eyes follow the cruel passage of the tugs until I was dizzy. Their wake churned up the white frothing blood of a wound, and scarcely had the wound closed in the calmer water than it was ripped open again by the cutwater of yet another tug. There were tugs by the dozen, ahead of us, astern, and on either side. After a while I became aware of a tension, of an expectancy among the crowd: even the Japanese upon their chairs and the engines in their housing were quiet, and then as we moved into a mist, a mist torn apart by the ship, they loomed up, the two long-awaited monsters, still far away but less so every minute, the two towers that even these unknowledgeable creatures knew to be the tallest buildings in the world. And all at once it came to me that I had misjudged the crowd; for they had come with some purpose, they had come for these twin towers that one sees after ten minutes on the Circle Line, and there was a general stir, a hurrying about among the chairs, exclamations, the noise of excited or crying children—much the same spectacle I imagine as one might see when fire breaks out, only here there was no fire, only the two highest towers on the planet, and I saw the Japanese, the fat one like a battering ram in front of the other, thrust into the mass, split it apart, and rush savagely for the part of the deck nearest the towers, there to squat against the side, where, leaning their elbows on the rail, they could get to work, thank you very much.

Now the towers were behind us. People sat down once more. The stretch of water had widened, and this gave me a happy feeling of the open sea. Shapes appeared on every hand, to port and to starboard and on great tongues of land where we were surrounded more by stone than by water. The mist reabsorbed the towers, and in agreement with my exulting mind I reflected that if I had had the delightful choice of my landing place and the power of exercising that choice, I should have chosen Ellis Island: and at that point, while we were running along the island, I sank into such a deep state of meditation that the record and the engines were no more than a vague background noise and I said to myself, "So that's where they first set foot on land, all those millions of Europeans, wretched or downtrodden, or, at best, poverty-stricken, reaching America at the end of a long and dangerous voyage. . . ." And my mind cut in, "The *Leibnitz*, 1868, seventy days from Hamburg to New York, 108 dead out of 544 passengers. The *Lord Brougham*, same year, 383 passengers and 75 dead." ". . . and that's where tens of thousands of them heard the doctors and the policemen pronounce sentence, condemning them to go back again, to return to that western or central Europe that they hated and that they had abandoned or to the East, either Far or Near." And I imagined

24

the millions of pairs of eyes fixed upon hope just over there on the other side of the island, the other end, a few cables' lengths away, the paradise whose lights they could see when night came on and whose rumbling breath they heard or thought they could hear—the paradise they had talked about with a great wealth of fantastic images back there on the threshold of their huts, cabins, hovels, shacks, and it seemed to me both absurd and touching that this island which had seen so many men, women, and children huddled together, weeping and filled with happiness, and which I was now discovering from the boat, should be a commonplace redbrick mass drowned in greenery, with rococo towers topped by fake pagodas in which nevertheless true gods might be worshiped—who can tell?

And I did not want the island to disappear. I turned, following it as long and as far as I could keep it in sight, and nothing shifted my gaze, not even the appearance of the twin towers in a diaphanous haze with their close-packed court of giants in the sky and of humbled buildings down at ground level. Then suddenly there was a prolonged outcry and I saw that all the people were crowding together.

They had rushed over to the right-hand side of the boat and they were standing there squeezed tight, shoulder to shoulder, those who had read the guide and those who had not, but who knew just as well as the others that at this very moment they were about to see, green from top to toe, the Statue of Liberty. I should never have expected to recognize anyone or anything in that jumble of ecstatic heads rising from a vague mass of necks, bottoms, and bodies; but there, with his raised arms higher than anyone else's raised arms, his camera waving higher than anyone else's camera, was the taller Japanese, his finger pressed to the object's button; and since I was not used to seeing the one without the other, I looked for his little fat companion and eventually in the slow ebbing of the crowd toward the chairs I found him, hidden by the tall one. He was working his crank with a feverish concentration, and I thought to myself that although I so disliked photography I would have wielded

25

a camera too if only I had been sure of even one chance in a thousand million of catching the opposite of reality—the only photograph I should have wanted was that of Liberty, breaking her statuesque eternity for once, bowing her head and stretching out her hand. But that day on the Circle Line I was wide of the mark.

Like the twin towers earlier glimpsed, the Statue of Liberty was soon astern, and I noticed that a kind of forlornness seemed to be coming over everyone: they had made the trip for the towers and the statue, for them alone, for the five minutes during which they could be seen and for the fifty high-speed photographs that could be taken of them, and now they had to resign themselves to the two and a half hours before the boat returned to its starting point. Sighing, some of them stretched out as far as their chairs would allow in the hope of sleep. We were off Governor's Island when I saw her. She had no camera: it was clear that she was like me, and she too clasped a guidebook. Somebody had gently tapped my chair, so I sidled up on her right and leaned my elbows on the rail. Then I watched the gulls and she did the same. We had reached the grim period when the children shout and snivel and wander about, fed up, when the parents, who have seen enough, start quarreling, when people take refuge in popcorn and hot dogs as in France they take refuge in sausages, and when those who are still wide-awake, still lively enough, still polite enough to stifle a belch or a yawn between two drafts, turn to cans of beer; and averting our eyes from the depressing scene we gazed at the shore, at a group of vast buildings with windows like the cells in a honeycomb and steel piers that seemed to be about to storm the whole construction, as though this same steel, which formed the fabric, were trying to overtake itself, to realize itself; then came an enormous set of cubes like those one played with as a child, building up a mass that gradually narrowed until it ended in a single block, high over the hundreds at the bottom; then came glass structures and, the sun suddenly overpowering the mist, a kind of gaiety came too, rather mad, rather

26

tipsy, iridescent colors that seemed to be running races; and our two hands on the rail touched, just as they do in books, at the very moment when we were passing under the Brooklyn Bridge, so thunderous with cars that I did not speak to her because I should have had to shout and perhaps I should long have regretted those first words though what they would have been I cannot tell.

We had passed Manhattan Bridge, both of us still standing in the stern, and in any case I could not have gone back to my chair; I could not tell which it was. People got up, marked their places with a paper or a scarf and one could guess—I guessed—the hour of the rest rooms, the hour when the children, as though they had been stricken with pollakiuria, never seem to stop coming and going, escorted by a mother, red-faced with the effort of climbing the stairs, and there was scarcely anyone but the tireless Japanese to forgo the consolation of drinking, eating, sleeping, or urinating. They were more active and overexcited than ever, and when the movie camera found that it was some way from the ordinary camera or the other way around, it called its mate with wide, imperative gestures, and the tall man or the short would hurry over, anxious not to miss the angle his friend had discovered: then together again, side by side, the little one under the big one's belly, their unwearying hands would set to work. . . . I had turned away from them to watch her when a movement of her head gave me to understand that I was to look up. She knew. My hand moved back to hers and together we gazed through the enormous lattice formed by the quivering lines and cables of the suspension bridge at the mass of buildings, close-packed now and of every shape the earth had ever formed to thrust up into the skies; and in this narrowing, this constriction, this tight array, there was as it were an aggression, an assertive urge to be the tallest, the strongest, the biggest, the widest, and indeed the phenomenon seemed to reach the point of direct conflict, of confusion, so that gradually the forms no longer stood apart but fused in a clinch like groggy, punch-drunk boxers at the end of a fight.

27

The crowd had grown lethargic, and heat and time seemed to have worn away the zeal even of the Japanese: we were coasting along a leprous New York made up of brown erections of no particular height and I would have laid a bet that black people lived in them—a winning bet, because boys could be seen playing in the mean little yards and gardens. Then came a building site with a huge structure going up; it was to be clothed with green sheets of glass, and where the glass was lacking, great black holes gave the monster a blinded, ravaged look; then without transition we ran by some really elegant houses and then there was the Williamsburg Bridge, then the United Nations Building, which stirred only the Japanese, instantly in place to shoot it through and through, and as I no longer saw anything to arouse my emotions, I took my hand away and hers remained there, quite alone, on the rail: the engines had never stopped throbbing, the record started up once more, and sailing along the Harlem River we passed the miserable dwellings of the blacks, and I increased my knowledge of New York by observing that unlike European towns the city did not spread out but soared in the air so that once again you had to look up to see and appreciate it. Then we went along by Inwood Hill Park with its great trees all close together, and I pictured the forest in that part of American history toward 1750, before the coming and the spread of the whites, and for the third time my hand covered hers—because of the George Washington Bridge, for here the river widens, and turning to look at Europe at the far end of the world I was amazed, stunned by the fantastic vision of the distant bridge with its parallel cables rising heavily into the sky to make angles with the arches, cables held by still more cables, upright cables that stood in an even file right across the whole breadth of the river, and at this my hand trembled upon hers.

We were at the point where our course took us into the Hudson again, that is to say into the river where the passenger on the Circle Line begins his trip, and she leaned toward me—the record had stopped and she spoke.

And I did not understand.

And I said, "What?"

And raising her voice she spoke and I heard something, a word that seemed to me to have no meaning.

And again I said, "What?"

And loud and spacing out the syllables she said a word whose sounds I heard, then she spelled it slowly, then she repeated it, and this time it was as though I were reading the word: Assemetquaghan.

And again I said, "What?"

She: "Assemetquaghan. It's a Micmac Indian word that means 'stream suddenly seen opposite you, after a bend, when you are running up the river it flows into.' I told you because we are leaving the Harlem for the Hudson. . . ."

I looked at her amazed and in a weak voice I said, " Is that really what it means?"

She: "It's in Rouillard."

We were about to land; I did my utmost to see how I should tread and I managed to ask her whether she knew other Indian languages. Yes, or at least one Five Nations language thoroughly besides Ojibway and Cherokee.

When we went ashore I felt I had known her so long that I walked on beside her.

There was something that puzzled me: to explain the Micmac word she had spoken to me in French—how had she guessed I was a Frenchman and how did it come about that she spoke my language so perfectly? And now I am about it, what is your name?

Luronne: and in a low, unbelieving voice I said Luronne, and deep within I stammered, "Dear God, what have I done to be so fortunate?"—happiness at such a pitch that you cannot bear keeping it to yourself, at such a pitch that it chokes you and you try to share it and now the share fell to God: I took Luronne's hand again, I did nothing but take and retake her hand, extraordinary first name, brilliant creation, and for the first

29

time she answered the pressure of my fingers and I suffered a fresh wave of happiness and without a sound I kept repeating Luronne, Luronne; at last I talked about the Huron and Iroquois countries, the source of that homesickness that was always with me as though I had known them and lived in them, and then she told me that her mother was American, her father, French, and that her childhood and adolescence had been divided between France and America, Paris and New York, her father traveling because of his work, her mother to follow her husband, and the only child always going with them for stays of about a year each time so that she had spent twelve in New York and the same in France and I said, "That makes you twenty-four."

Right: then, "How did you know that I . . ." and she replied that it was obvious, self-evident, and I reflected, "A certain way of dressing, standing, looking, maybe; the difference between a Japanese and a Frenchman amounts pretty well to the camera, but between an American and a Frenchman?" Trifles, the small change of passing thoughts, to be caught on the bounce and dropped right away for more important things, and as she was looking from side to side I grasped that she wanted a taxi: we got in, she called out a number, adding, "Riverside Drive," and to my question she answered, "Beside the Hudson," and all I could say to myself was, "Luronne, what have I done to be so happy?"

The library gave me something of a shock. The bookcases occupied several areas, first the whole wall running forward on the right as you came in, and they ran a good twenty yards, rising five or six, a regal height; and they had also spread along the full length of the left-hand wall, beyond the door. At right angles to this left-hand wall a vast bay window gave onto the Hudson, and in the curving panes I saw the book backs reflected and in front of them Luronne, who, right behind me, had closed the door and was waiting there silently: I admired a spiral staircase whose steps we did not climb, and Luronne led me to the far side of it, to her desk, a great stretch of oak that filled the whole remaining wall, and I no longer felt amazed because ever since the business of the Micmac word, amazement had become my settled state, so now my reaction to all this wealth, luxury, beauty, and gentleness was more a sort of dread, and instinctively I turned and walked toward the books, and just as I was raising my hand to take and caress them, Luronne's arm seized mine, held it motionless, and in a whisper I heard, "No." And we went up the stairs.

Sometimes I think I might never have come down them again. And Luronne believed in heaven too, often believed in it. Every time, I have to make an effort to recreate a true, living picture of those moments when we tore ourselves apart and either she or I went downstairs or sometimes both of us together if Luronne was overcome with the fear that I might not come up again for a long while, that I might disappear and perish alone far away from her and I went through that anguish too. Neither Luronne nor I went down alone without the other calling words of comfort from above. Sweetheart! For three days we scarcely left the bedroom except to spend a few minutes below where Luronne had arranged a kitchen behind her desk, and fortunately she had some provisions as well, so that by limiting ourselves we only went one day without eating. We would go up again, rather less brisk, just a little heavy. And the world went on in its usual worldly fashion while we knew nothing whatsoever about it—no papers, and Luronne had unhooked her telephone. It never occurred to us to switch on the television or the radio. For three days on end and with total generosity each did nothing but attend to the other, and to the other alone. Luronne lived and breathed only to see, sense, and possess me and my only aim was to see, sense, and possess her and our fatigue was not ordinary, commonplace fatigue but the gateway to a fresh glowing blaze, an extra outburst of energy and when, far beyond tiredness, almost entirely burned out after our wild mingling and entwining of bodies and limbs, both she and I like Buddhas and octopuses with arms, siphons, and

31

suckers, we could do no more, then I would feel that constriction in my throat which happiness makes: and when I asked Luronne whether she felt it too I wept at our harmony and perfect rapport.

Lying there quiet and good, getting our breath back, listening to one another's heartbeat, we were at the end of a long solitary journey and once she leaned over me, her lips like a flower, and she said, "It's as though I had been walking for a long, long while and then I had found you." The fantastic words spurred me on and at once I stiffened again for her and for everything I had discovered of her open, spread wide, crushed, closed, pierced; and everything that I had had from her, everything that she had given or that I had taken, spoke and proclaimed the miracle, and now for the first time in my life I filled my whole being entirely—no voids, no looseness: what I did, what I said, and what I delighted in were all in harmony. As I took her once again I told Luronne how for so long I had been unhappy—though without being fully aware of it, knowing it only at intervals—wretched at being unable to move up and down the length of her legs: the ten, the fifteen years without her, the geography, the orography, and the geology of the world I longed for, and with my hands and my lips I traveled upstream and downstream once again, with the current and against it, and when I reached the branches of her arms and I felt sure of myself, sure of my means, I thrust onto the mouth of the river and there in the estuary I fainted away, lost my strength, though not without having set up a tiderace that took a long time to die away in spite of our weakness—weakness, at this point in our relationship, being my settled condition, just as amazement had been six hours, twenty-four hours, and three days earlier; and it was now for the first time that the old enemy came to my mind. We had certainly knocked him out, Luronne and I, but I was thirty and I knew how he could hang on, the filthy, eternally prowling, elusive creep, the accomplished voyeur, and sometimes I thought I caught a glimpse of him in the half-darkness like a shadow on the wall, the ghost of a shadow, and I know he was already trying to snare us with those usual, commonplace, deadly dangerous traps of his that nobody had ever baffled before Luronne and me: the traps that are time and its passage, habit, death in all its manifestations. And in a single motion I turned onto Luronne and seized her and she cried out with pain and pleasure; then sad in my heart I said to her—and we both understood that these words came from a great way off, from where suffering has its roots and where anxiety grows—"I shall love you forever."

She lived in a world of shields, clubs, belts of wampum, bear's-tooth necklaces, kachina dolls, arrowheads, tomahawks, quivers, turquoise bracelets and rings, little figures made of the bone of whales or walrus tusks, fetishes carved in white stone, catlinite pipes of peace, and in a little ivory kayak she had placed three pieces of iron pyrite which she told me came from Labrador: and seeing them there, shining like gold, I understood why Frobisher, in his second and third northern voyages of 1577 and 1578, had taken a jeweler with him, a man of weight and substance among the sailors and the handful of colonists. She also possessed a portulan, a gnomon, a Klo-Kut fish carved out of bone—a lure, no doubt—from Old Crow in the Yukon. Also two pairs of moccasins, one pair of snowshoes, three pipes, and one ornament made of porcupine quills, the work of Athabascans of the eastern Mackenzie Valley, that is to say of Hares, Dog-Ribs, Yellowknives, Liars, and Chippewas.

Myself (croaking, bewildered, enchanted, lost, my head in a whirl): "What? What?"

And patiently she repeated: "Hares, Dog-Ribs, Yellowknives, Liars, and Chippewas."

All these things were wonderfully set out in a long, long, descending sequence, so that one's eye took them one by one: some hung from a white thread so thin that it was either invisible, or if it were caught in the sun, it quivered like a nerve in the dancing motes; others stood among the books to break the monotony; still others in niches; and on the few stretches of wall free from bookshelves there were reproductions—a black-

and-white drawing by Theodore de Bry of stags, and if you looked closely at the details, you saw that half the stags were Indians who, hidden under their deceptive hides, had come so close to the real herd that they were about to shoot their arrows; then another black-and-white drawing of two Indians as John White saw them when he landed in Virginia with Sir Richard Grenville's expedition; a Shawnee by George Catlin and a Cree by Paul Kane, both of them—I mean the Indians but it would also apply to the painters—strong and admirable. . . . And two maps, the one of Louisiana, the other of the country that runs from west of Lake Superior to Hudson's Bay, and here, south of the Nipissing territory and east of the Mandans', I recognized Nouvelle-France, where I had so often longed to be, back in the trading days. . . . Later she told me that after months of search and consultation with an architect, she had persuaded her father to buy this apartment: when the architect had thoroughly grasped what it was that she wanted and when she had told him that it was to be a place to live in reverse, to recede in time, that is to say to move forward in the years before these present years when movement is so rapid—and for my part, as I gazed spellbound at the artifacts, prints, and maps, I understood that we two, Luronne and I, were going to breathe in hundreds of earlier years, an impressive stretch of time, a protective screen, and I told her that if one lived two or three centuries before one's time then death was not to be feared—so when she had explained all this, the architect told her that she had to buy this particular apartment in this particular building and that she must order certain specific alterations designed to give her the space she was looking for, with precisely the straight lines and the necessary breaks to turn the whole into a dream for both heart and mind, and Luronne, overcome, vanquished (in my opinion she must have added to what the architect said and have spoken with even more conviction), had walked to the bay which was then, before the alterations, only an ordinary window, and her heart gave a leap, for the architect told her that she was in part of the island protected by law and that the screen of oaks over there on the other side of the river could never be touched: and Luronne, sure of living with what remained of the great primeval American forest, asked no more and all the rest followed like an uncovenanted gift. At this height she was sheltered from the noise of the street; all she heard was the wind and the cry of the gulls, the hooting and roaring of the tugs, those slow, stubborn, strong, stupid creatures, only just fit for towing, animals belonging to another age, river buffaloes as it were; and for that reason and from that point of view, Luronne had accepted them. And since she had defined them so happily I followed in her wake; I too gave them a place in my world as I heard them those summer evenings running up the Hudson as they might run up the river of time. Their noise, rising and falling, continually renewed—a noise that sometimes made the bay window vibrate as though it were signaling to them, echoing their passage— carried me off in all those vessels that plow American history, the galleons, pinks, caravels, carracks, curraghs, hookers, pinnaces, and the *pataches* whose sails I used to hear flapping in the wind when I was a child in Avignon and the mistral rattled the shutters.

July came, and in New York July is a hot month, sometimes downright sweltering, and every night we went out, so eager was I to see New York in those aspects that set it apart from European cities—the steam that rises from drain covers right in the middle of the street often in positive columns that never failed to astonish me, both on account of the life beneath the asphalt that seemed all the stranger since the whole town is up in the air, and because the steam, shooting up and spreading, would veil the shapes in the street for several seconds before it was wafted away like a cloud at eye level; and on those warm nights we loved hearing the whistles of the doormen—when the theaters closed, all the streets in those parts echoed with imperious whistling—and we went to Chinatown, where great stretches of unoccupied ground lie at the foot of the skyscrapers. This gives you the liveliest impression of having fallen into a hole, and for that reason the tall buildings soar even higher into the sky. . . . And sometimes, toward the end of a warm, humid afternoon, we would watch for the fog, and as soon as we saw it beginning to form we would hurry out, leap into a taxi and go to Sixth Avenue , where the greatest concentration of skyscrapers is to be found, and there we would watch it hood the spires, the pinnacles, the topmost towers and gradually come down the sides, where it usually stopped halfway, hanging there until the wind swept it clear. . . . But for all that, as far as I was concerned July was the season for bed.

We would go upstairs two and three times a day every day before the coming of the night, myself behind Luronne, pushing her as she climbed rather awkwardly, always stumbling on the steps, always the same, rather shy, rather blushing, rather bashful as I liked her to be and as she irritated me by being. . . . I would hold her with one hand and stroke her as we went up, often with both, and when we reached the bed she would never throw herself onto it but would always stand there a little more hesitant still, a little pinker, and in the seconds before our fall, before I pulled her down, one might have heard the beating of our hearts: and often I asked both myself and her what she thought about while we were going up and before I seized her, because when all is said and done there is no journey one knows less about than that ordinary passage from the bottom of the stairs up to the top. . . . I would rip from the bed the beaver skin she had bought from a Haute-Mauricie Tête-de-Boule squaw and fling Luronne onto the bed, diving after her, and then I would begin my continually repeated exploration of Luronne dressed, half-dressed, undressed, and under my fingers the marvelous substance yielded and swelled, and scrupulously, feverishly, jealously, tirelessly I checked that everything was there, her breasts, her belly, her *train* as I had spontaneously named her sex, from which, long before I made myself clear, I had expected the farthest-ranging journeys in the arid southwestern plains, and the taste of wild

36

sage and manzanita was already in my mouth. . . . And why *train*, why this semantic solipsism?

Because when I was looking in a dictionary long ago I found that the word *train* meant the hindquarters of a quadruped, and Luronne being only a biped I logically divided the expression in two to love her just there, at the junction of her two legs; and in the word *train* I also liked the sense of engine, locomotive, driving center, that infinitely tender belly into which I plunged so impetuously. One day, speaking of it to Luronne, I told her it was the heart of her lower half, by analogy with the other, her upper heart; and upon the first I flung myself with a fierce, rasping tongue, as do cats, wolves, lynxes. . . . So it was the season for bed. As I have said, we went upstairs two or three times in the day and there were also the nights, and one morning I discovered just how much I loved Luronne by finding that the word love had been written on the darkness; for waking, without the least idea of where I was or with whom, I saw that I (who can only sleep on my right side) was as it were wedded to her, my legs tight under the angle of hers and myself welded to her body as though I had been afraid that she might be taken away from me, as though I had needed her even in my sleep, had had need of her warmth, and, sweetheart, of your blood, like a child. So it was a season for bed, with the climbing of the stairs two or three times in the daylight without counting the nights and never have I talked to myself so much: "What," said I to my mind, pointing at my body, its brother, its opposite, its paradoxically antithetical twin, "what, he wears himself out, calms down, and goes to sleep, and you just let him carry on: you don't think of anything new, you don't help him, you don't urge him on; you cut me off, you divorce me, you leave me out in the cold . . ." And at this my mind, aiming through my closed eyes at those within my head, poured out fresh pictures of Luronne making love, crying out, sighing, swelling, collapsing, pressing down on me, playing, biting, dancing, so that I was on fire again and eagerly I returned to

37

the exploration of my territory and with the taste of Luronne in
my mouth once more I labored that good, rain-damp earth with
my plow and thrust my stem into the shining surface below
me; and I imagined great seabirds making their way up Luronne's belly right up into the heart of her country, which lies
in the two places I have spoken about, the upper heart and the
lower; and bending I searched for the taste of salt. . . . So it
was bed. The stairs climbed two or three times in the day, and
then the night. You can't spend your life in bed: a denial that I
utter and then instantly correct. What I mean is, spend your life
in Luronne. Yet sometimes, doubt gnawing me as worms gnaw
a wooden hull and I dwelling on the notion of my death, I believed that Luronne would save me. Would make me immortal.
In no place but in Luronne—and with Luronne always and to
the highest degree possible—have I ever felt that eternity was
so near at hand: I had only to stay a few seconds longer and I
should explode inside her. I never actually did so but I often
felt that I was on the edge of it. A question of willpower, physical strength? Surely not. Gripping my pleasure tight, I held it
back, I checked it as I might have checked a horse I was riding—and then I gave way. I always gave way. Every time. And
for some seconds every time. During those moments when I
was holding myself in, resisting pleasure, I could feel eternity
hovering there like a challenge, a defiance, and with clenched
teeth, stammering my love to my lover, I tried to attain it. And
at the last moment the pleasure that had drawn me close to eternity took eternity away from me, leaving me powerless on Luronne's moist body.

The weather grew hotter and hotter, and during the day we
climbed the stairs less often. Twice perhaps instead of three
times; or even once, when only just before the heat it had been
twice. Because of the tourists and the heat wave we decided to
postpone those never-ending visits to Rockefeller Center and
Central Park that we promised ourselves. There was the America of the present day, of the future, and of the past. It was

above all the last that concerned us, and the sickening heat in the streets also helped us to make our decision.

So we hunted America, just as one should perhaps learn to hunt time, in order to seize hold of it. The New York Public Library, Metropolitan Museum of Art, City Art Museum of St. Louis down in Missouri, the Boston Museum of Fine Arts, the Detroit Institute of Arts, the Smithsonian Institution, the New York Historical Society, the American Antiquarian Society at Worcester in Massachusetts, at Boston again the Massachusetts Historical Society, the Amon Carter Museum at Forth Worth—we went everywhere, by plane, by car, by train, everywhere in the states of New York, Connecticut, Pennsylvania, Texas . . . everywhere that colonial painting was to be seen, everywhere where it was preserved in the underground storerooms and the most obscure libraries of the most remote provincial American towns, and I do assure you we never had enough: we were hungry to know how America was born. And how she was now being born every day under our watchful eyes. At the end of each of our journeys, using these pictures, we tried to catch the living process of Americanization unawares, at the very moment it was taking place, to seize its totality, the colors and the lines that brought the scenes, characters, and landscapes into being; and there I tried to lose myself, forgetting Europe in order to be present in the art of those illuminators whose names I knew little or not at all—John Singleton Copley, John Greenwood, Robert Feke, who had painted seventy canvases by about 1750 and who just vanished one day, no one knowing what had become of him. Luronne, maybe? But Luronne shook her head: she did not know. It was above all the anonymous pictures that fixed our attention: the *Mrs. Freake and her baby daughter Mary* of 1674 and the *Pocahontas* of 1616, the one in the Worcester Art Museum and the other in the National Gallery of Art; and then the mantelpiece panel of the 1730s, when the Hudson country was Dutch. It shows Martin Van Bergen and his wife in their Sunday clothes

in front of their yellow, red-tiled house. Across the idyllic estate move blacks with nothing, apart from our knowledge, to
show that they are slaves, and some Indians too. A naive vision
of the rich, happy world of those days, whose colors and movement convey overflowing delight in merely being, walking, gazing . . . Luronne and I knew these pictures by heart, and as
though they were snatches of verse or pieces of prose we would
recite passages, details, and sections, and since the painters
were entirely unknown in spite of all research—no names, no
certainty nor even any likelihood—it seemed to us that this
gave us a better understanding of America's birth. Coming to
us without the men, as it were, she came stainless, begotten by
no one, without sin or blemish, an America of the world's beginnings.

We were charmed to read that Benjamin West, who made his
first brush from the whiskers of his cat, had learned their secret
of making vegetable colors from the Indians. For a whole hour
on end we devoured Le Moyne de Morgues' watercolor in the
New York Public Library, the only one left of all those he
painted, a picture that had escaped from time as the painter escaped from the Spaniards when they attacked and wiped out
the French colony the Protestants had established in that evil
dream which then made up the coast of Florida. We sought out
the works of Saint Merrin, who painted the upper Missouri Indians. Saint Merrin! What a curious name for an American.
The art of the "Indian" weathercock sent us from New England to South Carolina, and for a long while we were seized
with a feverish impulse to be on the go until our discovery of
the Deacon Drowne vane in the Massachusetts Historical Society at Boston, a weathercock that represents, guess what? An
Indian bowman! And every time Luronne thought of a new
trip and told me about it I asked her, "Are you sure we'll not be
disappointed?" But it was a stupid, meaningless question,
asked for the laugh, perhaps to disguise my intense happiness,
to keep me from crying, because I knew very well that we
should not be disappointed, and with my eyes full of these first

days of America I would say to her, "Just what is America?" impatient for fresh knowledge.

We went down as far as Virginia to look at the ivory-billed woodpecker that Mark Catesby drew in 1712, and I could scarcely believe Luronne when she told me it was extinct, that it had vanished long ago like the passenger pigeon, that fantastic bird, perhaps that one that comes most often into my mind and that is with me most. The passenger pigeon, or as the people of Quebec used to call it, the *tourte*. We know that in about 1800 they numbered something in the nature of five billion, and in the autumn of 1813 Audubon saw them when he was near Louisville, on the banks of the Ohio, and he says, "For three days on end these birds veiled the sun to such an extent that the country was bathed in darkness; there were more than a million of them in an area about two hundred miles long and a little under a mile wide." A million: five billion altogether between the Great Lakes and Florida, they alone amounting to 32 percent of all North American birds. And when great bands of them settled in Pennsylvania, Kentucky, Tennessee, Missouri, or Iowa, they broke the branches of the trees and the colonists attacked them with guns, sticks, and axes, using snares and wheat soaked in spirits, with such a ferocity, such an eagerness for death, that the passenger pigeon is an extinct species, wholly lost, for its last member gave up the bird ghost on September 1, 1914, in the Cincinnati zoo and I wept on learning of the final, definitive slaughter—I wept at having been born too late to travel to Cincinnati and perhaps to save the passenger pigeon, the last aristocratic bird, unrivaled for beauty, graceful with its long tail, small head and neck, shining, fiery-red eyes, purplish throat shading to white toward the belly, and the long, blue, tapering wings that gave the birds their general color when they were seen close up, so that the murderous rustics called them blue meteors—blue meteors that by 1831 were no longer to be seen, according to Tocqueville, who was there at that time, except "at long intervals." And moving on from the thousands of millions of man-slaughtered birds we wanted to

41

know Audubon's predecessors, and for a while, oh, for a very short while, we wondered whether we should go to London, where William Bartram's *The Imperial Moth of Florida* is to be seen in the Natural History Museum; but that was in Europe and the thought of Solange and the children spread a veil across my eyes and I said, no let's talk about something else, so we decided on Alexander Wilson's *The Little Owl* in the Harvard College Library, and there we were absolutely enchanted—they told us that the Historical Society of Pennsylvania possessed the picture called *Lapowinsa,* by that Swede, Hesselius; and for a long while we gazed at it silently, holding our breath, filled with love for him, for that Indian Lapowinsa, already so deeply sad, the first picture in the history of American painting that shows an Indian without false, unreal, evil-natured caricature. He is painted with his squirrel-skin bag, and on his forehead there are a few black lines. Tell, I said. And Luronne told me that he, the chief orator of the Lenni Lenape (the Delawares' name for themselves), had come with three companions, Nuntimus, Tishcohan, and Lesbeconk, and that Thomas Penn, William's son, had commissioned the portrait from Hesselius: this was in 1737, that is to say two years before the whites seized the Lenni Lenapes' best land, and on Lapowinsa's face can be read the foreboding, the certainty of theft, of rape, of the white man's unrelenting baseness: oh, Luronne, all those days, those days of July when we moved about in the dim museums, questioning mass, color, and line and when sometimes it seemed to us that we were touching the living flesh of America itself and that the flesh quivered between our fingers.

Then, after a visit to the Buffalo and Erie County Historical Society to see the peace medal of Red Jacket, the great Seneca orator whom Luronne and I preferred calling by his real name, Sagoyewatha—he had gone to Philadelphia to meet George Washington and the president had ordered a medal from an engraver of whom once again nothing is known, with the obverse showing an Indian chief dropping his tomahawk and offering

the pipe of peace—after Sagoyewatha, we decided to call a halt
to our raids on the museums, to which we should return after
other trips and other places; and one day in the Adirondacks
we got into the train that runs from New York to Montreal and
back, because we felt the need for vastness, an eagerness to
find it and to feel its impact on the endless shores of Lake
Champlain, and there through the carriage windows we also
beheld an impressive panorama of forest, of those interminable
monotonous stretches of flat country that we had been looking
for from the beginning of the ten-hour journey, and another
day we drove to Point Pelee, which juts out into Lake Erie at
the very tip of Ontario, to see the fantastic spectacle of the millions and millions of monarch butterflies, the dragonflies, and
the wasps hanging in heavy clusters over the lake, and this
high-strung airborne network was so tense as to lead one to
suppose that if a man were to adventure his head there, if he
were to stick it out, he would never find it again, because it
would instantly be cut off, stung and swallowed up by the hissing mass, and the execution would not have caused the slightest stir, nothing but a little many-colored snow of crumpled
wings and twisted wing cases, less than nothing, and then for
the sheer pleasure of it we ran down the Mississippi, where the
prairies are blue, between Wisconsin and Tennessee, and once
Luronne, who had restored her telephone to working order,
had a call and we traveled far into northern Quebec a hundred
and twenty-five miles from Seven Islands to lend the Montagnais Indians a hand, because the American Rayonnier Company's white employees were preventing them from reaching
their hunting grounds—for a song, the Canadian government
had granted the company cutting rights in a forest the size of
Belgium, Holland, and Luxembourg all rolled into one, no
less, and nobody had thought of telling the Montagnais of the
deal in which some thirty-four million trees were also to lose
their bark and their sap. Our greatest pleasure, and one that we
repeated a thousand times, was to go from New York to Staten
Island in a ferry that makes the trip in under half an hour.

Why? Out of love for the gulls. There are few sights to beat that of gulls working up against the wind. They always bring it off, but, you would say, only just. Sometimes a sudden gust would fling them right over, as though they could not resist at all; but then, having paid some kind of tribute to the wind, they recovered their balance with a single turning movement of both wings. At other times the gust stopped them dead so that they hung up there motionless in full flight for several seconds that seemed so many minutes; then there would be a calm until the next squall struck them from behind or in front, wresting from them anguished screams, that is how it sounded to us, although perhaps it was simply their way of expressing enjoyment of the sport. When the blow was so strong that they could not glide through it, we would see them literally vibrating there, almost motionless in the air, and at these times the ivory-yellow birds looked like something that an artist might have created, a masterpiece representing a half-somersault halted in midturn—the gull clinging stubbornly to nothing, hanging in the void with no force apart from its ruffled feathers: then, flight recovered, the bird sweeping over the ferry. And I would grip Luronne's shoulder with happiness, for every time a gull won against a renewed blast of wind, it seemed that Luronne and I had gained a victory, and we would go back to Riverside Drive, mysteriously overjoyed.

Then came August and the full height of summer and if possible we were hotter still. Observers said that the kind of heat wave New York was experiencing occurred no more than once in every ten or fifteen years. But we suffered from it only when we walked about out-of-doors. If we meant to go for a drive in Luronne's automobile, we would run from the apartment with its humming air conditioner straight to where another air conditioner was whistling in the car; and we always drove with everything shut up tight. Yet all this machinery directed against the heat rather displeased us, and we spent some time looking through books for descriptions of the burning summers that the explorers, trappers, traders, and missionaries had known in

44

Indian country. We went out for short walks and we came back soaked and exhausted. Nevertheless we stuck to it.

No doubt there was something urging us to realize that we had only recently come together, that we might never have come together at all, and that since our meeting had in fact come rather late, we therefore had all the more to do, particularly since we also knew with a deep conviction that one day the world would die and that we perhaps might die before it. We had to see everything, and in order to see everything we did not necessarily have to move fast but we quite certainly had to lose no time. And ever since my childhood discovery of America in books, I had wanted to see the forest close up, not merely from the train or from the air, and I said to Luronne, "Take me into the woods: there's so little left. . . ." She avoided giving any answer because by now she knew me well enough to be aware that waiting made me wildly eager, that it made things glow. And she liked that. She contrived to talk about the forest without referring to it directly and as though she had not the least intention of doing so: for example she told me the name of the tree that preserved the life of Jacques Cartier and his sick crew. At the time of his second voyage, when they were ashore in their fort, most of his men found that their arms and legs were beginning to swell, and presently the swelling spread to their bodies and they turned black all over and died—twenty-five corpses out of a hundred and ten men with only ten still healthy, and on one occasion Cartier ordered a postmortem in the hope of learning what was wrong and according to Luronne's quotation he found "the heart quite pale and shrunken . . . the color of a date." At this point the desperately anxious Cartier noticed that an Indian living nearby who had appeared to be as sick as the whites the day before was in bounding health the day after, and he waited for the working of the miracle the Indian had gladly brought him—leaves, branches . . . Luronne: "The anneda, the tree of life that cures scurvy."

Myself: "You must show me." And I told her, though perhaps she knew it already, that seventy years later Champlain's men were still dying of scurvy, for Champlain knew nothing about Cartier, whom he had never met, and I longed to hold, to breathe in great armfuls of anneda, and another time, as if it were of no importance, Luronne told me of the existence of the sarracenia, an insect-eating plant that grows in the marshes and whose leaves are like pitchers; and in these pitchers the rain-water sleeps as you might say with one eye open because in-sects come and drown themselves in it, to be eaten and digest-ed by the sarracenia, and I wanted to see that too, and one eve-ning Luronne said yes. It was an ardent yes, uttered during an embrace, and I was filled with a double happiness—that of en-tering the American forest and that of having Luronne show me this event, still another after so many, before so many, and in the night, thinking of all she was giving me, I took her and I took her again, and for a long while a comforting tenderness kept us awake; and because of that sleep only came in fits and starts and then went away so that night it never sank really deep down into us.

The alarm clock was set to go off at four in the morning and we were to drive to a forest she knew in Connecticut. We had to force ourselves out of bed. During the three preceding days we had spent several hours with a work on botany, looking closely at drawings of trees and flowers; the whole flora of North America was there, and Luronne, who had studied botany in the field for years and years, gave almost infallible answers to my questions on the conifers, the deciduous trees. . . . She was particularly brilliant at giving a detailed description of the leaves of any given species, even down to the variations be-tween different individuals. The evening before we set off we walked along the Hudson, and for a long time we watched the setting sun, quite round, bright red like a heated plate; it was extremely slow in vanishing, as though unwilling to give way to the night, and there was a rearguard action, with the ball hanging on, red against the blackness. According to Luronne, tomorrow was going to be as hot as a house on fire.

The sun rose later than we, the ball shooting up fast and then bursting in the sky; and after an uneventful drive there we were at the edge of the forest. As we got out of the car we seemed to step straight into a baker's oven. Yet it was only nine o'clock. I had taken Luronne's hand, but I dropped it very soon. In front of us, on the far side of a heath we were about to cross, there was the mass of the forest, dark at this distance, and immediately something struck us, something that brought us to the edge of uneasiness: it was the total immobility and silence of this landscape. When Luronne, speaking in what I knew was a rather tight, constrained voice, as though she had run until out of breath, began to point out the trees as we made our way into the forest—the white pine, the hemlock, the yellow birch, the sugar maple—we felt that we were disturbing, almost offending, a heavy, inimical order of things. Like the power of a tyrant. I looked for birds in the sky, found none, and looked down; there I saw green and yellow crickets jumping about in the midst of cotton wool and falling back onto the cotton-covered ground where nothing could support any weight and where nothing sent back any sound, and it was on what looked like cotton that the caterpillars were traveling—processions of caterpillars so long that when we looked back we could not see the tail end. Luronne had fallen silent. We were walking on spiders' webs, such enormous numbers of them that spontaneously the question arose: what are they doing here? And I said to myself that the sun had chased the spiders out of the trees—that they had come down to the ground to find a little coolness. Now no doubt they had been overcome by sleep or by death, because our feet, tearing the webs, caused no scurrying, no wild alarm. Sweating and gasping, we pushed on, squashing caterpillars as we went, and instantly the earth soaked up their blood, their lymph, a vile substance that quickly dried and crackled, and then Luronne, close by me, began to speak again, very softly telling me the species of the trees, and as she did so and as I studied each kind, looking attentively at the details, we discovered that they had suffered a great deal of damage; and later we made a general survey of it. The forest

47

mass that from a distance had seemed dark was in fact yellow, not the rich tones of Indian summer yellow, but of a sickly cast—a jaundiced yellow. The tips of the pine needles, usually so tender, had been eaten away, and the slim leaf stalks of the hemlocks had actually burst, and at one point Luronne showed me something that in a whisper she called the fir tree's fruit: no doubt the sledgehammer blows of the sun had ripened it prematurely, for the scales had fallen and all that could be seen was a wretched, wizened little stump. Where the sun had rasped them, the leaves of the aspens had no teeth left, and it had devoured the juniper berries, though in the summer they are harder than in the winter. Even more striking than all this was a tree that Luronne did not recognize straightaway; but after a moment the name came to her—the bitter walnut. The sun appeared to have attacked it with extraordinary force, as though through a magnifying glass, and the dark sap, its flow destroyed at various places on the trunk, petrified and twisted, looked like a cancerous excrescence.

At one time I wanted to go back to the car, but we were deep in the wood and I did not like to admit either to Luronne or to myself that I had had quite a different picture of the forest. So we continued on our way. At another time we saw a thin layer of mist lying at ground level, as though it could not find the strength to rise in this blaze of platinum light. I forced myself to look up. The sky, with its unmoving clouds, brought to mind the idea of a port suddenly drained of its water, so that the ships were stopped dead, fixed to the spot. My eyes hurt. Yet I had only kept them open a few seconds looking up and I had had to lower them quickly because something was piercing into my sight, veiling it, a shape like the slow creeping of a white silence shot through with fiery sparks, and I knew that dizziness was on me and that I was about to faint. Luronne saw and she flung herself forward to catch me if I fell but it was over already and I would not agree when she urged that we should go back. I could not bring myself to believe that this forest was devoid of birds: if they were not in the air, where the sun would have stunned them, then they must certainly be somewhere else, somewhere in the deepest, darkest, most sheltered parts of the forest where a little coolness would remain. That is what I thought as we plunged deeper, and eventually we did hear something, a sound like a sigh, a throaty noise; it was no doubt the wheeze of the birds' unavoidable breathing, and we reckoned that if they had exerted the energy required to push their breath right down their beaks they would have died of thirst. An unconscious law of conservation governed the slowed-down animal and vegetable life. With a slight movement Luronne pointed out a clump of trees twenty yards away, mad, maybe just foolish trees, so tall and so near the sun in the dry boil of this landscape we were passing through. Later, when I looked back on our walk through the fiery furnace, I was obliged to admit that if I had been alone I should have fallen prey to some kind of dread. . . . Once we set off a noise that seemed to us extraordinary for the moment: the twisted, stunted, truncated grass, growing as well as it could and as low as it could so as to reduce its upward thrust—this grass crackled underfoot like hardened snow. Yet the sound did not rise; it went along with us like an escort that could not be seen and that was therefore all the more threatening; and though I kept hoping to hear squeaks, rustles, grunts, and snorts, there was nothing but our feet striking the chords of a desolate music. We were reaching a stand of unusually leafy trees, and since our eyes were half closed against the blazing reverberation of the white-hot sun, we could not quite make them out until we were close, and then we saw that the leaf tips were all hard and shriveled. Death must have struck right in their nerve center, so that caught unawares they had rolled themselves up in a reflex action; then the sun's hot fingers must have improved on the corpses, rolling them tighter, blackening them still more, and it would only have needed a puff of wind to pluck them off and scatter them abroad. . . . At one time we thought we saw something moving at last; it was like a mist rising into the sky and you would have said that the forest, where Luronne identified white walnuts, willows, and witch hazel, was twisting in an enormous fire. The sun soared still higher in the sky and it must have been close to noon when at last we saw some birds.

We had left the dried, crackling grass far behind, and it seemed to us that the sound of our footsteps, stifled in the moment of their birth, pinned down by the direct blast of the heat or by its eddies, could not carry any distance, when all at once it flushed a pair of birds: we had almost trodden on them and they rose, heavy and torpid, not a foot away from us on the left, and Luronne whispered, "Blue jays." I had often seen the lively, noisy, quarrelsome, aggressive birds before, but today they could barely open half an eye: even so, they suddenly gave way to a panic that carried them ten yards over the burning ground in a rocketing flight. Then they summoned up enough energy for another burst that took them a little farther, and there they pitched, exhausted by the effort. We stood for a moment watching them as they sat there, suffering, breathless, their long eyelids drooping, and we saw that they had resigned themselves to the worst and that if death were to strike at them they would do nothing to escape it. And perhaps in fact it had come for them. We walked on, but we had not taken five steps before, following Luronne's sign, I looked up: above us, so low that we could have touched them with a stick, a couple of buzzards were fanning the air in the hope of a little breeze. They circled over the jays and we saw their beaks—beaks that closed only to gape wide again at once to force out croaking sounds; and although these cries were very faint we heard them with a kind of horror. It was as though the day had suddenly darkened.

Since the last great trees we had walked maybe five or six hundred yards, bareheaded, through a scrubland of tall, evil-natured bushes, when, without having had to exchange more than three short words, Luronne and I turned with one accord and made our way back. In the sparse shade of a bitter walnut, I collapsed. But for Luronne I should have stayed there a great while, in spite of the caterpillars, the spider webs, and now, just over me perhaps, the buzzards. With my eyes closed, I thought about nothing at all. There were sparks and broken lines of light dancing madly behind my eyelids and stinging as they danced; visions raced through my mind, vanishing the moment they were formed, and my only feeling was that of a harsh, rasping thirst that turned my swollen gullet into a foreign body, something alien to me, and at one moment an image of the buzzards pierced through with such force that it frightened me—frightened me so much that I cried out. Luronne firmly compelled me to get up. And we retraced our steps across that sick, baked, torrid landscape without looking at it, without even seeing it, going as fast as we could. It seemed that there would never be an end. Once, when in my exhaustion I felt that I no longer cared about anything at all, I had an urge to tell Luronne that we had gone too far, that we had pushed too deep into the forest; but all I was able to bring out was a series of short, hoarse, dry sobs that Luronne, three yards ahead of me, could not hear. In the end I took to scanning my calvary with half-closed eyes, Luronne's slim shadow traveling along between us. Now that combined suffering and fatigue were dulled by their very excess, I could have gone on and on without a pause, and in this twilight I did succeed in reaching the open space where we had parked the car. Sweat blurred our vision and soaked what little clothing we had on. The door handles gleamed and burned and Luronne had to muffle her hands to take hold of them.

Not the least recollection of the drive back, during which I slept. And none of reaching Riverside Drive, where I must certainly have made my way up to the apartment and have taken off my clothes, since the next day there I awakened, in bed. It was early afternoon. We had slept close to eighteen hours. As soon as I woke up I tested my body, and I found that my fatigue had almost entirely vanished. But when I wanted to talk to Luronne about our expedition I could not find the right words. And when, after an effort, I did find them, I had the uncommon experience of hearing myself say them, of feeling myself alien to them, as though they were being uttered by a stranger rather than by myself. My voice and I were talking at one remove, and I grasped that now I had seen it I no longer knew how to speak about the American forest, whereas only a little while before, having read about it, I could expatiate on the subject at length.

Something had failed to pass between the forest and me, something to do with its ugliness, whereas I had looked forward to beauty and surprises, and now it stood like a barrier between Luronne and me, a misunderstanding, a recollection not to be called to mind—in any case Luronne could not have done so: where the forest was concerned she too was unable to talk naturally. Like me, she could no longer speak of the forest or define our disappointment. Yet after all, we were not dead. After all, life was carrying on. What was it we had seen that we should not have seen? What was it that had not offered itself to us that day? The buzzards had never amounted to more than a ridiculous and no doubt imaginary threat. They would never have attacked us. It was only at the end of our walk in the unknown forest that we had seen them, when everything was over and when it was obvious that on this occasion we should not succeed as we had always succeeded everywhere else on our other trips, great or small, those of everyday life, in the fabric of time itself.

But the forest sent me back to Solange, to the children, to Europe, to all that Luronne had blotted out, or very nearly. My dreams about them were more frequent than my dreams about Indians. One night, according to Luronne, I shrieked aloud; and when she asked me about the reasons for the nightmare I did not tell her of the image, as terrifying as the buzzards, that had pierced me through—the single image of Solange's face. Then the children were with her, she leaning over them and they looking toward me, as though they were about to be photographed. Toward the lens. Nothing tortured in this image. The torture was in the dream and in me.

A few days went by and my vexation at the memory of my

weakness in the forest, my lack of resistance to the heat and fatigue, vanished, giving way to a feeling not unlike shame. Or rather awkwardness. We still did not talk about it. And underlying the failure of the trip I detected what might be called a flaw in reading and in books: as I read, day after day, perpetually, I had seemed to live my texts even to the point of dying of heat or of cold with those travelers in the America of former times—with *Les Relations* of the Jesuits, for example, where there are many accounts of canoeing, portages, and journeys on foot, for the Fathers never omitted emphasizing the contrasts and the similarities between the two extreme, violently marked seasons that make up the summer and the winter. Yet this death in books left me in fact more alive than ever with regard to America; and when I compared my book sensations with those I now felt after the forest, I found that I was wounded less by the disparity between the reality of experience and the reality of words—a disparity that I had experienced, though very much in spite of myself—than by the doubt thrown on the values of the imaginary world upon which I felt that I had based myself to so considerable a degree. I had been incapable of taking in or deserving all that vastness and savage immensity which is contained in the short, potent word, the *wild,* a word that you find in Jack London or James Oliver Curwood—to be sure they write about the Far North, but here the difference does not signify—and all at once a miraculous idea enlightened me, an idea that gave me both fresh assurance and shining visions. It was this: quite apart from me, the human undertaking, the human enterprise in the forest that day had for once been made to fail, through me, by means of me, and I said, Dear Lord, let that hostility, that foreboding sense of evil, persist, let people be thirsty, hungry, and frightened in the woods, let them suffer and let them go on feeling the life, the presence, the resistance, even the sickness of all that which is so usually brought down, killed, felled, hacked, rooted up and sawed to pieces, and Luronne found me deep in the blessed state created by that idea, full of desire for a Luronne I had not touched

53

these three days past and as though she had had a presentiment
that her shy, provocative approach would lead to happiness,
she said just the right things, made just the right gestures, and I
responded, and as we were now longtime drivers on the road of
pleasure, we set off once more with short pauses, stops, bursts
of speed, feigned freewheeling, double declutching, flicking
our headlights to make out the bumps and potholes and the
other driver too when he was running with no lights at all and
then the great slamming on of brakes that brings the two-head-
ed racing car to a halt in a moaning of delight and the pain of
overheated leather.

I loved the way Luronne, when I was in her, seemed to settle
down to a task immediately. I mean to settle down to succeed-
ing at a task, her closed eyelids rising and falling with the swell
that rose from her belly; and I distinguished, I recognized, a
most uncommon intelligence and sensitivity wholly concentrated on taking, holding, moistening, and quenching by
stages, each mounting higher, to reach the unbearable. Have I
said it clearly enough? However deeply and wholly she swam
in nonbeing, however she moaned and however incoherent the
monologue into which she plunged and at which she blushed
afterward, assuring me (reassuring herself) that the very next
time she would master it and force herself to a tight-lipped silence that in fact she could never accomplish—a proof of the
extent to which she was ruled by that sensual delight which enclosed her body like the wrappings of a mummy—I nevertheless sensed that an active awareness was at work in her, perhaps that rare sensitivity and intelligence I spoke of just now,
perhaps some particular quality of her muscles, her teeth, her
flesh. . . . Although it was tossed wildly to and fro, her body
remained sharply conscious. On the watch, even in the middle
of the breakers. The victim of the whirlpool and yet at the same
time controlling it. She moved toward my pleasure as she
might have moved toward the solution of a problem, getting
further and further into her subject, deeper and deeper still,
and conveying to me the feeling of her advance. Sometimes in

the convulsion of pleasure, with a drumming in my ears and an enormous, frightening pounding in my heart, I should not have been surprised if the lips of the praying mantis under me, reaching the final moment of suction, of swallowing, and on the point of giving me back my freedom, had made a single cutting motion, to fling me out in a blazing orgasm of blood, an orgasm never to be followed by another. Never again. But Luronne liked me alive, whole, lasting. . . .

And the slow drumbeat of time went on, scarcely to be heard except at intervals. Gradually I came to think about the incident in the forest less often, and Solange and the children no longer appeared in my dreams. Yet something had left me: a carefree, ardent something. Luronne and I talked rather less, and I shared less of my reading and my ideas with her. My desires. So then, as though we had felt some kind of threat, we decided to make a journey through our past, each speaking of his own, of course. The men in Luronne's life, the women in mine. What we had been, up until the time we met. Perhaps there, in the progress of that film and in our examination of it, we should find the reasons for our meeting, which obviously had not depended on the mere chance of our both being on board a boat at one particular hour of a particular day. This we did for several evenings until we discovered that we had said everything very thoroughly, even repeating it on occasion and often making cross-checks on the other's life (Luronne would take up some happening and expand upon it with her own remarks and I would set it in its right place in time, between other happenings or thoughts that she had told me about the day or the week before), and what she told me—a revelation, often enough—day after day was in itself the time of the tale, its own duration, and then when the tale was done it took its place between others or after others so that I saw Luronne's life stretch and grow at both ends, they being her birth on the one hand and the moment of our meeting on the other, and in the middle too: and as Luronne picked out events in her past, so she made holes in the fabric of an elastic, yielding time and then she filled them in. It gave me immense pleasure to hear her doing that. Then one evening with an autumnal taste—a rather absurd day that had strayed from the future, losing its way in the summer—we felt that we had said everything. In any case, what we had forgotten would somehow come to the surface. We had the whole of life before us. And the whole of the other's past life behind us, a past that would rise up of its own volition, unexpectedly, apparently unasked, to strike its chords.

It was after that evening that I did not speak to Luronne for two days. Without understanding this silence myself. Without being able to resist it. I just could not say anything to her anymore: perhaps it was much the same as my inability to speak about the forest. Not that day. But what if this silence, which worried Luronne, were to last tomorrow and the day after that—what if my dumbness were to carry on into a future without words?

I had to grapple with it. I had moved into a very unsettled period indeed: I felt weak and brittle and it seemed to me that I was going to pieces, leaking from stem to stern. Something in the nature of a ball where my heart was, ready to burst. I was deeply idle. What you lack, I said to myself, is a purpose. You no longer have your patients to keep you busy and you don't possess any other kind of professional life at all. Sure, you're on vacation here, but now your vacation hangs heavy on your hands. Before, you used to think about America, faraway America, and she filled what time you had left over, after your patients, after living. . . . Now you have her right here: she's become your daily bread.

And I had an uneasy foreboding, a feeling that something was needed—a distance, perhaps.

Luronne began preparing her lectures for the fall term, due to begin the first week of October, and we went out less. Her methodical arrangement and tidiness overawed me. She settled down at the left-hand side of the desk and I was on the right—unless indeed I was upstairs, lying on the bed. Settled down to read. Luronne did not talk. There were two or three books open on lecterns in front of her, and in a clear, careful, elegant hand she wrote on filing cards.

She had invented a kind of shorthand: one day she explained its rules and I had to admit that she needed only one card where I should have taken six to say the same things. Often, when she got up and disappeared for a moment, I went over and looked at her cards. Luronne's work was forging ahead. With their underlinings and their different-colored inks the cards were full and clear, and they displayed strength, natural ability, and mastery of medium. They gave me a better insight into certain aspects of Luronne's character. Her power of abolishing disorder, for example. After our tumultuous lovemaking she swept the battlefield clear with such speed and efficiency, remaking, smoothing, patting, and putting straight that the bed looked as innocent as a waiting-room sofa. Yet although I was fascinated by the tidiness all around her, the orderly method that I saw on the outward Luronne and at whose existence I guessed in the inward Luronne fascinated me still more. A fascination not without its qualms. I had seen her swell and tighten, I had seen broad red patches appear high on her chest, I had seen her utterly overwhelmed; and then, the tumult barely past, she would show a smooth, untroubled face, where my fingers stroked nothing but the usual curves and planes. And her eyes pellucid—no dark rings around them. Her heart beat slowly, like that of some top-ranking athlete after an effort. She got her breath back quickly. If I did nothing to stop her she was dressed in a moment, and already downstairs when I was only just crawling out of bed. She talked, as though to encourage me, and her voice was full of what we had just accomplished. Not emphatically so, not hoarse, but eager. She liked drawing comparisons: "That was better than the day when . . ." or, "This was the time I had most . . ." In the intellectual process of sorting and classifying pleasures, she was always way ahead of me. She had outstanding powers of assimilation, and that explains why she came up to the surface again so quickly. A strength that always leaves the man lagging quite a long way behind.

A strength that was sapping me. Combining with all the rest to take away my balance. One morning I had a fleeting suspicion that I was reading to pass the time. Dismayed, I looked at my hands: they were trembling. I—I who had always read in order to be in America, where time does not pass. I really had to get a grip on things; I really had to stop my drifting. On reflection it appeared to me that not long since France had sent me over to America, as a powerful racquet might send a ball, where I lacked strength, imagination, faith. Now America was sending me back to France, like a spent bullet. Then once again there was what I called Luronne's tidiness, her brain divided up into distinct segments that never overlapped, thus doing away with all confusion. On the subject of Solange this time. Solange, that is to say my past, which overflowed painfully into my present in spite of me. I was not Luronne: far from it. She never tired of questioning me about yesterday, about my tastes, my favorite tales, my fads, my loves: I had to tell her every detail of my last days in France and of that afternoon when I took off from Paris, and every time she avoided or sidestepped Solange and the children, and her questions were so phrased that I had to make an effort to remember that I did not go to the airport alone, a solitary bachelor. She never once asked me whether I wrote home. Nor what I thought of doing when I had spent the money I had brought with me—quite a considerable amount, luckily, because I had wanted to buy a chief's rattle on the Pacific coast, an Iroquois mask, a Great Lakes pipe of peace, a Plains headdress, and unforeseen wonders too, and it grieved me that because of daily living expenses I had had to give up my search and my possible acquisitions. Of course it must be said that I would not have renounced Luronne for any one of these things nor even for all of them together; but if only I could have had them and Luronne too! The thought came to me one day, with the impact of a slap, and I blushed when a voice inside me said it was dead certain that for her part Luronne no longer regarded herself as the sole owner of her Indian treasures now that I was in her life and the voice added that if I were to persist in thinking in terms of myself alone then she ought to say "We." I promised myself to behave better.

Basically what Luronne was looking for was just love. Just pure love and its free-springing impulse. Did it ever occur to her that I was not divided up into separate, clearly defined segments, as she was? I believe her thoughts or her once-and-for-all decision ran like this: "Let things come from him. Not from me. Since he loves me, let them come from him. I mustn't be a burden. What if I hurt him? He mustn't suffer because of me. Why be together if he isn't happy? If he talks, I'll listen; but I don't want him to force himself to talk because of me. . . ." Luronne asked nothing better than to help me, but she would not give me the wrong kind of help. It seemed to me that her attitude and her ways were saying, "Here we are, you and I, here forever, if you want it to be forever, as I do; a few difficulties will crop up, of course, but as it happens we have time before us, so let's wait, not stirring up anything nor anybody."

And I waited. I would drop off over a book, wake with a start, go back to my reading and find I could scarcely follow the thread: and at times I spoke to Luronne with something like hardness or resentment in my voice. Out of context. Although pleasure did not stay long in her eyes, pain left a lasting mark, and on three occasions it made me ask for forgiveness for having three times indulged myself in mean and ugly conduct.

And I wept. As far as I could remember my last tears dated back to my adolescence, and these struck me by their recurrence and their easy flow. There was no doubt that I had become morbidly sensitive, and this worried me. And if I did not always weep, then at least my eyes grew moist. Happenings in the world upset me beyond all measure. One in Jacques Cartier's third voyage to Canada, for example.

At least a dozen times I had read about Roberval, settled at the mouth of the Rivière Rouge and getting ready to spend the winter. With all the simplemindedness of the Europeans at the beginning of the conquest of the New World—this was in 1543. Scurvy began to attack his hundred and fifty colonists, carrying them off one by one, and I imagine that in addition to the blizzard there was a wind of desperation blowing, so little by little they took to circumventing the harsh discipline of those times, and the books say that Roberval reacted violently, having his men flogged, condemning them to walk about in irons, and even on one occasion sentencing a man caught stealing to be hanged. The Indians watched.

Hurons.

They had never seen a man flogged, men flogged, men in irons, a man hanged. Horrified, fascinated, they wept.

And as for me, I wept too, reading of their tears, although I, four centuries later, knew much more about the evil than ever they did. And I said to myself, "If you are already in tears, having seen nothing so far apart from the hanging of one man and the distress of half a dozen Indians, why, you won't go far."

Then, and they too were a danger, there were the illustrations in Luronne's old books, reproductions of engravings whose originals went far back beyond the publication of the books that contained them—the ancient in the old, as it were—and I let my feelings be worked upon by those which showed the deportation of the Acadians in 1755. A shore dotted with English soldiers, with white-headed peasants bowed in measureless woe; beside them, women in peasant bonnets; some priests with their broad-brimmed hats and bands; quiet children, not running about; girls praying. And as the tears ran down my face I wondered, deeply concerned, whether I was weeping over this deportation—though we have done so much better since those days—or whether, in a magically contracted time and with this two-hundred-year-old scene, I was monstrously, indulgently bewailing some moment of my childhood. And was it not a fact that thirty years back, before the passing of all this time that so distracted me, I was closer to them? So there I was, taking the deportation of the Acadians as though I had lived through it myself. Disturbing. Then there was what I shall call the *Newsweek* incident. We read the magazine every week and Luronne kept some of the numbers. In one that dated from Christmas of the year before, I found a double page showing a snowy landscape by night, and I tore it out. I meant to live with it, to look at it every day. In the foreground, a rider, his horse, and a mule attached to his saddle. These three heads, the man's, the mule's, and the horse's, were looking toward a cabin in the middle distance, a cabin with a snow-covered roof, a smoking chimney, a light coming from a small window. In the background, the dark mass of the forest, setting off the cabin and its enchanting farmyard, in which stood two horses, apparently welcoming the three travelers—cold and hungry travelers, one supposed—and all this absurdly enough, since neither Luronne nor I ever smoked—was Marlboro Country's Christmas greetings, and in the tender emotion that came over me I saw myself on the horse in the snow at the cabin door, on the borders between simplicity and silliness, and something that is not easy to define or pin down with a word, something that is not merely stupidity but superstupidity, not the stupidity that is the opposite of intelligence but stupidity in all that it can contain of softish, washy sentimentality . . . superstupidity. It was high time.

Yet I still needed another lesson, a last warning, and in a curious way it was Luronne's book that gave it to me. About August 15 she had a telephone call from St. Louis telling her that her mother was ill: Luronne was very fond of her mother and she decided to go to Missouri right away. Traveling alone, because she had not spoken nor written to her people about me, meaning to keep that for when she saw them: and obviously this was not the time for me to go with her. After a more or less sleepless night I drove her to the airport to catch the morning plane. We had neither of us had the least warning of a separation, and we were both overwhelmed. Luronne walked sadly up the gangway and I stood there watching the plane carry her away. Watching to the very end, until there was nothing more to be seen. Then, alone and unhappy at being alone, I had a purely masculine reaction. I decided to spend the evening out—and the night too—out or, in a manner of speaking, in. In places where Luronne and I had never been except for just once to see what it was like—prostitutes' bars, bars where people picked each other up for rather special parties, pornographic movies, shows where there was copulation right there on the stage. My heart was not in it. They say it's always like that. After a last and tolerably revolting bourbon just as three was striking, I made up my mind to go home. Without the least effort: and for five hours on end I had steadily refused the various propositions that had been made to me—all for cash, except for one homosexual. I went to bed in the Riverside Drive apartment, sour and heavy-headed.

The escapade was still with me the next day, like a regret or a reproach; I was at loose ends, even more lonely than before, and I set about a thorough inspection of the library. On one of the top shelves, so high that it could scarcely be reached at all, behind the first row of books, I found a whole mass of bound or paperback volumes, pamphlets, programs, all permanently yellowed, with a signature on the flyleaf or the cover of each one. Some crank, no doubt. The mass was made up of several parcels, and I undid the string. Lying on the first book in the first parcel there was an envelope containing a letter, which I read. It was the answer to one that Luronne had sent after seeing an advertisement, and I gathered that the writer had inherited the books a few weeks earlier, that he wanted to sell them, and that because of the subject Luronne had bought the accumulation as a whole, practically by weight. She must have thought that an Amerindianist's collection on the Indian in the nineteeth-century American theater might be useful one day. It was in fact a mass of plays, all written and performed in the last two-thirds of the century. I had to go up and down the ladder several times to get them all, and then I made several journeys up the spiral staircase to carry the whole collection up to the bedroom, where I meant to run through it, lying down.

Luronne telephoned as soon as she reached St. Louis. She was to call me twice a day, in the morning and in the evening, for the ten days she sorrowfully reckoned she would be away. Although I was capable of setting up a solitude for myself in the midst of others, I had in fact almost never been alone. I was now going through the experience for virtually the first time, and without being aware of it I reacted like a recluse. I shut myself up, waiting for time to pass. Later I worked out that during those ten days I only left the apartment three times, and then only to buy food at the Ninety-third Street supermarket.

She found me in every time she called. That pleased Luronne and it pleased me just as much as her, though she still worried about what I was doing. How I was living. I told her the truth, of course: that is to say, that I was reading. Once, when she called, I added, "I'm taking notes," by way of a change. Luronne had left on a Sunday: she came back not on the Tuesday after, but the Tuesday after that. The day of her return I went out some hours before the plane was due to buy her flowers and cakes. Which moved her to tears and which she took, smelled, and ate with joy and even wild delight, in spite of her mother's serious illness.

Then she wanted actually to see what I had been doing and how I had been living far from her, and in the bedroom I showed her, pulling the yellowed heap from under the bed. She recognized them and for fun she took the books one by one and looked at the titles down to the very last one and she read and I read: *The Manhattoes, Naramattah, the Maid of Wyoming, The Wigwam, The Indian Wife, The Last of the Mohicans, Miantanimoh, The Liberty Tree, Lamorah, Wacousta, The Pioneers, Oranaska or The Chief of the Mohawks, Kairrissah, Outallissi, The Yemassee, Sassacus, Tippecanoe, Sharratah, Osceola, Telula or The Star of Hope, Onoleetah, The Eagle Eye, Oua-Cousta or The Lion of the Forest, The Star of the*

West, The Silver Knife or The Hunters of the Rocky Mountains, Onylda or The Pequot Maid, Oroonska, Tuscatomba, Tutoona, Wissahickon, Mioutoumah, and a score of others.

And it was as though I were reading these titles for the first time. Astonished, I looked up at Luronne, and not understanding, she answered with a smile, far away, lost in the happiness of being together again; but then the same crushing thought that filled my mind came to her, and slowly her eyes met mine and there we sat, gazing at each other, filled with pain, overwhelmed by the fact that I had spent ten whole days amidst this faded, flyblown mass, all spotted like an old man's hands, the half-witted evidence of misled, corrupt emotion, impervious to the reality of the Indian, whom it served up with a white, syrupy, sentimental, idealizing sauce, and it was as though I had read without reading, without understanding this literature for shopgirls or Sunday-schools which ought to have bored me to death or to have repelled me with its stock, stereotyped, high-flown, lachrymose scenes, a whole false literature written by people not one of whom has come down to posterity, stuff that will never, never be acted again, of course, and that nobody has ever read again, either, for something like a hundred years, apart from specialists, thesis writers, and ludicrously enough me: and I had a kind of dizziness, with Roberval's Hurons and the deported Acadians whirling about in the phony cabin-of-happiness lit up in the night. Superstupid. In our shared confusion and distress we could neither of us find the words—no matter what words—that might have concealed our feelings: Luronne left my side, and there I was alone, with the evil taste of time past, of musty, wasted time, in my mouth. Superstupidity was leading straight to catastrophe. I had to react, to get a grip on myself. For the first time since I arrived in America, I knew what anguish was.

It was then, in this completely new distress, the very evening Luronne had come back to me, that I had the idea that she might tell, recount, relate America for me. As a child and an adolescent I had got along, I had grown up, conquered difficulties, made my way through time, all thanks to America. And later too, in my dual role as husband and physician. It was because of America that I was not dead. She had supported me, protected me. Borne me up. Kept me from falling. Helped me to my feet when in spite of everything I stumbled. What would have happened if I had not had her? What should I have become? What other kind of man? And with whom, at present? America had brought me to Luronne and now Luronne would have to protect us, both of us. And it was quite certain that she would protect us by recounting America for me, and for herself too.

Since she had a deep knowledge of it. Since I had less than she. Inevitably. Being an American, living half her time in America, she knew far more than I did, had read books unknown to me. More recent books. She spoke of publications I had never heard of. Frequented libraries. When I tried to follow her in our contests or to compete with her knowledge, I was always beaten. She beat me. Regularly. Put me right. Taught me. Yes, she had to tell me America. Since I should behave as one ought to behave, listening to a tale; and here it was a question of History made up of an infinity, a never-ending series of tales. Since for me the words that told America were always new! Hitherto unheard. Since they were lighthouses in the night that lit up and sent out the most wonderful pictures in the world, images in which I was happy, in which it seemed to me I might not die. Asturias tells us that the Indians (his Indians, those of South America), speaking of poetry say, "That is where words meet for the first time." . . . Since those words and others that you do not think of using on a particular day, words that you did use yesterday and may perhaps use tomorrow—words that you use in the course of a time that does not affect them, does not wear them smooth nor make them old—since these words speak to me, since for me they are a Pentecost, these America-recounting words that come down upon me as in other books the Holy Spirit came down on the Apostles. Words in whose heart beats the pulse of America.

There in a space as inexhaustible as a dictionary, stand words that tell America. Ready. And even if one were to say them all, there are yet others. A perpetual relieving of the guard. Words like soldiers who move up to the front line while the weary troops fall back to the rear. From which they will set out again, refreshed. Fresh regiments of words. You must use them, Luronne. Since they are waiting to be loved. Since they love us. Since I love you.

I knew that Luronne, being Luronne, would not refuse. That she would think about the plan and quickly make it her own. Entirely in favor of the idea. That she would be happy for us to play these parts, happy for herself and for me. The tales would be born and they would die in the evening: I mean Luronne would tell them in the evening with the dying of the day, just before sunset, with the day almost dead, cut short by the coming of the night. Her tales might give rise to dreams, visions, associations, music, colors. Vast landscapes. I should no longer slip off to sleep without companions. A crowd of them, sometimes. Sometimes just a single man, a single woman. Children. I should be less afraid of the moment of death: for the thought of that moment, I mean the word, grips my heart every time, every time in the same place, hastening its beat for ten unbearable seconds and hurting me whenever something thrusts from outside and says the word to my consciousness, which repeats it a second time: death, my death. The only word that escapes America. The only one where she is powerless. And therefore, implacably, the enemy. If only she could capture it! Kill it and quietly, slowly, pitilessly weigh down upon it. Until it smothered. Until it threw up its black bile. Or else shut it up in a cage, so as to look at it with a retrospective shudder throughout the whole length of eternity. Often I told myself that righting wrong was in America's reach and that maybe in her sheriff's star she had just brought it off, arresting death and holding it, handcuffed, in a county jail somewhere in Oklahoma, the former Indian Country, where it had been such a scourge. Only I did not know it yet. Perhaps one evening Luronne would tell me. . . . She would tell me: I could hear her cry, "Justice has been done!"

Until that evening came, life had to go on. And it might be that the evening I was talking about, the evening I cherished, the splendid evening would only come after many others— evenings when, plunged into the night for six, seven, or sometimes eight hours, I should be defenseless. That was where the limits of dreaming lay: I knew nobody whom dreams had waked, and he dead. Nor, she told me, did Luronne. Dreams do not wake a man who has just died. That is obvious: and perhaps the dead man no longer dreams. In that case dreams would not be any use; they would be no help in passing, in getting through the night; they would be of value only in the day, when you call them back to mind and tell them. One hypothesis remains, the perfectly enchanting hypothesis that the dreaming man is not dying. And although I knew no dead man whom dreams had awakened, neither did I know any dreamer who had been struck by death. Luronne!

When I felt sleep coming over me, and when according to my established custom I turned onto my right side, I took care to keep a piece of me in contact with Luronne—a leg, my back. Instinctively a part of me sought her out, touched her, kept in touch, and lay with her even more than I did; and she told me that at least once a night I would erupt and roll myself into a ball that looked for her. Found her and woke her in a soon-conquered panic. She would listen, soothe, and go to sleep again. She told me so.

In the evening, then. To dream, in order not to die. Just after dinner. We would be alone. Never anyone but us. America would open and flow out from her to me and I should open myself and receive her, hold her, and send her back again. Take her once more. I should have to help Luronne. I should do so with all my might. This is how I saw things: the history lectures she had been giving at Columbia these last two years: books: the card indexes: what she knew and what she would learn every day for me—for us. I should leave her some hours in the morning or the afternoon entirely to herself. The hours she needed for her night classes with me, her solitary pupil. The time she required. The books she required. And if they were not already here I should go buy them.

The time, I said. It was not a question of her talking, uttering a monologue, every evening. Only the evenings when she felt grace upon her and I felt the grace in her and in me—and my enormous need for America. Perhaps all these factors together. Or indeed separately. No absolute requirement. Nothing obligatory neither for us nor for American history. As far as that was concerned, things might happen like this: there would be an electric atmosphere of expectation: Luronne's tense feelings before her lecture. For we should have extraordinary emotions—in Luronne, the fear of disappointing me, of disappointing America, of not being up to the task, of frightening the words away, of handling them badly, saying them badly, summoning them up amiss, misusing them. Of keeping them earthbound. In me, the fear of her fear. At the beginning of her tale I kept my eyes shut. Held my breath. And here we come to two points which I feel I should get quite straight.

Luronne knew and I knew. Quite simply, her knowledge was greater than mine, as I have said. And naturally, the greater the knowledge the greater the wonder.

For example.

I grieved and I could not be comforted at the thought that I should never know the Missouri as it had once been and as it was not so very long ago before the whites undertook to control and spoil the Big Muddy, or the Grand Boueux, as the French explorers called it: the Missouri falls into the Mississippi, and once it kept its colors in a state of perpetual change; and often I was silent, shut in upon myself, when I called to mind that fast-flowing, turbulent river, a great carrier of tree trunks, an eater of cliffs, gnawing them away by the hundreds of thousands, continually weakening them so that in the end it bore them off, reduced to sand and marl, millions of tons of sand and marl that it swept down together with willows and cottonwood trees and the corpses of buffaloes, when the creatures had not retreated in time, and according to Luronne all this dead mass traveled right down to the distant delta of the Mississippi.

Myself: Surely not.

Luronne: Yes, indeed.

Myself: Tell me more!

Luronne: These trees and bushes and all this vegetation drifted to the delta at last, where pelicans and herons used it for roosting on and for nesting.

Myself (distracted by this vision of great birds, white and blue): More, more!

Luronne: You knew about the Red River Raft, above Natchitoches, in Louisiana?

I shook my head and she told me no one would ever see that again, either: since 1880 it had vanished, quite destroyed, though the French explorers had spoken of it as early as 1721—a huge, enormously long mass of old tree trunks, bushes, scrub, branches, foliage, mud, and everything that could float and that only came to a halt when the current bore it to the high-water mark, there to form a kind of dam. About forty miles long in the year 1800. About one hundred and fifty miles long in 1830. It rose and fell in rhythm with the turbulent stream: it raised up trees whose roots were caught in the tangled mass so that they stood as high as copses on dry land or even higher. Where humus had formed between the stranded trunks and branches, a jungle of vegetation thrust up in the dank, decaying earth. The monster's head, being torn, battered, and eaten away, continually dispersed, but more always came from its tail—vegetable, animal, woody, and aquatic matter— and I told Luronne to stop talking and I saw the Red River Raft, untouched by the river-borne colonizing whites, spread and overflow the banks, invade and swallow up Louisiana, then the United States, then the American continent and finally the whole world, and I saw the gigantic raft living and breathing for a century and a half, a colossus that took a hundred

years to ruin, crush, drown, carry off, pound to pieces, burn—
an act in which I recognized the white man's relentless eagerness to destroy the primeval America—and I could no longer
listen to Luronne. I said, "Stop! Stop and let me see and hear."
And I saw and heard the Red River Raft, above Natchitoches,
in Louisiana, in about 1721, and I said, "Why, Luronne, oh,
why was I born so late?"

Yes, the greater the knowledge the greater the wonder. . . .
Luronne would tell me of a thousand facts and situations, details and sights that I knew nothing about. And if I did happen
to know, it would turn out that my knowledge was unlike hers:
less complete, more anecdotic, less rich—but it might also turn
out to be the same. Just as full. In that case I should still be the
one who was hearing it for the first time. Who never wearied. I
should never interrupt you, sweetheart, unless you went too
fast, unless you hurt me or frightened me, unless you gave me a
happiness I could not contain, or lastly unless your words
struck a wrong note in me. If that happened I should stop you.
And if I were right and you were wrong, I should punish you.
Look at the beauty of the word—see it as I see it: in other con-
texts *punish* means something formidable, dreaded, badly carried out, and rightly shameful. A word that implies the disci-
plining of children. But I should punish you lovingly, in the
name of the deepest love. If I am right and I stick to it, that is so
that you shall be more fair, more beautiful. For your own good.
For the glory of America. I should not punish you except when
carried away by passion.

There was no question of her refusing me. Besides, the idea
would never cross her mind. My proposition, after all, only
amounted to being happy in America. To loving you still more,
Luronne. And to making that love have its beginnings far back
in time, so far back that it would merge with eternity. It would
in fact begin at the point where she herself began her tale. And
at the point where she chose to plunge into the history of America, which would surely be the very moment America plunged
into history, there, just at that point, I should love Luronne

even more. And America would come toward us, unhurried, borne on Luronne's lips. America would have time enough. All the time in the world. We too. Five centuries between Christopher Columbus and ourselves, five centuries in which to play and observe and skip around and make love and stretch out in time like on a sandy beach.

Two points, I said. Here is the second. A point that has an ingenious relation to time. In this way: we have Luronne talking to me. Not every evening. Only the evenings of grace. Fine. When she stops, there's the night and the whole of the next day before evening comes again. And if she prefers to wait, maybe other evenings too and other days, not feeling grace upon her and I not feeling it either. Four or six or eight days and nights might follow one another without any tale.

And it was at this stage that I thought of something important. A discovery that might change everything, a discovery that made my heart beat, like the thought of death. But the opposite of death. I'll give an example. Let's say Luronne stops in 1682, with the arrival in America of William Penn, one of the few whites whom I know we shall love, rightly and fervently. Who will make us love each other. There, with William Penn, Luronne stops a tale that has lasted maybe an hour, maybe two. Or twenty minutes. Two or three days go by, perhaps more, perhaps less—one or two or three or even four days that we spend without her being moved to speak. Days in which the history of America is, as it were, brought to a halt. Hanging in abeyance. Exactly so—hanging on Luronne's lips. A waiting history, in which nothing happens.

And that is where I have vast expectations from Luronne, from history, from America, and through them from time. I expect everything from all this time: by doing away with it and so giving history one or two or three or four days of respite. By obliging time to stop. And when you come to think of it, why not? It's a piece of luck history has never had before.

And by forcing it to stop perhaps we might force it to change. . . .

71

What if one night Luronne were to tell me of the historical existence of some event unrecorded, unmentioned in any book or in any living memory—of something that had happened during the silence of one of these one or two or three or four days I have mentioned, during the silence of history? William Penn lands in America, for instance, and for instance he does so on his first voyage—it was in 1682—and we give history three days off, three days of rest, before it starts up again, recovering its property, its past, its impetus, and setting the machinery in motion so that it moves forward once again. . . .

Dazzled, I watched history marking time, no longer recording anything whatsoever. . . .

Luronne had just come back, and I paused awhile: she was seated in one of the library's two armchairs. I told her. She did not interrupt, not even once. What I had to tell her was not always easy to understand in all its aspects and she had to make an effort to get to the bottom of my idea, above all when I expressed it badly. She could be relied upon, of course. Her green eyes were bigger than ever, even wider open. I was too far off to make out whether from time to time a shadow passed across them.

She did not answer. She was thinking. I took her lack of emotion for reserve. I had expected an outburst of enthusiasm. Myself, I was in such a heat of excitement! Was she hiding her feelings? Who could tell? Presently I found the silence and the immobility oppressive. And I was afraid. All at once I felt overwhelmed with weariness and although I could not think of any other place on earth, I wanted to be somewhere else, no longer here.

Then she said yes.

I seized her, hugged her, pulled her over, pulled her down, laid her flat, took off her clothes, lay on her, violated her, petted her, stroked her, caressed her. Kissed her. Stripped her. Very gently closed her eyelids as she lay there on the carpet. Watched over her. Five, ten minutes, until she opened her eyes again. Carried her upstairs. Laid her gently on the bed. Gazed at her. Dressed her once more. Brought her down. Put her into a chair. Wondered about whether she were hungry. Thirsty. What she would like. She could ask for anything at all.

I should have to look after her very carefully indeed. With total care. Take care she did not catch cold. Did not fall sick. The air conditioning was very dangerous. You never knew how far you could rely on it, trust it: always a little too cold or a little too hot and sometimes the contrast between the the temperature indoors and the temperature outside is bad for the throat.

I said to Luronne, "You must take care," and when, astonished, she said, "Care of what?" I replied, "I mean I shall take care of you, so you don't fall ill." And it was clear to me that she could scarcely make out what I was talking about.

We still had to fix the day she was to begin. Neither too early nor too late. Not too early because I wanted some days in which to relish my joy and hold in my eagerness; and it also seemed to me that she would need time to get ready and we both of us needed some days to be together and go out together and I told Luronne that if she liked the idea we would go back to our expeditions before her university reopened. About October 10. So from then on I went shopping with her every morning, and I selected, argued, added up and worked out prices, Luronne delighted that I should be so near to her in everything and I eager to try everything. In the evening I took her to a restaurant and then to places where the lights were low and the music soft, to tell her how I loved her.

Inexhaustibly.

When the Abenakis, the Cherokees, the Têtes de Boules, the Nez Percés, and the Indians of the Cat Nation came knocking at my head, as they might have knocked at a door, I told them to wait, to take it easy, to follow my example: I told them that thanks to Luronne there was going to be a great feast for them, a powwow—they would be the heroes of it, and the feast would last forever.

We lingered day after day, and night after night until very late, which was unlike us, because we usually went to bed early to get up at dawn. We went to the bars all along the streets that run into Fifth Avenue, and it took us five nights to try all the cocktails that America has in such profusion. Then because we knew nothing about them and wanted to know, we joined orgies on two successive nights, having drunk a great deal. In a way we were obliged to pass the time before the great evening: we had to feel that it was near and a great way off, we had to get ready for it, think about it and not think about it, summon it and keep it at a distance. Scatter ourselves abroad and give ourselves, before the concentrated deep communion. That was how we felt. We searched through books of Indian recipes to find out how to make sagamite, succotash, pemmican, and bannock, that corn cake the Abenakis love so much. Luronne and I cooked them, each at the stove in turn. And ate them. I telephoned an importer and he sent us two cases of Dom Perignon, that is to say twenty-four bottles. And a dozen of Bouzy. For the splendid evenings after the splendid evening. For happiness.

There still remained a duty—a painful duty for me and one that I had to perform without speaking to Luronne about it. That I had to carry through as she had sensed I should—alone. Without telling her. I broke with Solange, the children, medicine, and Europe for good and all. In exchange for the America to come. I asked an international lawyer to sell all my possessions for Solange's benefit. Everything was to go to her. He and I worked out that she could manage for two years without running short. There was plenty of time between now and then. Every day for a week I had to go to this lawyer's office; and once he had a long telephone conversation with Solange.

As for the beginnings, I thought about them with a kind of terror. Sometimes in less than a second I would be in a cold sweat all over. The way everything would begin. The first words. It was the beginning that I spoke about in those days, whenever I brought up the subject of the great evening. As I told Luronne, everything depended on the beginning; everything was there; if you began well, if you did not make a mess of the start, then everything was possible. My throat went dry when I thought of it. How ought one to behave, how ought one to feel? How would the words, the beginnings, like us to be when we made a start? The very first words? I thought up rites to make them look upon us kindly. On consideration it seemed perfectly obvious that everything revolved around the words.

So with them in mind we undertook five successful journeys. One in Quebec for the sake of the Ashuapmouchouan, which is the Montagnais word for the elk's meeting place. It is a tributary of the Saguenay. The next took us in two stages right down into the heart of Georgia to see the lovely Okefenokee Swamp on the one hand and to pay our respects to the Chattahoochee River on the other. We ate our lunch on the river bank. Then on to Ontario, full of love for Michipicoten, the infinitely amusing Michipicoten. An island, where I stuffed myself with ouananiche, while Luronne confined herself to a slice of ouitouche. Then the finest journey of them all, because these names have something wonderful about them, to Maine, to the two lakes that are called Mooselookmeguntic and Nesowadnehunk. Algonquin language. I said to Luronne, "It's as though one were purified. Yes, it amounts to a purification."

And the great evening came. We had felt it the day before, just as we were going to bed, and I took her all night long, to love her and encourage her, and we fell asleep at dawn in each other's arms. Before dropping off I managed to tell her that I should always be beside her, and spiritually (since physiology denied us a perpetual physical presence) always inside her. We got up in the afternoon and after careful preparation we put on our best clothes; we quickly lunched, still half asleep, not touching one another until the evening, when a snack was all we wanted. With the windows open, we waited for night to fall. Never had there been so many tugboats hooting and whistling, and the tireless gulls wheeled over the Hudson. And it was night.

And Luronne asked me to go down and wait for her in the library. And in the bathroom she closed the door behind her.

When she opened it again she told me to close my eyes, and I did so willingly. We had turned out the lights and the night outside mingled with the night inside, the same darkness: I dismissed impatience and dread, feelings that seemed vulgar at this moment and that Luronne certainly no longer deserved. My whole being was expectation, quivering expectation. When she came back to the library, Luronne asked one last question, learned that my eyes were indeed closed, and then she began.

And right away I knew that I had been right, that she was born to play this part, and that she was in her right place. The right tone of voice, the right snares (her accent and her way of speaking) set on their trail to trap the words; and I heard her say:

The earth, in the first place, the earth upon which we stand, you and I. The ancient earth, four billion years old.

Myself (clumsy, breaking in already and threatening to put her off): Surely not!

Luronne: Four billion years old, and I start with the beginnings of the ice age, one million five hundred thousand years ago.

(Myself enchanted that she should go back so far, to a period so remote: there would be enough to last our lifetime.)

Luronne: And during the hundreds of thousands of years of these ages the ice advanced and retreated four times and the last glaciation is still retreating even now, which perhaps you did not know. (And I nodded to say yes: yes, I did not know.) And at one point thirty-two percent of all the land above sea level was covered with ice, including the American continent as far as what are now the Ohio, the Missouri, and the Columbia rivers, that is to say the whole of the northeast United States and eastern Canada. Do you realize that?

(I nodded, my eyes closed.)

Luronne: But not Alaska, nor western Canada, nor Siberia.

(And I said to myself that I should have sworn the opposite: Siberia and Alaska free of ice—who would have believed it?)

Luronne: And in the south Yukon and Mackenzie valleys in

Alaska the grass grew thick—here, look at the grass and the ice side by side.

(I opened my eyes and I saw them side by side: a picture of grass growing right at the very edge of the ice barrier, and instantly I had a longing for the taiga and the tundra, where the poogie grows, smelling of sugar and honey; and the far northern grass sent me to another grass farther south—to that page in *A Brief Description of New York* which Daniel Denton published in 1670, six years after the Dutch colony came into the possession of the English, where Denton says that in New York the grass, and I quote, "came up to your waist," and full of dreams, quite overcome, I told Luronne that in one century things had changed more than they had in one million five hundred thousand years and she prized the powerful vision, this commonplace observation.)

Then Luronne: And now pay great attention. The great happening: where now there is the Bering Strait, a narrow sea some fifty-four miles across between Siberia and Alaska, Russia and the United States, in those days there was an isthmus, formed by the ice, a positive land-bridge twelve hundred fifty miles long; and the ancestors of the Indians crossed over this bridge into America. But listen now; it came to pass that the bridge vanished in the enormous melting of the ice and the isthmus turned into a strait, into what it is today, and there were the Indians, prisoners in America! The Paleo-Indians, as one ought to say. The bridge rose up, sank down, and rose up again several times and—just imagine it—as the first Paleo-Indians were crossing to America the ice began to melt again, to melt slowly, for as I told you it hasn't stopped yet, and these first Americans came at no one can tell quite what approximate dates, around about twenty or twenty-five or thirty-six thousand years before Christ, as they say, and maybe even earlier.

Myself: Stop, wait for me to see and feel and touch. You go too fast, no you don't go too fast, you go just right, forgive me, I love you, but stop. (And I set this series of millenniums straight in the sequence of time from the time before Time

77

down to the Pleistocene, which is synonymous with the Ice Age.)

Then: Go on!

Luronne: And the Paleo-Indians crossed over by the isthmus. To the continent which had been here for four billion years and on which no one had yet set foot.

Myself: Unbelievable!

Luronne: Crossed over and crossed back. And it is perfectly reasonable to suppose that some of them made the journey several times, dozens of times in both directions, not knowing they were going from Asia to America and the other way about: it was all the same ice for them.

Myself: Stop!

(These Paleo-Indians: something prodigious that I had to get clear in my mind—crossing the then nonexistent frontier as though it were a game, as though they did it for the laugh, crossing by means of a bridge that had no better foundation than the goodwill of the ice, and when the ice melted the bridge was underwater and there was no going back—hell, I've left my flints on the other side. Of course not: the ice takes thousands of years to melt—they'd have plenty of time to go there and back again.)

Luronne: Which they traversed in pursuit of game. The coming of men to America, the discovery of America, began with hunters tracking down large animals to kill them. Extinct animals: I'll tell you about them—long-horned bison, the imperial mammoth, the mastodon, several species of musk-ox, an elk-like creature, a sloth, a gigantic terrestrial sloth weighing about as much as an elephant, huge camels, the glyptodon, the wild horse, much sought after by the Paleo-Indians, and when they crossed the Bering Strait, hopping from island to island, what they found was a second animal paradise with all the creatures I've mentioned and the opossum too, the three-toed sloth, the saber-toothed tiger, the weasel, quantities of birds, and so on and so forth. Look at them. Men and women and children carried over in an exodus that lasted thousands of years, a diaspora: and these refugees wearing skins and furs had spears and pointed flints and perhaps the dog-drawn travois already. The dogs are known for sure. A procession on the march, moving south. Look at them—red Mongoloids, if I may use the term, with their javelins.

I looked.

Luronne: Paleo-Indians. Traveling in little groups, not knowing where they were going, and perhaps the first crossed the isthmus thirty-eight thousand years before Christ—Him again—and it was a great turmoil, a huge movement that lasted for thousands of years and there are vast stretches of time between the journeys of these bands, whole millenniums between the first and the last, no less, and look, here they are reaching Patagonia and Tierra del Fuego about 6700 B.C. when you in Europe were in the Stone Age, and it's been estimated that it took the Paleo-Indian two thousand years to travel from the extreme north of the continent to the extreme south. From then on he was all over it. Look.

I looked.

I looked, saying nothing, at the new-arrived Indian in Meso-America, and I observed the sparse campfires quivering in the icy air of the Andes.

And in a weak voice I asked how the Indians had . . .

Luronne, interrupting me: By following the foothills of the Alaskan mountain ranges and then the Mackenzie Valley, an ice-free corridor to the interior. And the Mackenzie brought them to the eastern side of the Rockies and to the great rivers (Luronne slid a map across, and reaching over with a flashlight she showed me), where they scattered. And some followed valleys and rivers eastward and some went west, crossing the Rocky Mountain passes—they were ice-free too.

She paused. Then: And the Paleo-Indians were then in that part of the United States-to-be that Lewis and Clark called the Great Plains and that did not change between 10,000 B.C. and some hundred fifty years ago, yes, until Napoleon I sold Louisiana, and listen, a hundred fifty years ago the white man saw

79

just about the same sight that the Paleo-Indians had seen ten thousand years back. Eternity, you'd say, but for . . . A vast flat country with sudden steep hills here and there and gentle slopes with clumps of trees like islands, trees that must have felt rather lonely, rather cut off in that ocean of grass, and now and then monstrous great canyons slashed in the prairie, thrusting down toward the heart of the earth. The first travelers in modern history described their stupefaction. Some amazed, their minds deep in thought. Others full of rapturous joy. Still others anxious and disturbed. In fact a paradise such as man had never seen before and now will never see again. The prairie.

Myself, overcome: You can see its tall grass in Fenimore Cooper.

Luronne: The prairie, now an arid plateau. In those days, toward the end of the last glaciation, rivers were born. The country had lakes and pools. And, as I told you, it was the big animals' paradise.

She said their names in a louder voice and deep inside myself I pictured their enormous bulk.

Luronne: The quiet flow, a seeping like menstrual blood, of the Paleo-Indians thrusting other Paleo-Indians before them, pushing them back, for thousands of years, and the last arrived some ten thousand years ago, Aleuts and Eskimos, and they did not come down. Stayed in the north. I said the word Eskimo but I shan't say it again. Some Indians invented it for the benefit of the Jesuits in Labrador. Appears in French for the first time in 1511. An Algonquin word for one who eats raw meat. A word that is supposed to describe them but does so badly, and the Eskimos do not recognize the description. Their own word for themselves is Inuit, Inuk in the singular—men, a man. That's the term we shall always use.

Myself: Yes.

Luronne: And by the time the whites arrived, after Columbus, the isthmus had been impassable for ten thousand years and there were many tribes who had not yet found the country they needed, the country they longed for, and they were still roaming about the North American continent.

Myself: Stop! (A sudden spring of imagination and knowledge carried me back to 1700 and I saw the Comanches traveling south from right up in the Platte River country down to the Arkansas, where they dispersed.)

Luronne (tearing me away from the Comanches): Then eight thousand years ago the temperature rose all over the world, caused the snows to melt and restored the water to the seas, which rose, thus submerging the isthmus, thus cutting the Indians off from their past. And now the Bering Strait has been there without a break these eight thousand years, the strait that divides America from Asia and that creates the Indians.

Myself: Stop! (And I asked her to repeat what she had just said and then stop to give me time to look, and I saw the prodigious upheaval and I said "Listen" and both of us listened to the mighty uproar some eight thousand years before Christ when that thick, extensive immensity of ice crashed into the sea, and we watched the water level rising, covering the land bridge.)

Luronne:

Pause. For a while she said no more, and we rested from the anxious, feverish crossing of the narrows and the journey down toward Patagonia, where Magellan, who passed by there on his way around the world, saw the Paleo-Indian in the distance, a sight that alarmed him.

Then without a word I watched the men of ten thousand years ago walking upon the earth, the four-billion-year-old earth.

Then Luronne: And they had dogs, as I said, and maybe travois: they did not yet possess bows and arrows—they came later—only throwing spears and lances with flint heads like the ones you've seen (she pointed at the Clovis, Folsom, and Sandia flints, obscure in the darkness), then later but still well before the bow and arrow they invented the *atlatl*, which you may know about. (She repeated the word, quite unknown to

81

me.) A spear thrower. And the specialists, who have managed to go back twenty thousand years with their archaeological digging and then to work down, have done all that can be done to trace the evolution of hunting techniques in this hunter's paradise that stopped being a paradise once it had undergone the great climatic changes that did away with the covering of vegetation. Seven thousand years back saw the end of the really big game, those mastodons.

Myself: What happened to them?

Luronne, put out: It was a little earlier than the collapse of the isthmus. About sixteen thousand years ago. When the ice began to melt the temperature rose, and there was less rain. The vegetable covering shrank and that caused the extinction I'm going to tell you about, the extinction of the North American mammals, the biggest the world has ever seen. Sixteen thousand years ago the mammals began to disappear, as did the dinosaurs sixty-five million years before. It would require six thousand years to effect their total liquidation, down to the very last one. From one day to the next—a day and a night that lasted six thousand years—no more woolly mammoths, no more tapirs, no more giant terrestrial sloths, no more bison, no more horses: the American horses vanished entirely, but in the Middle East in modern times they let themselves be tamed, then they reappeared in Europe and finally in America once more, after having been gone ten thousand years.

Myself, utterly galvanized: More!

Luronne: No more gigantic armadillos and no more pre-Columbian mammoths. None at all.

Myself, panting: More!

Luronne: Due to changes in climate, as I told you, also to the coming of mankind.

Myself: Already!

Luronne: Man had just made the discovery of fire.

Myself: Not possible!

Luronne: Big scale massacres, all the easier now that the country had grown arid. The animals were all crowded around what water there was, and the Paleo-Indians were waiting for them, ready to set the forests and the prairies on fire. . . . But apart from that, there may have been other causes. Nowadays it's thought that the dinosaurs may have been killed by angiosperms, plants full of strychnine and morphine.

I did my utmost to see. And as she was about to take up where she had left off, I checked her while I gazed within myself at pictures of her great animals, struck down, pierced by the sharp, biting flints: I had seen nearly all their surviving modern representatives in zoos, and I forced my imagination to make them seem bigger and taller like their ancient prototypes.

Luronne: There's also the possibility of something in the nature of a famine, food having grown scarce because of the changing climate; but all things being considered I come back to the Paleo-Indians' way of hunting (and here I felt she was smiling). Waste is no modern discovery, and to make sure of two or three animals they massacred hundreds and thousands, gradually putting the species in danger of extinction.

Myself: And what about the Indians?

Luronne: No one knows. Perhaps they disappeared along with the Pleistocene animals they lived on; or perhaps they were exterminated or just absorbed by other Paleo-Indians— the ones who came from Asia in little waves, you know, and who went on evolving from 10,000 B.C. until the fifteenth century of our era, when Columbus discovered the ancestors of the Indians of today.

Myself: Stop! (She stopped: I reached for her hand, found it, and held it so as to see that mass of humanity, these tens of thousands of Paleo-Indians, maybe more, who can tell? disappearing together with the animals of the Pleistocene.) I wonder what disappearance means, Luronne—disappearance, as applied to these men. Suddenly dying all at once, all together, in a fantastic simultaneous heart failure? Or fading away, drying up, slowly perishing, dying as we die? Or changing, turning into something else?

Luronne shook her head. She did not know. Then: The fact

remains that after the Paleo-Indian we have the archaic Indian. He lived in the vast solitary wilderness over toward the Pacific Coast and also in the eastern United States. He understood harvesting and he was still an everlasting hunter—deer, moose, raccoons, opossums. He was immensely, wildly inventive—harpoons, baskets, snares, stones for milling grain. He brought his mind to bear on plants, fish, turtles, very small game, shellfish, snails, mollusks. Yesterday the biggest, today the smallest, you see. With its ducks, geese, and all the migratory birds, this was still another hunters' paradise. And the archaic Indian evolved. Listen.

She was panting, not that she was short of breath but rather of inspiration. For the moment grace had left her. Faith. The exciting, disturbing images. Nothing rose from the darkness or the river anymore. The tugs were dozing: so were the gulls. And New York, so silent, might have been asleep.

Luronne: Then great civilizations arose in the deserts of the Southwest and in the woods and the plains of the Northeast: little is known about them, ridiculously little, but that little is enough to tell us something about the wonder we are both seeking: look, now. . . .

I told her I was looking.

Luronne: The Anasazis. Curiously enough it so happens that what we are looking at with them begins in the year 1 of history and carries on in Colorado, Arizona, Utah, and New Mexico until about 1300. In the Navajo language Anasazis means the old people, the people of olden times. From the very beginning they were wonderful weavers of plant fibers. They made baskets plaited and knotted so tight that water could be carried in them. Not potters: not in the least. But then in the second stage of their evolution, of their life, the Anasazis took to pottery and straightaway they were right at the top. Unrivaled. Yet their true genius lay in architecture: they invented the collective dwelling, and I know one in New Mexico that had as many as eight hundred rooms. Do you grasp that?

I told her I did.

Luronne: They had a Golden Age, and then a little before the coming of the Spaniards, they abandoned their great towns. In the thirteenth century. All their towns, one after another. Because of the attacks of the Navajos? Because of the sudden drought that lasted—and there is evidence to prove it—for twenty-three mortal years? Because of an epidemic? Internal strife? We don't know. The whole of the Southwest is full of these towns, these pueblos, abandoned centuries ago. . . .

I looked; I rearranged the causes she had given; I tried to understand, to make things out before she should start again, too soon.

Luronne: And the Hohokams of southern Arizona, another of these Southwest desert cultures. From a Pima word meaning those who have gone away. They are dated between 700 B.C. and A.D. 1400—rough figures, of course. In 1400 the Hohokams and every vestige of their culture vanished like the Anasazis I have just been speaking about. At the present day the Pimas and the Papagos are their descendants in southern Arizona.

Myself: We'll go and see them.

Luronne: The great irrigators of North America. One of their canals alone measured nearly sixteen miles. Others formed a series of networks, and we know of one system, provided with dams, that covered an area of over ninety square miles.

And they played a ball game on solidly built courts. And they too were great artists, and what's more: potters, sculptors, and architects who built their towns in circles, and can you imagine, they discovered engraving by the use of acid?

Myself, beside myself: Surely not!

Luronne, full of enthusiasm: I could name other cultures by the dozen and tell you about them, all mingling, interpenetrating, some alike and some unlike one another, all influencing one another and yet keeping the strongest marks of their original character, and what strikes us now and what astonished the whites when they first arrived is the variety of the Indians' attitudes, forms of behavior, thoughts, and expression, and I won't

85

mention all the aspects you're well acquainted with such as the towns, the pueblos in the side of desert cliffs, with the kiva, that kind of well for sacred rites that only men could enter.

Myself, after a slight hesitation: Yes . . .

Luronne: It must be clear to you that the heart of the matter is this phenomenon of the desertion of towns that had been inhabited for centuries; for sometimes it happened that other people came to live in them, coming as suddenly and for us as incomprehensibly as the earlier occupation and desertion. Sometimes they came long after, and then they too abandoned them, and for the last time—the desolation of those towns, now dead forever.

Myself: I can see them. (Looking at the great ruins rising straight up skyward among the sparse bushes of kochie, exomis, and mesquite.)

Luronne: And when the Spaniards came they found nothing but empty pueblos, empty as they are today, except right in the heart of New Mexico, and, farther west, in the Zuñi and the Hopi country.

I looked.

Luronne: The Adenas. We are in the northeast now. Earth-built pyramids. I know you've not seen the pyramids, because we've not been there, but (anticipating my question) we'll go. A people in Ohio, in Kentucky, and the northwest of West Virginia this time—huge tumuli where important personages were buried, their bodies surrounded by valuable possessions. *Mounds.* Remember the word, because you'll often come across it. Sometimes one mound might be built on top of another, and I know of some more than eighty feet high . . . but all that is—what did you say the other day? I've got it: small beer. All that is small beer. Now I come to the great Mound Builders, the Hopewells. From about a hundred years before Christ—always and forever Him—until five or seven hundred after.

Myself: What happened then?

Luronne: They vanished too. We'll come to that. As you see,

they were living and working there in the Northeast at a time
that runs parallel to that of the pueblos I was telling you about.

Myself: Hold on while I look. (And I saw, with Christ as the
pivot, the America of before Him and the America after Him
like a fantastic anthill.)

Luronne: Tens of thousands of mounds. I believe North
America has a hundred thousand, most of them in the Mississippi Valley. And just imagine this, whereas the Adenas were
brachycephalic, the Hopewells were dolichocephalic.
Mounds—I've seen masses of mounds: Fort Ancient: Great
Serpent Mound. They're on the top of a hill and they dominate
a valley. It's calculated that the building of Fort Ancient called
for about 817,450 cubic yards of earth.

Myself: Unbelievable!

Luronne: And that's nothing. It's almost small beer when
you compare it with another built by Indians who were not
Hopewells—the Cahokia earthwork, east of St. Louis in Illinois. That mound we owe to the Mississippi Valley tribes, and
to make it they had to carry three times as much earth as for
Fort Ancient.

(I gazed at this enormous transportation, this vast earth re-
moval, and my head swam.)

Luronne: And the Hopewells' influence reached out a great
way, as far as Minnesota, New York, Florida, Louisiana.

Myself: Wait. (Wait until I settle the position of these states,
travel about in them, take a long look. Then—) Go on.

Luronne: The Hopewells must have lived on a more exalted
scale than the Adenas, because their mounds were bigger and
their offerings to the dead richer. Mounds so high you can't see
the top. A single Hopewell earthwork in Ohio covers three and
a half square miles, and just one grave has yielded four thousand pearls from freshwater clams. You can speak of a Golden
Age when you're talking about the Hopewells. Fishermen,
hunters, and artists who worked gold, silver, copper, and iron.
Made ornaments of wood, mica, shells, bones. Great traders.
Picture that.

87

(I pictured it, though in this case without a very clear notion of what underlay my imagining.)

Luronne: The greatest traders in North America. They carried their trade to the uttermost ends of the continent. Picture it.

(And impatient to have my picture sharp and clear I interrupted—Faster.)

Luronne: Picture it! They had grizzly-bear teeth and obsidian from as far off as the Rocky Mountains, bivalves and other shells from the Gulf of Mexico and the Atlantic coast, mica from the Appalachians, lead and copper from the Great Lakes and the upper Mississippi Valley. Do you realize that?

Myself: Yes.

Luronne: A trade that threw the whole of North America into a fever a thousand years before Columbus.

Myself: Stop.

She paused for breath, and we contemplated that very high civilization, seeing it through its travelers, packmen, and carriers. Then:

Luronne: Morison states that the pipestone from a quarry famous for calumets traveled over nine hundred miles from its place of origin. Do you realize that?

I nodded yes. And I looked.

Luronne: Then, toward the year 500, the end of that splendid cult of the dead and the end of the Hopewells. True, after them there were people who built temples, just as they had built mounds. Only there's not a single temple left.

She stopped and I looked: the Anasazis, the Hohokams, the Adenas, the Hopewells . . . Their scattering and their disappearance. As though the earth had swallowed them up. Towns abandoned, inhabited again, lost once more. Nations that went away, that were absorbed, that vanished. Just before the coming of the Indian of modern times. And I said—

And I said, "It's strange, Luronne, but you've just told me about the arrival of the Indians in America—the Indians are in America—yet in order to do so you've conjured up lost and

vanished Indians. Indians whose trace is lost. To tell about life
you have told about death."

And I touched wood.

And all at once I was on her. Had flung myself upon her with
her look of one emerging from a dream. Coming from elsewhere. It was only now that I found she was naked, naked under a nightdress. One that I did not know. Transparent. A
nightdress that covered and did not cover her. I tried to control
myself and set my feelings in order and I said, "You are the Luronne of the beginnings, like the first Luronne, like a child." I
lifted her from her chair, I held her upright against me and I
clasped her. I was floating in the stream of her narrative as I
might have been drifting in the waters of a river, seeking for
the bend of a passage, the bed of a phrase, the sand of a word,
to stop myself. I looked at the Paleo-Indians, the red Indians,
the yellow Indians; I watched them die, find rebirth in the archaic Indian, die again, and resuscitate in a new Indian ten
centuries before the landing of Christopher Columbus; and
drunk with something I could not name, I said, "The Indians
shall not die a third time: they shall never die again," and
pressed against the mute Luronne I listened to the isthmus
foundering in the strait, the land sinking down, the sea covering it, and I carried Luronne away.

I kept her all night. And gazed at her for a great while. We
had not drawn the curtains and from time to time lights danced
through the windows, giving her skin the color of copper. I
took her once, just before opening the bottle of Dom Perignon.
Then a second time, toward the end of the bottle. Then a third
time, I'm sure: I remember it well, because just at that moment
I thought, in a blaze of joy—the sinking of the isthmus doesn't
matter in the least: the Indians are in America!

The grace had not dissipated during the night and as soon as
we woke we felt that it was there beside us. That like us it was
waiting for the daytime to pass. Oh, let it wait! It answered the
hundreds of prayers I had uttered as the hours flowed by. Ac-

cording to the rules I was not to know with whom and with what Luronne was going to continue until the last moment. Indeed, it was impossible to know. And Luronne had carefully prepared her line of approach. Unexpected. An evening full of laughter and fun.

It had hardly begun before I remembered that when I read my books about America in my childhood and right up to Luronne I felt a powerful dislike for those who tried to discredit Columbus, either by direct criticism or by not speaking of him. Full of envy and hatred. And devoured by eagerness to set foot on the continent, to land on the East Coast and then to make my slow way into the heart of the country that in my abounding love for America I magnified threefold, westward, southward, and northward—in this impatience I, both as a youth and as a man, had passed too quickly over certain moments of the pre-Columbian period and I had not sufficiently appreciated the stubborn and often ludicrous stupidity of those innumerable denigrators of Columbus. But now Luronne, scornful in her fierce, well-informed criticism of the would-be scholars who looked upon the world as a sieve, was providing me with proofs and arguments. When she had quoted some of their choicer statements I had a brilliant idea (I think) and straight away I called it *the stake.* Here now, said I to Luronne, on that high table over there we'll always keep a file, and every time either of us finds a particularly base or foolish remark, we'll put it in; and in another file, the *counterstake,* we'll put those statements that are beautiful or strong. In short, anything worth noting.

That first day, with much self-congratulation, we voted for this pronouncement of Cyrus Gordon, an American: in his view, around about the year 1000 (some five centuries before Columbus)—and here I quote—"The Caucasians arrived from Eurasia; the blacks from Africa [where does he suppose they came from, asked Luronne, Sweden, maybe?]; the Mongols, of the Chinese or Japanese type, from the Far East; and at different periods from the shores of the Mediterranean various

Semites (particularly Phoenicians, Carthaginians, Egyptians, Greeks, Ethiopians, Romans) . . ." Why, pre-Columbian America was a positive Fifth Avenue!

Myself: A Champs-Elysées!

Gordon and his kind reducing the Atlantic and the Pacific to the size of ponds that a vast crowd, a mob of people could take in their stride. . . . And since pretty nearly everybody was already treating himself to his little trip across the Atlantic, or the Pacific as the case might be, five centuries before Columbus, there naturally remained no element of chance. "The greater part of Atlantic traffic in the direction of the New World was planned," an extraordinary observation, still from the American, an extraordinary treasure that I begged Luronne to repeat and that I instantly put on record, darting to seize the stake at the other end of the room. A truly fine pearl. A hundred-carat pearl that would last our lifetime. And then Luronne exposed the unsound evidence upon which Gordon and his like based their hypotheses. A Maya head with its nose rising right up to the middle of its forehead: for these learned souls this was proof of a Near Eastern influence and therefore of the landing on American soil of the merchant princes from the Mediterranean. The Cretans' way of doing their hair? Why, it was modeled on the New World fashion, of course: and there was even no lack of inscriptions on stone to establish written proof that the Minoan and Phoenician sailors had landed on the shores of the New World long before Columbus. The latter was in fact the last, very much the last. The least gifted of all the swarming host of ocean crossers. The usurper. And just as all these people sailed across the Atlantic, each in the other's wake, so these misguided scholars raced one another in their vain search for the earliest crossing, a race to be won by the man who asserted that his voyage was earlier than all the rest. Shamelessly going back as far as possible in time, they challenged one another, their weapons being ancient or even extinct nations: one would maintain the priority of a Phoenician; another would retort with an Irishman; and this would bring a third scholar into the arena, armed with a Welshman: yet the palm fell, not as one might have supposed to the man who produced the Welsh original ocean voyager, but to an obscure person who affirmed that it was the redskins themselves who crossed the Atlantic! From time to time the sea threw up corpses on the coast of the Azores and occasionally even on that of Portugal, corpses rendered all the more mysterious by the fact that their race could not be made out: they were therefore those of redskins. Long before Columbus discovered America the Indians had discovered Europe on their own. Unhappily it so happened that for very good reasons not a single one was able to bear witness to it. And this perpetual silence was the basis of many works of priceless erudition.

But, Luronne, what's hiding behind all this pseudoscience? Behind all these confident statements? What is it that urges this Gordon to take the Pires Reis map and calmly to deduce that America was discovered at a time before the formation of the ice that now covers the North Atlantic Coast? In other words four thousand years before Christ? Not a minute less. What makes him set the first ocean crossing at the beginning of the Neolithic Age? Listen now, Luronne, does this Gordon of yours drink—does he maybe take drugs?

It did not take long to realize that these people were mondialists, universalists, internationalists, or, with the same artlessness, diffusionists. A fifth word: globalists. An unbelievable wealth of synonyms to express nothing, nothing at all. To hide the same thing—a total inability to conceive that a civilization might develop independently, of its own accord, in an evolution parallel with the others. In isolation. The very opposite of diffusionism. That works of art—and Luronne instanced those of the Mayas—could not be reduced to anything but themselves, with no explanation other than that of the men and the country which produced them—all this was something far, far beyond their comprehension. For if that were so then the world would be manifold! The notion sent them into a panic! And Luronne showed me the veil that covered all this high-flown, allegedly philosophic stuff: the unhappy people were filled with a longing, a nostalgia—for them the world was one. Basing themselves on this assumption, they delighted in working out endless extensions. The itch for unity! The great yearning for the One! The One, that philosophic idea . . .

Then there was what Luronne called the myth of lost knowledge. This is how the trick is done: you lay it down as a fact that the nations of preclassical times understood longitude, for instance: it follows that they had a thorough knowledge of navigation and mapmaking. And when we, who know more or less what kind of hell sailors went through until the middle of the seventeenth century because they could not calculate longitude—when we, rather stunned, rather at sea, say "Really? Oh, indeed? And where's the proof, Luronne?" "No proof! It's lost." And when this Gordon calmly states " . . . in the remotest times [of the earliest antiquity] there was a world-wide civilization [Luronne: of course!] whose cartographers drew up a survey covering nearly the whole globe at the same mathematical and technical level using analogous methods [as those of classical science] . . ." and when you ask to see and touch, hey, presto, it's lost. A certain Quinn asserts that the Bristol fishermen discovered North America between 1481 and 1491 and that they kept the discovery secret because of the prodigious wealth of fish on the Newfoundland banks, which they wanted for themselves alone. . . . The reason why the Carthaginians never said anything about their discovery was that they meant to take refuge there in case of disaster. . . . Once everything is lost or secret, the absence of proof for what you put forward is in itself a proof—*the* proof. Then after that you can decree anything you like—you can multiply the ocean crossings before Columbus a hundred or a thousand times; you can go so far as to make the discoverer of America a Pole or an African from Mali; you can even go so far as to write a book which, once published, bears this eloquent title: *They All Discovered America.* Why not?

There we were, Luronne and I, thoroughly worked up. She

displayed treasures of intelligence and humor and the art of penetrating another man's thought and dissecting it like a cadaver; and all this rendered her magnificent. I could hardly sit still. My arms reached out toward her: I had to keep myself from talking, crying out, echoing her words. But then I lost my self-control and I shouted, "More! More of them!" I saw learned men impaled like butterflies. And I longed for Christopher Columbus: I was sure he would come, in a few days' time, tomorrow evening, perhaps; and for him I was ready to castigate and revile all the Gordons in the world.

And there were plenty of them! Swarms. Almost all deserved this remark of Alexander von Humboldt: Luronne found it in Morison and I filed it in the counterstake: "There are three stages in the popular attitude toward a great discovery: first people doubt its reality; then they minimize its importance; and lastly they give the credit to someone else." A dunce's cap that fitted. Brilliant!

We had more fun when Luronne picked on another man, a Frenchman this time, or rather a Rumanian writing in French (well, a sort of French) and answering to the somewhat un-Rumanian name of Carnac. Pierre Carnac. A man tired of hearing it perpetually said that civilization was born in Sumer. So one day when he heard the news that great stone walls had been discovered under the sea off the island of Bimini in the Bahamas, east of Florida, his mind began to glow, and without waiting for the most competent authorities, who were on the spot, to give their opinion (they said the walls were a natural formation), he told us as a fact that the world had begun at Bimini. Still another diffusionist, of course. In dead earnest he stated that the Bahama plateau having been submerged, its inhabitants fled north, south, east, and west; and especially to Egypt. The rest followed as a matter of course: since the Bimini civilization had crossed the ocean to the land of the Pharaohs, Egyptian civilization was therefore born in Bimini more than ten thousand years ago. Leaving for America was something in the nature of a return to the cradle, to the birthplace;

and for Carnac too, that very questionable guide, there was a whole crowd of people who set off: in fact everybody—Phoenicians, Carthaginians, Ethiopians, Celts, Irishmen; and with a solemnity I was sure she had borrowed from Carnac, Luronne told me that he saw traces (together with obvious, self-evident proofs) of a Greater Ireland founded by Irish monks driven out of Newfoundland by the Vikings at the end of the eleventh century. And where was this Greater Ireland? Where did it lie? In New England, or if not in New England then in the Carolinas, or Georgia, or Florida. . . . Vagueness enabled Carnac to do wonders. From that point on, Columbus's goose was cooked. In this overcrowded Atlantic, swarming with mariners as a hive swarms with angry bees, the cunning little old Columbus set out to discover islands whose position he knew beforehand, islands that he camouflaged by pretending he thought they were part of Asia, by pretending that he meant to go to Cathay and Cipango, as China and Japan were called in those days.

And according to Luronne this was not all. These expert analysts, intent on bringing Columbus down to the level of a half-wit, were not satisfied with the assertion that he had discovered America after everybody else. Carnac, generous to his victim for once, grants him a fifth crossing of the Atlantic, a fifth voyage that he places first in the chronology. It was a trip to Greenland to take his bearings and make the task more simple. What's the evidence, Luronne? None, of course. Secrecy. Always this taking refuge in secrecy. And for the stake she read me this choice item from Carnac: "The nations living on the shores of the Mediterranean manufactured purple dye. The Phoenicians were great exporters of purple, which they produced more readily by the use of lizard blood obtained from reptiles living in the Canary Islands and from various vegetable extracts, also from the Canaries." There: you had quite enough to ponder. Furthermore, this allowed the indulgence of distinguishing between different kinds of secrecy. Here you have economic secrets and there secrets concerned with religion, geography, politics. . . . The Phoenicians keeping mum about their westward voyages in the direction of the Americas because of lizard's blood! Luronne and I just about split our sides laughing. I quoted, as well as I could recall it, a verse I had found in the prophet Isaiah: "Woe to the sails of the ships that go beyond Ethiopia." Perfect for the counterstake: and we felt that in his place in heaven or hell, Columbus was counting on us to set straight the crooked paths of history.

I sensed that Luronne was nearing the end. She chose a brilliant, most logical finale—hoaxes. The forgers. All those countless, often anonymous people who carved inscriptions on stones, buried them, and then, with expressions of amazement, discovered them. One of the best-known, said Luronne, was the stone from Kensington, in Minnesota, allegedly inscribed with runic characters. Certain learned men (!) deciphered them thus: "We are eight Gothlanders and twenty-eight Norwegians on a journey of exploration westwards from Vinland. We left ten of our seamen on the shore to guard our ships. . . . When we came back our ten companions were dead. Anno 1362." And Luronne told me that half the books on the discovery of America had become obsolete, discredited, because in their statement of the evidence tending to prove the reality of a peopling of America before Columbus, they had included the Kensington stone, an obvious forgery. Grossly obvious.

There were hundreds and hundreds of fakes, said Luronne, and I remember another she told me about that was, if I may say so, worth its weight in rocks: a "stone village" at North Salem, in New Hampshire, which some gravely pronounced to be Irish and others, no less gravely, Phoenician. This brought about a difference in nomenclature, the supporters of the Irish theory calling a certain megalith the Altar Stone, while the advocates of the Phoenician theory insisted upon Sacrificial Stone. In the end the "village" was found to be the work of one Pattee, a half-cracked Yankee farmer. And Luronne told me that if only we could both be sure of living rather more than twelve thousand five hundred years she would have proposed drawing up a catalog of the fakes in North America, a work that according to her tolerably exact reckoning would, at twelve hours a day, take us nearly half a century. But since this half century marked the limit of our lives, we only had time to attend to things that really mattered.

Here we paused for a while, rather shaken, rather disgusted, rather nauseated. All this to and fro of voyages, this churning up, gave us a feeling not unlike seasickness; and into the bargain I was unsatisfied. According to the learned men, the specialists as Luronne called them, everybody had set out for America and everybody had got there; but for my part I was still waiting for the great voyage, the first of them all, the voyage of Christopher Columbus. Was it going to come at last, after all these phony scholars and genuine crackpots, Luronne? I had the Indians: but for me to be wholly and absolutely in America, there still lacked the Genoese. She smiled, laughed, showed no kind of impatience: shook her head, saying, Take it easy, take it easy. . . . Plenty of time went by between the Indians and Columbus. . . . I could very well wait awhile.

We were moving toward September, moving quite fast. Two months and a half we had been living together, so close that we might have been on top of one another—apart from the ten days she had been obliged to spend in St. Louis. The Indians' arrival in America excited me very much indeed: thousands upon thousands of pictures ran through my mind, pictures that I should have liked to pin down with perfectly fitting and definitive adjectives, in the hope of slowing down the flow. I was impatient for what was to come, and at the same time I feared it. How one's sense of things alters as soon as one lives through the events rather than imagining them! In this way I had supposed that once the Indians were present in America and in time I should no longer have to worry about the origins. No. There was still Columbus, and even after him was I really sure that the beginnings might not still form an everlasting part of the scheme of things? All at once I did not want Columbus,

97

Columbus alone, to determine the future—besides, said I to myself, don't go too fast, just champ at the bit and take it easy, don't rush things, don't weigh on Luronne, let history stand awhile to work and rise, like dough with the yeast in it: and sometimes I strained my listening ear to catch the ruminations of history there in the time that flowed past day by day. Or that flowed no more, perhaps, because of us. Time that we spent talking, Luronne and I, waiting for the coming of Columbus. Never had we talked so much. No doubt we had already told each other everything and no doubt we had repeated that everything, with details; but now, just as Luronne was granted grace as a narrator, so I received that of words that seemed new, and I talked more than she did; and once, since she did not know it, I told her a story that I had had inside me these ten years or so—a story I sometimes shut myself up with, pencil in hand, to note down the thoughts, the new ideas it brought and the changes it made in me: furthermore, it was about the Apaches. A tale almost entirely concerned with their verbal taboo, which I either like or loathe: I don't know which. Probably both.

I told her, naming my sources—and with her very sound instinct for Amerindian matters she knew I was not making it up—that when an Apache died in Oklahoma, New Mexico, Texas—the Apache country—his name was never to be spoken again by the living. Because of this, Luronne, we know little about the Apaches, who have no writing of course. The taboo limits both the quantity of oral evidence and its transmission from generation to generation. That is what I said.

Then: death, and the name tabooed by death, deprives them of history, and I added—a people without history. . . . For a few moments we paused there, listening to that sound or silence inside us, the sound or silence of the void made by history's nonexistence. A sound or a silence perpetually reborn in cycles that follow the seasons perhaps, the nonhuman in an absolute degree, that is to say, the sun, the wind. . . . The Apaches, then. A brave dies: no doubt his deeds remain in the background of the tribe's conscious memory, but I imagine this to be a sort of *disincarnation,* lacking that kind of living memory provided by a name that can be uttered after its owner's death. Abstract spirits, forgotten with the passing of time. Then I went on to the revelation that was to excite us so: if the dead Indian's name was totemic—the name of a four-legged creature or a bird—then the survivors had to seek out and find a new way of referring to the one or the other at once: that is to say new words.

Luronne's lips moved a little: she wanted to say something but she could not—the words eluded her—astonishment made her pensive and we could not really tell (I sensed that she was trying to find out just as I had tried to find out these ten years past) whether we should feel delight or sorrow, and then we said: how splendid! How wonderful it would be if we too were now obliged to make up words every time a relative, friend, neighbor, or connection died, and I uttered something between a joke and a reflection—striking and full of meat though in dubious taste: if Luronne died, I should never again be able to say the word love in connection with her or anyone else, so if ever I found another I should have to use the alphabet, consonants and vowels, to make up another word—a shadow appeared in Luronne's eyes—how splendid, Luronne, this perpetual quest, this creation, and what a magnificent way of mourning one's family or one's friends, giving them a word, an offering certainly more everlasting than flowers or wreaths or inscriptions, and we were enchanted (though a certain uneasiness lurked beneath our enchantment) at this way of rimming and rejuvenating the vocabulary, and I told Luronne that someday I should shut myself up for a fortnight to study the taboo, its components, and its consequences, and I said it would be necessary to face up to the possibility—it must have occurred among the Apaches—of words deactivated almost as soon as invented. For example:

A living man's relative dies. The man finds a certain word let's say for beaver, the dead Apache's totemic name. How does that man feel, Luronne, when he uses the word, the term he has just made up, and finds that the word, the term is for his neighbor unutterable? You follow me, Luronne? You die, I make up a word meaning love, and when I try it on another woman, I find it's the very word she outlawed when death struck the man she once loved. . . . Story without an end, unbelievable conjunction, chance: and taking another example I showed Luronne the chain repercussion implicit in the verbal taboo. I cite another example: The aged Toothless Wolf dies. . . . Luronne: Nobody was ever called that! Myself, full of mirth: I know, I know it's a mere supposition. So Toothless Wolf dies, and the living members of the tribe must avoid, must forbid, three words: that which indicates the dead man, that which means toothless, and then that which names the wolf. And since from one end of North America to the other the Indian totem is primarily animal, we observed to one another that if the Apache taboo had spread over the whole northern continent, words would have been in a state of total and incessant ferment, but our excitement calmed down a little when Luronne pointed out that conversation between Apaches must have been difficult: which is true. From one generation to another it happens that a child Apache does not understand its grandmother, she having known quantities of dead people the child has never seen and there being words she no longer hears, words that alarm her and which she pretends not to hear.

We both of us paused for breath, lingering over the images that emerged from what I had been saying, an important subject with far-reaching implications that we had only just touched upon, following the consequences no great distance, a subject we should have to take up again, and as though jealousy had prompted her with a tale in answer to mine, Luronne told me (and she felt that her piece was closely related to mine) that the Bellacoolas of British Columbia, on the Pacific Coast, did not merely put to death the man or the men who threw filth into a stream when the salmon were running up, but they also, with the meticulous skill of long ancestral practice in using a

knife, removed the salmon's flesh alone—to eat it, of course—
taking great care not to break or disperse the skeleton or damage the tail; then they threw the perfect skeleton and tail back
into the river so that the salmon's soul and framework might go
back to their own country, which for them was something like
an inexhaustible paradise, and, moreover, the very opposite of
a dubious eternity, because there the salmon, restored to its
primitive shape, got its flesh back again. . . . A resuscitated
fish as it were, said Luronne, death done away with and she,
peerless and intelligent, was infinitely right; I took her hand
and in a lightning flash I saw the relationship—the Apaches
with graveyard after graveyard of dead men and dead words,
the Bellacoolas without graveyards, without dead men, without decay, but with words perpetually resuscitated in the salmon, leaping, splashing, then eaten, then given back, brought
back to life to leap and splash in the rivers once more, and I
saw in my mind's eye, first the Apaches riding over the thin
short grass of the Southwest and then the happy, laughing Bellacoolas, their life bound up with the exuberant vitality of the
fish up there in British Columbia, and at that moment the telephone rang.

I answered; it was for Luronne; I passed her the receiver. I
heard her happy exclamation; saw her skip for joy; she was not
looking at me, being wholly taken up with the pleasure of hearing the other woman's news, and I took the opportunity to file a
discovery of my own concerned with geography in the counterstake—the existence of Ha Ha Bay north of Newfoundland and
of the Chics-Chocs hills in the Gaspé (how can one fail to love
geography and words after such marvelous windfalls?), and as
soon as Luronne hung up she told me the news that her friend
had just given her—the reappearance of the bridled onychongale (Luronne wrote the word for me), a species that had been
thought to be extinct since 1937, a marsupial like the kangaroo.
Yes, but it wasn't in America. The friend had received a docu-
ment establishing the truth of the event. I thought of a bottle of
champagne to celebrate the reunion of man's estate and the

nail-tailed wallaby, but that was in Australia, in central Queensland. Oh, if only it had been a creature of these parts! I put the bottle back untouched, thinking it will never do to dissipate one's energies and we went out to see *Jeremiah Johnson* on Broadway.

Jeremiah Johnson or the return of the onychongale among us and perhaps the Apaches' verbal taboo as well, who knows? . . . I believe the notion of a journey to Louisiana had its vague beginnings there, with the Indian, the animal, the word. The next day Luronne asked me what I thought of a trip to Acadia, the Cajun bayou country along the Atchafalaya. She knew the answer of course, and it came like a thunderclap. To Louisiana! We spent the next several hours looking at maps, diving, swimming, breathing in visions of water smoother than the Dutch canals under skies that tired my eyes after a while, and we also wandered among the reeds, where the wind cuts whistles for itself and the coots proliferate underfoot. . . . To be sure, I knew that Louisiana was one of the American states, but because in former times, when it was French and before it had been lopped, amputated, diminished—because the name had once meant the whole stretch of country from the Appalachians to the Rockies, for me Louisiana still retained its immensity, and I found it hard to see my Louisiana confined within its present borders. I thrust them out far beyond those flat and liquid paunches that the Mississippi and the Sabine provide for it on the eastern and western boundaries. Not to mention Arkansas to the north, where in my splendid, flattering vision Louisiana reached as far as Mount Ouachita. A beautiful idea, Luronne my love, and one that may wipe out the evil memory of our trip in the Connecticut forests.

Louisiana! I must certainly have read at least three hundred books about it. There was no country in the Country that gave me a greater expectation of the roll of magic drums. And what are we going to see, Luronne? It was a secret. I should find out when I got there. So as waiting for Louisiana left me somewhat at loose ends, I went back to Christopher Columbus, but once again Luronne postponed his appearance. She laughed; she cried, We've plenty of time! Dismissing the Genoese, we plunged back into maps, books, and the preparations for a journey that was to last several days. Car to the airport, then plane to New Orleans. There hire a car and thrust deep into Louisiana. Myself: Shall we sail along the Mississippi (to me unknown) on a paddle steamer as we did on the cruise boat when I met you? Ships glided into my mind, which formed a sheltered harbor for them, and using my knowledge I controlled their speed, keeping them moving gently over the surface of my gray matter so that I could watch them. Then together with these images of peace, of rounded hulls, of gentle bows, of happiness, of day sinking into friendly night as I imagined it did in the South, I had a taste of unhurried love, of arms forever gliding up and down, and I was already in Louisiana, idle, languid, letting myself be carried on a smooth tributary current that relaxed me with none of those eddies or snags you find in the flow of ordinary time, for in Louisiana it does not hurry, it hustles no one, it has all the time in the world. As I remember that day, it was taken up by two motions, two motions that I took twenty-four hours to accomplish, voluptuous and filled with happiness: the first in which I took the unresisting Luronne's clothes off one by one, my memory reducing the four operations of removing the four garments that clothed her to a single gesture; and the second in which I gently pulled her toward me so that I might run up and down and up once more on the bayou of her belly, and perhaps go to sleep before the end of my voyage.

My first wishes, when the plane landed there next day, were very childish, but it would have been absurd to resist them. Luronne understood, and although it was so early we called for bourbon, the best to be had. Then when the car was hired we drove southwest on the road to Lafayette, where Luronne had decided that we should spend the night before making our trip to the banks of the Atchafalaya, from which I expected all the

103

more because of the beauty of its name. I said to Luronne, "Suppose this river were called Du Pont, the Du Pont River! Can you see us setting out from New York to see the Du Pont River, you who are half French and I a native of France?" She agreed that it was unthinkable, and for a while we talked about the exoticism of names; and as we talked, leaving New Orleans, we passed along by the university district: the columned houses were just as I had pictured them, read about them. On leaving the plane I had had that only too familiar feeling of stepping into an oven, but this time the heat was spread over my whole body, not concentrated on my head. What is more, this morning I was happy, and I had not been happy in Connecticut: I was driving through that richly luxuriant Louisiana I had been waiting to see and touch and breathe these twenty years; and since I was in Louisiana, springwater from within me had to rise as from a porous soil from the deep levels beneath my skin and spread over me. The power of words again, of course: of which I gave Luronne this striking example, and there was no doubt that the name Louisiana made me feel infinitely cooler than did that of Connecticut.

I asked her whether she meant to take advantage of our being there to tell me about the country, but Luronne shook her head. When, then? An evasive answer: she was obviously keeping her account of Louisiana for some place other than Louisiana, for some later time, and I observed to myself that Luronne was no doubt conservative and that she would begin with chronology, with the day of that year I have forgotten when Father Marquette and Joliet stepped into their Indian canoe. I saw them as I had seen them in drawings that were perhaps not drawings of them, though they are thought to show their features: but there is not the least proof, so these portraits, which I love, may not be portraits of them at all. The same applies to Cavelier de La Salle too, and Tonty and the two d'Ibervilles. They were there in my mind, next to us on the car seat, all along the road among the magnolias, hidden in the tracery of Spanish moss, and I thought, I'm never alone, all alone, they're waiting for me somewhere in time that is to come, whereas for everybody else they live way back in the past, in the history of the discovery and the exploration of America. But for Luronne and me they are ahead! The sign of a great upheaval was here, already. . . . And they were waiting for me not in time alone but also in space, out there beyond the hood of the car, long after Columbus, voyaging four times on the ocean sea, had tentatively probed a continent that he could never bring himself to believe was not China. Like me, Columbus had read about it in Marco Polo. Then after Columbus, the Spaniards, the Dutch, the French up there, and the English. All of them pawns on the chessboard whose lines were drawn by a knowledge of North America—soldiers, priests, trappers, fur traders, pioneers, colonists, and voyageurs, as the paddlers of canoes were called in those days. Luronne was driving, and I fell asleep with them all.

Only for a little while. I woke up thinking of the beginnings, when the history of America was being decided—an idea that came from them, perhaps. Something else too. I was never coming to an end of these beginnings. As though I could not see them clearly, did not know what to call them. Yet it was with these very beginnings that I had won Luronne's support. Why do we have to be wholly dependent upon those who began before us? The first? Traveling along these Louisiana roads, I thought of Strindberg's play *The Dance of Death*, in which an old captain whose name I forget says, "Cancel and carry on!" If I had to find a motto for myself I should choose "Wipe it all out and begin again!" If only I could do so. Once: just once. Recommence: no, I mean commence. Because those messed-up beginnings had nothing to do with me. Messed up: doomed.

Failure? Impossible. Besides, when you come to think of it, the impossibility of failure is what limits the power of the world's master. His own particular failure. To be quite exact, his failure lies in the impossibility of my failing were he to grant me the opportunity of beginning. Just once, no more. He doesn't risk it, of course, since with me success is certain. The master of the world's victory, his success, is our death. He can allow himself anything at all, except for giving me (and on this point I would believe in myself more than in Luronne) the power of beginning again. If he picked me to create the beginnings, to wield them in the sense of wielding a power, I should not commit the absolute error, the truly capital sin, of forgetting to bring in eternity, here, among us and within us. Of not giving it to me. Of granting me everything—except that. From which it is clear—self-evident—that eternity alone is what one needs. It covers all the rest. Wipes out evils. Evil itself.

And I said within myself: God, let it so be that I shall never die. And as I knew that was not possible and that the other, who knew a fair amount about it, would never give me the time for beginning, no, not even two seconds, I turned to Luronne.

She slowed down, sensing that I wanted to say something. What? The thing that interested me in this history of America that she had begun telling me—I'm still thinking about it, forgive me, Luronne—was that perhaps my knowledge was false. In that case it would only have to be slightly wrong quite often or even only once to become wholly wrong for good and all. Luronne: Explain. Myself: Sitting here beside you just now I was thinking about the master of the world. If just once he were to give me the power of starting everything, I'd set it all, the whole prostituted mess of the world, in eternity. You are looking into American history to find what I no longer expect from the master of the world—the possibility of saying and doing things differently, in a way unlike that in which they do exist and in which they do unfold. When you speak I can feel that power, that possibility in you. You haven't changed anything yet, but we're only just beginning. We're at the start of the beginnings.

(And I laughed. At the start! At the beginnings! No, because the fate of the world does not begin with the arrival of the Indians in America. In my own personal history it begins with Christopher Columbus. I should not be so impatient to reach him if I did not hope so fervently that somewhere they had got things wrong, that at some point the historians had gone astray, and that Columbus himself . . .)

And, I said to Luronne, "If you do change anything, it will obviously be because you are right. You will have found an error in what we have learned, in what we know. An error that you will remedy for us."

And, to encourage her and because I felt it very strongly I added, "I love you so."

Then, just when I thought I had said everything, a sudden fear came over me. I knew why, and turning to Luronne again, I said, "You must not lie! Not even to please me. Above all, not that. If you lie, you will only have told a story, when all is said and done; a lovely story no doubt, the loveliest in the world, but only just one more story, a story that will change nothing."

I did not tell her what I thought after that: If the Comanches hold out, if they beat the French or the Spaniards who come after them or the Mexicans who follow the Spaniards or lastly the Americans, the consequences will be enormous.

And another thought I did not utter: Consequences that lie in a moment of American history further off in time, in fifteen or twenty years.

The grief that came over me arose from this length of time: twenty years. Too much. And reacting against any such prolonged delay, I said to Luronne, "What's the point of our living together, we two, if we are only going to grow old and die, live and die like everyone else?"

A remark that I must have made earlier and that she listened to without interrupting, her body tense, her hands on the wheel quite taut. Luronne! Not only a magnificent narrator but a magnificent listener too: there she was, wholly absorbed in what she was doing, wholly absorbed in listening; she did not interrupt, she did not break my flow, although I was aware that my having held back some things for myself alone—things I had not said to her—made it hard to follow my general theme—how difficult it is to talk! She nodded; I knew she had understood; and I dived into the hollow made by her legs under the wheel and thrust home my tongue. Told her I loved her and unless we took care, unless we risked an accident, we should melt there in the car.

Then I straightened up, sat back, gathered my wits. And words came to me, simple words. I said: I have an immense love for the whole of you. We can't leave it at that and end up the way all stories do. There'll come a moment in what we are doing when something shakes the world and changes it.

Myself, to myself: What?

Myself, to Luronne: Something that may echo through the forests of the New World before the greatest environmental destruction recorded in the earth's history—it's not so long ago, less than a century, when the buffaloes amounted to seventy million head, and if I lay my hand on the ground away there in Nebraska I feel it tremble because of the running of six thousand buffaloes nearly twenty miles away from us.

I was wandering. I knew we were not in Nebraska, we were driving along the roads of Louisiana, but Luronne how can we fail to see that we are also in a Nebraska without a single buffalo, just as we are at Mankato, Minnesota, in 1862, when the whites are hanging eighty-five Santee Sioux at a single execution and at Sand Creek, Colorado, when they rape the women, cutting the throats of the Cheyenne and Arapaho children brought by Black Kettle in *Soldier Blue* and hacking them to pieces, and tell me it's not true, not quite true, that it's false to some degree and that if we start or restart properly, if we begin or rebegin properly, in spite of some failures that grieve me but one has to bear it! (I listed them: only twenty thousand buffaloes, five hundred passenger pigeons, and eighteen great auks saved), in spite of these almost total slaughters, tell me that in the time behind us, the time in which we are traveling, the two of us, coming down it step by step after having leaped back in one bound as far as the Pleistocene, tell me that somewhere in your narrative—somewhere not too far from the beginning, somewhere well before everything is done for, finished, dead from deterioration and neglect—you will be able to find and name something I do not know about, something that will make it so that we never die.

She stopped the car. She was staring right ahead and I looked at her eyes—they wavered. All at once there was something here unbearably frail: perhaps my motion of taking Luronne and holding her tight against me would do away with it. I was worn out. Utterly disorganized. It took me some time to see things again as they are in this mortal life; I did my best to adjust to it, and as Luronne, who recovered first, saw me recover from my trauma, something seized her at the very moment something left me, the same thing perhaps, and she said to me, "It's true, I'm sure of it: at some point everything will change." And exhausted, soothed, appeased, I gazed at Louisiana.

Luronne, looking at maps and working out distances (she wanted me to share in her planning and her sums, but I was a mere sleeping partner and she talked to herself), had plotted an itinerary that would start at New Orleans and carry us through half a score of parishes, and when I heard their names I repeated them one after the other, like fingering a string of precious beads—Lafourche, Terrebonne, Iberville, Pointe Coupée, Avoyelles. Then we would go down through Evangéline Parish, Acadia, Lafayette, Vermilion, and Iberia before dipping into the western part of Plaquemines Parish and coming up to New Orleans again; and then perhaps—if the wonders did not keep us somewhere in Louisiana forever—we would take the plane back to New York. In a hundred years' time. Luronne said that in our wanderings we would cross the Mississippi three times before the great moment on the banks of the Atchafalaya, by Fausse Pointe. Myself, enchanted: What? Luronne: Fausse Pointe. She had foreseen possible adventures and halts at Bayou Chef Menteur, Point Chevreuil, Thibodeau, at the Petit Lac des Allemands, Pointe à la Hache, Opelousas, Vacherie, Prairie Ronde, Katahoula, Cabahannose, Lac Cataouatche, Maringouin, Arnaudville, Broussard, Cortableau, Terre aux

Boeufs, Chataignier, and Grand Mamou, everywhere—and elsewhere—where the letters of the Indian, French, and even Spanish place-names wove their semantic spell. Once, earlier and without telling Luronne, merely to amuse myself, I had tried to make fun of the commonplace French toponymy; but on the other hand, I had often applauded the Jesuits' respect for the Indian place names in Canada: In the *Relations* one comes across rivière Pentagouet, lac Piecouagami, lac de l'Ouragastapi, rivière Mousousipiou; but later on, alas, Nouvelle-France was flooded by Sainte-Marguerites, Saint-Jérômes, Saint-Jeans, shoulder to shoulder in pious ranks, all saints' names for towns, villages, and rivers by the thousands, so that even the Piecouagami and Ouragastapi lakes were rebaptized, the one Lac Saint-Jean and the other Rivière de l'Assomption—short and silly—but here in Louisiana I was glad that the French names should be peasantish and beautiful. The proximity of Indian place-names suited them, and I passed from one to the other, feeling happy.

Luronne drove slowly, often stopping, either because she wanted to or because I did. As was but right, we had nothing to do with highways, keeping to the country roads. Regret at finding that the farm buildings, built of wood for the most part, did not come up to those of Europe. The sad gray of their walls, the paint flaking off under the attacks of the rain, the wind, and the sun, carried from one house to the next, like an echo. Here there was none of that beauty which is born of stone. But by great good fortune there was the sky, and when I remembered the glow of feeling that it aroused in me in New York and everywhere else in America, it did not take me long to decide that the American sky had a character of its own. I did my best to tell Luronne about it. The car had stopped, we had got out, and I had looked up. Straight up. And this is what came to me: in America the sky is not merely overhead, it is the whole space above the horizon, that is to say everything from eye level up. Once I had grasped that, the wonder became com-

prehensible. In Europe the sky is bounded, limited by sur-
faces, planes, the line of the houses, of the trees. . . . In the
American sky, nothing checks the range of vision. The sky
there is so vast that it does the diminishing: elsewhere objects
make the sky seem smaller, but in America it is the objects that
are dwarfed. But tell me, Luronne, what is this vastness due to?

We called New York to mind, and the answer came to us:
from the skyscrapers, of course. Luronne: They thrust at the
sky. . . . Myself: They push it away, thrust it upward. Luronne and myself: And so they stretch it wider. . . . And I said
to Luronne, "Louisiana is the flattest country in the world,
even flatter than the Low Countries [where she had never
been]; listen, I've invented a word—it's the country of *flatitude*," and we stood there for a while motionless so that happiness could inundate us, flood us without difficulty, and we
tried to define flatitude: a virtual absence of unevenness, of
rolling ground, of abrupt rises and hollows. Myself: The opposite of you— So it seemed that I therefore also loved Luronne's
opposite! We laughed, and once again we gazed out in front of
us. Nothing shut in the horizon: an immense, measureless sky
up there, a sky that only seemed to come down in the far, far
distance, a great way off, beyond the reach of sight. And I said,
"Is it really the sky that comes down or my eyes that cannot fo-
cus anymore?" That day we learned that in America the horizon is only a weakness of our eyesight.

And ten times, that first day, I made her stop to look at the
Louisiana sky. The American sky which Buffon spoke of as
"miserly," that it scarcely weighed at all on the "arid earth,"
drawing the conclusion that the animals of these parts were
therefore smaller than those in Europe. The fool. A blue all the
fresher—a newly washed blue—because, as we learned, there
had been continual rain until our arrival. According to Luronne, who had read about it, the winds coming down from
Canada met those from the Gulf of Mexico over Louisiana, the
first after a long journey, the second almost as soon as they had

111

got under way, and this stormy meeting, if I may say so, Luronne, was the cause of the birth and the fall of these rains.
"Don't you think so?"

(No need to ask her to stop, because she was not talking; she
only nodded, and we both looked up at the winds meeting,
blasting one another, intertwining, whirling, stabbing, opening—the winds that cause the Louisiana floods and make the
grass perhaps as green as it was in my imagination when it lay
next to the ice of the Pleistocene.) Heavy masses of cloud were
scudding across the sky and a warm, cheerful light poured
down on us, mingling with the water to flood the carefully
fenced meadows and their tall grass; stretches of savannah lay
next to these meadows, and as my eye ran over them it seemed
to me that neither man nor his domesticated creatures had ever
set foot upon them. The intense happiness of thinking that
there before my eyes I had the America of yesterday.

On these secondary roads, that would have been called main
highways in France, we met huge trucks, and I turned to look
at them, with their high exhaust pipes over the cab—in France
they are at ground level and at the back end of the vehicle—
belching black smoke that was absorbed and diluted by the air,
and for miles and miles behind me I watched the horizon swallowing up the trucks just as in animal films you see the big en-
gulf the little, the snake devour its prey, and I said to Luronne—it made her smile—that I should have liked to be a
truck driver in Louisiana, and I thought of my father—a keen
and painful vision. One day I was with him—I must have been
sixteen, so it was in the fifties—and we were driving along the
Nationale 7 toward Saint-Etienne with the Berliet carrying
eight tons of early vegetables. We had gone through Valence
some time back and Father, who was beginning to age, was
keeping rather too much in the middle of the road, this was before superhighways, when a blast from a horn that made us
quake made him swerve over to the right, and then, overtaking
us, we saw something slow and monstrous that went on and
on, startling Father; it was hugging the left lane, and squeezing

the right, grazing the plane trees and slowing down, and at last we saw the whole of this iron caterpillar, completely shut in, streamlined, a truck of a model and a shape we had never come across, and when we had the big boy's backside in front of us, there was a yellow plate and on it I read Pensacola, Fla., that is to say Pensacola, Florida, which struck me all of a heap and which perhaps made Father, who will never read what I am writing about him, say, "It can't be true!"—an American truck from Pensacola north of Valence in the fifties, that was really something, Luronne! And perhaps it was from that day on that I took to holding Florida close to my heart, only a little below Louisiana, South Carolina, Virginia . . .

We ran along bayous—from a Choctaw word meaning river—we crossed them, and Luronne took the car through lanes that were deep, narrow channels fringed with oaks so tall and wide that they made one uninterrupted line of shade as far as one could see, and where in their leafy coolness I thanked Luronne for everything she was giving me, and all along the roads we looked at the mailboxes, which are stakes driven into the ground with an oblong receptacle on top, and there I read Blanc, Leblanc, Blanchard, Landry, Dupré, Broussard, Lemoine, and I wished Luronne had already reached the expulsion of the Acadians when they left the seaboard provinces of Canada for Louisiana, but that was in 1755 and it would take us a long while to get as far as that, about two and a half centuries, close to eternity, and we watched the jays chasing one another as we drove toward southern Louisiana, and all at once I felt a violent yearning for the salt spray, the spindrift of the Gulf of Mexico which I had never seen and which we should reach tomorrow, taking the road that leads to the bank of the Atchafalaya; I wanted to be here in the heart of Louisiana forever and yet at the same time I longed to reach the seashore and the delta people, who preferred living in the woods with their snares and traps, hunting fur-bearing animals, and Luronne pointed out that all or almost all the houses were sheltered in little copses of oak, no doubt because it is much cooler in the

shade of such dense foliage, and as we were going along the
Bayou Teche, I asked her to stop again one last time before
nightfall to look at the sky, at its immense and luminous com-
position and to Luronne I said, on the verge of ecstasy, "There
is more sky in America than anywhere else," and once when
we were looking at a house with a garden I felt very close to my
childhood—I cannot remember that I had ever felt it so near,
never—and I was on the point of telling Luronne that she
should turn back, that I wanted to go up to the house and walk
about the garden to find the reason for this emotion, but I was
afraid that sorrow might be lurking there in ambush as had
happened earlier when something reminded me of my father,
now dead and gone; I kept these mental associations of the garden and of Father to myself and then it was twilight. And I
whispered, "It's the most beautiful country in the world." And
I shouted: "The most beautiful spot in the most beautiful
country! The most beautiful state. The marvel made flatitude."
And again I cried out, "Look!" and we saw it. White, its long
fair tresses gently stirring, suspended from the evergreen
branches of the massive live oaks, the Spanish moss. A jungle
in itself. Proud of being up there in the trees, it took a delight
in dangling, hanging monkey fashion. Night falls fast in Louisiana. It was essential to look at the Spanish moss during the
last ten minutes before the darkness, for the fast fading light is
all the stronger for its coming death. These are, in the literal
sense of the term, its last fires. It stamps—or etches—the Spanish moss as Henri Michaux does his India ink or acrylic drawings. It is beautiful, with a sophisticated delicacy whose great
value lies in the details. A pure, moving, complex drawing that
trembles there in an air still filled with the deafening cry of
thousands of blue jays.

We stopped a couple of hundred yards before the first houses
in Saint Martinville. Luronne was tired, having driven all day,
but all she felt was a sensation that we could not name, something that eluded us, something that was perhaps a word that
had to be discovered, a word that we vainly tried to catch by

groping for it with the help of others related to it: harmony, grace, plenitude, ardor. We did not find it, but we felt that so long as we committed no crime, no misdeed, so long as we in no way hurt anything connected with the evening peace, the mystery of the oaks, and the paranoia of the blue jays, the feeling would remain faithful to us and that when it chose it would come to stay for a long while. Gently laved by the mild warmth of the early evening, we walked slowly into Saint Martinville.

Where we spent the night. Which we left at dawn. Happiness and beauty there already. Waiting for us. With us all that day except when our eyes fell on the shoulder of the road: there the empty beer cans that drivers had tossed out, the thousands of empty beer cans on the state roads outraged our great bucolic rapture that only fools and murderers laugh at; then, dazzled by a succession of old Acadian houses, we set off in search of more. There was one, an unreal house, dated 1803, and another between New Iberia and Saint Martinville of 1827: the wood of which it was built was collapsing around the pillars that supported the balcony, and the pillars alone stood upright— the collapse of the gabled roof had smashed open the second story, which in its turn had caved in and shattered the ground floor, three levels intermingled, then in the cemetery of Saint Martinville, among two hundred other graves, we saw the simple, extraordinary inscription on an undated stone:

Here lies Lise Hault de Lassus

which instantly shook and stirred me: why did I have to be called Du Pont or much the same kind of name and why had my ancestors never roved the seas? Just when we were leaving the graveyard a furious storm broke out, and as she ran Luronne called to me not to go under the trees because of the snakes which had left the flooded bayous for the branches— and to keep to the very edge of the monkey grass. . . . She said that! She said that right there in the heart of the Cajun country, unbelievable—she said I was to look out for the snakes in the sky and walk on the monkey grass where the camellias were growing—they last the whole winter—and that jungle vision sent me almost out of my mind, then on the winding roads we amused ourselves by counting the bayous that played at hide-and-seek, making a straight line of gleaming water fringed with a tight-packed double rank of luxuriant trees, where one's eyes wandered, not presuming to pierce such a serried mass. How beautiful it is, Luronne! And then there was the delta and I cried, "I can smell the Gulf of Mexico!" The air was certainly sea air, and we could no longer follow the bayous, which were broadening, vanishing toward the Gulf, which seemed to be sucking them in. They had grown in number now, so that there were as many bayous as there are roads in France, and fishing boats were moving about on them. I breathed in the heady smell of iodine: I should have liked to detest the oil rigs scattered all over the fields along the shore, but I was forced to admit the beauty of those high-perched, flaming torches in the darkness.

We were to sleep in a house by the Chicot bayou, on the very banks of the Atchafalaya. Before going to bed we stood in the doorway, which faced right onto the marshes, and watched the shadowy forms that flitted by twenty or thirty yards away, and I wished I could have claimed to recognize the scent of the raccoon, the otter, the muskrat. But how could I, when I had only smelled them in books? Books: it so happened that Luronne had seen to it that we had some; this did not surprise me, because we always took some with us, but now I realized that this time she had managed to hide their titles from me. She was lying flat on her stomach on the bed and she had them open. Two albums and a guide. Birds! The albums showed them in all their magnificence, and in color. The guidebook described them most scrupulously, feather by feather, as it were. According to Luronne, all the birds of America were there, with their modes of behavior, their morphology, their habitat. Everything. Myself, as though in a fairy tale: Have we come to see birds? Yes, we had. To see Louisiana, and, on the banks of the Atchafalaya, birds.

And that evening, thanks to the birds, we never felt the weariness of a long day's drive at all. While I was having my shower I was impatient to be back with Luronne. Lying there on the bed she talked, turning the pages one by one, and she and I both looked at them at the same time. Oh, she could not turn me into a great ornithologist in a single night. But what about her? For five solid years in North and South America, and even in Africa, she had pursued birds, studying them in the field, and all this out of love for them. Myself, moved, full of admiration, forgetting that during our evenings in New York she had told me about this part of her life: How often? Thirty times she had made long trips to these remote countries, walking in the dawn or the twilight to watch birds through binoculars, and at her parents' house in St. Louis she kept sketchbooks filled with notes and drawings and straightaway I made her promise to go and fetch them as soon as we were back in New York, and then as I lay on the bed, pressed close to her, she told me about waterbirds: seabirds, coastal, and offshore birds, describing them in detail, explaining them by reference to their orders, families, species and subspecies. And lastly the individual birds. A whole vocabulary, often new to me, and one that I did my best to remember. Their different ways of flying. Their lovemaking. The influence of migration and the seasonal cycles. And everytime she had finished with one she said, "Look at it!" I closed my eyes, I waited, I looked, and if some characteristic or detail had escaped me, I admitted it and she filled the gap. We had put on our pajamas and stretched out on the bed at about seven in the evening. We closed the books toward two in the morning.

And it was they, it was the birds that woke us at about seven.

In the car I kept an eye out for the name Atchafalaya. Luronne had been here before: several times, perhaps. I sensed that she knew where she was going. She did not ask her way

117

while we were zigzagging among the bayous with their torpid water, stagnant water, comforting water, buoyant water, water that refuses any help to the hopeless and repels those that long to drown. Do you fling yourself into a looking glass? No. Violent death calls for violent water.

A subtle shimmering of the air and I knew we were reaching the Atchafalaya. It was hidden behind thick beds of reeds, and when Luronne pushed them aside I saw the running, wide-awake stream of the river, the antithesis of the bayou water. Luronne said we should leave the car there and go on by foot. The sun was high and we walked through the silence and the noise—that is how things are in the country on the edge of the Gulf and perhaps in open countryside everywhere, with the breeze gently wafting over the instruments formed by the grass, the trees, the flowers, and the water and the orchestration of the whole make a silence other than that which the mere absence of sound would produce, always supposing you can imagine such a thing—can you, Luronne? Luronne: Can you? We neither of us knew. That particular silence on the banks of the Atchafalaya was not absence or emptiness, not as one might say the silence of lifelessness and immobility, the silence of sleep and death, but rather a silence of such a kind that to hear it you have to stand still and compose yourself (your breathing, the lawless spontaneous movements of your hands and feet . . .), and when you do hear it or when you have heard it (you never hear it for long, which says a great deal about how hard it is for us to become impersonal and merge with Nature), then you know how to describe it—a silence that is uttered (as a note or a sigh is uttered) by beings used to living together for thousands and thousands of years, the outcome of the higher, perfectly worked out harmony of millions of little separate lives fused in the vast whole that Luronne and I traversed that morning and even if you succeed in isolating one given murmur, sigh, breathing, or cry as we tried to do and as, after a great deal of trouble, we did, still to our ears it seemed to suffer from the isolation in which we held it for a moment, and it fell

back into that remote, beautifully balanced orchestral music—a music that the waking wind would sweep away in a sudden savage blast, and then between two gusts you had to listen
closely, alerting your ear as it were, so that in the silence you
might hear that other silence. . . . We walked on again, and I
felt completely overcome at this wonderful companionship
with Luronne, this community of interests, coupling of desires, marriage of ideas by which I found myself increased,
magnified by two. By ten. Made much larger. Then at last we
reached our destination. Or almost. She made a sign, and from
that point on we had to move closer, slowly and quietly, on
tiptoe. This I did, and we were there: and in the instant of seeing the ravine below me I felt horror and pity as I had never
felt them before.

Luronne had brought me to the extremity of a kind of rise or
rather of a tongue of land overhanging an emptiness, and down
there below I saw a broad stretch of sand and stones with
skeleton shrubs and leafless bushes scattered about it. Opposite us, beyond this stretch, flowed the Atchafalaya. In the
course of time the alluvium had no doubt narrowed the channel, forcing the river to confine the greater part of its water to
that part where the bed was deepest. In this way the alluvial
deposits had gradually broadened this expanse, which the
birds had taken for their cemetery. A birds' cemetery! I had
never thought of the existence of such a thing and my mood
shifted from amazement to disgust and then to intense curiosity. A reek of carrion reached us from the seething mass which
was the first thing I made out. I recoiled—the stench was overpowering. And then I edged back to the sight, my head swimming. And once again I turned away, the wind bringing up the
appalling smell. And still I came back to it, sickened and fascinated. I could tell from her husky voice that Luronne, standing next to me, was equally upset; she told me we could talk
out loud, because the living birds were too weak to fly away. A
birds' cemetery! They must have felt the first touch of death
here in the South, either as they were coming down from the

119

North these last few days (for autumn was beginning) so that sensing death's approach they directed their last flight to this place, or they had felt it several months back, after wintering in the West Indies or Brazil or the Gulf itself, and when the time came to set off to summer in the North, they realized that their wings would not carry them so far, and rather than die on the way, somewhere along the Mississippi, they had preferred to save their strength for reaching the Atchafalaya graveyard, perhaps no more than a short flight away; and here they were already old corpses. That was how it appeared to me and later Luronne told me I was right.

On this expanse—some three hundred square yards, I judged—there were several hundred still alive, perhaps a thousand of them there on a substance that was not solid ground, for I saw their claws sink in when they tried to draw them out, a horrible, indescribable compost no doubt made up of their droppings and the accumulation of their rotting flesh, decomposed and then recombined, renewed by perpetual fresh supplies of rich dung and putrid, decaying flesh, and it was clear that the graveyard was in continuous operation.

For a moment I was surprised by the absence of vultures and I said so to Luronne as she stood there on my right, but she pointed to some trees a few hundred yards away on the other side of the river, with huge black birds perching on them, and in the binoculars I saw their bald, warty heads. Our coming had driven them away from this Cockaigne of carrion plenty and they were waiting, motionless, their heads toward the deathly bone-yard, for us either to go away or to stop moving. Then Luronne turned from them, and pointing, her arm stretched out, she told me the names of the birds. The common loon: and she reminded me of that point of identification mentioned in the books, the entirely black head. . . . I recalled that the loon, an excellent swimmer and diver, was growing scarce and that it had a far-carrying cry called an ululation, and in the books I had dwelt on that striking illustration that shows the loon taking off from the water in what I felt to be a steady, pow-

erful action, and then there was the accompanying picture of
its impressive landing in a long, planing sweep over the surface, the spray flying in its wake. . . . And here before me was
the common loon itself, silent, just moving, one eye closed, and
it struck at the empty air with its ancestral genetic reflex of diving under the water. Its checkered scapulars still looked fine,
but they no longer had any gloss, and I pictured its long flight
down here, still perfectly fit and well or perhaps already
sapped by age, who can tell? And who can tell whether it set off
from Waskaiowaka in the north of Manitoba, or from the north
of Saskatchewan, from the Grand Lac de la Plume? And next to
it, said Luronne, there was a red-necked grebe, a very large
bird, and its beak was still a lively yellow (does the horn of the
beak lose its brilliance in death, Luronne?) as it opened and
closed in a fruitless attempt in which the bird seemed to be ex-
erting the very last of its strength to utter a cry that I had never
heard but which both the books and Luronne described as
loud and ringing, and when the red-necked grebes gather by
flights of a hundred and a thousand strong on Lake Lillabelle
in Ontario for the autumn migration, then it is a huge orches-
tra, a positive brass band. And Luronne pointed out one, two,
three puffins, telling me their names, for they were not all of
one kind but members of the same species: the sooty puffins,
pink-footed shearwater, and then, brown-capped and black-
beaked, the great puffin, which is only seen out at sea, which is
mentioned by Jacques Cartier, and which for my part I had
never seen; then next to it, thrust against it, was an obscure little bird that Luronne, of course, identified as an Audubon's
shearwater, and in a whispering, choking voice I said, feeling
sick, "How do you manage to know everything about them,
recognize them with never a slip? . . ." and she told me that
these moribund creatures were wonderful sailers, long-
winged, incomparable gliders that fly low over the water, and
their wing tips shear the waves. Can you imagine that? There
were five or six of them, huddled together as though seeking
for a warmth that their own bodies generated less and less, and

they kept crowding closer and closer, it seemed to me, jostling as though they wanted to quit this envelope that death was stripping from them with its chill hand, and a kind of gasping came from their beaks as though death—death again—began by an inner strangling, a squeezing of that channel through which in the living yesterday passed the call, the outcry, and in which the death rattle was now having its difficult birth, and Luronne showed me some stormy petrels, first one, then another, just behind the red-necked grebe, then a Leach's forked-tail petrel, the only one of all the birds that she had named which appeared to see us and it made a rasping sound—come from where to die here, from what country, Luronne? Luronne: From the Charlottes or Vancouver Island. And once I turned away from the sight and buried my head in the grass beneath me to prevent myself from smelling the deathly musky reek, the deathbed stench, for the wind had veered; then I grew used to it as indeed I had to in order to spend three hours here as we did, our eyes riveted to the foul spectacle and filled with the same weariness, perhaps, that gripped the birds, and never before that day had I so strongly felt my own fragility, my approaching death, my loneliness, as I did there beside them, they governed by who knows what requirements, what instinct? At one point they almost all raised their heads, and just as the puffins had done a little while before, they lurched, jostled, and thrust against one another, a hideous seething motion, and I believe that if Luronne had been nearer I too should have huddled close, for protection from the birds, from myself, from death. . . . She had been here before, bringing friends to show them the death of the birds, and being more hardened she could point out a white pelican just as it slowly collapsed in a death that I took to be easy, its great sheathed legs bending under it—a white pelican, with its neck and plumage puffed out over its shoulders. Was the other pelican beside it the dead bird's mate? Or a companion from the same flight? I remember saying to Luronne that one day we should have to go up to the Great Slave Lake in the Mackenzie area to see them in their rookeries. Some person or some book had told me that when they come down on the water the wind whistles through their half-closed wings and that their squadrons, cleaving the sky in V formation, are a fabulous golden sight, and Luronne pointed out a gannet, a bird that I had read about in Jacques Cartier and Samuel de Champlain, who called it the *margaul*, and that I shall go to see one day on Bonaventure Island, its feathers were still a dazzling white, so its shroud would be the true plumage of the living bird, then a great blue heron and a whole group of other herons that she named separately: they were all treading the dung and carrion in time, as though they were trying to resist the soft grasp of that compost in which they were to dissolve, and I thought of the feeling of powerlessness that must have come over them when they saw the other migrants getting ready to leave, and I wept for them all, that impressive blue heron, upright and still retaining something of its former soaring splendor, the green heron, the cattle egret, to be seen in all the books perching on large animals and pecking their hides for insect larvae, the little blue heron, the American egret, which is on my list of threatened birds, having almost vanished, the snowy egret, the Louisiana heron, the black-capped night heron (it was perched on one of the bushes that had not been smothered by the flood of droppings, pecking at a branch), the bittern, whose deep guttural voice I shall go to hear some summer evening on the Great Whale River, and the tireless Luronne, in an even-pitched, sometimes hesitating, self-questioning voice, identified the glossy ibis, the bald eagle, which I had observed in Audubon, the fishing eagle, the prairie chicken—it was an extraordinary thing, but the charnel house contained both migrant and sedentary birds—then the whooping crane, long legs, outstretched neck, quite white, almost extinct, and I said, "Luronne, there are almost no whooping cranes left," and Luronne said yes, but here this bird, wonderful in life, was dishonored and brought low by filth on the ridge of its beak; then the king rail, the piping plover, the American golden plover, and on its wing coverts there was a stain of something that looked like blood, and I pictured it on the Mackenzie where I knew it lived, between migrations, by the Great Bear Lake, though sometimes it preferred Artillery Lake, or to both of these the Prairie Lake, whose vast expanse of water I tried to visualize in order to counteract this cruelly distressing scene and turn my mind from it to some degree— the lake and the moon setting over it as night falls, when the owls blink, their eyes encircled by a golden wedding ring. Then the snipe, the long-billed curlew, the western sandpiper—it could no longer control its poor wobbling head—the Hudsonian godwit with its upturned beak, and this one trailed a wing, no doubt wounded by a hunter at some point in its flight from the Mackenzie to South America, a flight of well over four thousand miles; a herring gull that was pecking at the dead bodies around it—there was something fantastic about the gull with its beak open, just as there is in Audubon's osprey and magnificent frigate bird, and I fully realized that they had come here at different moments of their lives, of their deaths-to-be, and that each of these half-dead creatures, under suspended sentence of death, had reached a unique and, as it were, a solitary stage in its predeath, in its death agony; and the last-comers could be made out from their greater vitality— there was a nervous aggressiveness about their wings, their muscles, their leg articulations; to die the death that perhaps they did not yet quite believe in, they would have liked space to themselves, a territory of their own, so they struck out with their beaks right and left, in front and even behind, and as time went on I noticed that the pecks grew less fierce, less frequent: and from the charnel heap, rising together with the stench, came a hideous noise of groans, whistles, ululations, grunts, snufflings, moans, strangled cries, sibilations, croaks; and I was wondering whether this cacophony could possibly represent a related manifestation of the stench itself, when silence fell.

Absolute silence. After three hours. And as it so often happens, we did not hear this silence immediately. And when at last we were aware of it, I knew that it was not Nature's usual silence, not of the kind that we had experienced that morning on the path along the Atchafalaya and that we had talked about, nor yet the silence of death, of the void. What we were hearing was a third kind of silence, one brought into being by the paralyzing terror that had now seized the hundreds of petrified birds there before our eyes; much sooner than we they had seen, high in the sky and like great opaque clouds against the blue, the vultures. Slowly wheeling, they planed on the wind, letting it bear them up, though presently they would tear it apart as they dived, plunging happily for the kill: we must have looked too big there in the grass, and some inhibiting wariness was holding back the carrion eaters that we had forgotten but that had been watching us for three hours on end, creatures that I could picture only too well, with their yellow eyes, sharp talons, and the ominous black pall of their wings, and I cried, "We can't go! We can't go, Luronne!" then again and then a fourth time, each cry rather weaker because I knew we should have to go.

And if not in an hour, then in a day.

And because vultures also have to eat.

We left the observation post and its pestilence, we walked to the car never once looking back, and during the four-hour drive to New Orleans, I said to myself, "Why, in America, do there always have to be birds of prey hovering over my happiness and my adventures? Louisiana vultures after the Connecticut buzzards, the ill-omened birds," and Luronne spoke, for she particularly wanted to let me know that death was not always like what we had just seen; sometimes it was—Luronne searched for a word and found it—cheerful, yes, cheerful. Myself, shocked: How can you say that about death? But she held to her point and she undertook to prove that it was so when we reached New Orleans in a little while. Perhaps she was wondering whether it had been right to show me the birds' cemetery: all I could say about it was, "It's beautiful, it's vile," without being able to give any fuller or better explanation of my feelings—maybe women have an easier, more resigned, and fatalistic relationship with death, who knows? And suppose Luronne felt she ought to provide me with an antidote after the birds' cemetery? By Canal Street in New Orleans, another cemetery. Myself, dumbfounded: Another? Luronne: Yes, but not for birds.

A cemetery for us: men, women. And I understood why Luronne wanted to show it to me. Because it was happy—almost. Almost joyful. The miracle had to do with the graves being high-standing recesses or alcoves; and at once I perceived that the overwhelming sadness of our European graveyards is due to the fact that the dead are buried in the ground, whereas here they lay them at eye level, so that we feel they are close to us. There they lie at this height and your eyes do not have to make a painful downward journey to reach them in their subterranean grave. They are present in the living world of sight. Almost alive. Luronne was right: something in the nature of cheerfulness did beam from these alcove tombs, and I was grateful to the ground for being below the level of the sea, which made it necessary to raise the dead and their resting-place.

I had something to ask Luronne. The question filled my mind for two hours on end. How to put it? I waited until the last moment, and then in the darkness of our bedroom just before going to sleep, I said—and it was no longer a question— "If I die, promise to put me in a columbarium in Louisiana. So that I shall see your eyes, forever."

She promised.

In fact I had lied. Oh, a poor little lie. It was not to see her eyes that I wanted the columbarium niche. But to reassure myself. To feel happier in my death as I dropped off to sleep. Almost comfortable in the stone.

The birds came with the night. Luronne told me that they came to her too. All we could describe when we woke up in the morning was whirling feathers, emaciated necks, bodies torn to pieces, sightless eyes; and in my case a huge bird with a

126

dull, elusive look that for a while preempted my whole dream. In the plane that took us back to New York we sat for a long while without speaking, each deep in reflection, and it occurred to me that hitherto it was only the life of the birds that had interested me, their life, because it was lived in the springing impulse, splendor, strength, or exoticism—in which I had been taking refuge from any consideration of their pitiful vulnerability. I said to myself, "Living birds are mortal," and I kept that word mortal in my mouth for some time, and there it made my breath smell foul; I should have liked to turn it around and spit it out, cure myself of it and go back to the birds as they were before death defiled them, but Luronne and I had gone too far, to that far point you no doubt have to reach in order to lose a certain foolish lyrical innocence, and just as the plane was getting into bumpy air I realized that I never wanted to lose anything ever and there was a pounding in my heart— my heart that would stop for sure one day maybe: I sweated heavy drops that Luronne wiped away; she knew that rough air horrified me and that every time I took off I was afraid I should die in the plane, so much less safe than a bird: I wanted to throw up and she suffered for my suffering and at one point she said, "What can I possibly do for you?" and I answered, "Columbus."

It was yes right away.

An ordinary yes. I mean she did not say it because I was sick. But because it was time for him to come. What if I were lying there dead in the shattered plane before the landing? Columbus's landing. After the forest I had lost the birds, a whole section of my great picture book torn out in America itself; but there was still Columbus and I detested Luronne for having delayed, for having held back, yes, I detested her, and there was something tugging at the plane from beneath so that now it did nothing but go up, go down, go up, go down, down where I had seen too much of death ever to get used to it, I hated it with a profound, irrevocable hatred; the plane just would not get on; it no longer went forward but only up and down, up and down long enough for me to be completely emptied, long enough for me to die, and when we landed I knew that Columbus, stronger than technology, stronger than engineering, stronger than the pilots' skill and knowledge—that Columbus had saved Luronne and me. I availed myself of my remaining consciousness to say to him: "If I died, I'd carry with me the grief of not knowing you well. And the grief of my death—the death of perhaps the first man ever destined to die no more." And again: "If I do not die, then thanks to me you will hear what Luronne says about you. And what I shall add." Columbus stronger than the storms. Those that batter ships and those that planes encounter. And perhaps Columbus himself did not know what Luronne would say; might not the passengers and crew owe their lives to his curiosity, as eager now, I imagined, as it had been about China and Cipango? What was Luronne going to teach him about himself? What was she going to set in motion?

An ambulance had drawn up by the gangway. Many of the passengers were ill, but Luronne looked as though nothing at all had occurred, neither the storm nor that unsteady plane. Nothing. I left, following in her wake, and we went back to Riverside Drive.

There were still thirty-two hours before the great day: the remainder of this afternoon and the first half of tomorrow. We went to the Bronx to see John Ford's *The Cheyennes,* which I had seen long before in France, then immediately afterward Arthur Penn's *Little Big Man,* to which I had treated myself under the title *Les Aventures d'un visage-pâle* on a trip to Paris from my provincial home. No question of going to films that showed Westerns, since we were not even in 1492! The year we were about to reach at last.

From seven o'clock that evening onward I could hardly keep still. Deep within I seemed to feel the night getting ready and slowly, too slowly, coming nearer. At one point, at about half-past seven, Luronne went to the bathroom. I took advantage of this to go upstairs, and there I gazed around the bedroom. On the bed lay her nightdress; I took it and convulsively I held it

to my lips. Without undoing the folds, I buried my face in it.
Clean! I mean, after the first day, the day the Indians arrived in
America, and after the second, the cheerful evening of the
hoaxes, she had sent it to the laundry. All I could make out was
a slight trace of her scent. Clean! She wanted to be clean and
new, even to her nightgown! Perhaps she thought, "It's possible to spend an evening like that time with the hoaxes and all
our fun in a yesterday's nightgown, but with the Great Admiral, no."

Emerging from her bath, she unbolted the door and stood at
the top of the spiral staircase. According to our ritual, she asked
me whether I had my eyes shut. I heard her come down and the
faint rustle against the leather of the armchair as she sat in it,
then:

(Hell! She had not said three words before I thought, Hell!
The Vikings! I had just plain forgotten them. Between the Indians and Columbus there were the Vikings. Around about the
year 1000, or some five centuries before him. No time to be disappointed, furious. They existed, and that was a fact! I always
forgot them. Not without good reason, by the way.)

(And I resigned myself to the Vikings, knowing that after
them and before Columbus there was nothing, nobody. Nothing but the silent passing of time, half a millennium that I
figured Luronne could compress into five minutes, once the
fate of the Vikings was settled. Since there was just nothing,
nobody. Five hundred years that she would require only five
minutes to leap over!)

By the time I left my line of thought in order to follow her, to
catch up, she had reached the knarrs, whose name she spelled.
I used to say drakkars like everybody else, but she put me right,
telling me that their boats were knarrs, not drakkars. Fine. And
in the same way you ought not to say Vikings but Norwegians:
this according to the great authority Morison, whom Luronne
liked very much and so did I. The Vikings were pirates, coast
raiders, and Morison distinguished between them and those
traders and peasants who sailed westward and whom he called

Norwegians. Fine again. And in Luronne's mouth everything began with Eric the Red, when he discovered Greenland and founded a colony in 986 which lasted—I had no notion at all of its long history—three hundred years, and which had a population of five thousand by the middle of the thirteenth century.

Myself: A mere five thousand!—A trifle! (Luronne did not understand my meaning—it was meant to express my amazement at five thousand colonists right there in Greenland in the thirteenth century: almost as amazing as the truck from Pensacola, Fla., that overtook Father and me the other side of Valence in the fifties—so I explained it.)

So there is this Eric the Red, discovering Greenland, and he beheld, said Luronne, the biggest island in the world. . . .

Myself: The biggest island in the world!

Luronne, put out: Shit.

And I was aghast; she never swore except when making love, which is not swearing at all—but I saw I should have to stop interrupting.

Luronne: "He beheld the biggest island in the world, like a blue and terrible mountain standing on a broad green land." The very words, according to Luronne. A choleric, disturbing character, this Eric, and he would have made me anxious and uneasy for America but for the fact that he only discovered Greenland—an island I'm perfectly willing to call American. . . . But still, he never saw, smelled, touched, or trod the American continent. . . . A killer's son: Eric's father had a quarrel with a neighbor in Norway and slew the man. And now we have Eric himself, obliged to leave Iceland after having killed his neighbor's two sons! Father and son: three killings between the two of them. To say the least, these Norwegians were not what you would call neighborly folk. And here I felt one of those fears that they call retrospective: I reached out, found Luronne's hand, squeezed it, and in a shaken voice I said, "Suppose it had been Eric the Red, a killer's son and a killer himself twice over, who discovered America! What a heredity, what a taint! What History! They say it was only man-

slaughter, but what do they know? Maybe he was a real mur-
derer! These things are touch and go. . . ." Leaning over I
covered her bare arm with kisses, and by the time I had
finished she had reached Eric's son, Leif Ericson, a killer's
grandson and the son of a killer twice over, but by immense
good fortune he overcame the curse, the fate that lay on two
generations, he broke the jinx of the Indian sign—delighted, I
said, "The Indian sign," a fantastic expression that, as I expected, Luronne did not know, and I explained it to her. When she
began again this slayer of nobody in the year 1000 exactly, discovered Vinland.

And I bawled, "America!" Just for the laugh. I knew perfectly well that Vinland was not quite America, but merely Newfoundland. And that Helluland and Markland, where Thorfinn
Karlsefni landed after Vinland in 1005, were only just America.
Helluland is Baffin Island and Markland, the southern coast of
Labrador. I called out to Luronne, "Leave it!" as though we
were playing football, and before she could speak I recited the
splendid litany aloud: "Vinland, Helluland, Markland," and I
should so have loved to be there to shout to Thorfinn Karlsefni,
"You're getting warm!" Yes, not quite America; and that infuri-
ates Columbus's detractors, who see Norwegians all over the
place, far beyond the American landings—everywhere, from
Ungava Bay up on the northern tip of Quebec right down to
Florida, and they have located Vinland in ten different states,
in Rhode Island, Massachusetts, Illinois, and even Minnesota.
Even wilder—in Oklahoma!

Myself: It can't be true! We laughed, I loaded the half-wit
forgers with insults, and I repeated Humboldt's beautiful, definitive remark which we had put in the counterstake quite
some time back, that cheerful evening of the hoaxes.

Then Luronne went on to a passage in one of the Norwegians' sagas, *The Tale of the Greenlanders,* a passage in which
Leif speaks: he says that he and his companions "plucked
handfuls of the dewy grass, tasted it, and found they had never
eaten anything so delicious." The Norwegians were at Belle

Isle then. Splendid. I stood up, ran over to Luronne, pulled her nightdress up as far as her waist, bit her wherever I could, and told her I wanted to taste the same dew as Leif, to taste it on her. . . . Luronne disliked having things mixed up—bed business and the Norwegians, for example. She did not react, and calming down I went back to my chair.

I asked her whether the Vikings, excuse me, the Norwegians, had described Vinland, Helluland, and Markland. Sometimes, and according to her, when one read the sagas one had the feeling that they thought of Helluland as something not far from a paradise—not quite paradise itself, because of the cold (Myself: There, you see, it was not really America yet!), but they did see stretches of white sand, fertile valleys, and deep forests, not at all what Jacques Cartier, five hundred fifty years later, found in Labrador, which he called "the land that God gave to Cain"—words that I carry within me, that live and travel with me, and that will follow me until I die. Wonderful. In Vinland, these Norwegians' Newfound-land, there was a little of that fabulous America whose reality was later to become legendary. Go West! That was what I said to Luronne, and I told her that when I was a child I loved the Ancients because they set the earthly paradise in the west, beyond the Gorgons and the Fortunate Isles. Then my mood clouded over at the thought that nowadays there was no West left, no more lands to be discovered, no hope, unless Luronne . . .

I told her that what we ate that night perhaps and again tomorrow would taste of Leif's dew; she smiled, and I said that one day we would set off from the Faroes for Iceland, then Greenland and Baffin Island, and then Labrador, a journey that maybe no one had undertaken for a long while, and at this point she interrupted and asked me to visualize, to recall again the Greenlanders, that is to say these Norwegians settled in Greenland: in the summer they discovered the high mountains of Baffin Island, and we too contemplated them with our eyes closed, lofty, impressive, unbearable because of the sun blazing on the icy peaks and scorching our eyes, and when I opened mine, Luronne, who had got up without my hearing her, showed me Baffin Island on the map, far away at the world's end, and she pointed out the two-hundred-mile-wide Davis Strait that these Greenland Norwegians were obliged to cross to reach Vinland, Helluland, and Markland, a feat that dumbfounded and amazed us—they had no compass, for it was only invented at the end of the twelfth century at Amalfi.

Incredible! And who knows whether their belief that Newfoundland plunged straight down to Africa was any comfort to them?

Then in a subdued voice Luronne said she still had the saddest part to tell. I searched my memory, found nothing, reassured myself with the thought that we were not really quite in America yet, and she told me that Leif had a brother called Thorvald, to whom he entrusted the leadership of the expedition that followed his to Vinland. And one day after their second wintering came the first meeting between the whites and the (almost) Americans, the Skrellings of the sagas—the Eskimos. Maybe Indians. Without any reason or pretext the whites killed eight of the nine Skrellings who made up the little group.

Myself: How could that have happened?

How could Luronne tell, since the sagas give no details? The Skrellings would surely return, no doubt embittered and angry—how can one know the minds of men who possessed no form of writing and who very clearly had had no contact with the whites? And in their turn the Skrellings struck: Thorvald was mortally wounded. I observed to Luronne that it was the well-known process, the usual unhappy sequence, and then she told me that on his voyage to Vinland, whose beauty he described, Thorfinn Karlsefni touched at Labrador, where he seized two young Skrellings that he carried off as captives to Greenland.

Myself: You hid that from me!

For a little while Luronne said nothing. And I reflected: Leif Ericson set foot on Newfoundland in the year 1000; five years after Lief, with Thorfinn landing on Labrador and Baffin Island, we are already in the midst of crime! She recounted several other incidents of this abruptly darkened history—Karlsefni and his men killed five more Skrellings; a bull suddenly appeared among them, with terrifying effect—they had never seen one, and it was no laughing matter; the bowman who killed Thorvald with a single arrow had only one leg—he must have belonged to that race which is calmly described by Jacques Cartier as living in the mythical realm of Saguenay. No laughing matter either. Nor was the battle three weeks after the appearance of the bull, when the Skrellings attacked and were routed: Freydis, Eric's bastard daughter and Thorvald's wife, pregnant and enormous, seized her breasts, bared them, and struck them with her sword. No wonder the Skrellings fled.

I thought about the murder of the eight. What if it was a forewarning? What if something of the same kind was going to happen from Baffin Island to Tierra del Fuego? And I knew that, like me, Luronne was thinking of the abductions and the killings that came after, tainting American history with blood and ugliness. Of the ships loaded, overloaded, with Indians whom Frenchmen, Spaniards, and English were sending for their kings' galleys. No, Luronne, this is not America, this is not American history, and yet . . .

Luronne: And yet . . .

Myself: We're not far off.

We paused for some little while, as though poised, and then she laughed. Not far off! Here were the Norwegians imprisoned in time as they were imprisoned in the ice. Their encounters with the Skrellings had taught them a lesson. Impossible to live in! This almost-America was impossible to live in! Let it be spread abroad! They spread it abroad, and for five hundred years nobody else set sail for America. The curtain, so barely, so slightly lifted, fell once more. A new virginity. Five hundred years for the Indians, the buffaloes, the birds, the great trees. America forgotten. So entirely forgotten that in the six-

teenth century a Portuguese from the Azores, setting Greenland on a map, believed it to be a new discovery!

I breathed easier. I was pleased. Five hundred years: plenty
can happen in five hundred years. Or rather, and much better,
nothing at all. No continuity whatsoever between the Norwegians and Columbus. A five-hundred-year emptiness in history, wiping out the blood.

And I said, Go West!

Then: No, wait—and I hurried off to chill the wine.

When I came back Luronne had not stirred: we listened to
the silence and then, on August 3, 1492, we watched two caravels and one ship putting to sea from the port of Palos, in Spain.

Luronne, looking back nine years earlier, to 1483, saw the
birth of that passion in Christopher Columbus that was to
change both his fate and the shape of the world—the finding of
a way to the Indies shorter than the Portuguese route, which
took them right down the whole length of Africa. The Indies:
that was China, Japan, Indonesia, Thailand, and those countless, those innumerable countries that were between them and
India properly so called. The Indies, far away to the eastward;
and Columbus yearned to reach them by sailing west, by way
of the Atlantic, the Western Ocean. He lived in Lisbon with his
brother Bartholomew, who kept a shop for maps and charts;
and silently Luronne and I watched Christopher handling, caressing the navigation manuals, the atlases, the planispheres
crisscrossed with rhumb lines. By the time the vessels left Palos he had already spent nine years trying to find a patron to
back his plan—John II of Portugal, then the Spanish sovereigns, then, by means of his brother, the king of England, then
the king of France. In vain. Luronne: Nine years, can you imagine that? And the dream, the devouring passion, growing
stronger and more obsessive year by year.

I told her I could imagine it.

She went on to a story that had me frightened for thirty seconds. On April 17, 1492, Christopher had a last interview with

Ferdinand and Isabella, the King and Queen of Spain at that time. Once again they said no. So he saddled his mule and got onto it. Rode away. He had already ridden three or four miles along the Seville road when an alguacil, galloping from Granada, caught up with him. The court had had second thoughts; the queen had changed her mind.

Myself: And what if he had killed himself or got lost in the crowd? What if they hadn't found him?

(I looked hard, and in the darkness I saw lack of knowledge, ignorance, emptiness, the world with half of itself lopped off; I saw America—hidden in the fog for how much longer?)

Then, to Luronne: Go ahead.

She unrolled those great fantastic tales, which were true, spread them out like a parchment scroll. The belief of those times in fabulous islands in the regions of the setting sun—the Isle of Brasil and Antilia, also called the Island of the Seven Cities. Then beyond them, Cipango, as they then called Japan, which, according to Marco Polo, that accountant-explorer, was washed by a sea with 7547 isands in it. Then Cathay, which no ship had ever approached and from which no ship had ever returned: this was China, where Marco Polo—Marco again—had lived for sixteen years. The realm of the Great Khan, in the land of spices. Luronne listed them: cloves, pepper, nutmeg, mace, cinnamon, coriander, and I begged her to stop long enough for us to breathe in and smell their powerful, heady scent. . . .

Thule, that is to say Iceland, right up there, was the world's boundary. After that, in the Ocean Sea, began mystery. Just as it began lower down, after Flores, the last of the Azores. Once, exactly forty years earlier, in 1452, a pilot by the name of Pedro Vasquez de la Fontena sailed beyond Flores—the Portuguese Diego de Teive was with him—in the direction of America in order, said he, "there to seek the Indies"; but he had to give up and make his way back again, because of the Thick Sea.

Myself: The what?

Luronne: The Sargasso.

(I stared into the darkness before me, and there in my mind's

eye was that vast sea of grass which I had never beheld: nor
had Luronne.)

Then Luronne: There were quantities and quantities of people obsessed by the idea of India: swarms of them, like Mes-
siahs in Palestine. Only one succeeded in this case—Columbus—and only one succeeded there—Jesus. With a great deal
of luck, at least as far as Columbus was concerned.

She paused for breath, long enough for me to take in the
comparison and perhaps to admire it, then she made me understand the nature of Columbus's luck which lay in the errors of
his time, its mistaken science, its wholly misleading represen-
tation of a skimpy, limited world. All sixteenth-century cartog-
raphy borrowed from Ptolemy, and he gave Eurasia 180 degrees of longitude, that is to say 50 percent more than it really
possessed, so that the size of the Atlantic was made less by so
much, by exactly so much. They even supposed that this Western Ocean washed both the shores of west Europe and those of
Asia! Columbus thought the world was made up of fifteen percent water, whereas in fact the figure is seventy percent.

Myself: Surely not.

Luronne: Yes, and here Pierre d'Ailly, in France, a cardinal
by occupation, added his contribution by publishing the *Ima-
go Mundi*: Christopher Columbus had a copy, and he covered
it with notes. Here's one, and Luronne quoted: "The ends of
the habitable lands eastward and the ends of the habitable
lands westward are quite close and there is only a small sea between the two."

I asked her to stop, because I wanted to note down that lovely remark for the counterstake; Luronne smiled and told me
she was going to produce some more. Illustrious ones. It had to
be said that the erroneous science of Ptolemy and of Pierre
d'Ailly, which dwarfed the Atlantic, was based on the Ancients. She quoted Aristotle: "The same sea washes the region
of the Columns of Hercules and India." Then Seneca: "This
sea can be sailed across in a few days."

She stopped and waited. I remained silent. These were utilitarian observations, if I may say so, devoid of beauty. Amused, she saw my indifference, my disappointment, and she laughed: "Listen, listen carefully," she said. And she went on: This is Seneca's prophecy in his *Medea*: "A time will come, in the last years of the world, when the Ocean will loosen the tie of things. A vast land will be revealed, for a navigator will appear, a navigator like him whose name was Tiphus and who was Jason's guide, and he will discover a new world, and Thule will no longer be the earth's end."

We paused there for a while, saying nothing, she who had spoken and I who had heard; and the words kept ringing in my head, making my breath come short, and deep within, for myself alone, I repeated, "A time will come, in the last years of the world, when the Ocean will loosen the tie of things." So beautiful, so beautiful. The queen of the counterstake. Luronne did not go on right away, but left me time to tell her, in my ecstasy, that I loved her—a time in which I felt she was happy—and then she added that to be exact, and she meant to be exact, she should tell me that Columbus thought Japan was twenty-four hundred nautical miles from the Canaries, whereas the distance is twelve thousand, five times greater!

We cried out in astonishment.

When I think of all those jealous, evil-natured, envious creatures who assert that he had a great deal of knowledge! He did have it, but it was wrong—and that was his good luck. No knowledge: only foreknowledge, Luronne, if I may say so!

We came back to the ocean, to the sea where our vision had begun, with this squadron of three vessels carrying eighty-six men, and Columbus on his flagship at 28 degrees north, the very latitude of Florida. Go West! And when, in the silence of the night on the Sea of Darkness, we had watched the swell and the heavy seas breaking over these fragile craft of less than a hundred tons that sailed by dead reckoning alone, the logline not having been invented until 1577, we came back to Columbus, who set Japan, in relation to Spain, just where the West Indies lie, and we thought about the crews, tough men always ready to mutiny; about the captains, whom their leader once had to promise to turn back if land did not appear in the next three days; about their diet of salt pork, ship's biscuit, and foul water, with never, of course, a hot meal or drink, not even once; and Luronne told me that Columbus lied to his sailors, they being on the edge of panic, thinking they were sailing on and on nearer and always nearer to the brink of the world, to its last verge, where the antipodes are to be found, that is to say literally those whose feet are opposite to ours: Columbus lied to these unruly, violent men, who did not doubt that the earthly paradise bloomed over there to the west, where they were heading, but who also believed that hell boiled somewhere in those regions too—the hell that St. Brendan and St. Malo said they had met with in the . . .

Myself: This lie, Luronne, what form did it take?

Luronne, after a pause: On September 9, when he saw land for the last time, Christopher Columbus decided that he would keep two reckonings of the distance run day by day, a true reckoning for himself and another for his men, so that they should not be frightened by sailing so far from land and from Spain—a reckoning that concealed the extent of their progress.

I laughed in admiration.

Luronne: When he did discover America, he had no doubt that God had chosen him for this undertaking, just as he took it for granted that God had prompted Isabella's favorable reply— that favorable reply at last, which decided the voyage at Granada. The Holy Spirit enlightening the queen! The spirit was seen everywhere, sometimes even setting itself to homicidal tasks. Listen to what Las Casas says about Felipa, who died just as her husband Columbus set off: "God saw fit to take his wife from him, it being to the advantage of his enterprise that he should be freed from all anxiety."

I laughed again, and while Luronne was drawing breath I recreated the vision of the squadron that Columbus was leading,

139

as he supposed, to Japan. And always louder and more threatening, I heard the grumbling of the crews, up until September 14, when the *Nina*'s men saw first a tern and then a tropic bird.

Myself: I should so have liked an osprey, since it seems we are getting near the land! (I had never seen one, not even on the shores of the Atchafalaya.)

Luronne laughed and moved on to September 17, when Columbus, who was now four hundred fifty leagues from the Canaries and twenty-five days from America, wrote in his journal, "All the sailors were competing for who should be the first to sight land." Here we grew excited, and Luronne pushed on to September 23, when the crews were very discontented because the sea did not run high in these parts. And if the sea did not run high, how could they get back to Spain? Fortunately it did grow rough, and over this sea Luronne glided fast until she reached September 25, when Martín Alonso Pinzón thought he saw land. Columbus was aboard his ship, and at once he fell on his knees and chanted the Gloria in Excelsis. There was no land.

Myself: Faster.

Luronne: October 7, flocks of birds migrating southwest, and Columbus altered course in their direction. The whole night of the ninth was filled with the cries of birds heading west like Columbus and flying over the ships; and listening to them the sailors could not sleep, their hearts beat so violently.

Myself: I like having Columbus sail toward America with birds all around him.

We gazed at the shimmering picture of the vessels on the sea and the squadrons in the sky, and I watched the lookout on each ship, staring straight out ahead until his eyes were tired. Apart from the fact that each wanted to be the first, for nothing, for the glory, perhaps for history, to cry "Land," there was also, said Luronne, the promise of a reward.

That was what I was thinking about when at ten o'clock on the night of October 11, Columbus, standing as he always stood, on the poop of his flagship, saw a light or a will-o'-the-wisp, who can tell? so unsteady, frail, and doubtful a light that he dared not shout "Land" but merely called for Pedro Gutierrez, the king's upholsterer, and Rodrigo Sanchez de Segovia, the comptroller of the fleet. They saw nothing.

Luronne said, "They saw nothing," and I looked into the darkness of the bedroom, a darkness even greater than on other evenings, as though it wanted to be in tune. My heart throbbed like that of a sailor yearning for the Indies. I watched Luronne's lips for Columbus to cry "Tierra! Tierra!" his happiness, his immortality, his fortune; and I waited until close on two in the morning of October 12, 1492; but it was not Columbus.

It was Juan Rodriguez Bermejo de Triana. He shouted, "Tierra! Tierra!"

(And I shouted with Luronne, I echoed her, I flung myself upon her, and like Christopher Columbus caressing the navigation manuals, the atlases, and the planispheres, with my palm and fingers I ran over her, feeling, stroking, up and down, from her lower to her upper heart, and it was long before I calmed the quivering, tremulous tenderness in me, and I told Luronne to wait until I had uncorked the Dom Perignon for just one glass, no two glasses, each, since it was twice that Juan Rodriguez Bermejo de Triana had proclaimed the discovery of America.)

Tierra! Tierra!

We drank.

Time passed.

I collapsed in my chair, dead tired, dead with having lived too much.

And that incredible story, the first Luronne told me immediately after the discovery. Christopher Columbus did not give Juan Rodriguez Bermejo de Triana the reward that Juan thought his sight and his shout had earned him. Columbus persuaded himself that it was he who first saw land—saw it yesterday, when he observed the flickering light. So he appropriated for himself the prize of ten thousand maravedis a year!

141

I laughed, I was amazed. I said to Luronne "How was that possible?" and she led me to dry land.

Where Columbus, not losing a minute, instantly set about trying to recognize the China and Japan he had read about in Marco Polo's *Book of the Wonders of the World*. Yet the little coral cay of Guanahani in the Bahamas (which were to be called the Lucayes) was nothing like the flat, green, wooded island of Marco Polo's Japan, with its gold-roofed palaces. Columbus decided that he was just next to it, on one of the 7457 islands. He called this one San Salvador.

I asked Luronne to stop and let us both look. I wanted her to touch me, to hold me; I wanted to hold her tight and love her with great strength in this first-discovered land of the New World, and I stood up, raised her up, set her on my knee, and we observed everything—the wild, delirious excitement of the crews, the thanks to God, the scores of men falling on their knees, the worst, the scoundrels, those who had not believed in the discovery that made their leader—the leader they had challenged, threatened, only yesterday—the Great Admiral of the Ocean Sea! Kissing his hands, they begged his forgiveness: Luronne had been right earlier on, when she compared Columbus and Jesus. A messianic picture, and one that delighted us there in the dark. Since it was in the darkness that we had reached land. We could find no more to say: The images ran through us, dwelt in us, and we were not in the least sleepy as we waited in that Manhattan apartment for day to dawn in the Bahamas!

When the sun rose, we and Columbus looked out, and for the first time since our arrival we beheld Indians. Indians, of course, since it was the Indies he had reached.

Luronne: Tainos, belonging to the Arawak-speaking group.

I did not have to ask her to stop. When I left the armchair in which we sat, Luronne on my knee, she knew where I was going. Together with the discovery of America, we were about to celebrate the rediscovery of the Indians all night long with Dom Perignon—the Indians of whom I had heard nothing since Luronne had finished with the Anasazis, the Hohokams, the Adenas, and the Hopewells, far back, at the beginning of modern times.

And I said, "I see this rediscovery as the second greatest thing that ever happened in the world after the crossing of the Bering isthmus twenty-five thousand years ago. That was the first."

We did not talk anymore. I arranged a gentle, filtered light that carried no more than twenty feet, and slowly, as though partaking of a sacrament we drank, happily watching the happy Tainos.

For they were happy.

They had hidden at first, but now they were running about on the brilliantly white coral beach, shouting their happiness.

Columbus and his men landed, loaded with quantities of gimcrack goods that they meant to give or exchange—red caps, bead necklaces, colored hats, brass tambourines, cheap lace.

The first meeting of Indians and white men: we watched it, imagining, reassembling, listing the details. And I told Luronne that privately I could wish that there had been no other meeting than this, begun over and over again indefinitely.

(Perhaps it was at this moment that she felt her power; perhaps deep within, while she sat there silently watching the Indians and the whites, she tried to change certain incidents in the tales she was to tell me later, and no doubt she felt she was too much of a novice at this work, which was moreover a task that came too soon, since everybody knows what happened later, from Columbus's second voyage onward, and how relationships between these Spanish whites and the Indians developed. . . . To delude History you no doubt have to strike where it is secret, hidden. . . . Where you can take it indirectly and almost from behind.)

Myself: What happened then, Luronne?

Luronne, having put out the light: There was something that struck Columbus right away—the beauty of the Indians. These men and women running on the white sand, running as nobody ever runs today except on the white sand in travel agents' brochures, these men and women were completely naked, young, well-made, and—I quote Columbus—they had "very large and beautiful eyes."

Large and beautiful, I saw them, the Tainos' eyes. And, under their helmets, the eyes of the Spaniards, which nobody had ever described as large or beautiful.

Then Luronne: And now for their innocence and their generosity. Deep. Absolute. All that Columbus wrote speaks of the innocence and generosity of the Indians. Not only of the Tainos. Of all the Indians. In no matter what island he came to— and he discovered twenty large and hundreds of small islands—everywhere, except for Jamaica in the second voyage, he was received with a delighted, artless welcome with gifts. Listen to Columbus: "They invited us to share everything they possessed and they displayed as much love as though at the same time they were giving away their hearts."

Myself: How beautiful!

Luronne: ". . . they are all gentle and they have no evil knowledge, neither of killing nor of capturing." Still from Columbus. It was about these Indians that Peter Martyr said, and I quote, "They seemed to dwell in that golden world of which the writers of Antiquity speak at such length, a world in which men lived simply and in a state of innocence, without the burden of laws, without quarreling, without judges or legal documents, happy in the satisfaction of their nature." You can see it was not difficult for the myth of the noble savage to come into being there in what Columbus wrote. And it's not altogether a myth. Sometimes it's reality. Ten times, twenty times, from whatever island he visited, large or small, from his first voyage to his fourth, Columbus tirelessly reported the Indians' beauty, their generosity—unexampled among the whites—their marvelous welcome. . . .

A pause, then Luronne: He did not know that the Caribs, pursuing the Arawaks from as far away as the Orinoco, had almost exterminated them. . . . A slaughter, as I might put it, a bloody slaughter. . . .

(I was well aware that this slaughter did not grieve me as much as if it had been perpetrated on the Arawaks after Columbus.)

What then, Luronne?

Luronne: On October 21 he was at Crooked Island, which he called Isabella, and there he had a revelation of paradise. Of its existence. On earth. The earlier islands were paradise, nearly. The near-paradise. Here it was paradise entire. Listen: "The forest is a marvel. . . . And the singing of the birds makes you long never to go away again; flights of parrots darken the sky; and then there are trees of a thousand varieties, each with its own fruit, and all of them smell so good that it is a wonder. . . ." And whatever island he visited, large or small, from his first voyage to his fourth, Columbus called it paradise. He did so when he was speaking of himself in the third person. Listen: "He dropped anchor in a river of no great size that ran among wonderfully beautiful hills and plains. A small carp jumped into the boat. He heard a nightingale singing. . . ." This was at Haiti, during the first voyage. And on the second, still at Haiti, listen to Las Casas: "Columbus reached a fruitful valley, so beautiful and green that it seemed to him that he was in some part of paradise." Jamaica filled him with ecstasy; and in Cuba, according to Bernaldez, "two springs of fresh water gushed out close to the shore; they all lay there on the grass amidst a wonderful scent of flowers, surrounded by the singing of birds." Columbus himself, on the subject of Cuba: "the most beautiful land that eyes have ever seen. . . ." And he had exquisite turns of phrase to describe the splendor, a splendor that was repeated day after day as they sailed from one island to the next.

(As Luronne was putting out the light that had been switched on to quote Columbus and the others, I tried to memorize their words.)

Then: On October 28, the three ships reached Cuba. It was in vain that he gazed about, asked questions, sent out expeditions—there were still no gold-roofed temples, no dragon-mouthed bronze cannon. Sailing at random among the islands in the days before this, he had not seen the gold he so passionately sought, but he had seen the first maize that any white man had ever set eyes on, the first hammocks, the first potatoes, the first dyewoods, the first yams. . . .

Myself: Stop. (And together with these beginnings, these firsts, I lingered over what she had told me that Columbus wrote about the parrots: with their darkening of the sky they reminded me of my passenger pigeons.)

Then Luronne: He decided that Cuba was Japan, that is to say Marco Polo's Cipango. Imagine the scene: he sent an embassy deep into the island, bearing the credentials that Ferdinand and Isabella had signed before his departure, and these letters were to be delivered to the Great Khan. There was an interpreter with the band that plunged into the Cuban forest: Columbus had taken care not to overlook him when they left Palos, and this interpreter was skilled, for better or worse, in the languages they hoped might be familiar to the Chinese Great Khan, that is to say Hebrew, Arabic, and Chaldee.

Myself: You don't say so!

Luronne: Yes, I do. I am not lying. I never invent either. Just listen to this: A hundred and twenty years later the white men were still haunted by the idea of the Great Khan. In 1626 Jean Nicolet, one of those remarkable "Champlain's young men," as they called them, since it was Champlain who trained them, set out from Lake Huron that Champlain himself had discovered eleven years earlier, the first white man ever to see one of the Great Lakes of America. . . .

Myself: Surely not!

Luronne: Nicolet passed through the Straits of Mackinac, crossed Lake Michigan and paddling and portaging, he reached Green Bay, and there at the mouth of the Fox River, in what is now Wisconsin, stood a Winnebago village. For Nicolet there was no doubt about the matter: he was very close to that Southern Sea, later to be called the Pacific Ocean, and

146

watch out now, because this is my point—are you paying attention?

(I nodded, meaning, yes, I was paying attention.)

Luronne: In Nicolet's opinion the Winnebagos were as like the Chinese, whom he had never seen, as—how do you put it?—as two drops of water. And do you know what he did? For his meeting with them, he put on—and I quote—"a Chinese robe, all sprinkled with flowers and birds of innumerable colors."

(And we lingered over these dreams, this foolishness, this pertinacity, and the immense confusion and turmoil then reigning in what is now the most firmly based and thoroughly settled kind of knowledge.)

Luronne: Columbus was obsessed by gold, and what I have to tell you won't come easy after the Indians' beauty, innocence, and generosity, and the glory of the Caribbean paradise.

She stopped; I switched on the light and saw her, deep in thought, searching; then she turned it off again.

Luronne: What I have to tell you is connected with several aspects of the Indians' character. On the one hand, their inclination for the marvelous, their love of it; and on the other, their talent for providing the whites with what the whites so totally expected from them. And what did they expect? The disclosure of the whereabouts of the gold and silver mines. To avoid disappointing their new friends, the Indians lied. Made things up. They so wanted the white men to be happy! They wanted the gleam in their eyes to last forever! And that charming kindliness that a man displays when he hopes the other will give him the moon and the stars! So every time the whites asked where the gold was to be found, the Indians answered, "Over there. A little farther on. When you leave here, it's straight ahead. A little to the left. A little to the right. Two or three days from here."

Myself: Not possible.

Luronne: Yes. Out of kindness, to begin with. Later, when the whites had shown their real nature, to get rid of them.

Things had not reached that stage yet. And it's funny enough when you think of the interpreter translating the Tainos' Arawak by means of his knowledge of Hebrew, Arabic, and Chaldee!

We laughed.

Then Luronne: For example, Columbus landed on Cuba, and the Indians—Ciboneys or Subtainos—told him that farther on, over that way, there lay the province of Magon, and by that Columbus understood Mangi, Marco Polo's name for southern China! These same Indians added that in those parts the people had tails. . . . That love of the marvelous I was telling you about. . . . And when another time, still in Cuba, the Indians told him of a man who wore a white robe reaching to the ground, and in this vague description he thought he recognized the mythical Prester John, that priest-king—still from Marco Polo—who ruled various states in the neighborhood of the Great Wall of China. . . .

(Dazzled, I gazed at China in America.)

Then Luronne: And just as he was leaving Cuba, he chanced upon some Tainos who were smoking cigars, who thus, with Columbus as their intermediary, revealed to the world, tobacco Nicotiana rustica.

(We contemplated the millions of human beings all over the planet, drawing on their pipes and cigarettes.)

Then Luronne: On December 8 he reached Haiti, which he named Hispaniola. Here again you see everything I've been telling you about—the paradise (Columbus called the estuary where he anchored the Valley of Paradise), the innocence, the generosity, and the friendliness of the Indians. The local chief came aboard the flagship, and I quote Columbus' observation: "Let it not be said that the Indians are openhanded only with what is of no great value, because they give pieces of gold with just as much liberality as they give a gourd of water." The white men's one dream, now that they were loaded with gold, was to discover the mine. Columbus prayed to Jesus: "Help me!" Christmas was coming, and during the night of December 24, while Columbus was asleep, the *Santa Maria* ran aground. The chief, the cacique Guacanagari, hearing of the disaster, sent canoes at once, and quickly and skillfully the crews unloaded the stranded ship, and listen to Columbus: "Without so much as a needle being lost. The king and his people shed many tears. . . . These are people filled with love, devoid of cupidity. They love their neighbor as themselves. They speak very gently and they always smile. . . . None of them, and particularly this virtuous king, is in the least covetous of what belongs to others."

She paused, and I looked at the picture called up by Columbus's words as Luronne spoke them, and for twenty seconds I said to myself that she ought to break off forever at that point, because no one would ever do better than Guacanagari's Indians, not even maybe other Indians in other parts of America, but she went on:

Luronne: Columbus decided to make a fort with the wreckage of the *Santa Maria*, a small fort to be called Navidad, the first attempt at a settlement in the New World since the Norwegians. There he left thirty men with arms and stores, under the command of Diego de Arena. Then, convinced that in Haiti he had discovered the Indies, Columbus turned his mind to the voyage back to Spain, and set out, escorted by fork-tailed frigate birds and gannets.

Myself: The American gannet!

Then, after a pause, Luronne: You know I never lie, not even by omission; so I must tell you (and suddenly she seemed to me a great way off; and I felt she had drawn back there in the depths of her armchair) . . .

Then: At San Salvador he seized six Tainos.

Myself: Like the Norwegians with the Skrellings!

(And I thought, Suppose there was a curse coming down from them and their botched beginnings to set its mark on Columbus's undertaking, five centuries later?)

Luronne: I must also tell you what he thought about gold

149

and what he sometimes planned to do with the Indians. As for gold, he said that the more one possessed, the more heathens one could convert. You grasp this dubious alliance between the metal and religion?

I told her I grasped it.

Then Luronne: I've read a piece in his Journal, meant for the sovereigns: "Later I shall bring some Indians back to Spain to teach them our language. In any case, your Highnesses could always have them taken away or keep them prisoner, since it would only need fifty men to make them do anything one wants."

Luronne broke off, and in a low voice I said: Disturbing.

Then Luronne: Columbus again: "These people are amenable to servitude, fit to be made to sow, to build towns, to be taught to wear clothes and to adopt our customs."

And as she said no more, I murmured very quietly to myself: Disturbing, disturbing.

Then Luronne: And lastly this remark, which connects with the first and develops it: "How easy it would be to convert them and make them work for us."

(Yes, and if we do nothing, if History carries on in this ugly way, following the same ugly beginning, if Luronne does not divert it, then the whole story of the relationships between the nations, between men, is there as early as 1492, a story that can still hurt and kill just as well in 1976 as it did then.)

Luronne paused so long that Columbus had time to reach Spain, and through the eyes of the child Las Casas, who later described the scene, we watched Columbus riding in procession through the streets of Seville with the crowd running behind his horse, with half-naked Indians close behind, carrying parrots whose claws dug into their shoulders.

Seville, with its colors and its celebration, faded away, and nothing remained in me but the remarks of Columbus about gold and the Indians. Disturbing. Sickening. Luronne had stood up; I switched on the light, and the morning discovery of the frail, shivering Luronne there in her nightgown like the

150

New World in its gauzy veil of mist made me say to myself that it must not be in vain that she had been talking, that she had poured out this great narrative right through the sleepless night till dawn, and all I remembered was the beauty and the excellence, the splendor of the Caribbean islands there at the gates of the American continent, the magnificence, the liberality, and the innocence of the Indians—no, it was impossible that things should go wrong, that relationships should turn bad there on the stage of the New World and in the arched bow of the Caribbean—God grant that Columbus had not botched his beginnings! God grant that with his obsession about gold and his questionable notions about the Indians, he might not have sown the evil seed! I looked at the mute, exhausted Luronne and I thought of those words of Montaigne in the chapter entitled "Coaches," where he writes, "Our world has just found another. . . . This other world will step into the Light only when ours leaves it. The earth will succumb to paralysis, one limb impotent, the other strong."

I recited the quotation for Luronne. It was indeed my turn! She smiled at the newfound world and I went to make the coffee.

While it was brewing we finished the champagne. Rather forcing ourselves. It did not taste the same as it had that morning when the Indians, crossing the Bering Strait, spread over America. But who can account for these bottles you do not drink up as soon as they are uncorked? Then we set about going to bed. I beheld Columbus's voyage uncoil within me, and in the darkness and my battle against the confusion of sleep, its rings were like so many lightning flashes that lit up landscapes, Indians . . . There blazing with their brief fire. In a voice sleepy, husky Luronne urged me to relax, as she was doing, but I did not want to go to sleep, ever—I wanted to stay there wide-awake, poised between this voyage that had just taken place and the other that was to come tomorrow: how is Diego de Arena going to behave without Columbus, Luronne? She had given up. She was asleep. And I thought of what I had promised myself, of what I had told her about—a fantastic celebration of her body, a religious office in the gleam of dawn, a lucernary of love, a penetration and a libation of her until we reached the limit of mortal endurance and our thirst was quenched. Rapturous ravage to celebrate and accompany the discovery of America. But she was asleep. And from the first moments of her sleep, no doubt, her strong, gentle right hand had closed upon my left. Our two arms along our bodies, and they pressed close, matching each other. Let the night last long. If ever we wake, Luronne, I shall certainly take you after the second voyage. I shall do everything I told you I should do.

Then, no doubt, I fell asleep.

We slept until about two in the afternoon. Badly: a feverish sleep on my part, and again and again I was jerked out of it. Because of my dreams. The most vivid was of Vitus Jonassen Bering, the Dane who gave his name to the strait up there. He set sail in 1741, discovered Kayak Island and North America in the neighborhood of Mount St. Elias on the Alaskan peninsula, and then a storm drove his ship with its scurvy-ridden crew onto an island. And there, on what was to be Bering Island, he died. I saw him in my dream, ending as I know he ended, as Luronne had read it to me; I watched him in the shelter that they had dug for him and where he lay, sick and dying: the sand slid inward, threatening to bury him, and in reply to the seamen who suggested pulling him out, the shivering man said, "Leave it alone, leave it alone: the sand warms me."

Bering finding warmth in his shroud!

Appalling.

And exactly twenty-seven years later was shot to death the last rhytina, the sea cow that Bering discovered. Between the revelation of its existence and its extinction, twenty-seven years!

And in my dream the dead rhytina lay by the dead Bering.

I did not go to sleep again, and when the alarm clock went off at about two in the afternoon, Luronne got up as well. That afternoon after the discovery of America she was to give her first lecture. Two hours on Tuesday, and then she had another three hours to do, two of them together on Thursday. I decided to spend the afternoon at the Museum of the American Indian and not to come back until it closed. Before going I felt an urge to glance at Luronne's desk. At her files. At her card indexes. She had run far beyond the last voyages of Columbus. In her files I found evidence of extensive reading and the taking of notes on *La Historia general de las Indias* by Francisco Lopez de Gomara, Antwerp, 1554; the *Principal Navigations, Voyages, Traffiques and Discoveries of the English Nation* by Richard Hakluyt, London, 1582, in eight volumes; *Historia general y natural de las Indias* by Gonzalo Fernandez de Oviedo y Valdes, Madrid, 1535 and 1547; *Les Voyages de découverte et les premiers établissements (XV–XVI siècles)* by Charles André Julien, Paris, 1948. And many others.

Myself, from the bottom of my heart: My love!

She had moved far into the sixteenth century. I need not fear that the gift of words would ever find her short of knowledge. I did away with all traces of my curiosity. Then, after my return from the museum and hers from her lecture at Columbia, it was nighttime.

Scarcely had he come back from the western antipodes before Columbus was wholly taken up with the thought of setting out again. He sailed from Cadiz, and twenty-two days later the viceroy of the Indies appeared in the Caribbean with his seventeen ships and twelve hundred men, charged with Ferdinand and Isabella's injunction that the Indians should be treated—and here Luronne quoted Isabella—"with love."

Myself, happily: Good!

Myself again: This is beginning well.

We watched Columbus sailing in the arc of the Lesser Antilles, bumping into Dominica, bouncing off onto Marie Galante, and then pushing on through the scattering of little islands he called the Eleven Thousand Virgins, moving from one to the other; and Miguel Cueno, who was aboard, states

that Columbus intended to point out the birthplace of Baltha-
zar, one of the Magi, which legend sets in India.

Myself: With him we are always either in Marco Polo or the
Bible.

Luronne: Right.

Then we saw Columbus landing on Martinique, with its
man-eating Caribs, and we felt something of his horror at coming across the remains of a cannibal feast. We reached the island of Santa Cruz, where there was fighting between whites
and Indians, Caribs in this case—the first of those battles—and
we looked at the first of the dead, a Spaniard.

I made no remark, and we discovered Puerto Rico, which the
admiral described as "the island with singing rivers"; I told
Luronne I liked that, and we touched at Hispaniola, where the
Santa Cruz corpse was buried. On November 27 the fleet
dropped anchor in a bay. During the night a canoe manned by
Indians came alongside, calling, "Admiral! Admiral!" There
was an interpreter aboard, one of those Tainos Columbus had
captured during his first voyage, a man the admiral had had
baptized by the name of Diego Colon, and he told the horrifying story. . .

(Upright and motionless, I waited for what was to come—
Bering had prepared me for it.)

Luronne: Gathered in a pillaging, killing band, the Spaniards had ravaged the middle parts of Hispaniola, looking for
gold, for women. . . . Caonabo, the cacique of Maguana, had
wiped them out. Caonabo marched on Navidad, where Diego
de Arena had ten men under his command. A second extermi-
nation of the whites . . .

Myself: No!

(She stopped: because she knew me and she knew that while
I looked upon death and evil with no sort of indulgence at any
time, I was utterly overwhelmed by seeing death and evil
there, beginning their work in America.)

Then: And he founded another post called Isabella, like Navidad during the first voyage, only on a larger scale this time. An important trading post. He had been away from Spain for a month, and the undertaking was very expensive. He absolutely had to find gold.

We turned aside from Columbus to consider Columbus's policy.

For example, at the foot of the northern range of mountains, he organized an expedition under the command of Alonso de Ojeda, and this expedition was lucky enough to find some gold. Great rejoicings on their return. Columbus sent twelve of his ships back to Spain, that is to say the greater part of his fleet, under Antonio de Torres, carrying cinnamon, pepper, wood, sixty parrots, and thirty thousand ducats' worth of gold.

Then Luronne, after a pause: And four hundred Indian slaves.

(I looked at them first.)

Luronne: Two hundred died between Madeira and Cadiz. The others died of sickness after the Archdeacon Fonseca had sold them in the market of Seville.

I looked at them again, and when I had wept for them deep within myself, I followed Columbus, who had launched an anabasis, a military advance. According to Las Casas the country was so beautiful, so smiling, green, and fresh, and the going so easy, that it began in cheerfulness and gaiety. Columbus did not bring back any gold, so to raise his men's spirits he sent out another expedition under Ojeda. Ojeda's orders were not to touch the Indians. Then Columbus left Isabella, with his brother Diego in command, and went off to explore Cuba. Ojeda's first act was to cut off the ears of an Indian who had filched some old clothes from him. Then he sent a cacique to Isabella in irons. Carrying on as he had begun, he stole the natives' gold and their food, and put their children in chains: the boys were to be slaves, the girls, concubines.

I looked.

And carried myself over to Cuba, where Columbus was frantically searching for gold, yet at the same time he noted that all along the coast the land breathed out a wonderful scent, and he collected all kinds of aquatic plants, cacti, and sea shells.

Luronne: But Cuba did not contain gold. So Columbus set sail for Jamaica: the Huereos attacked him; Columbus retaliated, and at one point he let loose his dogs on them. With the Huereos of Jamaica, Spain once more set about committing the vile crime perpetrated on the Guanches of the Canary Islands. Until the death of the last man. There are no more Guanches.

(And with a knowledge that dated from before my meeting with Luronne—a knowledge that I was not yet to possess, it being before its time—I knew that there were no more Huereos either.)

Then Luronne: He reached the Bay of Pigs.

Myself: The Bay of Pigs?

Luronne: Yes: he called it the Gulf of Pigs. Still no temples nor junks. As though the culture of Cathay had not reached this remote part of the Great Khan's dominions. But listen: He sent a notary to the three caravels, to speak to the seamen one by one. Each was to bear witness that Cuba was the mainland marking the beginning of India. If not, a thousand maravedis fine and his tongue cut out. So of course, with a horrified earnestness, they all said that Cuba was the Indies!

Myself: Incredible.

Luronne: Yes, and after a long, strenuous voyage, beating up against the wind, Columbus returned to Isabella, which he had left five months before; and there he found his brother Bartholomew, who had come out from Spain. Now here the worst is to be told.

She stopped; I waited.

Then Luronne: Columbus turned himself into a slave hunter, just a plain slave hunter. In 1495 his men took fifteen hundred, holding them at Isabella. Five hundred were sent away to Spain, the Spaniards of Hispaniola were invited to help themselves, to take as many as they wanted, and the rest were set free.

156

(I looked at the crowd of shocked, stupefied, overwhelmed, terrified, horrified Indians.)

Luronne: In the first set battle between the white men and the Tainos, the Spaniards put two hundred infantry, twenty horsemen, and twenty mastiffs into the field.

(And I watched this first confrontation, white against red, horses against bipeds, dogs against Indians, muskets against Indians who only had bows and arrows and who advanced naked against the Spaniards in their armor and high-crested helmets.)

Then Luronne: Columbus then organized the country, inventing the *repartimiento* system of forced labor that was eventually to flood the whole of Spanish America—the Spaniards were given estates, with the power of life and death over the Indians who lived in the concessions. You can imagine it.

Myself: I can imagine it (the scenes that Las Casas, monotonous in horror, describes in pages dripping with blood).

Then Luronne: In 1492 there were two hundred fifty thousand Indians in Haiti. By 1538 there were five hundred left. In 1686 Marie Galante had just fourteen Caribs. And I say nothing about Peru after Pizarro, where the population dwindled from seventeen million to one million in fifty years. Nor about California, where there were a hundred and fifty thousand Indians in 1760 and twenty thousand in 1880: nor about Brazil, where there were three million when the Portuguese arrived and a hundred and eighty thousand in 1970.

Yet still she said it, and bewildered, wretched, I gazed at this profound unhappiness, this depopulation of the Indies, this unexampled genocide. . . .

Then Luronne: He went back to Spain. We are now in 1496. During this homeward voyage he came into conflict with Carib archers in Guadeloupe; they were women, and he therefore concluded that Guadeloupe was the Island of the Amazons.

I did not laugh, I did not cry out. I was a vision, a scene behind, for my mind was still set on those countries Luronne had spoken of—Haiti, Marie Galante, Peru, California, Brazil. . . . I barely had the strength to follow the accursed Columbus when of his own accord he put on a coarse gown out of humility, as though he sensed that he had failed, that he had not done well, and that he had slipped into crime. . . . For a long while we said nothing; we could hear each other breathing; and when I came back to ourselves I asked Luronne to hurry with the third and fourth voyages, let's be done with them, I'm listening, Luronne.

The third voyage took place in 1498. Luronne gave me an account of it and said that at night Columbus guided himself by the position of the Guards.

Myself: What?

Luronne: The Guards, the stars that make up the tail of the Little Bear.

(Steeped in fervor, I gazed at the tail of the Little Bear.)

Luronne: On August 5 he landed, and this was the first time a European set foot on the American continent.

Myself, torn two ways: I can't rejoice in it anymore.

Luronne, vexed: You'll have to make up your mind whether you're for the discovery of America or against it.

(What could I reply? Though sick at heart, I was for it.)

During his fourth voyage, Columbus was wholly absorbed by his Asiatic illusion, and he set himself the task of finding a strait between Cuba (which, as everybody knew, was an outpost of China) and the mainland, which he had discovered when he landed at Venezuela in 1498. The strait that Marco Polo, leaving China, had taken in order to come out into the Indian Ocean. And as Vasco da Gama was now making his second voyage around the Cape of Good Hope, the Spanish sovereigns, who thought of everything, gave Columbus a letter of introduction to him: they were expected to meet somewhere in the Indian Ocean.

We laughed.

These same rulers forbade their admiral to land at Santo Domingo. He went there, nevertheless, because he saw a storm in the offing: he told the governor about it, but the governor took no notice. Columbus had scarcely taken his ships under the lee before the storm broke, destroying not only the town but also the ships of the armada that was preparing to leave for Spain, nineteen of them being sunk with a loss of all hands, as well as cargoes, six capsized with a few men saved, and four badly damaged. It seemed that the natural world wished to forbid Columbus this last voyage of his. Never had such blasts of wind been seen, nor such floods, which drowned everything, drowned men and their hopes. Columbus stubbornly coasted along, first by the south of Jamaica, then the south of Cuba and Honduras. Then, after a tempest so furious that every man aboard, having resigned himself to death, was astonished at coming out of it alive, by Nicaragua and Costa Rica. As he ran along Costa Rica, Columbus was convinced that only a narrow barrier lay between him and China.

Myself: Bitchy America!

Luronne: If you insist.

And that haunting idea of a passage which lasted for two centuries dates from this voyage, this fruitless search for a strait. The men who were obsessed by the notion knew nothing of America, did not want America, only thought of going beyond it, getting around it, crossing. . . . The search for the passage to the Great South Sea was to exhaust the energies of very nearly all the explorers, as you'll see. . . .

Myself: Yes.

Luronne: They searched for the passage in the northwest, then when they were tired of that, in the northeast, then in the south, and Baffin swore it was to be found north of Davis Strait and then later denied it though he had been right in the first place.

It was Amundsen who found the Northwest Passage, in 1906.

(My inner vision of explorers sailing along the eastern edge of the continent for four centuries and saying, perhaps, that goddam America!)

Then Luronne: It was a wretched voyage. Hunger, thirst,

159

rain, Indians; and in their worm-riddled ships they reached Jamaica, where they were to stay, a hundred and sixteen of them, lost and abandoned for a year.

Myself: Surely not.

Luronne: Yes. And fed by the Indians, as usual. Before their eyes, the white men fought among themselves, and listen, at one point . . .

I listened.

Luronne: The Indians, whose stores were running out, had had enough of these turbulent people. So Columbus, and a brilliant man he must have been, thought up a stroke of genius. Listen. . . .

I listened.

Then Luronne: He had kept an almanac by him, and it forecast a total eclipse of the moon for the last night in February 1504. He warned the local cacique that he had just received a message from heaven telling him that if the Indians did not supply food the moon would die that night, swallowed up. The Indians only asked to be shown. Scarcely had the moon appeared before it vanished, leaving a profound darkness, and this terrified the Indians. They hurried to Columbus and begged him to make the moon come back. He stayed in his cabin for as long as the eclipse was to continue, and when it was nearing its end he emerged, stated that he had spoken to the Almighty and that he had been promised that the moon would return if the Indians undertook to provide continual supplies of fish, game, maize. . . . The moon reappeared; so did the provisions.

Myself, amused, disgusted: How beautiful! How base!

Luronne: There's Columbus for you. When he went back to Spain in 1504 after the most disappointing of his voyages, he had two years left to live.

And these two years being past I looked at Columbus dead, the Columbus I had so loved until his second voyage.

Before our eyes the discoveries ran by for the last time: the Bahamas, Cuba, and Haiti on the first voyage; the Lesser Antilles, Puerto Rico, Jamaica, and the south coast of Cuba on the second; Trinidad, Colombia, and the South American mainland on the third; and on the fourth, Honduras, Nicaragua, Costa Rica, and Panama. I should so have liked to be happy there. I could hear Isabella's indignant voice when Columbus brought slaves back to Spain after the second voyage: "Who authorized my admiral to dispose of my subjects in this fashion?"

But, Luronne, should we approve of this remark? For although it expresses a proper revulsion, and expresses it well, it also presumes to call the Indians Spanish subjects. In any case, the queen died in 1504, and Ferdinand officially sanctioned a policy that consisted of making slaves of those Indians who resisted the white men. He so stated.

Then inside myself I listened to the sermon preached at Santo Domingo by that Dominican Antonio de Montesinos, who had the courage to outline a charter of Indian rights. How I loved him! But that was in 1511—already too late. Too late also the appearance of that splendid agitator Fray Bartolome de Las Casas, the bishop of the Indians. His *Brief Relation of the Destruction of the Indies* told the tale of the Indians through infanticide, fire, the sword, and slavery: certainly the fullest, the most overwhelming, the most horrible, the most thorough, and the most varied of all the accounts that have ever aimed at enumerating and describing crime. Nothing can match it for crackling flames and lopped off heads, set to the hysterical music of a lust for gold—but this was in 1542, and too late.

Too little and too late. And quite suddenly I realized what I always knew anyway. Released from fatigue and tension, I proclaimed to Luronne: There is nothing left but you—you alone!

For several days Columbus's last three voyages left me heavyhearted, which alarmed Luronne. Once, when she was questioning me, I told her how I should have liked the tale of St. Brendan and St. Malo to be true—St. Brendan and St. Malo, with sixteen Benedictine monks, in a wickerwork boat covered with tanned hides, crossing the Atlantic in the sixth century, well before the Norwegians and Christopher Columbus, and coming upon hell, which they spoke of as "a savage island, all rocks, with no plants or trees, full of smithies"! Luronne did not laugh; she asked me not to go out alone anymore, not even to the Museum of the American Indian, the days she was giving her lectures. I was to stay at home and wait till she came back. In the evenings it was she who saw to the beginning, raising my desire for her with her hands, her mouth, and the Little Canyon between her breasts. Then she got on top of me. One night, feeling that at least once and as a sort of reminder, I ought to take America for the Indies like Columbus, I turned Luronne over, carried out Columbus's error for a few blazing, painful minutes, and named that means of access the way to the Indies—a route that I never took again. And to hold me tighter, no doubt, to keep me to herself, to do away with any risk of my being bored, she took to running two sets of lectures at once—one set that she gave me in the morning of the days when she gave the other set at Columbia in the afternoon. Those afternoons I was to learn my lessons and review them.

Three times a week I had to tackle exercises that had to do both with pronunciation and with memorizing. And with the Indians' culture and the sense of the wonderful. Oh, the happiness I owe to Sacajawea, the first woman to cross the Rockies: this she did when she was acting as a guide to Lewis and Clark in 1803. She was a Shoshoni, captured by the Hidatsas and then sold to Toussaint Charbonneau, who begot the little Baptiste upon her: I loved her because of her name, Sacajawea, and I was wonderstruck on learning that it meant bird woman in Hidatsa and boat woman in Shoshonee. When Luronne showed me this double meaning of the name, this double image, this crowding mass of images, I embraced her and took her among all the cards and books that had fallen on the carpet, calling her Luronne-Sacajawea, bird woman, boat woman . . . But there were also harder, less amusing exercises. The list of the Algonquin groups of Quebec and Ontario

162

might be looked upon as a pleasant pastime, but no more: I was very good at it, and in a convincing, liturgical tone, my eyes shut, I recited:

Abenakis	Montagnais
Algonquins	Naskapis
Crees	Ottawas
Delawares	Ohios
Foxes	Ojibways
Illinois	Penobscots
Mohicans	Potawatomis
Malecites	Sacs
Massachusetts	Shawnees
Miamis	Têtes de Boules
Micmacs	

in two columns, without forgetting the Winnibagos; but I found the divisions and subdivisions of the Montagnais of the north coast of the St. Lawrence very difficult. In reply to Luronne's question I was, without a fault, to recite:

The Astouregamigoukhis
the Attikiriniouetchs
the Betsiamites
the Chisedec
the Escoumains
the Espamichkons
the Kakouchakis
the Mauthaepis
the Miskouahas
the Mouchaouaouastiiriniocks

and place each one of these Indian bands and tribes in its own village, that is to say:

Appieelatat
Ashuapmuchuan
Attikamegue
Chicoutimi
Itamameou

163

Kapiminakouetii
Mauthaepi
Mingan
Moisie
Mushkoniatawee

The separatist tribes of the Huron nation were a torment to
me: these were the Tahontaenrats, that is to say the people of
the roe deer; the Attignawantans, or the people of the bear; the
Attingueenongahacs, the people of the rope (or the cable); the
Ahrendarrhonns, also called the Contarearonons, the people of
the stones; the Ataonthrataronons (from an Iroquois word), the
people of the otter . . . and I skip the rest. The semantic and
the somewhat imprecise sociohistoric evolution made my head
whirl. Broadly speaking, the Indians, when referring to themselves, used a word of their own language meaning "the people," and at the time of the white men's arrival they spoke
thousands of languages. I had to learn—and to remember—that
the word Comanche, the name of those splendid horsemen
who were the Apaches' enemies, came from the language of the
Utes, who, like the Comanches, were of Shoshoni origin, and
that the Utes also used the word Komantcia, which means "all
those who want to fight against me all the time," for the Arapa-
hos, the Cheyennes, and the Kiowas. To make things more
difficult, the early French explorers did not call the Comanches
Comanches but Padoucas, a name that some Sioux use for
themselves. A positive madhouse! And what about the Arapa-
hos? They called themselves *Inuna-ina*, which means "our nation, our people." But the Caddos, the Comanches, the Shoshoni, the Pawnees, the Wichitas, and the Utes called them
"dog-eaters," while the Cheyennes and the Dakotas called
them sometimes "men of the sky" and sometimes "men of the
blue clouds." For the Kiowas they were "the men who wear
knotted leggings," while for the linguists, Arapaho is derived
from a Pawnee word with the meaning of "traders." Extraordinary semantic processes! Like my teaching Luronne to say *"A
la bonne vôtre!"*

Here books were of no great help to us. Luronne thought highly of a passage in Father Duchaussois's *Etude philologique des langues sauvages de l'Amérique*, a passage that she extended to all Amerindian languages: "Sir Alexander Mackenzie, who gave his name to the great river, brought back from his travels an Algonquin dictionary of 364 words. But of these scarcely six are to be found faultlessly written; many are shortened or badly deformed; some are incomprehensible; and about a quarter are poorly translated."

The close attention required by these studies turned my mind from Columbus and his abortive undertakings, particularly as Luronne set about the sixteenth century without delay. She was to make a general survey of the whole and then come down to details. The fourth evening after Columbus's last voyage, a Saturday, we watched John Cabot leaving Bristol in the *Mathew*, bound for the great cod banks, Labrador, Newfoundland, Cape Breton Island; and when he arrived in those parts, he was to take it for granted that he had reached the Land of Spices.

Myself: Once more.

Luronne: Yet again.

Then we saw him return and set out again with the intention, as he put it, of "establishing a trading post in the country of the Great Khan," never to come back—four ships lost with all hands and the disappearance of John Cabot, who was the first man after the Norwegians to discover North America, and who gave England the vast country east of the Rockies and north of Florida. I mourned for him.

Then we looked at certain Portuguese, the brothers Corte-Real, whom I hated. It is quite enough that their surname should have passed into history: I shall not mention the Christian names of either. In 1501 and 1502 they dropped anchor off Newfoundland, where the Beothuks lived, the people who are at the origin of that highly successful expression "redskin" —they painted their bodies with ocher to ward off the mosquitoes. One of the Corte-Reals seized about sixty Beothuks, men, women, and children, and crammed them into his two ships while the sailors fired at every Indian they saw.

And unhappily the whole Beothuk nation lived in Newfoundland, where all the cod-fishing vessels moored. In 1506 Jean Ango of Dieppe captured seven and took them off to the French court. In 1610 at Saint-Malo the king's attorney complained that the Newfoundland savages (as they were called) harassed the fishing fleet, and he successfully petitioned for two men-of-war to subdue them. They resisted, and throughout the seventeenth century the authorities mounted campaigns to exterminate them. In 1492 there were ten thousand Beothuks; in 1760, five hundred.

Things reached such a pitch that on November 8, 1769, John Byron, the king's governor, issued a decree "forbidding all his subjects to hunt Beothuks under penalty of prosecution according to English law."

Myself: So they hunted the Beothuk!

Luronne: Yes, and the Newfoundland English ignored the decree. In January 1786, at a place called Grand River Exploit, some Englishmen found a Beothuk village and instantly opened fire. Thirty dead, including women, old men, and children. The survivors killed themselves by thrusting branches down their throats. This is a known fact, because their bodies were found. In 1810 some inquiring souls wondered whether there were any Beothuks left; they organized an expedition to the interior of Newfoundland and found one couple, the woman with a child at her breast. One of these Englishmen, feeling an urge to touch the young woman, raised his hand: the husband leaped at him. The wicked creature was shot and his widow carried away. The child died three days later, and Waunthoak—that was the woman's name—was given into the care of a priest. I am telling you nothing but the absolute truth.

Then, after a pause, Luronne: That was not the end of the Beothuks. Their last representative was another woman, Shanawdithit—the English called her Nancy right away. She was captured in 1823 and she died at St. John's in 1829. With her

expired the English huntsman's last hope of bagging a Beothuk by way of dispelling boredom on a Sunday.

(Empty, emptied, I consider the ten thousand Beothuks reduced to nothing, to no one, reduced to a mere name, like the
Tainos.)

Luronne: You see—an ugly tale that began with the Corte-
Reals.

(I spat upon their name once more.)

Then we watched John Cabot, the Corte-Reals, and Sebas-
tian Cabot, John's son, seeking the passage to the Orient by the
northwest. And then happy at last for the first time that evening, we looked at Florida, as it existed in 1502.

A fleeting moment. As early as 1513 in the Bahamas and 1521
in Cuba there was no more than a handful of Indians left; and
we saw Ponce de León setting out for Florida with the intention of finding slaves, according to some, land according to
others, or, according to still others, gold. Some historians affirm
that all the fifty-year-old Ponce had in mind was the Fountain
of Youth, which he looked for at Bimini. He clashed with the
Timucuas and the Calusas, who fought him furiously. Because
they knew the white men—they had seen them before! We saw
the Spaniards founding St. Augustine in 1565, and we watched
Ponce de León come back to Florida, fight the Indians again,
and go away to die, wounded by an arrow. Well done. Then we
saw Verrazano: and you can get ready to spend a good hour
with him, said Luronne. I liked Verrazano. In 1524 he reached
the coast of North Carolina: he sailed up the coast and landed,
paying great attention to the Indians, whom he described at
length, an accurate and a learned man. He fraternized with
them. He was a friend. Then he sailed along Virginia and we
saw him miss Chesapeake Bay: then on by Maryland, Delaware, New Jersey, and then it was the bay of New York. He
landed north of Staten Island, he saw the mouth of the Hudson, and he was struck with astonishment at the beauty and the
courtesy of the Indians.

Myself, overjoyed: Good! That is really great!

Luronne: Just imagine—when he was between Cape Look-out and Cape Hatteras in North Carolina, he thought he was in the sea that washes the coast of India and of China.

Myself: No.

Luronne: Yes—and the country was so beautiful that he named it Arcadia. He was the first to see the Wampanoags in Massachusetts and then the Abenakis in Maine. As I told you, he was looking for a strait, a passage, the equivalent of Panama but in the north. He thought he had found it off the Carolina Banks. That is why after him all those maps and globes came out, showing America much narrowed in the neighborhood of North Carolina, which meant the flooding of forty percent of the United States.

We had a good laugh.

Then Luronne: He came to a bad end, killed in Guadeloupe by the Caribs, who ate him before his brother's eyes.

I wept for Giovanni da Verrazano, a Florentine serving the king of France, an intelligent, sensitive, observant man.

Then we saw the Spaniards busying themselves with California, and we saw the Timucuas kill and eat the good fathers Las Casas sent them, for they had learned from Ponce de León that the white men brought disaster. We watched the French settling in Florida, building Fort Caroline, and, under Jean Ribault and René Goulaine de Laudonnière, taking a *tatouille*, a thrashing, that irritated me, because it came just after our failure in Brazil.

Myself (having told Luronne the meaning of *tatouille*): When I speak of us, of the French, I say "goofs" as usual.

Luronne, evasively: As you like—and she told me that things began to turn nasty when Laudonnière shoved his big nose into a quarrel between two caciques. But at that point it did not amount to much. Then the Spaniards, under Pedro Menéndez de Avilés, joined battle before Fort Caroline; the French lost, of course, and Menéndez de Avilés put all those who professed the Lutheran faith to the sword: quite a few people involved, exactly two hundred murdered in cold blood.

Luronne: The women and children were destined for slavery, and as you can well imagine all this aroused a good deal of strong feeling in France, where a Gascon, Dominique de Gourgues, after two years of preparation, launched an expedition against Fort Caroline and seized the Spaniards: he hanged them all out of hand, all of them, that is to say—and I am very exact—three hundred and fifty men. Then he went back to France and was heard of no more.

Then we watched the Spaniards growing interested in the region of Chesapeake Bay, where they kidnapped a young Indian whom they baptized Don Luis de Velasco, instructed him in the Christian faith, and ordained him priest. The Jesuits, disappointed in Florida, sent a number of priests, including Don Luis, to the country watered by the James and York rivers, where Powhatan was to reign in later years. Here, in the Chesapeake hinterland, Don Luis found his own people once more; he let the Spaniards forget him entirely; and then one day he fell upon them, slaughtering them to the last priest.

I made no comment.

According to Luronne, the origin of the frightful crime lay in a casual meeting of the Jesuits with Don Luis; they reproached him severely, accusing the renegade of living in a state of sin. Don Luis took it much amiss.

Myself: Because he had a pious horror of sin!

We couldn't help laughing.

Then we watched Hawkins and Sir Francis Drake harrying the Spanish trading posts, settlements, and ships; and Drake in the *Golden Hind* accomplishing the second voyage around the world after Magellan. He too was haunted by the idea of the passage, and he sailed up the west coast of North America as far as Vancouver.

Myself: So far!

Luronne: Yes.

Then we observed the death of Sir Humphrey Gilbert, something of a crackpot and equally obsessed by the passage. Indeed, they all were. After a storm, his ship sank off Newfoundland. He would not leave her, and standing there in the bow with a copy of Thomas More's *Utopia* in his hand, he called out this quotation from it just as the sea took him: "We are as near to heaven by sea as by land."

Myself: I've read *Utopia* too.

Then we saw Frobisher make his three polar voyages, doubling the southern tip of Greenland without recognizing it, sighting the coast of Labrador, pushing on still farther northward, crossing the eastern mouth of the bay that Hudson was to discover in 1610, and making his way into Frobisher Bay, the most southerly in Baffin Island: and here, lost amid the ice, he supposed he had found the passage. He was the first to chance upon the Eskimos of the Canadian Far North, and, what is extraordinary—are you paying attention?

Luronne: Three hundred years later, when the American Charles Francis Hall found the Inuits, they told him all the details of their ancestors' historic meeting with Frobisher: you must realize the strength of oral tradition among the Inuits.

I told her I realized it.

Then we watched John Davis fail three times in his search for the Northwest Passage, sailing farther north than anyone before him, reaching 72°12' N along the Greenland coast, and, during his second voyage, playing football with the Eskimos on the ice floe where the English had landed. And, said Luronne, and here I quote, "The Englishmen threw the Eskimos to the ground every time they tried to kick the ball."

Myself: That doesn't surprise me.

Then, under the leadership of Sir Walter Raleigh, who was consumed with eagerness to found a colony in the New World, we saw the English land settlers on Roanoke Island in that Virginia which Verrazano had discovered, and then take them aboard again after they had ravaged the Indians' corn and burned a village, all because of a stolen silver cup. Then they tried a second settlement that Raleigh had intended to be on Chesapeake Bay but that ended up on Roanoke Island once more—fourteen families settled there, who were never seen

170

again, never heard of, a total mystery even now and one that
has given rise to countless books and articles—two hundred
people who vanished into thin air but whom Luronne, following Morison, believed to have joined the North Carolina Indians, some of whom have blue eyes and fair hair. . . . The
Roanoke colonists adopted by the Croatans!
 Then Luronne said she had something prodigious to tell.
 Myself, eagerly: I'm listening.
 Luronne: The Saint-Dié nonsense. Picture Saint-Dié, a remote village in the Vosges, where there lived a group of geogra-
phers, cartographers, craftsmen who made terrestrial globes,
printers . . . An account of a voyage appeared, the voyage of
Amerigo Vespucci, a Florentine like Verrazano. This Vespucci
alleged that he had made four voyages to the New World, the
first in 1497, that is to say before Columbus's third voyage,
which made him the real discoverer of the American continent. . . . The voyage is utterly improbable, but that struck
nobody in Saint-Dié, at the other end of the world, and Martin
Waldseemüller, the best-known of the Vosgian craftsmen, put
out a large map of the world, a globe-shaped map upon which
he wrote, basing himself on Vespucci's tales, he wrote America, a neologism that he had formed from the name Amerigo as a
tribute to Vespucci. This was the very first use of it.
 Myself: Wait—I rush to get the champagne; I always keep a
chilled bottle ready for use.
 Then, when we had clinked glasses to toast the birth of
America Luronne went on: Vespucci was all the better known
because his account contained some very racy stories, almost
porno, whereas Columbus, who dedicated all his writings to
the very Christian rulers of Spain, laced himself up tight in a
severity that left no room for any flight of fancy, any wanton
nudge or wink.
 We laughed.
 And we were absolutely delighted with that place at the back
of beyond, with Saint-Dié in the Vosges, where they took the
fake for the genuine article—Saint-Dié, which brought forth

171

America on the basis of Amerigo, whereas they ought to have produced Columbia on that of Columbus. Prodigious.

Then Luronne came to a halt. She sat there without speaking for a long while, and I said nothing: I was ruminating over what I had heard. It went away, came back, dwelt in me, left me, struck against me, flooded in, withdrew. Seized me once more.

And after this silence Luronne told me she was about to plunge in deep, as she had said she would.

She began with Jacques Cartier, right up there in the north, in 1534. We watched his ship and his sixty-one men on their first voyage, and then, on the west coast of Newfoundland, the terns, the puffins, and the great auks, which he called *apponatz*. Then a swimming polar bear, which the seamen killed, and the walruses, and then presently the Magdalen Islands, and then Prince Edward Island, which in August was a paradise of fruit, where the sailors filled their bellies with wild currants, gooseberries, strawberries, and maize. And thanks to the Micmac Indians of Chaleur Bay, they ate migane. Cartier speaks of the scenery with love. So beautiful that he forgave Chaleur Bay for not opening into a passage toward China. In Gaspé Bay he met Donacona and two hundred Hurons, who had come up from Quebec to fish for mackerel.

Luronne: In Iroquois, Quebec is a strait, a narrowing of the waters.

Then: And like the Micmacs of Chaleur Bay, these Hurons sang and danced, showing every sign of great joy. No doubt they were eager for allies, because the Etchemins of Maine were giving them a hard time, but all the sources bear witness to the North American Indians' happiness at their first sight of white men. Champlain too speaks of the positive feasts of joy by which the Indians celebrated their meeting with the whites; and many people have pointed out this feature of the American Indians' character—their overflowing spirits, their love of fun, of games, of feasts, of their never-punished children; and Scott

Momaday, a Kiowa, the greatest Amerindian writer of our day, speaking about those of his own blood, says, and I quote:

(She lit the lamp.)

". . . The Indian has always had a great capacity for wonder, delight and belief . . . The love of fun, which is a basic characteristic, they owe to the joy with which they view the world and to their pleasure in life itself."

(She switched it off.) Then Cartier met some Montagnais, and seeing that autumn was at hand, he went home—a disappointing voyage, since he had not found the Northwest Passage nor the gold mines he had hoped for. Still, you must bear in mind that he had discovered the St. Lawrence, the means of access, of penetration into the American continent, and that in the following century the French made their way up it to reach the Great Lakes, the Dakotas, and beyond them, the Mississippi and the Gulf of Mexico.

I told her I should bear it in mind and I said how very happy I was that this first voyage should have caused so little talk, and how happy I was at the great names he flushed, like game.

Then Luronne: He set out again the next year, 1535, and it took him five weeks to reach Newfoundland in the *Grande Hermine*, the *Petite Hermine*, and the *Emerillon*. Still looking for the passage to the elusive Cipango and Cathay. I forgot to tell you he'd taken two Hurons back to France with him, Domagaya and Taiognagny who, soon as they had learned a little French, began telling about the wonders of a kingdom in the west called Saguenay, which Cartier recognized as Cathay with his eyes shut.

Myself: We'll never get out of this.

Luronne: The same old tale, and when Cartier saw that he would never find the strait, he now confined himself to looking for Saguenay. And now here were these guides telling him he was on its borders, or to be exact, on the great Hochelaga River, that is to say, in Iroquois, the beavers' highway. Cartier was consumed with impatience. There was this dazzling vision of

173

another Peru taking form only a few cable lengths away. He worked up the Hochelaga and anchored at Tadoussac. Then he reached a place which they told him was the beginning of the realm of Canada; and Canada, still in Iroquois, means village. Donnacona, his acquaintance of the first voyage, was the lord of it, with the title of agouhanna. He was the father of Domagaya and Taiognagny, and he came aboard the *Grande Hermine*: he had not seen his sons since Cartier took them away.

(We contemplated the touching picture.)

The Hurons celebrated Cartier's arrival and instantly gave a feast. A great array of warriors and great bringing in of food.

(Myself so happy that for once, for this once, everything was going well.)

Luronne: Cartier wanted to go on, to make his way up the river, but Donnacona did not like the idea of his going to Hochelaga. The Frenchmen disregarded his objections and reached the beavers' highway, where a thousand Hurons gave him an enthusiastic welcome. Perhaps they too hoped for help from the white men, because the unfortunate creatures lived in a place where their enemies were continually passing through—the warriors of the Five Nations.

(I looked at what I had not yet the right to know and which in any case I only knew in its broad outlines: at the hatred between the Iroquois and the Hurons. A hatred that I knew was going to hurt me in a hundred years' time.)

Then Luronne: Cartier named a hill Mont Royal. All night the Hurons danced. And sang and caroused and heaped up the fires. Cartier, and the white world with him, discovered wampum—you know, the beads the Indians make out of clamshells and wear in belts. It's their money. Their dollars and francs and they get it by plunging the correctly mutilated corpses of their enemies and of criminals in the water. The clams deposit their pearls in the wounds of the dead.

Luronne: Then Cartier recited to them from the Bible—the Passion according to St. John.

Myself: Not really!

174

Luronne: Yes he did. He viewed the Lachine rapids and asked a great many questions about Saguenay. The Indians pointed to a country in the unknown regions, over toward the Ottawa and Lake Superior. This was a little after the half moon when the roebuck courts his mate, or, more prosaically, the second half of October. Overcome by the power of the autumnal beauty, Cartier decided to stay all through the winter, the first winter that any white man had ever spent in Canada, or (still in Iroquois) in the village.

In their custom of putting all the nubile girls without exception in huts where the men made use of them, Cartier discovered the Hurons' brothel. He also smoked a pipe, the first mention of tobacco in the northern parts of North America. He speaks of it as being "like ground pepper." From November 1535 to mid-April 1536 he lived through the abominable Canadian winter. His men suffered from scurvy. And from syphilis, which Columbus had discovered, if I may so put it, in the Caribbean islands, and which he had carried to Europe, where it was unknown before his first voyage—did I mention that?

I told her she had not.

Luronne: Donnacona: another teller of wild tales. Eloquent. Lavish. Tireless on the subject of Saguenay, which he had visited, where he had beheld mountains of gold and rubies, where the people were as pale as the white men, and where some possessed no anus, a fact that delighted François I. Pygmies, too. Donnacona had seen them, just as Thorfinn Karlsefni had, you remember?

(A pause.)

Then Luronne: So Cartier, wishing to show François I this blessed creature who had seen Saguenay and who talked about it, kidnapped him.

(A pause.)

Then Luronne: And he seized ten other Indians too, not one of whom was ever to see his own country again.

The first stroke of sadness I had received from Cartier, and I said, "They're all the same."

175

Luronne: The end of the second voyage, even more disappointing than the first, when you think of its aims. The third and last took place in 1541; its chief aim was no longer this undiscoverable Northwest Passage but the wealth of Saguenay. This time Cartier was only second in command under Roberval, the "viceroy" of Canada. The noise of the expedition's departure spread even before it got under way, and this alarmed the Spaniard Charles V, who ordered Havana, San Juan de Puerto Rico, and San Domingo to be fortified.

She laughed. We both laughed.

Then Luronne: He took settlers and convicts aboard and set sail without waiting for Roberval. The Indians no longer seemed so friendly after the kidnapping. Cartier decided to set up a colony at a place he named Charlesbourg-Royal. The Indians attacked and killed thirty-five of his settlers. Scurvy broke out again, and as Roberval did not appear, Cartier concluded that he had been lost at sea. He loaded his ships with gold and precious stones, diamonds and rubies, which of course turned out to be mere worthless flashy minerals, and then left Canada forever. When he reached the port of St. John's in Newfoundland, he could not believe his eyes: there were Roberval's ships! Refusing to obey Roberval's order to return to Canada, he set sail for St. Malo. Roberval wintered at Charlesbourg-Royal, where the cold killed fifty of his colonists. Then he too gave up and went back to France. There was no more talk of Saguenay, that other Mexico in the Laurentian snows, except as the name of a pleasant but unexciting river.

(I saw and I heard the collapse of the dream, a collapse so generally understood that no one undertook any landing in Canada for more than half a century.)

Then Luronne: Now for the south. Look at Pánfilo de Narváez, one of the worst butchers of Indians. Cortez had put out one of his eyes. He sailed along the coast of Florida at the head of three hundred men.

(Through the eyes of the Pensacolas, wide open with amazement, we watched Narváez' four ships.)

Then Luronne: In April 1528 he landed at Tampa Bay and ordered a raid in the direction of Apalachen, a northern province where he had heard there was gold in abundance. This was the first expedition penetrating the interior of America. The ships followed up the coast, with the intention of picking up the marching men when it was all over.

Then Luronne: The Indians systematically avoided contact with the Spaniards, who suffered from hunger, from disease, and from tramping through the jungle. And when the Apalachees did appear, it was to attack; and their arrows struck the Spaniards in the gaps in their armor, in the places where the plates were fastened together.

Myself: Bravo!

Luronne: Diabolical. Against them the matchlocks, snaphances, and wheel locks, fired leaning on a rest, were merely ridiculous. Apalachen turned out to be a bog on the shore of Lake Miccosukee, with forty huts on it. A fruitless wait for the ships. Narvaez ordered boats to be built. Out of nothing. The Spaniards had to forge every nail that went into the making of their nine open boats. Once they were beyond the mouth of the Mississippi they all sank, but not before some men, driven to madness by the sun and by thirst, had jumped overboard and drowned. All the boats were lost, except the one carrying Núñez Cabeza de Vaca, the expedition's treasurer.

(A pause.)

Then Luronne: They landed on the coast of Texas, where the Indians, appalled at finding these whites had committed acts of cannibalism, seized them and made them slaves—they had to dig edible roots for their masters. One by one the Spaniards died, and in time Cabeza was quite alone. And so he remained, a white among the Indians, for five years, from 1529 onward. To make a living, of course, but also to get to know the country and to escape from it one day, he became, with his masters' consent, a messenger, a peddler, a carrier of shells and ocher— fantastic traveling to and fro from the coast of east Texas to the interior and back again. The Indians moved as their supplies of

177

food obliged them to move: acorns at the beginning of the year, then roots and spiders, snakes and rats. In the fall, fish and pecan nuts. One day in the winter of 1533–34, Cabeza de Vaca chanced upon three survivors of the Narváez' expedition; Alonso Castillo Maldonado, Andrés Dorantes, and Estebanico, Dorantes' black slave. Look at them.

I looked at them.

Then Luronne: Now began one of the most extraordinary adventures I shall ever tell you.

(My heart beat high.)

Then Luronne: Picture these three white men, naked apart from a loincloth, their long hair held back by strips of deer hide. Their bodies burned by the sun—in one place Cabeza de Vaca says, listen, "Twice a year we changed our skin, like snakes."

Myself: Striking.

Luronne: Because the four of them still had three years of wandering to go—that makes eight altogether—wandering from tribe to tribe across Texas and as far as the Pacific. Eight years in southern and northern Florida and then Texas. The first men to cross North America from east to west: four thousand four hundred miles in eight years.

Myself: Eight years.

Luronne: Take notice of the black man: I'll be talking about him again. Picture him. Very well built, a giant of a man, six foot eight, with flowers in his hair. It was the season for nuts, then for cactus fruit. In August 1539, when they were on the Texan coast, they decided to try to reach Mexico. They traded deer skins for dogs, and they ate dog until they could eat no more. They traveled among a swarm of Indians, several hundreds of them, a crowd that was continually renewed; and Estebanico marched in front with his hollow-gourd rattle. Cabeza de Vaca found that he had gifts as a medicine man; he cured with all his might, and the four men's reputation flew from tribe to tribe, where they were spoken of as great shamans. Listen. . . .

(Myself, thrilled: I'm listening.)

Luronne: Listen to them, look at them when they hear about the buffalo, which were grazing not a hundred miles from there, to the east of the Pecos River, the buffalo that no white man had ever seen, and that these four were never to see either, though they ate buffalo meat. At the beginning of 1536 the Jumanos of the Rio Grande took them in. It had not rained for two years and the ground hogs had eaten the standing corn. Nevertheless the Jumanos fed the whites and the black man.

Myself: Admirable.

Luronne: The first whites ever to see the southwest of the United States. The first whites ever to set foot on the continent to the north of Mexico.

(Myself, excited and enthusiastic: What a quantity of beginnings! What a quantity of firsts! This wonderful brotherhood, in spite of Cabeza de Vaca's sufferings, in spite of the Indians' extreme poverty. . . .)

Luronne: In 1537 they left the Rio Grande valley and made for the Sierra Madre, which they were to cross.

(Fascinated, I watched these men, day after day in the wilderness for eight years on end, day after day once they had left Florida.)

Luronne: They may have seen Apaches up there by the pueblos; and then after eight years they ran into a group of Spaniards, slave-hunters working for the governor of New Galicia. Silent, hostile, scarcely recognizing the three white men: "they were so astonished at seeing us," says Cabeza de Vaca, "that they did not utter a single word." And for a long while the slave hunters scarcely believed their story, or that they were the survivors of Pánfilo de Narváez' lost expedition.

(For my part I gazed, picturing them, pitying them, struck with admiration, perhaps with envy.)

And when my eyes hurt with staring at them in the Texan desert I told Luronne, and I said she would never have a greater, more powerful tale to tell; sweetheart, you ought to have kept Cabeza de Vaca for the end.

Luronne: Coronado. The logical continuation of Cabeza de Vaca, who was no fabricator of dreams. When Cabeza told what he had seen, he did not invent gold and silver in the fabulous Seven Cities of Cibola in the far north of the Spanish territory. So they suspected him of keeping quiet about the facts; they suspected that his dissimulation was proportionate to his real knowledge; and when Don Antonio de Mendoza, the viceroy of New Spain, organized an expedition, he tried to engage the three miraculously preserved Spaniards, approaching them one by one, starting with Cabeza. They all refused.

The viceroy's choice then fell upon a priest, Fray Marcos, and upon the black man, Estebanico. They were to be the advance party, and they were to be followed by a great expeditionary force under Don Francisco Vásquez de Coronado.

(I hated these Spaniards, but I loved the Christian names and surnames that rang and rolled and sang, whistling and hissing when they came to an *s*, a *z*, an *r*.)

Then Luronne: Now you must picture Estebanico's swelled head. It was he who had gone beyond the Opata country and upper Sonora. He was the one who had been there, and who knew. Who understood the healing art. The one whom the viceroy had chosen to bring about the revelation of the Seven Cities of Cibola, all overflowing with gold. See him traveling with his tent, his dressing gowns, his mastiffs, his huge set of cutlery and dishes that he would let no one else eat from: see him going along and waving the rattle he had acquired from the Texan Indians during his wanderings in the emptiness of the South with Cabeza de Vaca. As he advanced so he built up a harem, and this grieved Fray Marcos, though he dared not say anything. Estebanico was corrupt through and through, and as you put it the other day, he wrung everything he could out of the Indians. So Fray Marcos, in order to be rid of him, in order not to have him carrying on there before his eyes in a state of sin, ordered the black man to go ahead. He was to tell Fray Marcos of his discoveries by sending back messengers with a cross whose size was to vary with the importance of the find: the greater and more splendid the marvel, the bigger the cross.

Then Luronne: Estebanico reached the Zuñis of Hawikuh, in New Mexico. They were suspicious: what these logically minded Indians could not swallow was Estebanico's tale about a great body of white men who were coming along behind him, the subjects of an all-powerful king who had the ear of an all-powerful God. A black to announce the coming of whites? Lies, decided the Zuñis, and they put Estebanico to death, cut him into small pieces, and killed every last one of his three hundred followers.

(Sadly I watched Estebanico being carved into small pieces, the black man who had discovered Arizona and New Mexico.)

Then Luronne: The news reached Fray Marcos, who turned back, horrified. A little later he showed the stuff he was made of—a mythomaniac, asserting that from a distant hill he had seen Cibola (she put on the light and quoted) "larger than the city of Mexico," whereas Cibola is nothing but a Zuñi pueblo, of the most modest pretensions.

(She switched off and in the darkness I gazed at the Zuñis in their pueblo for the first time, and satisfied I said, "It's not only the Indians who are mythomaniacs.")

She agreed, then: Fray Marcos' tale excited the viceroy, who instantly sent an expedition on foot, entrusting the command to Coronado. Look: two hundred and fifty horsemen, eighty foot soldiers, some women and children, a thousand servants, and twelve priests brought by Fray Marcos, together with herds of cattle, sheep, pigs, pack mules and a thousand horses.

(Impressed, I looked at this great movement of humans and animals, this vast convoy.)

Then Luronne: Mendoza sent a certain Melchior Díaz ahead to scout: look at the map.

(She put on the light and unfolded one of our maps.) We watched Díaz advance toward the Colorado plateau, where the cold, the snow, and the ice soon stopped him. He met with some Pimas: he did not enter the Pueblo country though he was told about it, and he had not returned by the time Coronado gave the signal to move off on February 23, 1540, between Jacques Cartier's second and third voyages.

(I waited.)

Then Luronne: Following river courses, Coronado made his way from Arizona to New Mexico and reached Hawikuh, that is to say Cibola, where Estebanico had got himself carved up. An enormous disappointment, of course. The Spaniard seized the pueblo and dismissed Fray Marcos. Never-ending disgrace for the mytho.

(We looked at the pitiful creature.)

Then Luronne: After the taking of Cibola, Coronado organized several expeditions, sending out small advance parties: one of them met with Hopis, others discovered the Colorado and the Grand Canyon, the greatest gash in the earth anywhere in the world—it did not impress them.

(Quietly I relished these firsts.)

Luronne: Coronado advanced in a country entirely unknown to white men, through New Mexico, the Rio Grande valley, and then the Great Plains, leaving behind him a trail of blood and death, studded with ravaged towns. A journey through hunger, where the reality of corn ended up by counting for more than the hope of gold: a deathly journey. Coronado and his men were the first to see the Tewas, the Tiguas, the Jemez, the Piros, the Keresans, the Pecos, and the Apaches.

Myself: The Apaches.

Luronne: Yes: and to Coronado we owe the first description of the Pueblo Indians, whom the Spaniards deceived, tortured, and murdered in their pueblos.

(She stopped, and I no longer relished or savored these firsts; nothing went down my constricted throat anymore. Something tells me, Luronne, that from now on we shall be drinking less and less champagne.)

Then Luronne: See Coronado's lieutenant, Hernando de Alarcón, discovering the mouth of the Colorado, then passing close to Yuma in Arizona, and turning his head to gaze at California, the first white man to see it.

(I gazed at California with all my might.)

Then we followed this third exploration, when Coronado sent Hernando de Alvarado to look at the Acoma pueblo: he reached the Rio Grande and found a number of pueblos, many of them deserted in that tragic, desolate, abandoned land. The white men were impressed by Taos; they left it for Pecos, the pueblo farthest to the east. The buffalo plains began just after that.

Myself (and I felt my eyes stretching wide, like those of Narváez' Pensacolas): The buffalo plains!

Luronne: At this point Coronado decided to make for the Rio Grande, since the pueblos to the east were friendly. Winter came upon the Spaniards, and there were too many of them. They had to be fed, and as usual the task fell to the Indians. Coronado seized a pueblo by force, and so that the whites might spend the cold season by themselves, he expelled the inhabitants. This provoked a big uprising among the pueblos: twelve of them. The Spaniards replied, as usual, with the worst of crimes, tying Indians by the hundred to stakes and setting fire to them.

(I suffered.)

Then Luronne: The reconnoitering party that had gone to Pecos kidnapped an Indian, whom they brought to Coronado. The Spaniards called him the Turk. A mytho!

Myself: Still another!

Luronne: Yes—the old story all over again. This Indian was maybe a Kansas or a Nebraska Pawnee. Cibola's dead, so long live Quivira, a place invented by the Turk, every detail of it made up. Golden details. Another of these fabulous cities! So as to reach Quivira as soon as possible, Coronado left the valley of the Rio Grande, made his way eastward from New Mexico, followed the Pecos River, and crossed the Llano Estacado. This was in June, a splendid month down there in Texas and

Oklahoma. They forded the Canadian, Cimarron, and Arkansas rivers, reaching a place that was one day to be Dodge City; then he came to Smoky Hill River in Kansas, and there on the vast, rich, grassy plains of the north, Coronado, the first white man after his lieutenant Díaz, saw the buffaloes.

(No, I did not have the heart to celebrate the buffaloes: from now on I knew how things were going to turn out.)

Luronne: Jaramillo, who took notes, was absolutely amazed. This enormous woolly mass left him speechless. Buffalo by the thousands: more of them, says he, than there are fishes in the sea.

Then: Coronado came across some Wichitas, all of them tattooed from head to foot. These were the Indians of Quivira. The Spaniards ate buffalo until they were ill.

(I could not tell what it tasted like: I should so much have liked to know.)

Then Luronne: Quivira at last! Exactly the same as Cibola. Coronado's heavy heart: his furious anger. Look. . . .

And I looked at the horror she related: the Turk garroted at dawn, the death of the mytho.

Then Luronne: The expedition turned back, following a route that was later to become the Santa Fe Trail. An uneventful journey from the heart of Kansas to the Rio Grande. Coronado and his men had traveled farther north and they had covered a greater distance than did Cabeza de Vaca, and they brought back invaluable first hand information on the culture and the character of the Indians of the Southwest.

(I looked at them before they turned, before they set out for home: I looked at them there in the north where no one else was to go for a hundred years, and I should so have liked to see little herds of buffalo in Kansas and a roaring stampede in Texas; take me there, Luronne.)

Then: At one point in 1541 Coronado and de Soto were riding within less than three hundred miles of each other, though neither knew or ever was to know it. As far as de Soto is concerned, history begins in 1538, that is to say two years before

Coronado, and ends in 1543, one year after him. For five years on end de Soto marched about the country from Georgia to Oklahoma, the greatest criminal in North America, as I told you once.

Myself (torn by conflicting emotions, and as it were in spite of myself): Go on.

Luronne: De Soto was already an old hand when he landed in Florida. At the age of fifteen he had been with Pedrarias, ravaging Darien, Panama, and Nicaragua. He had accompanied Pizarro, as one of the conquerors of Peru, and he had helped himself to some of Atahualpa's enormous ransom. He knew all about sacking temples and palaces, and he dreamed of importing this kind of behavior to the lands of North America, into which he led the greatest expedition that had ever been sent on foot.

(I watched myself hating him.)

Then Luronne: He was the governor of Cuba, and he sailed over to Tampa Bay with six hundred soldiers, accompanied by the same number of Indian carriers in chains. Herds of swine followed him or marched ahead. Scarcely had he landed before he exhibited his true form—butchery, burning villages, Indians thrown to dogs trained to attack them.

(Bewildered and distressed, I looked at Hernando de Soto's true form, at his way of behaving. What is in store for us, Luronne, if he breaks out like this when he has only just set foot in Florida?)

Luronne: He was in the country of the Timucuas—you know, the Indians who attacked Narváez—and striking north, he went beyond Apalachen, where Narváez suffered his resounding defeat.

Myself: That was good.

Luronne: Yes—to a country where he had been told that there reigned a woman whose physical proportions were quite unheard of. And where there was unheard-of wealth, too. As you see, we are still in the midst of lies, fables, myths.

Myself: And mythos (as she put it).

Luronne, smiling: Yes. Of course the queen was just like you and me, apart from the fact that she was ugly and that she lived in utter filth. De Soto fought a battle called the Battle of the Lakes; he won it, and put some three hundred Indians in chains. Then, with his herds of swine following or going ahead—they were having a fine time, and they always joined up with the main body—the Spaniard moved from the Timucua country into that of the Apalachees with five hundred whites and five hundred prisoners, and there he received the unrivaled assistance of a certain Ortiz, a suvivor of the Narváez expedition. The Calusas had captured him and they were about to put him to death when the chief's daughter, who was in love with him, intervened and begged that his life be spared. Pardon granted: first example of all those stories recorded by History of white men saved by Indian girls.

Myself: Maybe it was true.

Luronne: Certainly it was true, and Ortiz' work among the Calusas consisted of keeping the carrion-eating wolves away from the graveyards—a what do you call it? A not-very-appetizing calling. He despaired of ever seeing another Spaniard; but then, ten years after he was taken prisoner, there appeared de Soto, whose interpreter he became. So here we are with de Soto. Inevitably he chanced upon a mytho. The mytho of duty. Named Perico. A prisoner from the Battle of the Lakes. He told amazing tales of gold far away in the north, and de Soto felt that his new Peru was within hand's reach.

Next you see him in northern Georgia, and then at Cofitachequi, which was ruled by a Cree queen. Perico had lied; they put him to death, burned a few other Indians for good measure, and carried the queen away a prisoner. And de Soto marched on from the Savannah to the Tennessee. Then across South Carolina as far as the foot of the Blue Ridge Mountains and into North Carolina. Pillaging temples and graves. It was something of a feat: look, in five days he covered nearly a hundred miles in that difficult broken country. The pigs came along behind, thank you very much. In the Cherokee country a chief brought him three hundred dogs to cook and eat: the Spaniards thought them delicious. Then, following the Indian trails, he reached the Tennessee.

Luronne stopped and drew breath for a while, long enough for me to see clearly, to picture and to bring to life that fantastic march through a terrain that I had read about and that I loved.

Then Luronne: He carried out the first crossing of the Appalachians, and it was a hundred years before any other white man did the same.

(I listened, I admired, I suffered.)

Luronne: He continually renewed his stock of slaves, and look at him now among the Creeks in Alabama, then in the Chickasaw country along the Tombigbee, then the Mississippi.

Myself: Stop!

(She had to stop, because I wanted to take a long look at these Indians she had spoken of; they were Faulkner's Indians, and not only Indians: Chickasaws, Choctaws, Creeks, Seminoles, Cherokees, but also Faulkner characters, droll, bitter, the victims of a fate outside their control.)

Then: Go on.

Luronne: Between the Tombigbee and the Alabama, about halfway through October 1540, a great battle took place, swords and arrows against muskets; and in the blazing town, where the cavalry charges broke against the Indian resistance, the historians number two thousand dead. Don't interrupt. At Quigaltam, a little later, he ordered all the men to be put to death: and the town had five to eight thousand inhabitants.

(I looked away.)

Luronne (pitiless because she had to be, because she had to tell the whole truth): He achieved at least one genocide. The killing off of the Kaskinampos, in a region of the Arkansas. De Soto exterminated them, except for ten or fifteen who went off and were assimilated by the Alabama Koasatis, wiped out of history.

(I told her that she must stop, that I no longer wanted to hear

187

nor to see: I know nothing worse than this disappearance of a people, of a name, vanishing into death forever.)

But since she had to go on, "Go on," I said.

An immense river appeared before them. Under the eyes of the canoe-borne Indians who were keeping watch on him, de Soto crossed the Mississippi, which Alonso Alvarez Pineda had discovered in 1519. De Soto was the first white to cross it north of the delta, and then along the bayous and the marshes he advanced along the Arkansas. He may have made his way into the Ozarks, to the Missouri. Then among the Sioux of the Kansas River Valley he saw tepees. There de Soto spent a third winter. The North had disappointed him; the West, or the buffalo country, was disappointing him now. The South was to disappoint him later. Never any gold.

(I contemplated this shortcoming.)

Luronne: Toward the end of 1541, when the Christmas snow had fallen, he made his way into the country of the Kadohadachos, who formed the Caddo confederacy in northeast Texas. Another very hard-fought battle. To escape from the horses, the Caddos climbed onto the roofs of their houses and from there they shot down upon their opponents. They leaped from roof to roof, holding out so long that the horses dropped with exhaustion. De Soto withdrew. And reappeared three days later to occupy a town deserted by the Caddos—from a word meaning real chiefs—who, hearing of de Soto's return, came back at four in the morning of that first night of occupation and attacked in two divisions with bows, arrows, and stakes. A slaughter. Prisoners by the hundreds. De Soto ordered six of them to have their right hand and their nose cut off and he sent them to the cacique with a message. If he did not come and swear obedience, all the prisoners would have their right hand and nose cut off. The cacique yielded.

And I entreated: Stop, Luronne! And stop him! Bring de Soto to a halt there with the Caddos! Oh, Luronne, if only you could!

Luronne: Ortiz vanished. A great loss. When he attacked the

188

towns in Louisiana, de Soto committed the vilest atrocities. Then, as I did not tell you before, he caught a fever, and there in Louisiana, at the end of May 1542, he died.

Myself (a heartfelt cry): At last!

(And relieved, happy, suddenly relaxed, I looked at the dead body of de Soto, which Luis de Moscoso de Alvarado, his successor as leader of the expedition, threw into the Mississippi by night, near Natchez.)

Then I turned away from the survivors, who reached Mexico four years and four months after their psychopathic chief had left Havana.

Luronne, exhausted, had done with the subject: too many deaths, I told myself, too many atrocities, too much blood in so short a time. One century. Almost nothing. I loathed death, that other death which comes through illness or loss of vital strength: but what of death given by a mortal man? Almost as base and vile as the other, although more cunning, more insidious. And implacable. Written in our blood. In me; in you, Luronne. Unavoidable, unbearable death is quite enough. Why did they all of them have to add to it, there in America?

De Soto's contempt for Indianism . . . The Corte-Reals' and Jacques Cartier's abductions: but that's nothing, Luronne! From Narváez to de Soto, the evil of conquest and destruction never stopped. And again I saw that four-and-a-half-year march from Florida to Mexico by way of Georgia, Alabama, Mississippi, Tennessee, Arkansas, Oklahoma, and again Mississippi. All of them lands where I had never been. And I saw the procession of the Indians they had met: Hitchitis, Creeks, Chakchuimas, Chickasaws, Choctaws, Alabamas, Mobiles, Tuskegees, Chiahas, Yaquis, Cherokees, Tunicas, Kaskinampos. All of them Indians I had never seen. And half of them Indians I should never see, Indians it would have been impossible for me to see these four centuries past.

Still without speaking, Luronne switched off the light, as though she wanted us, each for himself, to take a last look—a look filled with an indefinable decent reticence toward each other and from each toward America—at those two arrows of sinister portent, Coronado and de Soto, striking deep into the fleshy flank of America, which jerked in convulsive spasms and wept.

And when she turned it on again, she told me, in a low voice, that in this sixteenth century death was busy everywhere in America and in the direction of America, and she quoted Morison saying that less than one in four of those who so cheerfully set out from Europe came back to his starting point. To emphasize this she mentioned only Alonso de Ojeda's shipwreck on the coast of Paria, with thirty-five survivors out of three hundred; Diego de Nicusa's on the coast of Brazil, with sixty survivors out of eight hundred; and the loss of Pedro Alvarez de Cabral's four ships with every soul aboard just after he had discovered Brazil. She had a whole list, which she held out but which I did not want to read; and together with this list she had another, just as long, containing the names of all the vanished Indian tribes of North America. I won't read that either, Luronne, not this morning; it's late.

Less for herself than for me, Luronne had already emerged from the sorrow, from the impotent rage in which we had shut ourselves up all through the sixteenth century. She stood up, she walked about, she smiled, and I had a strong feeling that she had something to say to me, as though she did not want to leave things on the note of death and evil. And automatically I said, "Go ahead."

She went ahead. Straight into what she called crazy geography. Cabral, for example: he sets out for the Indies, of course, like everybody else; he sails wide out from the African coast and then a sudden thump and Cabral bangs into Brazil. Not the Indies: Brazil. Vespucci and Frobisher discover a bay, and they're convinced it's a strait. You put to sea to reach the Pacific—thump again, and it's the Arctic Ocean.

I smiled. Luronne took a map and showed me, made me understand. All at once the revelation, the revelation that made me stutter. From which I recovered just enough to say to Luronne, Look, look. What at? said she. Myself: Look here, look—when the sixteenth century came to an end in 1599 there was not a white man in America from the Arctic Circle to the Gulf of Mexico—nothing but Indians, except there, where it's marked on the map, the military post at St. Augustine, held by the Spaniards in Florida.

She smiled scornfully. I didn't have to worry about that. A miserable little post. A mere fortlet. Of no importance whatsoever. So it was true that America was still to be discovered, still to be explored.

We drank. To the Indian and the almost virgin America, a hundred years after its discovery by Columbus. Luronne had a wonderful opportunity coming up, if she would use it to good advantage. If she could do it. The past was safely behind her. With one hundred years to go, in the century to follow, how the devil could she miss finding a way to manage without having to throw everything overboard? To America, Luronne: to us.

We drank and I held her, stroked her, with first one hand and then with the other, running over her as I would have run over a map, a planisphere, a globe; Luronne was smooth like the America of the globe. America there is likewise as smooth as a naked belly, and I feel no friction—not a single Spanish helmet, nor a musket, no thick blood sticking to my fingers. So I laughed and I drank—tough luck for the dead of sixteenth-century North America, Luronne, we couldn't do a thing, you and I, especially you. Sensible folk say, Don't look back, don't look back toward the dead but look forward, turn toward the living, and now do you see, Luronne, I'm looking right ahead of me at the seventeenth century and I'm sure we're going to be happy in it, there among the living. The great century.

We laughed. We drank.

For several days the history we had just lived through kept us in a state of excitement; we talked of nothing else, and every now and then it shook us like a sudden bout of fever, and once in the confusion of a nightmare that Luronne cut short—a nightmare that she had perhaps started herself—de Soto came back to haunt me. He was entering Louisiana, the land of alligators, and at the same moment I felt something grab me in the belly, crack: I started up, groaning, and Luronne, disturbed, went right back to her work, to her pleasure, to mine, to ours, and her gentle, persuasive mouth carried on at my belly, crack, and with a life rattle I said, "My love!" We were happy there at the end of the sixteenth century and the beginning of the seventeenth—between 1599 and 1601 to be exact—so comfortable, so happy that we should have liked never to leave but to live at the meeting of the two centuries forever and to die there if we had to, far back in the line of time: we felt that History was giving us a break, and that we should make the most of it. Luronne wore her hair long, because I had often told her I liked it, and I made love to her powerfully, continuously, without the least hint of sadness. Without any anxiety at all. And in order to know the seventeenth century better while I was waiting for it, in order to be able to move about in it at my ease, I learned the names and the positions of all the French, English, and Spanish forts built and spread abroad between the Atlantic and the Mississippi, Hudson's Bay and the Gulf of Mexico, in just one century. As I did so I strayed into the eighteenth century, but I kept strictly to the names of the forts and their position on the map: I did not want to know anything about the following century's tragedy or happiness.

We spent two hours of one evening changing the lighting system. When the time came for Luronne to take up her tale again, we should scarcely have to move more than a finger or a foot to light up the scenes she described, the stages whereon, with a little luck, no more massacres would be enacted.

Then we left for the Grand Canyon of the Colorado.

Once or twice, when she was speaking of Coronado, she had mentioned the Grand Canyon and the Colorado River, and I wanted to go see them. We had to get ready at once. Summer is the time for going down the Colorado, and it was now the beginning of winter. Luronne spent some six hours on the telephone, and she got pretty well what she wanted. The trip was promised on condition of our being there on the spot tomorrow at the latest, down there in Arizona. Some winter days could be warm and full of light, like a last echo of summer. With a guide, we were going to take the chance.

Of course there was no question of going down the two hundred seventy-five miles of the river from one end of Arizona to the other, from the Utah border to that of Nevada, running along the bottom of the Grand Canyon, sometimes two thousand feet down. Since it was winter we should have to be satisfied with a two-day trip of a little under ninety miles, going down to a point set by the guide, and there, on a cliff landing place by the Bright Angel trail, a helicopter would pick us up. Luronne had no more seen the Grand Canyon than I had. We knew it was a wonder. But it was a wonder that eluded the fanciful operations we mounted to capture it. One by one we tried the words by which it is usually described, at first in a quiet, meditative rhythm, then at a faster pace. These words painted no more than a faint, sickly picture. We were sure that the Grand Canyon was beyond and above the accounts of those who had written about it. We knew with a deep inward truth, a truth that we both possessed and that each had wept with joy on discovering in the other, that the world is contained, absolutely contained, by words, and that nothing in the world eludes them. Everything hinges on gaining the cooperation of the words. In a way we had applied this inward truth wherever we had been; we had applied it in the Connecticut forest as we had on the banks of the Atchafalaya. We should be the first to recount the Grand Canyon, a rich and magnificent tale of its splendor. Calmly we dropped off to sleep, proud to face the challenge.

The guide was waiting for us at Lee's Ferry, south of the border between Utah and Arizona. He was a Havasupai Indian. Later we found that he had studied at the University of California at San Diego, and that having got his degrees he had gone back to live among the Indians of his tribe on their reservation.

193

In short, he had chosen the Grand Canyon. In this we saw a good omen.

We never did get to know anything but his American first name—in this case dull and commonplace: John. Perhaps he thought a white's mouth could only mangle an Indian name. Spoil it, as a fruit is spoiled. So he pretended not to hear, concealing his Havasupai identity from us. In any case, the trip provided little opportunity for conversation. He showed us our tent and our sleeping bags in the dory, the flat-bottomed row boat that was to carry us. He had his own tent and bag. It was only the food that was to be shared.

The sun had scarcely risen that Monday morning when the guide launched the dory. We had arrived in the darkness, so we had seen nothing of the Grand Canyon, although it was already in evidence at Lee's Ferry with its cliffs that showed higher and higher still as the mist thinned out, our gaze continually rising and sometimes running ahead of the immense, wafting veils of cloud. This wall of America towered at least two thousand feet above us. The guide dipped his oar into the slack water, and Luronne and I, pressed tight together in our life jackets, were filled with that enchanting intoxication which comes over townspeople when they are suddenly brought face to face with nature, an intoxication that arises from the meeting of air and water. We went along at the average speed of the current, between three and four miles an hour, and the great walls of the canyon closed in on us, narrowing the channel to such a degree that we could even distinguish the rocks in their diversity, their personality, their beauty. Luronne pointed out the rising strata and their colors, first cream, then light yellow, white, red and brown, then red all by itself; and these she recognized, from bottom to top, as Kaibab limestone, Toroweap limestone, Coconico sandstone, Hermit schist, and Suprai limestone—hesitating only over the Redwall limestone, of an indefinable color that morning—all of them formations which, in that trembling light, seemed to be alive, to be pushing, helping one another to climb and make their way upward; and thus there

was a double movement, the one up at the top with the crests
tearing free from the clouds, and the other down below, with
the sunlight playing on the colored rocks; and between them
they thrust the cliffs up to pierce the dark covering of the sky.
In the huge, irregular, broken wall before us, almost round
holes were to be seen, gashes that were lengthened by downward curving processes, like the mouths of those black women
who distend their lips with plates, and then ten oar strokes
downstream you would have sworn that some enormous top or
whirligig had spun madly on the stone surface, always on the
point of stopping, but spinning still and leaning over so that its
rim had chiseled, cut, ground, worn, smoothed, and bored
deep, so that the rock, vertically over the river, was hollowed
out in steps and rising outthrust tiers that only a bird could
have walked around; and you would have said that this fantastic, industrious antediluvian top had often changed its center
of rotation, thus churning up areas several dozen square yards.
It was then that we heard the roar.

The moment it began, the guide turned and gravely uttered
the single word rapids, which explained the phenomenon. The
noise made by the rapids. I guessed that we were traveling over
deep water here, and that although the guide was no longer
rowing, the boat moved on because at this point the stream
flowed down a somewhat steeper gradient. Yet it would not
have been surprising if the noise, under the water, had thrust
the boat back. For it was everywhere. As though the very air we
breathed were part of it. As though everything around us—and
even ourselves—were made of it. The noise did not penetrate
us, yet we were filled with it. Luronne and I, taken up with the
single, amply sufficient spectacle of the cliffs, the leaden sky,
the light, and the water, had not exchanged so much as a glance
since the beginning. Now our eyes met, and each saw that the
other was trembling. For the Colorado River is a train and on it
you quiver as though you were aboard an express, a *rapide*—
oh, this same word to say a very fast train and the turbulent water—and it roared, puffed, gasped, pushed, and thumped, a

rich, fantastic music that would turn one's mind from any view, however beautiful, and we experienced something like dread when, with a gigantic grinding, the torrent sharpened the stones of the riverbed against one another, stones that we knew to be the size of houses; and then the Colorado, rattling and panting, ran over the switches. The train's thunder was inside us, inhabiting our blood, and it was outside us too as we neared the Soap Creek rapids, on whose shores there were to be seen banks of gravel and rocky projections at the base of the cliffs, they too thundering and trembling under the enormous, tireless blows of the mass of green water. The guide had stood up to peer into these rapids, and later we learned that the water here was a good sixteen feet deep.

He picked the best course among the eddies, steering the boat by slewing it around with such force as to tear Luronne and me apart and then fling us together the next moment so violently that I felt I had been shot from a catapult. Several times the canoe bounced off a rock face. Telling myself that I had to hang on, that the rapids wouldn't last, I was gazing right and left at the river and straight ahead at the guide when all at once I no longer saw anything at all beyond him. And for the first time I no longer heard the thunder. It was blocked out by my fear, and it seemed to me that I had stopped breathing. Staring at the now nonexistent river, I grasped that we were coming to the edge of a fall: in its mounting spray, strange, hallucinatory shapes rose and plunged down again, shapes I could not name; and all the time the guide doggedly worked his oar to steer us through the waves, the eddies, and the rocks, perhaps in vain, because something that had just taken hold of the boat was pulling it—and then I realized that we were plunging into the whirlpool at the bottom, there where the furious heart of the rapids roared and thundered. Waves, some of them maybe ten feet high, rushed swelling and hissing at the boat and struck it, and at one point, when we were in the midst of the rapids, we very nearly dived into a hole—the guide avoided it by inches, thrusting with his oar. Now the riverbed had narrowed, and the furious waves came at us from both sides; one last blow sent the dory over onto its right side, then it yawed and began to spin at such a rate that I knew we should never survive. And perhaps I heard Luronne scream. Or myself, maybe. Both of us. The boat had scarcely recovered an even keel before a wave swept over it and engulfed all three of us. It's all over—if only I'd known—to die like this! Then in the midst of an enormous din the returning wave flooded the boat. It was filled to the gunwales, and no doubt only the watertight compartments kept it from sinking. The guide thrust down his oar to change course as we began bailing out the mass of water which at this juncture was less the boat racing along between the rocks and eddies than the Colorado itself.

We must have shot about fifteen rapids, or one every two or three miles. None were as formidable as those of Soap Creek, and presently Luronne and I came back to ourselves, to the sky, the cliffs, and the less furious water. And to the thunder. The guide was relieved too, and in a better mood for a little conversation he told us that we were about to reach a part of the Grand Canyon called Vasey Paradise, that we had traveled over thirty miles, and that we should camp on a sandbank a little lower down, a dozen miles below Vasey Paradise. Then suddenly there we were. The guide fell silent, no doubt as dazzled as we were ourselves.

After the rapids the river had broadened, then it narrowed again, and under the midday sun the Colorado, enclosed between its cliffs, made one think of a ring reversed, with the jewel in its setting upside down. Springs by the score gushed from the rock face, sometimes in a powerful jet, sometimes in a seeping trickle; and in the dampness around them flourished lush fern brakes and those plants whose flowers we might have admired some months earlier. And the dory ran on down the nine-million-year-old Colorado, between the mossy, fantastic rocks, piled on top of one another without the least sense of proportion, and there were boulders that seemed to be balancing on the weathered surface by no more than a ridiculous corner of their massive bulk; then we went along beneath cave dwellings with a huge arch cut from the stone above them, and I gazed at it in amazement as it stood there without falling, held up by nothing, and at our request the guide, from down there in the boat, managed to point out the trails high up on the cliff, telling us whether they were made by deer, mountain sheep, Indians, or white explorers; then, the river widening again, we passed by a waterfall, and we saw it plunge a hundred feet in one blue-green jet down into its basin, and Luronne, who had recovered her voice, identified poplars, willows, watercress, and negundos under the trees, wild vines, nettle trees.

Myself (as in the Riverside Drive apartment, and enchanted): More!

Luronne: Arrow grass, maidenhair fern, cattails, monkey flower cluster.

(Myself, deep within: Who can ever tell the wonder of words?)

And we saw several cormorants and some wild duck, and then it was the halt. The guide pulled the boat out on one of the few sandbanks we had seen in more than forty miles of running downriver, took out the tents—we set them up—and went off to gather juniper wood to make a fire. He gave us a great quantity of pinecones and opened them to get at the kernels, which he placed in a heap. His only words to us were a remark about the lateness of the season, which prevented us from eating the trout he would otherwise have caught. When the very early twilight fell, before five o'clock, he retired to his tent, twenty yards from ours. Then we looked at the sky, which had turned yellow, and in this sulfurous tinge we perceived the brewing of a storm. We moved to the tent and sat there in its opening, Luronne leaning against me and both of us covered with a blanket: half in, half out, we watched the clouds gathering above the flying bats. The clouds rose and the yellow fever of the sky seized them, swallowed them up as they mounted fast, breaking free from the shifting perspective of the horizon in huge black masses. Presently not a single one was left, and then, night having fallen, the storm broke over us.

Pressed against each other, we listened, our hearts beating. Its wrath spoke louder than the canyon's thunder, which was deadened as soon as the first drops fell. Deep within us, coming up from the remotest ages through us, through the skin of time and the bones of the dead, we felt ourselves caught in an upsurge of panic. The dread which men, sheltering in caves as we were sheltering in our tent, felt when the elements were let loose. The ancient fear of primitive things. There was bare rock at ground level in front of the tent; the drops struck this surface with such force that they seemed to bounce, and steam rose up, the water's anger. This spectacle, this close-packed, roaring, fuming downpour conveyed such power, such a feeling of harshness and impenetrability, such force of will, that neither Luronne nor I could say a word, each of us struck and weakened as though by a blow or by bad news, and for my part I had the impression—and a very strange impression it was—that no time was left to me, no future. Or almost none. The rain had been falling like this since the beginning of time. And would go on falling forever after us.

The roar woke us the next morning. According to the guide the storm had stopped in the night, and he pointed to our watches. Eleven o'clock! We had slept fifteen or sixteen hours. Luronne and I looked at each other, unaccountably happy. If we still retained anything of those feelings that had so disturbed us during the storm, at this point we were no longer aware of it. We strolled about the camp, all clearly to be seen there at the edge of a little wood of piñon pines, juniper, yellow pines, and a few gambel oaks. The guide awoke early, long before us, had seen a few snowflakes fall. They were the forerunners of a drop in the temperature; but lower down, where we were going, we should be spared. In his curt way he asked us to get ready. The sun would rise, he said, about noon, in an hour's time.

He had not been rowing the dory above five minutes before

the sun appeared, and this in so beautiful a spot almost at the heart of the Grand Canyon and still far from the next rapids, that the guide stopped. And for no reason that I could make out, we no longer heard the din that had been with us all the way until now. The light invented a geography for the Grand Canyon, endowing it with continents, islands, peninsulas, headlands, gulfs, straits, and isthmuses. Lakes. I could make out striations in the rock, but I was too far away to see more than the general outline, bringing to mind the pre-Columbian world that I bore within me, visions fed and increased by knowledge. Coming up, over the horizon, the sun chased away the mist, turning it into clouds that slowly rose and then disappeared. An Indian summer day, here at the beginning of winter. We watched the rays, stronger and stronger, warmer and warmer, as they moved down the cliffs to seek out and work upon the moisture at their feet; and now the warmth caused fresh mists to rise, scattered at first, then joining to form a dense haze that thinned out and vanished in the upper air. We felt that there were long, splendid hours stretching out before us, and tirelessly we watched the light, so pure in this dry air, strike across the strata of the rocks, which go half a mile and more into the earth, where they are at home among their relations, ten or twenty of them all together, just as they are on the surface of the earth too; and we recognized the gray limestone in the yellow, sandstone in the white and grayish-brown, the pink granites, the almost black schists, and still other formations that I did not know, and as the rays beat down on the Grand Canyon I asked Luronne what, as she saw it, they were revealing there and she instantly replied, "High bluffs, rocky overhangs, volcanic craters, pinnacles."

Myself: More.

Luronne: Needles, precipices, amphitheaters, buttes, slopes, peaks, temples, crags, spurs.

Myself: More.

Luronne: I don't see anymore.

Myself: Prows of ships, rugged crags, a Métro train, beggars, kidnappers with scarves hiding their faces, each behind his hostage, bald, red-faced old gentlemen, walking sticks, several disemboweled ships, bones, ocelots, gunstocks with their tank turrets behind them, grown-up people and children, puffy faces with mustaches.

Luronne, delighted: More.

Myself: Streets, mosque roofs, the muezzin, bolting horses and overturned automobiles, a lady in a tutu among swirling clouds, monkeys, overloaded barges in heavenly water, the blue of fairy tales and some nostalgic greens, graveyard voices and cathedral Gothic, a postman on his rounds, a weeping woman, stonecutters and cut stones, a clubfoot, a red cosmic scar from left to right and back again, beaten children, drug addicts, a wind of panic, a shepherd with a flock of a thousand head at least.

And maybe when I drew breath Luronne said, More, our evening and night-time password, the word of love in America, but the guide had started to row again, and rather than have the litany perish of starvation or of my inability to maintain the tension, and the pitch I had reached, I preferred to let my visionary transports drown in the plashing of the oars, together with the shepherd and his flock of a thousand head at least.

Soothed, wholly satisfied, we watched the marvels glide by, both of us filled with a diffused inner happiness, and Luronne, who had taken my hand, squeezed until it hurt.

The helicopter was waiting for us, as we had arranged, at the landing place below the last five rapids after the junction of the Colorado and the Little Colorado, there where the Hopis locate hell.

As time went by after our return, my feeling of wonder gradually diminished, fading as colors fade. Or rather it underwent a transformation, so that eventually the Grand Canyon in the sunlight merged, in my memory, with the evening of the storm. I told Luronne, who thought that the same evolution was tak-

ing place in her. With our urge toward the beautiful on the one
hand and our liking for the dramatic on the other, it was as
though something in us chose the drama and dedicated us to it.
And it was in vain that I knew that the rock was lashed by the
wind, scored by the rain, roasted by the heat, frozen by the cold
and the snow, split and cracked by seeping icy water; although
it was broken and shattered I still envied its eternity. It has
been reckoned that a Grand Canyon pebble takes five hundred
thousand years to fall into the river, and even there it does not
meet with its death! And that the oldest rocks in the Grand
Canyon are two billion years of age! My inward suffering at the
knowledge that I should not reach even half the age of these
stones . . . Such was the impression, the sad impression, that
this journey left upon us, a trip in which we had found how little we counted, how little room we occupied, how short a time
we lived. . . . Then there were the books.

In order to live longer with the Grand Canyon and to refresh
our memory of it, we set about gathering books on the subject.
And what we read had a depressing effect. From these emi-
nently authoritative works we learned, for example, that the
Colorado, after its fourteen-hundred-mile journey from its
source in the Rockies to the Gulf of California, no longer falls
into the Gulf as it did for thousands of years. And it no longer
falls into the Gulf because at the end of its course it no longer
amounts to anything. Nothing but a meager trickle. A wretched
little channel is all it has by way of a mouth, and in this channel rises and falls the tide, which plays with the remains of
what was not so long ago the very formidable Colorado. The
towns, villages, and factories have simply taken the river's water away from it, so that at the end of its run it no longer flows, a
sovereign stream, but dies away in the mud and sand for mere
lack of water. Dies of thirst. Unbelievable! A stolen, embezzled
river. Torn from its bed so that air conditioners, hair dryers,
televisions, radios, electric guitars, irons, and can openers may
function. . . . Luronne and I read about this mockery and we

learned that the river would never overflow its banks again
now that it had been shackled with dams, those prison wardens
for rivers, and that its flow varied between 182 and 577 cubic
yards a second, a miserable trickle when you consider that in
the days of the Colorado's brutal splendor it would leap from
41.2 to 8240 cubic yards a second; and filled with wonder, admiration, and unhappiness we read that before the dams the
Colorado carried five hundred thousand tons of debris and
rocky sediment through the Grand Canyon every day, a load
that might rise, in time of flood, to twenty-seven million tons,
borne along by a current of such force that if it were so inclined
it could carry, roll, sweep down six-foot masses of rock. Do you
realize that?

We realized it. At the drop of a hat we would have laughed at
the recollection of our fear when the storm raged. We should
never know the terror of the Navajos, the Hualapais, the Hava-
suapis in the days before the white men came, when a storm
broke over them—what shall I say, Luronne, a real honest-to-
God storm? Surely more real than the one we went through, because in the enormous downpour they saw the anger of the
gods, and they were by no means sure that the anger was going
to spare them. Believe me, Luronne, it no longer rains now,
and just as they harness the rivers, so one of these days they'll
harness the rain. From now on the sense of solitude in the face
of nature is completely artificial. Seldom felt, moreover. We're
no longer allowed to experience even this romantic feeling.
Look.

(I said, Look, just as in the Grand Canyon I had asked her to
go along with my fantastic visions.)

And since this collapse into mockery had to be, we listed all
the great Colorado's petty assassins once again and turned
them inside out—the air conditioner, the hair dryer, the television, the radio, the electric guitar, iron, and can opener, in
which our feeling of dread and magnificence had vanished
there in the Colorado of the Grand Canyon; and that evening,

for the first time since the discovery of America, we drank a great deal, but we drank for no good reason, because this time there was nothing to celebrate but ill-omened woe.

Perhaps we never went out so much as we did during the time that followed our trip to the Colorado. We took advantage of the fact that now, at the beginning of November, the cold weather was bypassing New York, which had no snow, and we went out to look at New York by night between First and Sixth Avenues and between Central Park and Thirtieth Street.

Myself: The most beautiful city in the world.

The world, in any case, took to knocking at our door as though it felt that from now on we had given it a right to do so, since the sixteenth century was over and all in all we had not come out of it so badly, with just that little Spanish fort of St. Augustine, an absurdity in the vast expanse of Indian Florida and America. Once Luronne was asked to give a lecture on the Plains civilization at Abilene, in Kansas, and there in the hall I counted 329 people, not one of them a child; and on another occasion, at an evening party people could not take their eyes off Luronne, who more than usually inspired, beautiful, and earnest, explained and displayed the notion of exoticism for a score of people who surrounded us: one day she planned to write (from her wink at me I understood that for her *one day* meant a long while ahead, after the discovery of America) an Apology for or Treatise on Exoticism, and since our return from the Grand Canyon we drank heartily—always bourbon, the champagne being kept for the great events in America the Happy. I had gone back to my Master of Passion rôle, and now it was I who made the first moves, who took the initiative, and I made love to her twice or even three times a day, as I had at the beginning of our relationship, and I no longer felt the weight, the fear, and the tension of Coronado, de Soto, and the others who had given me a bad taste in my mouth for many days on end, and if I were to add it up night by night, we must have walked some hundreds of miles in New York, our heads in the air.

Myself, tirelessly: The most beautiful city in the world.

We had agreed that on reaching the neighborhood which was to provide us with our field of view and with a great many reasons for delight, we should look down. Then, at her command or at mine, we should look up. It might be midnight or one in the morning. Sometimes later. There are three factors that render New York's night incomparable: the skyscrapers, the electricity, and the darkness. It might happen that on raising our heads we would catch sight of a square of light (which was a window) in the darkness before us. Very high and quite alone. Like a living eye. Then we would listen to the common sense inside us stating that the square poised up there in the air could not rest on nothing. It presupposed the existence of a wall and therefore of a building, a tower, something rising up—and the higher the window, the farther the rise into the sky. Quickly we would form a picture of this skyscraper, although only a minute part of it was revealed by the light. There is nothing that spurs the imagination so much as a skyscraper. It excites and inflames one's spirit. Provokes searching. Scaffolding. Building up. It is a gigantic erector set for grown-ups; but one night at the foot of a skyscraper, Luronne, in the grip of strong emotion, told me that if one day we had a child she would take it into the streets to play this game, which rejects the manual in favor of the visual, subtly stimulating the perceptions of the mind.

The electricity that pierces New York's space shows at varying planes, and this difference of level applies both to height and to depth. So that a skyscraper is something other than itself. A space-scraper. A scraper of the great beyond. To be quite exact, that which lights, or scrapes the depth in front of itself; and for still other rewards we loved those lights that, disregarding alignment, made the windows gleam in no kind of order at all, one halfway up, another lower down, a third way up on the left. Or on the right. They played with the hundreds and thousands of lights in the other skyscrapers near and far with an infectious, overflowing enthusiasm, so that Luronne and I had the illusion of taking part in a shifting exchange of signals and replies, and between the soaring and the plunging of the half-seen walls, we were aware of empty space, of a gulf in which even the notion of the sky was lost, so that it was no longer perceived as a dome but as an abyss. We never missed going to Park Avenue, one end of which is blocked by the mass of Grand Central Station. At night, of course, it is impossible to gauge the dimensions of the obstacle, but we found that because of their relationship with the darkness, the lighted windows here and there helped us to take in Grand Central Station, and we literally printed it on ourselves so that later we could talk about it in bed.

Even more than Grand Central, a light in Forty-sixth Street occupied our minds. We had picked it out at once because of its likeness to others that we had noticed and that had moved our pity—single, isolated, lonely lights—yes, that's it: lights that seemed to be suffering from loneliness. And sick. Without strength—or with so very little. Pallid rather than luminous. All over New York they silently proclaimed their suffering, with a cry that you have to listen for, begging for a glance, as though a face looking up could revive them. And the Forty-sixth Street light moved us by something that it possessed to a higher degree than the others and that struck us as though it were a signal of distress. It was a dreary, wavering yellow and it seemed to be there to say farewell. We used to stare at it for a long while, and once we thought it had died. We went back to look at it four nights running, hoping each time that it would have broken out of its loneliness, that others would have joined it in the windows of the next-door skyscraper. In vain. A long death agony: we did not want to be the witnesses of it any longer and we stopped going down Forty-sixth Street.

Scarcely more than ten days had gone by since the last night of the sixteenth century with Cabeza de Vaca, Coronado, de

Soto . . . I felt the next installment coming. It was the night of that afternoon when we went to see *A Man Called Horse*. Luronne was silent, answered with monosyllables or not at all, and I saw that she was preparing the seventeenth century. When she came back from the bathroom, I looked up just before putting out the light and I noticed that she was wearing the white nightdress with blue trimmings that she had put on at the time of Columbus's first voyage, her favorite, I believe.

Scarcely had she begun before she carried me away from Port-Royal in Acadia, where Pierre du Gast, a Calvinist from Saintonge, had planted the first permanent colony in northern America, to Quebec, founded by Champlain in 1608, and then from Quebec to the *Hopewell*, with Henry Hudson aboard; and almost immediately after that I was to land in Virginia.

Myself: Not so fast.

Myself again: Tell me about Henry Hudson (I was glad that this Englishman, who gave his name to a river, should himself have a river's name).

Luronne agreed and we watched Hudson sail farther north than anyone else, up toward Baffin Island, where the ice barriers alarmed him as much as the whales. During a second voyage he saw polar bears drifting on icebergs, and for the first time in the history of mankind in America, he recorded an eclipse of the sun. At the time of his third expedition in 1608, on the 17th of July, Hudson, sailing in the *Half Moon*, discovered more of America, the coast of Maine, where the Indians at the mouth of the Kennebec River gave him a hearty welcome.

Myself: Naturally.

Hudson had a second-in-command named Juet, in whom evil seemed to have chosen to incarnate itself. He had the guns fired upon a village, and in his chief's absence he ordered it to be sacked. On September 2 the *Half Moon* appeared at the mouth of the river that was not yet called the Hudson, and sailed up as far as Albany. It was delightful. Wonderful countryside. Wonderful Indians. Nevertheless, Juet fired at them, blazing away with a falconet. Result: the Hudson Indians rose up against Hudson.

Myself, much distressed: That Juet ought to have been put in irons! Hudson had no authority.

Luronne admitted this and we watched him sail away for a fourth voyage, in the *Discovery,* which took him to Ungava Bay, where he saw those birds that the English so charmingly call ptarmigans; and then there he was in Hudson's Bay, into which he penetrated.

Myself: Wait.

(This was where I wanted to travel, both by summer and by winter, and I looked at it.)

Then: Go ahead.

Luronne did not go far, because Hudson, who believed he was in the open sea and who was still another of those who wanted to discover the Northwest Passage, found that he was surrounded by land. A bay! Disillusion on the part of the captain, discontent on that of the crew. Then a storm. Hudson, making for the strait, struck a rock, and all hands had to leave the ship. A wintering in the Arctic.

Myself: How are they going to manage?

Luronne: For long months on end, the men ate ptarmigan.

Myself, with some difficulty: Ptarmigan.

Luronne: And when the mutiny broke out, after the melting of the ice, Hudson, his son, and seven loyal hands were thrown into a longboat. The ship sailed away and Hudson and his party were never heard of again.

With a heavy heart, I watched Hudson, his son John, and the seven seamen die of hunger and thirst, cold and despair. In Luronne's mouth, the seventeenth century had begun with death. Bad sign. Luronne, if you can, if you know how to, tell a story with no death in it!

She smiled: she did know one. One man in America, who died a natural death: Samuel de Champlain.

He crossed the Atlantic twenty-three times, and before fixing upon Quebec he landed in Acadia, where abound those names that make my life happy on certain days, raising my heart to the pitch of exaltation: Passamaquoddy, Chibouctou, Mistigouèche, Chedabouctou. Luronne's lips and mine breathed in these words, rolled them about and caressed them, and then, with a wafting sigh, we breathed them out. We saw him explore the Saguenay, treading in the steps of Jacques Cartier, making his way up the St. Lawrence as far as Sault Saint-Louis, and then go off all by himself to Gaspé Bay, we'l into Chaleur Bay and along the coasts of New Brunswick, Cape Breton Island, and Nova Scotia. And we saw him reconnoiter the Bay of Fundy. Indefatigable. The next year he explored Acadia as scrupulously as if he were looking for a needle in a haystack, going as far as the Kennebec, then traveling up the Penobscot in Maine as far as Bangor. He was in the country of the Etchemins, also called the Malecites.

And I cried out that she must stop, that I wanted to relish this taste of forest and salt spray, both in the words she spoke and on her lips.

I gave her a long kiss. Then I tore myself away, and happily, easily, she followed Champlain to Cape Cod and Martha's Vineyard and we watched him complete a three year journey in the Iroquois country, ending it by going up the Richelieu, and what did he discover there?

Myself, foreseeing it: Lake Champlain.

Luronne: Right: then he fought against the Iroquois near Lake George in New York State before making his way into Ontario, where he traveled up the Ottawa River as far as Ottawa and beyond it to Allumette Island, where he entrusted Brulé, one of his lieutenants, to the Hurons, so that they could teach him their language. And that's not all: listen. Champlain would not give up the idea that the best way of getting to China was by the St. Lawrence, whose source, thought he, must originate somewhere in the baffling mysteries of the Orient. In 1615 he took a birchbark canoe, and together with Brulé he followed the Ottawa and reached the Mattawa, which leads to Lake Nipissing; then he took French River to Georgian Bay and went on to a point close to Lake Simcoe. Do you want any more?

Myself: More.

Luronne: Brulé headed south and Champlain east: Champlain skirted the tip of Lake Ontario, reached Onondaga in the Iroquois country and then Syracuse in New York State, while Brulé got to what is now Pennsylvania by way of the Ohio. In the fall of 1615 Champlain fought against the Iroquois and then wintered with the Hurons, following Father Le Caron, who was evangelizing seven nations, village by village.

She paused, and I set myself to reconstructing those endless, fabulous journeys that my memory had retained in part, fragments and episodes burning there with a religious ardor; and I urged her to speak of the encounter that I had read about when I was a boy—nine or ten I must have been—and had reread a hundred times since then, always with the same fascination. It took place at dawn on July 19, 1609, where the river leaves Lake George. Champlain was with his Huron and Montagnais allies, who had persuaded him to carry the war into the country of the Iroquois Confederation, or the Five Nations, which the French called the People of the Long House. Surrounded by sixty braves he advanced to meet about a hundred Mohawks, who, believing this to be an ordinary battle, having shot their arrows, were preparing for hand-to-hand fighting. At a given moment the Montagnais' ranks opened, and Champlain, who had picked out three tall chiefs wearing feathers and roebuck antlers, fired three times. They fell.

Champlain describes the scene. He says that at twenty yards he saw the Mohawks' eyes widen as they caught sight of him. At this time the Five Nations warriors had never seen a white man nor yet a firearm. And I never tired of looking at Champlain looking at the Mohawks. I never tired of looking at the Mohawks looking at Champlain. A white man. Completely white. Their first white man and their first firearm.

Can you imagine the tale they told, these flying Indians, Luronne, when they reached home? A white man, abruptly appearing from nowhere and carrying a stick that spat fire and flames. And all at once the Mohawks' world, thousands of years old, beginning to totter. . . .

We went back to Champlain. I had read everything he had written, which is saying a good deal. The American landscape fills him too with wonder, but he takes America—how shall I put it?—calmly. No crying out. If it were not for other texts of the period that prove the existence of the exclamation mark, you would think it had not been invented. He was a stranger to emotion. Here he is confronted with weather of the most extraordinary violence: "We were thwarted by a great tempest, which seemed to be made up rather of lightning than of wind, and which continued for the space of seventeen days." There. Just one reserved, modest little sentence to describe a thundering storm that lasted for seventeen days! Canada? Far superior to Florida, in Champlain's opinion: but superior in what way? Here: "There cannot be smoother nor better land than that which we have seen." Frigid.

He is above all a reckoner, a counter. Land surveying in the blood. He spends his time measuring, estimating, calculating. Measures everything—rivers, bays, channels, everything that opens, closes, broadens, narrows. No one so exact as Champlain. If he speaks of a day, then he also gives its date. Of a ship, then its tonnage. In Champlain, to be sure, we see the careful precision of a seaman who knows that the slightest negligence may cost him his ship on a rock or a sandbank. But Luronne saw something else—a response to the unknown and to immensity. Champlain peopled his world in order to tame it. Into an unknown expanse of land, water, trees, and rocks, he introduced the human factor of number. Yielding to the need to carry out a transposition, a tranquilizing act, the mapmaking Champlain drew his lines less for the sake of knowledge than for that of protecting himself.

As perhaps I was doing with America.

We watched him live threescore years and ten, marry without ever having seen his wife, never take a mistress, and attain a kind of perfection, for he was a great man in whatever he undertook—exploration, navigation, warfare, the command of men, evangelization, the setting up of the fur trade, colonization. A perfection that did not conceal a very grave defect, one that Luronne hated in him as much as I did and that kept us from setting him in our pantheon—a place, it must be admitted, where there were few white men. Never once did he wonder whether he might be interfering in what did not concern him, whether he had the right to shoot Indians, wreck their faith, burn their harvests, and, using God as a pretext, bring misfortune on them.

It took us some time to emerge from the depression into which we had been plunged by the not quite admirable, not quite odious Champlain. In 1609, on the sparkling shores of Lake George, he was three days' march from Hudson, who was making his way up the Hudson. They were never to know it.

Then Luronne announced what was perhaps the greatest event in this seventeenth century. For the first time in the hundred years that they had been trying, the whites at last succeeded in setting up something more than a little fort or bridgehead in the northern reaches of the North American continent. After eighteen weeks at sea, a hundred and twenty colonists settled down at Jamestown in Virginia in 1607.

Myself: How difficult America is!

Luronne agreed and then brushed all the glamour off this attempt at colonization: Elizabeth of England authorized the expeditions because they took paupers out of her kingdom! The important men went to America only for the gold. Arduous, even wretched beginnings at Jamestown. These Englishmen had no idea of how to use their hands, and for two that lived, one man died.

(This rather pleased me, because there was not the least doubt that others would come over, and there was everything to be feared from too considerable an immigration.)

Myself: How difficult America is!

Luronne was of the same opinion.

Myself again: America is only hanging by a thread!

Luronne: Yes: and by the Indians.

Myself: Which?

Luronne: The Chickahominies, the Potomacs, the Mona-
cans, three independent tribes, then the Pamunkies, the Paspaheghs, the Kecoughtans, the Nansemonds and the Chesa-
peakes, vassals of the chief Powhatan, who in fact was called
Wahunsonacock. Powhatan suited the lazy English better. He
saved them from starvation. John Smith, at the head of the colony, confiscated the Indians' canoes and burned their houses
and their crops. It is said that but for Pocahontas, Powhatan's
favorite daughter, a girl with an unaccountable liking for the
whites, Smith would have been even more homicidal in his
dealings with the Indians. On several occasions she risked her
life, telling him the tricks her father meant to play. Smith returned to England, and the colony sank into anarchy and the
horror of famine and manslaughter. In October 1609 there
were five hundred settlers: six months later there were sixty.

Myself:What a difficult birth America is having!

Luronne said yes and told me this moving tale: in 1610 the
desperate colonists were going aboard their ships with the intention of leaving Jamestown forever when suddenly there appeared other vessels from England bearing a certain Lord Delaware, who had the title of governor of Virginia. So everybody
went ashore again!

Myself, repetitiously: America only held by a thread!

Luronne: Yes—and by the Indians. The reason for their anger was that the English had lied to them, saying that they were
merely passing by.

Myself: Swine!

Luronne: And murderers too, for when they attacked the Kecoughtans' village and that of the Paspaheghs, they killed the
children. And Governor Dale kidnapped Pocahontas in order
to blackmail her father, Powhatan. When she was set free she
married John Rolfe, in April 1614—the first marriage between

an Indian woman and a white man. Powhatan did not attend, but sent a brother.

(I ponder these nuptials, not knowing whether I should bless them or not.)

Then, deeply unhappy, I watched blacks being landed, the first to tread the soil of America, where their masters at once began to lead them a wretched life. This was in 1619. Powhatan announced that he would no longer fight, and under the leadership of his brother and successor Opechancanough, the Indians, tired of feeding the whites and anxious to preserve their last remaining territories, launched a fantastic attack upon the Virginia colony: 350 English killed, others mutilated, the plantations wrecked—yet Virginia carried on, because the Indians had not been able to destroy Jamestown, and the English lost no time retaliating. With unexampled cruelty. A guard killed Opechancanough in his prison.

I mourned for Opechancanough, and we turned from him to watch James I granting charter rights to two companies, the one in London and the other in Plymouth, with territories stretching from 34 degrees north to the 45th parallel, from the mouth of the St. Lawrence to Carolina.

Myself: Not possible!

One day when Luronne was at the university I went over to her desk, and idly, without any clearly formed idea, I fingered her books, her notes. Up until this time only once had I been so indiscreet. Then I opened her drawers to look inside, doing so automatically, with no reason. All the drawers except one, which was locked. That drawer I wanted to see immediately.

So I looked for the key. Luronne had hidden it under a pile of nightdresses in the bedroom. The drawer contained nothing but papers and notes. Into which I plunged.

Among them was a detailed outline of her history of the seventeenth century, ending with Pennsylvania. But with Pennsylvania after its founder, when, like the other English colonies in America, it became a graveyard for Indians. Luronne had not gone as far as that: she had decided to stop before reaching one of the greatest atrocities in American history, the massacre of the Conestogas, who were Christian Indians. Later, when he was speaking of the perpetrators of this hideous crime, Benjamin Franklin called them "white savages." And now Luronne had left out this episode, although it made a logical end to the seventeenth century, that century of death. Seeing that she would have to end with murders, she had changed her mind and had chosen hope. Wishing to make me happy, no doubt, she had falsified history to that end. On one occasion Luronne had boasted that she never lied—she was almost haughty about it. She was lying now, although it had been understood that she would always tell me the truth—the whole truth. I should have to beware.

And we saw the birth of New England with the colony of Plymouth, founded in 1620 by the hundred and two pilgrims of the *Mayflower,* who brought with them Puritanism, the source of all those sects in which a cat could not recognize her kittens; then we watched the Puritans set up the colony of Massachusetts Bay in 1628. Other Puritans settled around Boston, and as early as 1634 they numbered ten thousand in America. They adopted the *Body of Liberties* that guaranteed men, women, and animals freedom from barbarous punishments.

Myself: What men, what women, and what animals?

Luronne: White ones.

Myself: And the Indians ?

Luronne: Nothing for them.

We saw three new colonies taking root in Massachusetts, among them that of Rhode Island and Providence Plantations, founded by Puritans of the extreme Left, who already found the atmosphere of New England stifling. The people of Boston were fanatics, and they would not allow nonconformity. Their religious intolerance provoked the setting up of new colonies, just as in London the king's absolutism had provoked that of Boston. Always the same old story, you see: and the Puritans made the Quakers their scapegoats. The Puritans hated the Indians. One Pilgrim, a man named Johnson, settling in a district

215

from which the plague had swept the Indians in 1616, proclaimed, "God has thrust out the heathen to make room for His people."

We spat upon this Johnson.

Then we gazed long and reverently at Roger Williams, the founder of Rhode Island colony, and we loved the heresy that he put forward—that in God's eyes the beliefs of the Indians were of the same quality and the same value as Christianity. Clergyman that he was, Roger Williams did not go in for converting the Indians. He was admirable: we admired him. On one occasion he withdrew to live among the Delawares, in order to meditate. Then in 1684 we heard Cotton Mather invent the word American, referring to a European settled in America; and looking back a little earlier, to 1638, we saw bees introduced in America.

Myself: Were there no bees in America?

Luronne: No.

Unbelievable.

Then having spat, with all our might this time, on the Boston Puritans who banished Mary Dyer, a Quaker, and who, when she came back to the town, hanged her, we looked at New York and the Dutch governor building the wall of Wall Street to protect the farms behind it from the wolves and the Indians; and then, clenching our fists, we watched the Dutch massacre the Wecquaesgeeks at Pavonia in 1643, and we hated those English kings who, to reward their faithful followers or to get rid of extremists, granted lands in the country of America that did not belong to them. Thus, in exchange for two Indian arrows to be presented every year, Charles I gave Lord Baltimore that magnificent expanse that stretches from the latitude of Philadelphia to the south bank of the Potomac, a country that Baltimore meant to turn into a refuge for Catholics, just as New England was a refuge for Puritans. When Charles I expelled his convicts, we saw them peopling America, where, after seven years of enforced labor, they were given back their freedom;

and then, overwhelmed, we heard Maryland, in 1664, pass a "black law" according to which any black coming to the colony should, merely because of his color, be a slave as long as he lived—so that we scarcely applauded at all when a little later this same Maryland passed the Toleration Act, which laid down that no one, in any circumstances whatsoever, might attack any religion, be its nature what it might; and in any case we scorned this Toleration Act when Luronne told me that it condemned all those who denied the Holy Trinity or the divinity of Christ to death by hanging! Then we observed the economic life of Virginia based on tobacco as a medium of exchange—everything, including wages and prices, being calculated in tobacco—and that pleased me, because among the whites tobacco was neither more nor less than the equivalent of belts of wampum, the Algonquins' shell money—then Luronne gave me figures showing the growth of population in this colony: twenty-four thousand Virginians, three thousand blacks.

Myself: That's not bad.

And we moved on to Nouvelle-France, where Maisonneuve founded Montreal in 1642. In this mid-seventeenth-century Canada, New France was a fantastically long, fantastically thin village stretching along the St. Lawrence from the rock of Quebec to the shadowy trading post of Montreal, with the little bulge of Three Rivers between the two. Barely three hundred Frenchmen! Who bothered with nothing but the beaver skins and the souls of the Indians, whom they called Savages—a word you find in Cartier, Champlain, and all the rest of them.

Myself: I hate that word.

Luronne: So do I. And she told me a story that delighted me, a story she had found in a report dated September 8, 1719, and written by Francois-Marie de Brouage, the king's commandant in Labrador. Brouage had captured an Eskimo woman: "She told us," he says, "that in her band they had a man who knew how to write: he had long been married among them. I asked

217

her whether he were a man of their nation. She told me he was a Savage, and from this I learned that they call us, both Frenchmen and those from Europe, Savages."

I laughed; I clapped my hands.

Then we watched the fur trappers mingling with the Indians, traveling north along the rivers, hunting and trapping all through the winter and then, with the melting of the ice, crossing the Great Lakes and coming down the St. Lawrence or the Ottawa to Montreal in their heavily loaded canoes—a single one might carry as many as six hundred skins.

Myself: Surely not!

Fantastic fur trade. We considered the fifty thousand Hurons scattered in twenty-five villages between Lake Simcoe and Lake Huron and on the shores of Georgian Bay setting themselves up as the controllers of the trade in vegetable substances and acting as a buffer between the Iroquois of the south and the Algonquins of the north. Luronne explained that when the Senecas of the Five Nations wanted birch bark for their canoes, they had to buy it from the Neutrals, who got it from the Hurons, who in turn had it from the Algonquins! The rise in the value of birch bark made war inevitable, all the more so since the Hurons also claimed exclusive rights as fur jobbers. The Iroquois, seventeen thousand of them in twelve villages, who had been battling with the Hurons since 1570, wiped them out in 1649. We watched the triumphant Iroquois, whom their English allies had armed, and the slaughtered Hurons, whom their French allies had been unable to help. When the overhunted beavers grew scarce in the Great Lakes, the Crees and the Assiniboines of Manitoba and Saskatchewan acted as intermediaries between the Indians of the northwest and the whites of Hudson's Bay, where Médart Chouart, Sieur de Groseilliers, and Pierre Esprit Radisson built a fort, and we watched these wonderful surnames, these wonderful Christian names, travel north to the bogs and the marshes, where in the spring, among the reindeer moss, they may have seen the ouaouaron leap.

Myself, amazed: What's that?

Luronne: A giant bullfrog. And perhaps they saw goglus, those migratory passerines, and perhaps they smelled the poogie, which has the scent of sugar and honey.

(Which I breathed in too, at that very moment.)

And we watched the collapse of Louis XIV's great dream of peasant colonization for the Canadians, who for their part dreamed of nothing but trade; and all the while the Iroquois led the French a hard life, attacking them and torturing them with the utmost zeal until the expedition of 1666, when the troops of Tracy, the military governor, helped by Indians, mounted a hitherto unparalleled operation with more than three hundred boats and struck right at the heart of the Long House Confederation, compelling the Iroquois to bury the hatchet for a good twenty year respite: and then the French advanced westward, to the country of the Potawatomis, the Sacs, and Foxes.

Myself: More.

Luronne: Listen to this story. The missionaries converted the Hurons and Algonquins with all their might, but since with these Savages (she laughed scornfully and I with her) there was always the risk of apostasy, they baptized only those who were on the point of death. And who indeed played their part by dying: so that the Indians soon detected a relationship of cause and effect between baptism and death.

This absolutely enchanted us and once again we joined in derisive laughter.

Then in 1673, a great sorrow, for the Jesuits stopped sending their *Relations* back to France. Excellent descriptions, accounts, and meditations that I had been reading ever since my arrival in America, and Luronne for a longer time, and every day we looked into them for pieces for the counterstake; we found them, so that when Luronne quoted, "We shall die, we shall be taken, we shall be burned, we shall be slaughtered: very well. Bed is not always the best place for an exemplary death," I could reply, "We die every day from our lack of faith," and she could come back with, "But his heart spoke louder than his words and it could be heard even in his silence"—magnificent, high-souled quotations whose discovery filled us with a keen happiness, and we observed a long meditative silence in memory of the *Relations,* themselves now forever silent.

A silence that Luronne broke with King Philip, as the English called him. Metacom by his real name. The great sachem of the Wampanoags. He made war on the Puritans, who hated him of course.

Luronne: Suppose the Indians had invaded England and had declared that all those who did not accept them were rebels. That was the Puritans' attitude, and in fact they went further—the Massachusetts government made a law subjecting the death penalty to any Indian who blasphemed.

Myself, depressed: All very well for the whites, but for the Indians . . .

Metacom succeeded his brother Wamsutta, who may have been poisoned by the English. Wamsutta's widow, Wetamoe, was the Squaw Sachem of Pocaset. Philip knew he could rely on his sister-in-law. He was twenty-four, and the New England Indians numbered twenty thousand, against forty thousand English.

Myself: As many as that?

Luronne: Yes. The whites' racism and greed for land: you don't have to look further for the cause of what they called King Philip's War, as though it were his alone.

Our blood boiled.

Luronne: Philip had won over Canonchet's Narragansets and the Wymucks, tribes numbering four and three thousand. Now no more than a spark would set things off. . . . It came when the English, by way of avenging the death of a converted Indian, seized three Wampanoags, including one of King Philip's closest advisers, and hanged them. The flame swept over the southern part of New England, and the Indians carried fire to all the places inhabited by white men.

We watched them attack Worthfield, Deerfield, Hadley, and

all along the Connecticut Valley. New England was in danger of death. Total war. Philip, who needed warriors, traveled up the Hudson some twenty miles north of Albany, but the Mohawks were too busy with the fur trade. The English, who had raised several thousand men, took a fortified Indian village at the far end of a marsh, a village held by Philip. He lost six hundred of his people, braves, women, and children—a figure that shows you how fierce the battle must have been. In spite of the disaster of the Great Swamp Fight, as it is called, Philip escaped. His allies, the Wipmucks of Monoco, and the Narragansets of Quinnapin, all great tribes with great chiefs, carried the war throughout Massachusetts. Out of ninety white settlements in New England, fifty-two were attacked and twelve were utterly destroyed.

Myself: Stop.

(An immense hope had dawned in my mind, and I wanted it to last for a long while—Luronne must not speak, not yet.)

Myself: Let's have a drink.

We drank.

And when we had finished, Luronne had to go on: she had to go on and tell what I had foreseen from the start.

Luronne: Springtime came. Traditionally, the Indian bands dispersed in spring, because then they no longer thought of anything but sowing. Furthermore, it so happened that many Indians had taken the side of the English, in some instances out of fear, in others—and this was the case with Punca, the Mohegans' sachem—out of hatred for Philip.

Myself: Harkis.

(And I explained the meaning of the word. Harkis were North African soldiers in the French army: during the Algerian war many of them fought on the French side.)

Luronne: The end began, if I may so put it, with Canonchet—you know, Philip's Narraganset ally. The English took him, shot him, and gave his head to the Connecticut authorities.

Myself, in a low voice: What then, Luronne?

Luronne: The Indians surrendered in great numbers, and in great numbers too the English hanged them or sold them to the slave traders. They found where Wetamoe was hiding— Philip's sister-in-law, you remember—and she was drowned in trying to escape. They cut off her head, too, and exposed it to public view.

Myself (and perhaps she did not hear me): What about Philip?

Luronne: He had been fighting for a year by now. Alone, or practically alone from this time on. The English, informed by an Indian renegade, went with a swarm of what did you call them?

Myself: Harkis.

Luronne: Yes: they surprised Philip at dawn on April 12, 1676, and killed him as he was trying to get away. He was beheaded and then quartered. His head was exposed for twenty-five years on top of a pole in Plymouth.

We gazed, mute and horrified, at this only too imaginable head.

Luronne: One word more. This war made such ravages that the New England settlers were scarcely beginning to get over it two years later—it was still continuing on the borders of Maine, and the ports were swarming with refugees.

I did not have the heart to curse these whites who, merely because they were white, could afford the luxury of keeping away from the battlefields filled with braves, squaws, and dead papooses.

Then, unutterably weary: What then, Luronne?

Luronne: Popé. At the other end of the country, far away in New Mexico. For a hundred years the Spaniards, with their hatred, their scorn, and their greed, had been oppressing the Indians, who did not possess the right to be armed or to ride on horseback, but only the duty of working. In 1680 Popé, a Tewa medicine man and Philip's contemporary, rebelled.

Myself: No, no. I know only too well how it's going to end.

Luronne: Listen. He traveled about among the pueblos. See

him talking, explaining, exhorting, recalling the past at Taos, Santa Clara, Picuris, Santa Cruz, Pecos, Galisteo, San Cristobal, San Marcos, La Cienega, Popuaque—everywhere. Then, bursting from their pueblos and hunting down the Spaniards, Popé's Pueblos massacred four hundred of them while two thousand five hundred more ran in terror for the frontiers of New Mexico. Popé besieged the capital, Santa Fe, and the Spaniards, having killed their prisoners, abandoned it. Total triumph. There was not a single Spaniard left in New Mexico: Christian names were proscribed and the objects of Christian worship destroyed. A year later Fray Francesco de Ayeta, basing himself on his spies' reports, could write that the Indians "so valued liberty of conscience and so admired Satan that no sign of their former Christian faith remains."

My spirits had so recovered that I clapped my hands: still, I did not dare to believe in it entirely, not yet. In a reserved tone: What then, Luronne?

(My voice full of hope in spite of myself.)

Luronne: As it always happens, I have to end up with the worst.

Myself: I knew it.

Luronne: And indeed the worst of the worst, if I may say so. Picture the Indians just simply incapable of going back to their old ways. Of returning to the life they had led before the Spaniards. Of reviving the ancient man, the Indian in them. You see, the Spaniards had brought to the pueblos some of the benefits of white civilization, some of the material advantages, and the pueblos could not understand Popé's desire to do away with it all and start over again from scratch. They resisted him, and all the more forcefully because Popé began to behave like the Spanish masters he had got rid of for them. A tyrant. The Spaniards took advantage of the Indians' dissensions. Exactly twelve years after their flight, they came back to New Mexico.

We did not give them so much as a glance. We looked beyond them to see that unhappy, unfortunate people, made for victory perhaps, but certainly not made for what followed it. After Philip, Popé. I should never have been able to bear a third failure after an uprising, but that was all for the seventeenth century.

So then, still quite downcast, I sought peace with Father Marquette, the great *black robe*—both priest and explorer. Father Marquette, who knew seven Indian languages. I loved him. Together with Joliet he went down the Mississippi as far as the place where it is joined by the Arkansas: and with him we found that, contrary to the firm conviction of many other men, the Father of Waters did not flow into the Pacific. Then came Robert de La Salle, and I watched him indulge in the great dream of a French America stretching from Hudson's Bay to the Gulf of Mexico. I loved him too, that magnificent friend of the Indians; and in 1681 we saw him and thirty-one of King Philip's former followers make an attempt at continuing farther than Marquette and Joliet, right down to the mouth of the Mississippi, which in fact he reached. Thinking nothing of it, he simply appropriated Louisiana, that is to say the whole valley of the Mississippi, including its tributaries!

Luronne: Listen: less than three years later, in 1684, he reached the Gulf of Mexico, this time by way of the sea, and he looked for the Mississippi that he had sailed upon. And believe me or believe me not, he couldn't find it!

Myself, though amazed: I believe you.

Luronne: By sea he couldn't find the river that he had found by land—because in those days they did not know how to figure longitude.

And we noted the death, on the nineteenth of March, 1687 of Cavelier de La Salle—among Indian friends he was killed by white men. At about this same time, equally culpable white men in Salem were putting to death women accused of sorcery. I did not want to see them—I've had enough of this death-ridden seventeenth century, no, Luronne . . . but she must have smiled as she heard me. I should never have enough of William Penn, one of the greatest English figures, with Roger Williams, in America: there, in his Pennsylvania, he established complete religious freedom, and we watched the Quakers hurrying in: they were hated everywhere else in America—whipped and imprisoned in Rhode Island, tortured in New York, hanged in Boston. We heard Penn proclaim that all forms of government had but one aim—men's happiness: and at the same time we switched on the light, Luronne and I, to see one another, to see ourselves, together and happy! This word *happiness,* given to the politicians as their chief, if not their only task! Penn founded Philadelphia and set up mixed juries of whites and Indians. He signed a treaty with the Susquehannas and the Delawares; and it is known that in 1685 no white man killed an Indian nor any Indian a white in the colony of Pennsylvania with its nine thousand inhabitants.

Myself, overcome, filled with euphoria: It is impossible: I knew it.

And I collapsed, worn out with fatigue, worn out by too many, too often disillusioning emotions.

It was two in the morning. I told Luronne that our nights always finished like this, with bitterness in the dawn twilight. Penn was too exceptional, Pennsylvania too isolated—the beautiful note of hope at the end of the tale rang false. Out of place. That was my feeling, though Luronne laughed at it. When at last she stopped, she took a book, the *Oxford History of the American People* by Samuel Eliot Morison, the admiral. The great Morison. She opened it, pointed to a passage, and there I read that the number of whites in America when the seventeenth century died in 1699 was three hundred thousand. It was written. There. Three hundred thousand plus six thousand two hundred in Canada. Surely not! That was nothing! Two centuries and some odd years after Christopher Columbus, almost a century after Jamestown, and there were still no more than a little over three hundred thousand people and there it was written in the great Morison! All at once I no longer wanted to go to bed. We opened a bottle of wine—come, hope's not entirely lost—and we talked and talked, Luronne and I. She dressed as though we were going out: indefatigably

I read and reread that passage in Morison, page 166. And the next day, when I told Luronne I had dreamed of that book and of that page 166, she quoted to me the latest gem she had found in the *Relations:* "So that no foolishness should be wanting, they also believe in dreams."

And thereupon we dreamed. . . .

The snow came in the first week in December, falling day and night, thick and beautiful, and I spent some time at the window, watching it drown in the Hudson: and there, between the seventeenth and eighteenth centuries, between the finished tale and the tale yet to come, I passed through good periods and bad, periods unequal in effect, the bad striking deeper than the good. My high excitement at reading in Morison that in 1699 and 1700 the whites occupied only the Atlantic seaboard and that only to the ridiculous number of three hundred and six thousand two hundred—my excitement no longer bore me up, and, disillusioned, at the breaking point, I was sometimes afraid that—all the more so since you can make figures say whatever you like. Then came this incident.

I thought Luronne was coming near to the time when she would be obliged to step in before it was too late, and fearing that she would fail—or that she would cheat—I wantonly spoiled all the possible evenings of grace by taking her out on each one of them and staying out until the early hours of the morning. Holding her tight against me, tighter than ever before so that although she was happy in her pain she still cried out, I carried on as if I were trying to make something of her pass into me and something of myself, something that I dreaded, go from me. And always: What is going to happen in the eighteenth century? If things turn bad ultimately, will she be able to intervene? Then—and this was a new anxiety—will she not lie?

We were approaching the conquest of the West, and we decided to give ourselves leave to see Westerns. As many as three a day. When they turned out to be bad—and a bad Western can be detected in ten minutes—we left at the end of that time. Going out as often as this, we inevitably met other people. We liked some and saw them again more or less regularly. I wondered how I should understand this continually increasing presence of friends and acquaintances, since during the first months of our life together no one had ever come near us. And at that time we needed nobody. To struggle against these people and against my own apprehensions I drew Luronne away toward the Indians, and we took to looking at them as we had never done before.

For example, among the tribes of the Plains there was the Society of Contraries, which we had discovered in *The Adventures of a Paleface.* It would sometimes happen that certain warriors, certain braves, would carry bravery to an unheard-of pitch. And that the warriors would have hallucinations of thunder. It was understood that in the midst of the greatest perils or in the fellowship of thunder, supernatural beings revealed themselves to these braves and that this grace rendered them different from the other Indians. From then on the chosen man, a Heyoka, belonged to the Society of Contraries and he led his life back to front, leading his horse by the tail, riding the wrong way about, washing with sand and drying himself with water, answering yes for no or the reverse, complaining of the cold and shivering in times of the greatest heat: and after a night of very great pleasure, Luronne and I tried to turn ourselves into Contraries.

For a whole day we tried to drink food and eat water, break paper and tear china, stand upside down, walk on our hands and write with our feet, weep through the hair on our arms and sweating through our mouths and drool from our eyes, she behaving like a man and I like a woman, brushing the hair of our heads; but neither she nor I had dreamed of thunder and neither of us, in spite of our love and respect for the Indians, ever attained their sense of the sacred, so that I resigned myself to loving them as an outsider, at a respectful distance.

Luronne had spoken of the Five Civilized Tribes down in

the southeast, that is to say the Creeks, the Chickasaws, the Choctaws, the Cherokees, and the Seminoles, and she had told me how they took to white American ways, apparently without giving up anything of themselves; they turned to stock raising, farming, and the crafts and skills of those times, the squaws using spinning wheels like white women, while marriages between the races increased in number; this made my heart beat—rather marriage than massacre—and it caused me some anxiety too: what if they ended up by losing their soul? And during this period I would ask Luronne every morning, as I got out of bed: "How are things with the Five Civilized Tribes?" every morning, as I got out of bed; and for a while all went well, so well that it was possible to wonder whether someday a southeastern Indian state might not come into being, a state that would have to be admitted to the Union.

To the Indians I also owed some hours of fun, hours that touched my heart and made me feel that Luronne and I would know an everlasting love. Her preference went to the Iroquois, the Natchez, and the Hopis, which just happened to be feminist tribes. We read that the Iroquois were ruled by a council of fifty chiefs or sachems, all of them chosen by women.

At this point, Luronne: You see.

Myself, thoughtfully: Yes.

And the Iroquois women had the right to remove any sachem who turned out to be an indifferent politician. They confiscated his antler headdress, the symbol of his authority; and turning our eyes toward the Hopis, with their system of matrilineal descent, we saw the man going to live in his wife's house (in him I recognized myself), the child taking its mother's name, and the woman dismissing the husband she no longer wanted by putting the poor man's blanket and foot gear outside the door of her house.

Myself: Unbelievable.

And we looked at the Natchez, with their hierarchical society divided from top to bottom between Suns and Strong-smelling Animals or Stinkards: if a Sun woman marries a Strong-smell-

228

ing Animal man, he eats at another table and stands when she is present. If she had had enough of him, she is allowed to sentence him to death and take another.

Myself, deeply shocked: No!

(Within myself: What if I had been born a Strong-smelling Animal?)

We were filled with wonder at the fact that the Algonquin squaw should be so free, so liberated, that before her marriage she could take her pleasure where she liked, a form of behavior that the Recollets and the Jesuits deplored, misrepresented, and denounced, calling it savage and licentious, perfectly typical of these barbarians.

Myself: The goddamn fools.

Although I still thought Montaigne was making a general statement in defiance of the truth, Luronne liked the passage in the chapter "On Cannibals" where he says: "The whole of their [the Indians] political science contained no more than two articles—resolution in war and affection for their women." In this love of the Indians for their women, Luronne readily discovered a distinction that I shared with them.

We also liked seeing them move about, and this they did in every direction, making fantastic migrations far in the dateless times into which we both plunged deep. Intoxicated as though with the racing wind or with wine, I held Luronne by the hand, pulling her after me, and we watched the Kiowas come down from their high plateaus in western Montana and undertake their long march southward and eastward, kindly received by the Crows as they passed through.

Myself: How happy I am!

Myself again: More!

We watched the Blackfeet leave their remote forests northeast of the Great Plains before the discovery of America, a widely feared confederation that came to occupy a territory stretching from Saskatchewan in Canada to the sources of the Missouri in southwestern Montana; and with the Navajos, the Iroquois, the Apaches, the Cherokees, and the Sioux we bathed in the words of American geography, hydrography, and toponymy, and once I said, "If I die, I want to be buried in words. . . ."

And it was above all the horse that rejoiced my heart. With him we almost finished the champagne. I saw the Spaniards advancing north of Mexico, forbidding the Indians to possess horses, and then, with the rising of Popé's Pueblos in 1680, I saw the creatures escape, run away and reach the prairie, a scattering, a spreading that completely changed the buffalo hunters' way of life, and with it the history of the West; and now there rose up the Pawnees, perhaps the first of all the Indians to capture horses, horsemen before the Comanches, before the Utes, and I cried out to Luronne, "Wait!" (meaning that she was to wait for me to see the Utes launch their expeditions against the Western Shoshonis, whose stock they raided).

And I saw the Nez Percés buying horses from the Shoshonis as early as 1730, and then all the Plains Indians without exception, from the sands of Texas to Saskatchewan, becoming horse-borne, and panting as though I had run a race I could say no more to Luronne than, "More, more," for my distracted mind was exalted with visions of horses galloping over the dry grass of the prairie—and it was then that she must have conceived the idea of including the Comanches some day soon.

Other Indians led us in that direction too. Those who must be called the tragic Indians and who, because they suffered, made me doubt Luronne's success.

I looked at them for a long while, right through a whole evening. Each time that Luronne either told me about their end or left me to guess the tragedy, it grieved me. Grief for the Delawares, who did not know how to choose their allies—the French, who were to be beaten by the English, then the English, whom the Americans sent back to Europe. The Delawares are extinct. Then grief for the Shawnees, perhaps the finest trappers, hunters, and warriors of all the Indians. The most intelligent—and I saw that Shawnee Nika, in the seventeenth century, discovering the Ohio with Cavelier de La Salle, and dying like him, with him, murdered. Two friends. The last of the Shawnees died in Oklahoma in the nineteenth century: the Shawnees are extinct. Grief for the Tunicas, who, in their country of Louisiana, were too fond of the French, and who were wiped out by the English. The Tunicas are extinct. Grief for the Illinois, who were turned into a nation of alcoholics by the Frenchmen's firewater: on the eve of the American Revolution there were no more than two hundred left, and they were degenerate. The Illinois are extinct. Grief for the Osages. Audubon met them in 1810, and in his opinion they had an even deeper understanding of nature than the Shawnees; and I never tired of reading and rereading their cosmic, visionary myths of the creation of the world—myths that inspired their name Osage, which means the States of the Middle Waters, on the banks of the Missouri—a territory that they had to give up to the white men and that amounted, listen, to just about the whole of the state of Missouri.

Myself: No!

Grief for the Assiniboines, the handsomest, the best, most richly dressed of all Indians, as one sees in Catlin's paintings and drawings, the most sociable, and the happiest too.

Myself: No!

All of them characteristics reported by admiring travelers—so much so that they seem to be copying from one another—but this admiration did not save them. The Assiniboines are extinct.

Myself: No!

Luronne: Killed by smallpox, venereal diseases, alcohol: in 1830 an observer counted twelve, the entire population.

Myself: No, no!

Luronne, pitilessly: The Kansas. The most silly, as you would say. The worst warriors, the worst hunters, the most conceited too, and indeed the stupidest.

Even so, I grieved for the Kansas.

Luronne: The Kickapoos, from an Algonquin word meaning "He moves: now he's here and now he's there": they displayed the finest military organization of any Indians. In their raids they were as formidable as the Apaches or the Navajos, and they ravaged America from the Great Lakes to Georgia. They fought, crippled, hated, with greater determination than any other tribe, and finally fled the white man right down to Mexico, where, in the state of Chihuahua, they are now called the Mexican Kickapoos.

(And maybe because of this hatred of the whites that I understood and felt, I was closer to them than to any other Indians.)

Luronne: The Tuscaroras, the most robbed, the most defeated, the most punished, the most humiliated, the most imprisoned, the most massacred of all the Indians, first by the English, then by the Americans, so that one day in 1711, a day of great despair, they fled from their homeland in North Carolina to the State of New York. And there the Senecas and the Oneidas, more humane than the white men, welcomed the last of the Tuscaroras.

(And all at once drained of strength, overwhelmed, as wretched as the Tuscaroras, I grieved for them too.)

Then the Mosopeleas. The only Sioux to live in the Ohio Valley, and Luronne quoted this from John R. Swanton who knew the Indians better than anyone in the world: "In 1784 their village was on the Western bank of the Mississippi eight miles above Pointe Coupée, but nothing more was heard of them until 1908, when I found a single survivor living among the Tunica just out of Marksville, Louisiana."

Myself: The last of the Mosopeleas—and I grieved for him.

Luronne: The Susquehannas, near the river of the same name—are you listening?

I told her I was listening.

Luronne: In 1763 there were just twenty of them left: twenty, no more. On June 21 of that year the whites, who wanted to avenge some atrocities committed by other Indians, slaughtered them all. The last twenty.

And I did not grieve for anyone anymore: now I grieved only for myself alone.

There was something that always astonishes me—the fact that these killings, these murders, this genocide could go on and on and that I myself should be there, doing nothing but listen to Luronne, nothing but make remarks about what she said and add to it; and that she should be there, doing nothing but recount and expound two centuries of absolute evil from Christopher Columbus on, and what will things be like tomorrow, in a hundred years or later still, if Luronne and I do nothing about it?

I was still at this point in my thoughts when she moved on to the Comanches. With scarcely a pause, hardly stopping to breathe. Relentlessly. As though to overwhelm me. As though to take all the Indians she knew about and throw them in my face—and after the Indians of tragedy, the Indians of horror. Fascinating. Revolting.

When Luronne showed me the Comanches, in the middle of the seventeenth or eighteenth century, no one knows quite when, they were getting ready to migrate south from their prehistoric Rocky Mountain country in Wyoming, above the source of the Missouri, a country whose harsh beauty lies in three stages, the high peaks with their perpetual covering of snow, then lower down the wilderness of wooded canyons, and then the level where the racing torrents tear their way through the rolling, flower-studded carpet of the prairies.

(I looked right ahead at this wildly savage country she had described.)

Luronne: These last words only apply to the short, fleeting springtime. In winter, the scars made by the torrents in the long-frozen prairie increase and the harsh, savage country looks as though it were wounded, sick with the never-ending cold, deeply saddened at never producing anything at all. And over this country, always hungry, wandered the Comanches. (A pause.) We know a little about them, though at the same time we are deeply ignorant. No writing, of course, no records—not even those sketchy but efficient Kiowa calendars. All nations have their legends: not the Comanches. No songs.

233

On entering history they had so little recollection, so slight an account of themselves, that for a while it was thought they had tried to forget their past. But they had nothing to recollect and therefore nothing to tell.

(Another pause.) Knew nothing about their origins. They thought that one day, the first morning, they had come into being by magic, rising from an animal copulation, and they believed this all the more because they felt close to animals, so close that they recognized the animal in themselves. In the wolf they revered a possible ancestor; they respected the coyote, his cousin; and they refrained from eating dogs, which as you do not know are also cousins to the coyote and thus to the wolf. Extraordinary symbol! And indeed the Comanches were very like wolves. Savage creatures with a deep sense of the responsibilities of the clan; and although they hunted in packs, love and ardor flourished among them. As cunning as the coyote, as relentless as the wolf in tracking down their quarry, dealing out death recklessly.

I listened as I had never listened before.

Luronne: Stone Age hunters in the midst of the eighteenth century, and then later gatherers and grubbers who did not build a temple nor set up a house nor cut down a tree nor sow a seed. Never. They made their pipes and bows according to a technique that never changed until the white men made their way into Comanche territory. I include the skin drums, the bone rattles, the reed pipes by which they produced a monotonous music, and they painted their faces with colors that were chosen to clash, they tattooed their chests, they dressed their hair—a whole ritual of customs and body adornment to express something as profoundly ancient as their origin. Look.

I looked as I had never looked before.

Luronne: Do you know what they called themselves? Nermenuh, which means Men. Not *the* Men, but Men. There were Men—that was they themselves—and then there were the others, *the* men. In this case the article does not designate or point out; it scatters and sets off at a distance. Dismisses. The Nermenuh, or Men, were all alike; spoke one unvarying language, followed the same pattern of life, the same taboos. The difference lay not in them but elsewhere, in the others, *the* men. The non-Nermenuh. You follow?

I told her I followed.

Luronne: Conservatives, in the strong, even rigid sense of the word. Did nothing but conserve and carry on. Never acquired anything, never began anything, never made any fresh start, any innovation. Added nothing. Perhaps the only people on earth whose future was in the past. Not a single one of their actions that, in the course of these thousands of years, was not an ancient action, precisely repeated. Reproduced. When they killed a buffalo they did so according to laws which have always governed the death of the buffalo. When they died of hunger, their collective tragedy reenacted a tragedy already experienced in exactly the same way. Do you see this world in which nothing can ever change?

(Hesitantly I replied that I did see it, and in order not to break her train of thought I added nothing, meaning to go back to the subject later—there was a good deal to be said about it.)

Luronne: See them hurrying about, small, dark, short. Not at all well-proportioned. Stocky legs: thickset muscles. Mountain men, and the absolute antithesis of those beautiful Indians I was telling you about, the Assiniboins. Listen.

Myself: Yes.

Luronne: The men averaged five feet five and three-quarters inches tall and the women just under five feet!

I cried out.

Luronne: Black hair, deep-set slit eyes, almost no body hair, no beard. Big round heads, among the biggest since the days of the Cro-Magnon man.

I looked at these huge heads, and they made me feel uneasy.

Luronne: They spent their whole life looking for food. The deer was too cunning, the moose too big, the bear too dangerous for these archers. Ate rabbits, reptiles, small rodents, never gutted—ate skin and all. An ancient taboo forbade frogs and fish. When buffalo came into their country the Comanches set fire to the prairie to make them stampede.

(I saw the Plains swept by the crackling fires that I had read about in Captain Mayne-Reid, those fires that did so much damage.)

Luronne, doggedly: Drank the hot blood from the creatures' very wounds. Groped for their kidneys, which burst under their tightening fingers. Delighted in hot entrails and in the testicles, which they ate raw and greasy.

Myself, sickened: No?

Luronne: Yes, and because they swallowed the whole of the animal, not only its meat, they provided themselves with vitamins—without them they would have died.

Then: Tough men—but not noteworthy for their longevity. They put up with extreme privation, but nevertheless hunger and lack of hygiene made great inroads on their numbers. Pneumonia found them an easy prey, and rheumatism attacked them very early. Intestinal disorders at all ages. The Nermenuh became arthritic when they were young. Blind, too. They died from thorn wounds, snakebites, broken bones, injuries.

(And perhaps, thought I, Luronne should have stepped in at this point, not, as I had expected, in History, but in this barely human humanity.)

Luronne: Not that they had no medicines. They knew how to dress a wound with grass and suck poison out of their blood. They made poultices out of pears and ointments out of animal fat. They treated toothache with tree moss and they filled hollow teeth with dried fungus. They made laxatives from willow bark. Yet they still died at a great rate: Look.

(She was talking about death again just when I, together with the Comanches, was beginning to feel better, because of the medicines she had spoken of.)

Luronne: It was because they associated medicine very closely with magic and the observation of taboos. Their women had a very difficult labor and most of the newborn babies were carried off by infection. When they acquired horses, the wife rode behind her husband, and this killed fetuses wholesale. Look at the women, old when they were twenty-five, and at the men, impotent very early, at the threshold of old age when they were thirty. By the age of forty-one most of the Nermenuh were ancients, with death just at hand: yet for all that their hair did not turn gray.

(I looked at the Nermenuh vanishing, cut down at the threshold of maturity, passing straight from adolescence to senile decay without transition, without those intervals of living that might be called time out.)

Between five and seven thousand of them altogether; never more at this period because they could not change their environment so as to make it feed a larger community. And split into groups of three hundred, their life swinging from an orgy of eating when they had killed a buffalo to the passive despair that comes from long-lasting hunger. Once they had the horse, they became the best riders in America. Even more than that: the best riders in the world. More gifted for riding than the descendants of Genghis Khan or Tamerlane, whatever people may say. No people attained a greater skill in training horses and riding them, and I know of a band of about two thousand Comanches in the eighteenth century who possessed fifteen thousand horses, as well as four hundred mules.

(I listened to the sixty thousand hoofs of these fifteen thousand horses thundering on the drum of the earth.)

Luronne: War was their prime justification for living and their chief pleasure. Not merely waging war, but the total devastation of the opposing side, the mutilation of the dead whom they thus deprived of everlasting life, the raping and the slaughtering of the women, the stealing of the children or the clubbing them to death. Do not think them inhuman. They adored children and they adopted orphans without the least hesitation. The babies spent their first ten months in a cradle, which consisted of a plank covered with skins and furs, with a hole for urinating: they were enveloped in moss, they were changed every evening, and they were bathed and rubbed with animal grease.

(This vision of them, suddenly so tender.)

Myself: Go on!

Luronne (and I heard her laugh): See the Comanche wearing his talisman surrounded with secret knots and magic herbs and firmly fixed to his penis, the most magical of all his tools.

I did not laugh.

Luronne: They were incapable of conceiving anything massive or elaborate or of carrying it out, for being nomads they were perpetually on the move, and if the old people did not kill themselves, they did it for them. Usually the old man or woman withdrew from the group and went off to die alone. Like an animal—and here again you see the link. The incurable were abandoned all the more readily because of the fact that a sick person was surrounded with swarms of evil spirits. They killed cripples, put unfaithful wives to death, and smothered twins as soon as they were born.

Myself: No!

Luronne: Yes, because this incomprehensible double birth terrified them. And in any case, life was so short.

(She said, "Life was so short," and as she spoke it wrung my heart. What a mockery if the difference between a Comanche and a white man lay in the thirty or forty extra years that the white man has to live! What do thirty or forty more years really add? Apart from traveling a little further, just a very little further into life and a little more certainly toward death, with those inevitable periods of despair and resignation from which the Comanche, old at the height of his youth and dead in the fullness of life, was perhaps protected by his beliefs. . . .)

And when I came back to myself I said to Luronne, "Go ahead!"

Luronne (as though she had guessed my thoughts and meant to surprise me by using my own words): They were seized with despair when a young man died. If that happened, they would spend months mourning him. For his kindred the source of food had vanished with him. The Shoshonis solved the problem of the widow: they sacrificed her on the dead man's grave. In these very small societies there was nothing more tragic than the death of a young warrior.

Luronne again: As you can imagine, they had little room for feelings. The aim of sexual intercourse was reproduction, which ensured the economy and thus the life of the tribe. No homosexuals, no polygamy, although it was allowed. The elder brother lent his wife to the younger, and when in his turn the younger brother married, he thanked the elder with his own wife.

(A trifling, frivolous thought—regret that Luronne had no sister.)

Luronne: Listen. They had a horror of menstrual blood. When the women bled the Comanches looked upon them as sick and accursed. The women withdrew of their own accord and the men never touched them until the menstruation was over and the women had washed and scented themselves. Menstruation abolished all magic, all medicine, and it reinforced the women's position of inferiority. To be sure, the menopause wiped all this out, and the Comanche woman could attain the rank of a priestess or shaman. But there were few of them who ever reached the menopause.

(Once again my heart was wrung.)

Luronne: And it was these bands—not a nation but a collection of tribal groups—that wrecked the old dream of a Spanish empire in North America, that plunged the Mexican border into fire and blood, that blocked the French advance in the Southwest, and that delayed the Anglo-American conquest of the northern continent for sixty years.

Luronne had stopped speaking and I sat there without a word, slumped and huddled in my armchair, quite insignificant in all that vast panorama she had unrolled, where I was but a passive participant. I turned the details over and over in my mind, caressing them with my eyes, touching them with the tips of my fingers, looking away and coming back, attracted, fascinated, disgusted, above all when it seemed to me that I could smell the Nermenuh with their dirt, grease, clotted blood, every kind of rotten filth, where, as Luronne had discreetly hinted, lurked countless running, scratching, sucking vermin, and I knew that the Comanches had just added to my febrile vision of the Indian, a new element; I would be better off if I no longer knew what was waiting for me, that is to say failure, time, and death: and that this factor would affect my view of them and of myself. I still had strength enough to ask Luronne what had become of them.

Luronne: In 1910 eleven hundred and seventy-one Comanches were numbered, and in 1931 it was reckoned that only ten percent of them were of unmixed blood.

(That meant that in 1976 there would not even be a last of the Comanches in existence.)

And in the silence that had once more fallen between us, I should have liked, once my horror and disgust for them had passed, to keep the pictures of their life and death: for here, inexplicably, it seemed to me that I identified myself or rather discovered myself, another self. A possible self. I only had to have been born a hundred years earlier—three or four hundred years before my time would have been better—to have felt akin to them, and maybe I should have been one of them, in that America where they would have formed me, who can tell, and with space and time wiped out, it all happened as though they had given me something of themselves, something that I should presently break by living my own life and because I was not a Comanche. Or was one no longer. When I turned away from them, utterly weary, I saw the sign they had made me die away, and at the same time the strong feelings that their fate had aroused in me died away. The Comanches were leaving me. All the Indians would leave me. I should be left by everyone. In my death I should be alone.

But from now on I was too big a man to take it tragically.

Up until this time, Luronne had given me love with that kind of somewhat cold and prudent ardor that was natural to her; she was generous, but in her case—unlike mine—it was not expressed in sudden outbursts, gusts, waves that flooded over her and stripped her, waves from which I emerged for a couple of hours or three days. And emerging, appeased, I would set off for America. Luronne's prodigality lay in steadiness, not in accumulation (kisses, caresses . . .) nor in feverishness, and she abandoned herself to unrestrained passion only in the bedroom. Running over the same distance—a distance that we took for granted we would share our whole life long—she went at the pace of a long-distance runner and I at that of a sprinter. The day after the Comanches she changed, and I believe she changed because of them and of me.

It must be admitted that they had shaken me. The physical prostration that had come over me while she was speaking was still with me three days later, and I had no appetite for anything at all. All the less so since I saw a dark future beyond the eighteenth century. The future of whom, of what? I evaded exact definitions, and watching Luronne sideways or out of the corner of my eye, I thought her less powerful, less capable. Less unique, if I may put it like that. Immediately after the Comanches I slept a great deal, more than usual, as though I were trying to forget or escape. Happily Luronne did not feel the inspiration to speak during those days. I could not have borne her telling of misfortunes without doing anything about them.

No doubt she too was aware of my feeling of having changed. And perhaps this strange alteration in me disturbed her. However that may be, about this time I am speaking about, three days after the Comanches, she became affectionate, filled with tender concern, so much so that she never stayed more than five minutes with her books after she had been talking to me or kissing me. She kept coming back to me.

Then she made up her mind that we should travel again. After the Colorado, she wanted Niagara Falls. I wanted an Indian reservation. We could not make both trips, because of her mother's health, which was beginning to make her anxious once more, for the two together would have kept us out of New York too long. There was nothing to be seen in the reservations she said obstinately. And once I said, "You're trying to cut me off from the Indians." A serious accusation, and one that she denied. Then she yielded, particularly as she had already seen Niagara ten times.

We picked on the Caughnawagha reservation in Quebec, because according to our guidebooks, it was modeled upon the other reservations all over North America, and we hired a car in Montreal. As far as Indians were concerned, I had known millions of them in the course of time, but they were all in books and all in History. I wanted to see them alive, living in the flow of time as it passed through a whole day and not, as it nearly always happened in books, through ten years or a couple of centuries. I wanted living contact with Indians.

Luronne drove, as usual; and sitting on her right I gazed down, once we had passed the Mercier Bridge, down at the Indians on the banks of the St. Lawrence in that reservation which was once a strategic Indian locus, dominating the rapids just beyond the point where the Ottawa River joins the St. Lawrence. The Ottawa! Luronne had often spoken of it during the seventeeth century. Here History caught up with us, and we made room for it between us, just a little room, that particular evening. Poised on the edge of my seat, I sat straight up to catch the very first glimpse of the scene below; and I saw wooden houses in bold relief against the snow down there, houses coated with faded paint, just as they are in the poor or not so poor countryside all over America. I also made out some caravans; and as we were coming into the village, after the run down from the bridge, we saw countless pieces of washing hung out to dry and outhouses like those that stand at the end of the garden in the outskirts of French towns. Rather a dismal sight, made worse by quantities of signs I pretended not to read—Hot Dogs, French Fries, Soft Drinks—that alas had nothing Indian about them. Had it not been for a kind of thicket of little sumac trees covered with clusters of red fruit that caught my eye, I should not have thought the Indian village of Caughnawagha in any way different from American villages. Here it was Nature that spoke of a race, the race that had loved her most. I clung to the sumac trees so as not to see the rest.

For we had seen everything. That is to say nothing and nobody, apart from the huskies and some Father Christmases standing inside the windows, according to the custom in North America. It was enough to make you weep for sorrow: we preferred to laugh. We passed the church again and again, simply because Luronne was waiting for me to say let's go and I was thinking we can't go just like that. Then we went into one of the souvenir shops, and there, in the presence of an American Indian woman, we looked at and fingered the mass of junk, the wretched collection of glass geegaws and models, dwarf totem poles, cardboard tepees, dolls with synthetic leather skirts like Scottish kilts, belts pricked with artificial bristles, rickety pipes of peace, moccasins made of the skins of domestic sheep or goats or cattle that I should never put on my feet out of respect for the original and for the deer, stout pasteboard Indian canoes—and the unmeaning, lamentable quality of these little small-scale objects arose not from their size but from the fact that together with the total absence of soul and of the Great Spirit one felt the lifeless workmanship of these machine products—the Indian has been dying these five centuries past, and now the machine is finishing him off—and seeing that we bought nothing, the Indian woman turned toward the kitchen behind; she called out, and we started in astonishment, for there in the doorway appeared a fat Indian wearing jeans and a red-and-yellow checked shirt with a bottle of Coca-Cola in his hand and on his head, its feathers moth-eaten and sad, a huge Plains Indian headdress of the kind that the movies have popu-

larized and that the Quebec Indians never, never wore. To
amuse the whites, this Iroquois was dressing himself up as a
Sioux.

So we took to the car again to pursue the only dream that was
given to us, in the only space that would allow us to hide the
vulgarity, the ill-omened farce—to pursue it on the roads. No
one had troubled to lay them out or level them: they wandered
in every direction, cutting across one another without any kind
of system right in the village itself, full of bumps and potholes
that jolted the car, planted with bushes that seemed to have
sprung up by themselves without the help of any white man or
Indian, and this mingling of natural paths and a vegetation
growing according to its own laws warmed our hearts. The
dream had taken refuge there, among the sumac trees and the
plains covered with black, sickly, utterly wretched maples. All
that remained of the American forest. At least these remains
were not adulterated. The memory of them stayed with us all
the way back to New York, where we did not hide our pain and
disappointment either. I said, "There are no Indians left," and
we bowed our heads as though we were guilty.

So Luronne had been right. It would have been better to go
to the Falls. She did not make me feel it. She just said, almost
as soon as we had got home, that she wanted to set off again.
Maybe she thought that another trip would wipe out my disappointment in the last. For my part I wanted whatever she wanted. The Caughnawagha Indians had sent me back to the Indians of books. Since they no longer existed. So I agreed when
Luronne told me about her idea for a fresh journey—going
down to Virginia to see a nineteenth-century village restored to
its condition of 1825 or thereabouts. I was charmed right away.
At that time it did not occur to me that Luronne was probably
trying to use the whites to cure me of my disappointment with
the Indians.

As always on our trips, a car was waiting for us at Richmond
airport: and Luronne had introductions to the authorities, so
that we could visit the restored village before the crowds began

flooding in at ten in the morning. With the curator and his wife we passed through the white fence that ringed the whole. Slowly pointing out one wooden structure after another, the curator enumerated successively: an apothecary's, a baker's, a blacksmith's, a saddler's, a gunsmith's, a bootmaker's, a cabinetmaker's, a miller's, a candlemaker's, a printer-bookbinder's, a dressmaker's, a goldsmith's, a clockmaker's, a weaver's, a wigmaker's, and the list not being full, he told us that because of the time of year we should not see the flax dresser, nor the potter, nor the papermaker, nor the soap boiler, nor the slate worker. Apparently these craftsmen, in their stalls, stores, or workshops, dreaded the winter. So we should have to manage without them.

We walked into the first house, Luronne and I rather nervous, for although at our age we had had plenty of time to get used to automobiles, we were by no means accustomed to the horse-drawn carts and buggies that brushed past us, driven by some of the three hundred and fifty people employed in the village; they took some time to go by, and in the interval we feared for our feet—it would scarcely have surprised us at all if they had been crushed. We were in the harness maker's and we observed, hanging from a stable rack, harnesses, collars, bridles, halters, saddles, lines, hemp, and rope yarn on a rack; and there, by an undoubtedly subtle analogy, the authorities had also placed a spinning wheel with many spindles, together with its wharve and its flyers. When we had looked at it from a distance, without touching, we smiled at our hosts, who at once led us out, and after the inevitable ordeal by buggies, which made us walk with our toes turned in, we went into a cooper's: here, in a space of some three hundred square yards, rose a barrel, poised on supports as though upon a throne, a barrel certified as old, of course, but not antique, perhaps an instructive object; it was railed off from the public by a double range of thick-looped rope, and the bilge, the head, the chimb, the croze grooves, the crosspiece, the spigot, the bung, the iron hoops, the wooden hoops, the wedges, and the horses were thickly covered with labels from which, by leaning over the rope, one could learn the name, origin, date of manufacture, or use of each piece: and I told Luronne that here, in this extreme compulsion to name, number, and identify in time and space, I detected something of the anxiety we had observed in Champlain; then, smiling at our hosts once more, we walked out.

The blacksmith's presented us with a fully equipped smithy, with its hearth and slack table, the pipe connected to the bellows, and we were cold in there, filled with a desire to light the nonexistent fuel under the metal hood, where, as though they were logs, the authorities had placed an anvil, some horseshoes, and some hammers, and every object had its label at the end of a length of pliable wire that made one think of the shrunken arm of a policeman, and we moved three steps farther on to look at a plow with a moldboard to turn the earth, a pair of tilts for steering, a coulter for the upright cut, a share to cut lengthways, a slade (also called a sole) to support the moldboard, a clevis to hold the coulter against the beam (also called the shaft) of the plow, and next to the implement lay a horse hoe upon which Luronne and I fell without the loss of a minute, feigning a close interest in the working blade, the turner, and the carrying wheel, these being followed by a team harness, a breast holder, some scythe blades, and a turnwrest, all dusty and all of course labeled with their provenance, name, and date, and here I felt a first weariness, a first spinning of the head, wondering whether one should credit this mass of information or look upon it with distrust as upon a useless, preposterous luxury.

We knew that our smile was rather forced, a half-smile, but on the faces of our untiring, dangerous hosts it had not changed at all, and we resigned ourselves to going through the whole of the restored eighteenth-century village, house by house, a museum into which there fitted still other museums, dreadful to the worn and harassed visitor, and in showcases lined with blue linen we saw two thousand three hundred and twenty-four locks, then in the wine and cider press museum we

saw a Kentucky model, of which there were thirty-three speci-
mens, without counting the other presses stored away which
Luronne and I unanimously declined to visit and then we were
shown a wooden washing machine, a stone gatherer, and, lined
up against the whitewashed wall, a number of wood-turning
lathes, topped by scrolls. Then maybe three hundred pewter
measuring pots. We passed through the weaver's and the bootmaker's shops without seeing them. And, drawing fresh
strength for hypocrisy, we managed to follow our beaming
hosts; almost smiling and more drunk with objects than ever
we could have been with wine, we followed them as they led
us at the double (for the first visitors were flooding in) to the assault of one final collection, a kind of hymn to the craftsmen of
which I remember only the bootmaker's paring knife and the
currier's skiver, and, because their names were amusing, the
gunsmith's breeching piece and the cooper's chimbing iron.

Then we came out again. At least I had learned that the mind
infinitely prefers the images produced by words to those im-
printed on it by things themselves. We felt something like hatred for the curator and his wife. Yet since we had a certain curiosity about their home, which they had mentioned on our arrival, we had accepted their offer of a meal.

The curator (his wife was his assistant) told us that in fact he
was quite disillusioned about his restored village where, in
spite of all his efforts to keep it out, the twentieth century
would seep in, getting a hold, gaining ground, and striking its
worst blows where he least expected it. The twentieth century
won its easy victories all the more readily because, unlike the
curator and his wife, the staff did not possess the sacred flame
of devotion to the past. Too indifferent, too contaminated by
the present age. Besides, what could he do with three hundred
and fifty employees who, having worked in the nineteenth century all day, went home at five o'clock and there found the soft-
ening, enervating modern and even ultramodern comfort for
the night and until nine the next morning? And the transition
from one time to another, across the abyss of a century and a

half, did not seem to worry them at all, the bootmaker buying his children ready-made shoes at the supermarket and the candlemaker lighting himself with electricity. I could feel Luronne giggling inside, as I was doing myself, but we solemnly agreed with our host's remarks, and he, growing confidential and expansive, told us that the innkeeper did not sleep in his nineteenth-century inn but in his own modern house ten miles away and that the saddler rode not a horse but an automobile. And so it went. Then came the almost whispered revelation: half an hour from the village he ran a farm; and there, on a more modest scale, he had very nearly retained or rebuilt the spirit of the nineteenth century by means of authentic artifacts: he and his wife went there on three consecutive days every week, from Friday to Sunday, to refresh their souls.

Myself: Not possible.

The curator, beaming: Yes. And he added that he had three servants, as in a farm of that period.

Myself: What?

The curator: Three servants.

Luronne and I exchanged glances, each privately observing that the worthy soul had certainly succeeded in his transformation, at least in one aspect, since without turning a hair he had used the word servants for his employees, a word that has fortunately grown quite obsolete.

So, consumed with curiosity, we let ourselves be taken there.

Hold Tight Farm (the name was eloquent of its owner's aspirations) covered two hundred and thirty acres, and we were told that it represented the first attempt ever made in America to recreate the life of a rural community of a hundred years earlier. Here the couple insisted upon the strict accuracy that they had been unable to impose upon the village, using tools and methods that they assured us were 100 percent nineteenth century. Both horses and cows belonged to the most common breeds of former times. In an authoritative tone, the curator called an employee who was passing by. The man did not seem to us to have the respectful, even submissive behavior to his master that one would, perhaps mistakenly, have expected in a servant of the last century. When we reached the pigsties we lost our host, who set off at a run: he came straight back with a paper and unfolded it above the hogs, and seeing it we agreed that he was absolutely right—from snout to corkscrew tail, they were just like the old pigs there on the old engraving—then we went to see the guaranteed true-bred chickens, then the granary. The grainheads had seeds with curiously notched edges, the result of what is called backbreeding; the delighted curator and his moist-eyed wife assured us that both with the poultry and the grains they had reproduced the breeds of the last century to within a feather's or a hair's breadth. These crops gave him a great deal of trouble: not only were they attacked by the enemies they had always had—and these the curator coped with—but they were also plagued by the Japanese beetle.

Luronne and I; By what? The curator, sadly: By the Japanese beetle.

All the more damnable, we understood, in that it had not existed in 1850.

Myself, kindly: It doesn't matter if the evil has a different origin: the trouble of dealing with it is the same.

He thanked me for this understanding remark with a broad smile, and confidentially he told us of several other pests that left him in doubt—did they belong to the twentieth century or were they carrying on with their ancient obsessions in this world that had been restored for their benefit too? A hundred and fifty years ago, did the raccoons devastate kitchen gardens as they did now? Did the mealy moth ravage the harvests? All these were questions that made up the torment and the salt of his existence: questions about which the farm inventories that he continually consulted said nothing. The "farmwife" chatted with Luronne, and I heard her say that her husband and she were working on the very same tobacco-exhausted land that their predecessors had labored. . . .

At one point, as we were strolling along a path some distance from the house, a vile stench swept over us, and in less time

than it takes to tell we were enveloped and smothered. Before I
had found the handkerchief in my pocket, Luronne was fifty
yards away. Gathering my wits I fled from the reek, and we
waited for the couple to join us, both of them as amused as
though they had played a funny joke on us. Each tried to get in
first with the explanation—we had been smelling fermented
urine, which they used by way of insecticide, like the peasants
of the good old days. Yet for all that, there were years when the
crops stubbornly failed. When that happened, they turned, in
despair, to chemical products. When, glad to score a point, I expressed a hypocritical astonishment, the curator abruptly
turned more sour than his urine and retorted that if the farmers
of those days could see him now, they would not blame him for
this deviation, for taking this easy way. Then, "When the crops
failed, they didn't go to the supermarket and buy food. They
just didn't eat, and that's all there was to it." Overcome by this
capricious logic, I agreed: I did not say, "Since you, for your
part, can treat yourself to the supermarket, why don't you carry
the experiment right through to the end?"

We went into the dining room of the farmhouse, where we
were to take leave. The pots were genuine antiques; so were the
chairs, and we were asked to sit in them with care. Which we
did, poised on the edge of our buttocks. Here, as we had tea—a
drink that scarcely compromised them at all, since Americans
have always drunk it—we listened to complaints about the disappearance of the hardwoods such as hickory and chestnut
which used to provide tool handles and which had now been
swept away by the bulldozers, together with the last remaining
forests. Many recipes involving the sturgeon, now no longer to
be seen in the streams. . . . And how do you manage, asked
Luronne, to keep your clothes in the nineteenth century? I too
had noticed that they were wearing somewhat peculiar garments. She had said exactly the right thing: this was their highest claim to glory, and they had been on the point of telling us
about it. The curator-farmer took off his coat and gave it to us to
feel, explaining that he had successfully combined cotton and

wool: what is more, he had discovered a name for the result—
linsey-woolsey. It's like wearing steel wool, added our good
farmwife.

Steel? The word was risky, to say the least, but I had no time
to ponder over it. For some while Luronne had been darting
significant looks at me, and when at last I followed her eye, I
knew that never again should I experience such a monstrous,
outrageous contradiction: for there on the spinning wheel, like
a huge wart, hung a *plastic* bag.

Luronne was very fond of traveling, but these two trips convinced her that we were going through a bad period and that it
would be better for us to confine ourselves to New York. This
we did, waiting for the time when she would be given grace to
recount the eighteenth century, and we put as much zeal and
energy into walking about the streets as we had put into our
longer expeditions. In any case, as far as I was concerned, this
diving into New York amounted to a journey—a journey slight
in distance, great in the emotions it aroused in me. By evening
I was dropping with weariness. It was to fatigue, I believe, that
I owed a series of impotent lapses that were to change our life
together.

For of course it was obvious that these embarrassing lapses
could not be ascribed to my age. So it was fatigue. And maybe
something else that it hurts me to name, because I detest the
word: habit. The first time I fell asleep over it, and although
she was eager Luronne did not hold it against me. The second
time I was angry with myself, with life, and with the city. The
third time I cursed myself.

To begin with, when I could not manage, I would call up
pictures of a Luronne naked, lascivious, and acrobatic beside
Luronne herself. Then Luronne's face would dissolve and I
saw nothing but her body, and that made me vigorous again.
One night even that failed me. Although Luronne was there, I
was quite alone. That was why I urged her to make other con-
tacts, so that she could tell me about them and excite me vicari-

ously. It's not betraying me, I told her. It's not betraying your lover or your love for him. I'll love you even more. We'll be as happy as we were at the beginning.

Now she took to going out every afternoon. I never knew when she would come home. Sometimes an hour after she had left. More often, the next day. In the course of a week she did not stay with me in the apartment more than forty-eight hours. She liked her adventures. Every time she came back I had her at once, and every time I made a triumph of it.

Then she calmed down. She only went out for two nights a week and one whole afternoon. I knew she had set about the preparation of the eighteenth century, and now I became positively superstitious!

Taking Luronne with me, I picked out very expensive nightdresses for her, making her try them on there in the shop; and I said to myself the finer the nightdress, the more I gave the miracle a chance to work, with Luronne in tune with it and History maybe yielding to the temptation.

This time grace took longer to come down on her than it had on the two occasions when she told me of the sixteenth and seventeenth centuries. Christmas was coming, and the last account was five weeks behind us! Her adventures did not explain everything. I knew that she was capable of learning the whole century in one evening. On thinking it over, I saw that Luronne had been most thoroughly at her ease in the period from the arrival of the Indians in America to that of Christopher Columbus. The deeper she plunged into the violent world of the white men and the death of the Indians, with and because of History, the less willing the grace of words had been to anoint her. Why? And what about me?

I had contradictory feelings, longing for the tale and at the same time dreading it. I knew that we were playing for high stakes, and although at a given moment of the day I would be full of hope, an hour later I would be pessimistic. My hopes found some support in John Adams, the venerable second president of the United States: "Yet if I am to believe the weak lights that remain to us, it appears to me that we can say that despite all its errors and all its vices, of all past centuries the eighteenth will have done most honor to human nature." On the other hand, my anxiety found sustenance in Benjamin Franklin's advice that the Indians should be given rum in abundance "in order to exterminate them and leave room for farming white men"—a piece that I had stuck to the stake and that tortured me. So how could I tell whether I should pray for the arrival of the eighteenth century or whether I should only want it to come a long, long while later? I gauged my confusion of mind by this memory that kept recurring to me many times a day: As an adolescent, on the road from Châteaurenard-de-Provence to Avignon on the evening of a blazing day, I watched the sun go down in flames behind the wind-break hedges and slowly vanish. Then, with the darkness hiding the shape of things, a sadness drowned my happiness in life that day, and in this twofold assault I recognized death, death felt for the first time. I must have been fourteen: and it was this recollection, which had never come to mind before, that sustained me more than countless others.

The grace of words delayed its coming so long that I suspected Luronne of preparing herself badly. When she was there I took her with a kind of fury. I had found a way of doing it so deep and straight that if I had been set going I should have spun around her like a top; and once I thought I should go on forever and ever. How long should I have to wait? Then one evening I was brutally rough with her, and without my knowing whether I had anything to do with the phenomenon or not, grace came down on Luronne.

We saw Sieur Antoine de la Mothe Cadillac found Detroit in 1701 and Lemoyne d'Iberville, New Orleans in 1718; and spitting on him several times we listened to Cotton Mather, the preacher whose fanatical excesses prepared the way for the Salem witchcraft trials, state in 1712 that the presence of the Indians in America was connected with the Devil and his works.

YVES BERGER

With Lemoyne d'Iberville dying of yellow fever at Havanna, we saw the death of the dream of a French America stretching from Hudson's Bay, Acadia, and Newfoundland to the Gulf of Mexico by way of Louisiana. Luronne dodged here and there in the century, and in the Boston of 1721 we liked Dr. Zabdiel Boylston, who adopted the practice of inoculation, unknown in America up until then; he inoculated two hundred and fifty people, of whom only six died in the smallpox epidemic—and the mob abused him, threatening him with death. We watched the English of England and America organize expedition after expedition to destroy the bases of French power—expeditions that were scattered by storms and devastated by the intolerable Quebec winter; and in the other direction, we watched the French of France and Canada organize expedition after expedition to retake Louisbourg in Nova Scotia and burn Boston—expeditions that were ravaged by scurvy and scattered by the almost unbeatable English fleet. In Acadia, the Micmacs, who fought on our side, loved us so much that it made me grind my teeth. Acadia. In 1755, forced into exile by the English soldiery who had burned their houses and slaughtered their cattle—

Myself: The swine!

Luronne: —eight thousand Acadians put aboard ships, and this deportation of a whole people, the first in history, scattered a diaspora far and wide, in France, in England, in the West Indies, and indeed in Louisiana itself, and there in New York Luronne and I, enchanted by their music, both sighed for the big drum, the accordion, the fiddle, the harmonica, and the triangle.

We saw the Canadians prefer trapping and trading with the Indians to sowing and reaping.

Myself: How well I understand them!

Luronne: A choice that angered Louis XIV and that was to bring about the death of Nouvelle-France.

I was moved by Colbert, who wanted the white and the Indian races to be but "a single people and a single blood." Much affected, we saw the black slaves of South Carolina rise up and

254

then collapse in 1739, rebel again in the following year and
once more collapse, the whites taking advantage of it to hang
fifty of them; and two years later there was in New York the
hysterical rumor of a conspiracy, which resulted in the death of
thirteen blacks, burned alive, and fifty-eight hanged; and when
the French had exterminated the Foxes in Wisconsin (Luronne
went so fast that I let them die without a word, without a tear),
we saw the birth of Georgia, which James Oglethorpe banned
to both blacks and Roman Catholics. We liked the Frenchman
Pierre-Gaultier de Varennes, Sieur de La Vérendrye, who made
his way into a country where I took a deep, happy breath; and
La Verendrye traveled with his three sons—we thought this
touching—toward Rainy Lake, then to the Lake of the Woods
at the mouth of the Winnipeg. His craze: the building of forts.
Here were three on those singing, powerful streams, the Red
River, the Assiniboine, the Saskatchewan. The Ojibways and
the Crees gave the party a splendid welcome. We saw his sons,
alone now, carry on their father's dream, crossing the South
Dakota plains in 1743 and reaching the Rocky Mountains, the
first white men to see them. We left them there, in the Black
Hills, on the border of Wyoming and South Dakota, to follow
Pierre Mallet and his brother Paul as they traveled up the Missouri and the Platte between 1739 and 1741, at the same time as
La Vérendrye, crossing the high plateaus and the mountains
with the help of the Pawnees, and reaching Taos and Santa Fe,
the first Europeans to cross the hitherto unknown country running from the Missouri to New Mexico. Then they went down
the Canadian and the Arkansas rivers, thus making the round
from the mouth of the Missouri to that of the Mississippi.

Myself: How splendid it is!

Luronne paused to catch her breath, and I struggled to recover from the vertigo engendered by that marvelously dazzling
historical account from the horses' hooves drumming on the
trails, to the canoes with their paddles swishing in the water.
Next we watched General Braddock leave Virginia, cross the
Blue Ridge and the Alleghenies, strike into a country that no

one had yet crossed, and march through it in the direction of Fort Duquesne, which is now Pittsburgh. He reckoned on thrashing its French garrison; but in a forest almost impenetrable to anyone but an Indian, Braddock was mortally wounded, having had several horses killed under him: and then, surrounded by Delawares, Caughnawaghas, and Mohicans, all thoroughly enjoying this one-sided slaughter, he saw the Indians win the greatest of all their victories: out of one thousand four hundred and fifty-nine officers and men, nine hundred and seventy-seven killed or badly wounded.

Myself: Hey, hey!

Luronne: A bashing, as you would put it. After this victory the Indians ravaged the Shenandoah Valley and the Seven Years War began, the one the English call the French and Indian Wars, as though they washed their hands of it; one in which the French of Canada, numbering sixty thousand, made war on the English colonies with their million inhabitants.

We saw the English fleet move up in three weeks, to lie before Quebec, without the loss of a single ship or a single man.

A bad omen: I saw Wolfe, the attacking general, down there on the river, observing the fourteen thousand Frenchmen that the Marquis de Montcalm had gathered in and about Quebec. Then, together with Wolfe, I raised my eyes and gazed at the citadel.

Luronne: Montcalm did not trouble about the south bank. He was wrong. Wolfe sent his troops there and seized Pointe Lévi, from which he could fire on the lower town. Then he landed on the north bank, upstream from Quebec. Listen. Wolfe's scouts made a discovery—oh, scarcely anything at all—just a little footpath so narrow that Montcalm had not seen fit to guard it: the path wound up to the cliffs on this north bank which led to the Plains of Abraham. At sunset on September 12, 1759, the English moved up the river in small boats, unseen by the French, who in any case were expecting a supply convoy; and while Wolfe recited the "Elegy Written in a Country Churchyard"—Gray, you know—your countrymen mistook the enemies who were landing and filing up the path for friends.

Myself: There must have been treason somewhere.

Luronne: The operation was carried out all the more easily because when a sentry called "Who goes there?" a French-speaking Scotsman replied, "France," just as you or I would have done, and then "De la Reine," which was the password.

Myself: There, you see—a traitor!

Luronne: Maybe. Probably. And you know what happened then: the five thousand Englishmen all landed by dawn, finished the French off with the bayonet and made Nouvelle-France English, France keeping no more of all the splendid empire that Champlain and Cavelier de La Salle had given her than the paltry islands of Saint-Pierre and Miquelon.

Myself, on edge: What about the Indians?

Luronne: I'm just coming to them.

Then: Listen. He was called Pontiac. An Ouatouais, or as the English say, an Ottawa. He came from the country between Lake Erie and Lake Huron. Born about 1720. As the leader of the Ottawas, he was one of those who smashed Braddock. Capable of the most provocative arrogance and also of the humblest spirit of submission. A forest Indian who drank the blood and ate the hearts of his brave enemies, believing that he derived invaluable qualities from them. But he was more than that. The only Indian of his time to grasp that in order to resist the whites something in the nature of a holy league of the Indians was called for. He had a sense of leadership. Style. See him, tall, well-built, tattooed, pearls in his ears, a stone in his nostrils, bracelets. A great orator into the bargain.

Whom I devoured with my eyes, already believing that I could hear him speak.

Luronne: He could not get over his grief for the defeat of the French, who, unlike the others, did not take the Indians' land away from them and who were generous with their brandy in exchange for furs. Couldn't believe they had gone forever. Look at Pontiac, at the end of November 1760, unable to believe his eyes as he saw the British colors flying over Fort Detroit.

I looked at him.

Luronne: Sir Jeffrey Amherst, commanding in North America, had nothing but contempt for the Indians. Listen to what he said on one occasion: "The only way of behaving with savages is to keep them in the most complete submission and to punish all those that resist without exception." You see the type. The English made a total break with the French policy which was founded on presents. They walked about arrogantly, as though they were in a conquered country. Now look at Pontiac.

I saw him impose his leadership and his great plan on the Ottawas, the Chippewas, the Potawatomis, all the Great Lakes tribes, and send scores of messengers to the Shawnees, in Ohio. A war was being set on foot, a war unlike any other.

One that I awaited with feverish impatience.

On April 27, 1763, Pontiac, uneasy at the spread of the English in western Pennsylvania and confident of the support of the tribes, made a blazing speech to four hundred warriors gathered around him. They besieged Fort Detroit, ringing it about with trenches. The order was given to slaughter all whites except the French traders, who were to be preserved by a passport—a strip of birch bark with Pontiac's totemic seal, the otter. The war spread to Michigan, Ohio, Indiana, Pennsylvania, and Wisconsin; and one after the other the English forts fell under the attack of the Delawares, the Hurons, the Potawatomis, the Mingos. On the lakes, fleets of boats were stopped, pillaged, and sunk.

Myself: If only he could succeed!

Luronne: Now the Kickapoos rose, and the Weas, the Mascoutens, the Chippewas, the Sauks, even the Senecas and the Shawnees.

Myself: All of them!

Luronne: By the end of June, after two months of war, the English had lost all their forts on the Ohio and the Great Lakes except for Detroit and Fort Pitt, which were besieged. Never had the Indians, usually so changeable, shown such patience, steadiness, and strength of will. From New York to Virginia, the war spread like a prairie fire, with countless atrocities on both sides; and it was at that time that the terrible words were born: "The only good Indian is a dead Indian."

Words that hurt me.

Luronne: However rapid and effectual Pontiac's successes, they were not enough. The English pulled themselves together. Amherst sent a certain Colonel Bouquet with thousands of soldiers, and, you know, he proposed an unbelievably base and shameful action—infecting the Indians with smallpox by means of contaminated blankets.

Myself: Are you sure?

Luronne: Absolutely. And Pontiac's tragedy lay in the fact that he could not manage to take Fort Detroit. The Indians grew tired of the siege. Tribe after tribe they defected.

First, after one last desperate attack, the Potawatomis. Then the Chippewas. The last to leave Pontiac were his own people, the Ottawas. The last straw was when a French officer came up from the south to warn Pontiac that the kings of France and England had buried the hatchet and that the peace covered America too.

Heavy at heart I saw Pontiac's wretchedness. After so many victories.

Luronne: What remains is sad, as usual. Pontiac held out, sending messengers as far as the Mississippi, to the Tunicas and the Choctaws. In vain. In vain, too, to the Illinois territory, where he himself moved about unseen, traveling in spite of the price set on his head. In the spring of 1765 he agreed to meet the English to make peace. He signed the treaty and he would have respected it if he had been given the time. But on April 20, 1769, near St. Louis, for some unknown reason a Peoria stunned him and stabbed him. To death.

I looked at the dead Pontiac, who had raised eighteen tribes from Ontario to the Mississippi and who had taken eight of the twelve English forts.

I felt that Pontiac, even more than Philip and Popé, was going to dwell in me. His dream in mine. I no longer had the spirit to follow Luronne. Nor the heart either, no doubt. I switched on the light and she agreed to stop.

The next day, endowed with grace or not, Luronne began again. I had spent the day in feverish expectation and perhaps I had some foreknowledge of the great, the splendid news and suddenly we were back in those crazy days when I used to have her on the carpet to celebrate our happiness. Listen: by royal command, the English forbade the whites to cross the Appalachians. The whole country to the west, and from the 31st parallel to the Ohio, became Indian territory. That historic date—October 1763. What if the English were seeking to people Canada, Nova Scotia, and British Florida by means of this prohibition? Of no importance. Philip's, Popé's, and Pontiac's sacrifice would not then have been in vain. This great decision, which did honor to the English, was called the Proclamation Act! At once I saw merchants and politicians who had influence in London forming themselves into companies to speculate in land, companies that approached the Crown with proposals for the purchase of enormous areas, one of which took in Illinois and Wisconsin, no less. Franklin dabbled in this affair. Another proposition concerned half Kentucky and Tennessee, and a third covered the whole of what is now Michigan. Every time London said no. And I uttered the war cry of the free Indians: Whoop! Whoop!

We had to celebrate this Proclamation Act. And London's firmness too. I looked in the cupboard and found one bottle, the last. Yet we had not had many happy events since Columbus. We must both of us have been very free with the champagne. As I filled her glass I said to Luronne, "From now on there's no room for anything but misfortune." But I didn't believe it.

And here we were at the year 1775, at the American Revolution, the independence of the thirteen colonies. Three years earlier, the Americans, as the English of America were soon to be called, had concluded a treaty with the Delawares, the first of the three hundred and seventy-one treaties between whites and Indians, every one of which the whites were to break. Independence withdrew me from the Indians. Good-bye: see you again sometime!

After the British victory over the French in Canada, we saw London try to raise fresh taxes in the colonies: the colonies thought it natural that the English should have come and died for them, but they thought it quite unnatural that these same English should set about getting money from them. If the English have run themselves into debt to give us peace, so much the worse for them! Suddenly, in 1775, the English were hated, hated as heartily as they had been loved ten years earlier, when they were hammering out the victory! I saw the Americans indulge in smuggling on a huge scale, at the expense of the British administration, never drinking any tea but that which had paid no duty. Agitators, who were called the Sons of Liberty, organized the resistance, inciting their countrymen to turn on the higher officials of the administration, and when the English created the stamp duty they lit bonfires with heaps of official papers.

Amusing.

I guessed that things were going to warm up, and very quickly at that. We saw the revolution being prepared in the Atlantic ports, where the most disaffected, the most uncompromising colonials—those who were called radicals—combined with the merchants, and in the South with the planters, all over, from Portsmouth to Savannah, from New Hampshire to Georgia. Patrick Henry impressed me when, at the First Continental Congress, he declared, "I am not a Virginian, I am an American."

Had I been English, I should have felt uneasy.

But the English were not the least bit worried.

And the reason why they did not worry was that they despised the colonials: the English soldiers who had fought in the New World despised both the American military and the American civilians, and the English in England despised them too, from a distance. A kind of set idea—a fashion. Luronne insisted on the point. This claim to superiority was to have grave consequences. One day in March 1770 passersby in Boston caught sight of a sentry and threw snowballs at him; the situation grew tense; the sentry called for help; soldiers came running. One shot was fired, then two, then ten: result, three dead and two who died from their wounds, all of them on the civilian side. Luronne: Do you know what the Americans call this clash? The Boston Massacre.

I nodded. I was acquainted with the inflationary power of words. If five dead out of an attacking mob constituted a massacre, that meant that the words, to say nothing of the dead, were against the English, who had set off on the wrong foot. And indeed the news spread throughout the colony, carried by scouts, by runners. . . . The course of events was staggering along when in 1773, still in Boston, some Americans disguised as Mohawks (which did not exactly please me) went aboard a ship from London, seized three hundred and forty-two tea chests, and flung them into the sea! So much for the duty on tea! That was the turning point. The radicals persuaded the colonies to send representatives to the Congress to discuss the problems raised by the English. I watched the revolutionary committees in the thirteen colonies choose their delegates. It had started.

Myself: What about the people?

Luronne: There: it's a very odd thing—the people were filled with a hatred that can't be explained by the taxes. Listen to this conversation between Judge Mellen Chamberlain and a former soldier he interviewed sixty years after independence, when the ex-rebel was ninety-one.

"Did you take up arms against intolerable oppression?"

"Oppression?" replied the old man. "I didn't experience anything like that."

"What, were you not oppressed by the Stamp Act?"

"I never saw one of those stamps. I certainly never paid a penny for one of them."

"Well, but what then about the tea tax?"

"I never drank a drop of the stuff; the boys threw it all overboard."

"Then I suppose you had been reading Harrington or Sidney and Locke about the eternal principles of liberty?"

"Never heard of 'em. We read only the Bible, the Catechism, Watts' *Psalms and Hymns*, and the *Almanac*."

"Well, then, what was the matter? Why did you go off to fight?"

"Young man, what we meant in going for those Redcoats was this: we always had governed ourselves, and we always meant to. They didn't mean we should."

Shocking. According to Luronne, everything was clear from that point on: without knowing it, the English of the colonies had become Americans! Their hatred of the English, of the English soldiers, was the hatred of the oppressed for the tyrant, even if the oppression did not amount to much.

Perfectly clear. So I watched the Redcoats, as the Americans called the king's soldiers, fight the militiamen at Lexington and Concord while the disturbed, uneasy country took up arms. Eight dead at Lexington, and here again the choice of words was revealing: the messengers galloping with the news spoke of a massacre of the country people! Of all words massacre is the one that does the least harm and makes the most noise in the history of the struggle for independence! But still, the king's subjects had fired on the king's soldiers: the Revolution had begun.

We watched this war that lasted eight years, a war that ought to be called civil—a war between those who wanted independence and those who remained loyal to the English crown. The first were the Patriots, the second the Loyalists or Tories. A worldwide war, which was joined by Holland and Spain as well as France and which spread from West Indies to India it-

263

self. We considered it in its men, its ideas, and its consequences. Far over on the other side of the water, we saw
George III of England. By 1775 he had been reigning for
fifteen years and he was to go on reigning for another thirty-
seven after the War of Independence. Couldn't read until he
was eleven. Pathetically attached to his mother. One day when
he was walking in the streets of London, some wags called out
"Are you going home to your wet nurse?" Didn't marry, but
was made to marry: to Princess Charlotte of Mecklenburg-Stre-
litz, of whom Horace Walpole observed, "There were not half a
dozen people in England who knew that any such princess existed." She was seventeen, snub-nosed, large-mouthed, yellow-
complexioned: she reached London at three o'clock in the afternoon of September 22 and they were married at five.

He had twelve children by her before she was forty, and a
year after his marriage he was afflicted with madness. Apparently after that it spared him until one day in 1788, when he
was in Windsor Park: he got out of his coach and bowed to a
tree, taking it for Frederick the Great!

Myself: No!

Luronne: Authoritative, obstinate, and vindictive in the bargain: yet not without some good qualities.

Luronne did not name them, however, and we watched the
Second Continental Congress create an army, appoint George
Washington commander in chief, give its consent to war, and
try to win over Canada—all these being decisions taken in the
name of the king! Such were the Americans of 1775 and 1776:
they made war but they recoiled at the prospect of independence. Between the first conflicts and the famous declaration,
fourteen months went by. Furthermore, the State of New York
abstained from voting. And the author of the Declaration of Independence, Thomas Jefferson, went so far as to observe, in a
melancholy tone, "Together we might have made up a great
free nation."

Luronne: Besides, the people did not want war. Don't you
believe that this American nation rose up, full of wholehearted

conviction, fully determined to seize its independence. It has been estimated that the Patriots amounted to a third, and the Loyalists to another third, the remainder being neutral, neither the one nor the other. An unpopular war, one that the soldiers, enlisted for a set period, wanted to leave on December 31 of every year; and when the French arrived, the Americans would willingly have let them fight alone! Do you know that the State of New York provided more soldiers for the king of England than for George Washington?

I did not know it.

Then Luronne went back to the Declaration of Independence, because there Jefferson spoke of the "pursuit of happiness" as an inalienable right. And in the darkness of the room we searched for each other and each fell into the other's arms, enchanted that after William Penn, Jefferson should have thought about happiness, about us. And we fell apart because Jefferson also said that all men were equal and excluded the blacks from that equality.

Then, moving into the war, we watched the arrival of the thirty thousand mercenaries that the English had hired in the German principalities and duchies and that the Americans called the Hessians. Twelve thousand of them were to stay in America for good.

Myself: Of course!

Then we turned our attention to George Washington. The most conventional of pictures, as Luronne warned me. The muckrakers have been at work for two hundred years without finding anything but trifles. A great gentleman and one who took almost morbid care to keep the commander in chief—that is to say himself—subordinate to the decisions of Congress, except, of course, in the field of military operations. He accepted his appointment but refused to accept any pay, preferring, as one might put it, to give of himself. A great general with something about him that evokes Bonaparte. Whereas the English generals continued the practice of going into winter quarters, Washington chose the winter to move his army and to attack—

that night march on Princeton, with the wheels of his guns wrapped in cloth to muffle the sound! If one day he lost on the Hudson, the next day he won on the Delaware, and he always recovered from his defeats, gaining the battles that really mattered. We watched him start from nothing with the militia, and build up an army, train officers and men, and persuade his soldiers to reenlist at the end of their contracted term of service rather than to waver perpetually between camp and farm.

His dignity, his strictness, and a hint—no more—of haughtiness inspired respect. So did his integrity and his capabilities. He was by no means a phlegmatic man, but he never broke out in public. Washington was never so great nor so alone as he was at the end of that winter of 1776 when he only had five thousand men to face forty thousand of the enemy. He was humane, though not too much so, and he wept for his soldiers who, because of the farmers and merchants, were cold and hungry, in want of clothes and shoes. "You could have followed the army . . . as far as Valley Forge by their bloody footprints," said he. Soldiers who had not a penny in their pockets because of the errors of Congress. Later their wretched state astonished Lafayette and Rochambeau, and Washington was ashamed of it. He solved the problem of making his army, in which Northerners disliked Southerners and the other way about, into a homogeneous body. He dealt with the endemic desertion. The troops mutinied: he brought them to terms and gave Congress an exhaustive explanation of the reasons why they had gone to such lengths. Later he said, "History offers no example of an army subjected to such extraordinary labors and sufferings." Washington displayed imagination, and in comparison with the ridiculous, slow, stupid, scornful, shortsighted English generals, he possessed all the good qualities. We saw him resist Congressional intrigues and baffle mediocrity, self-interest, and treachery. Luronne: Did you know that his second-in-command, yes, the deputy commander in chief, was a traitor? We saw him stop the rout of Lee's troops at Monmouth and give the example by advancing alone. Lafayette: "I never saw so magnificent a man."

Luronne told me an anecdote in which Washington, who had already foreshadowed Bonaparte, now did the same for de Gaulle. General Howe, wishing to avert war, sent to Washington a lieutenant with a letter. The officer waved a flag. No shots were fired. The Americans approached: he produced the letter. They took it and set off at a gallop. Came back and asked to whom it was addressed. The officer, surprised and polite, took off his hat, bowed, and said it was from Lord Howe to Mr. Washington, New York. "We have no one of that name in our army," replied the Americans, and they handed the letter back. When the puzzled Englishman asked just how the letter should be addressed, he was told, "General Washington!"

I laughed admiringly.

Then Luronne went on to another anecdote: the scene was Yorktown, where the English had just surrendered. Washington, mounted and in full-dress uniform, was waiting at the head of the whole Franco-American army, drawn up in parade, for the defeated commander in chief, Cornwallis, to appear and to give up his sword, as custom required. Here he was— no, it was O'Hara, a lower-ranking officer, who stated that Cornwallis, being sick, had asked him to take his place. At this the imperturbable Washington waved him away, pointing out the American, Lincoln, who had the same rank as O'Hara. In the face of History, Mr. Washington treated only as equal to equal.

I laughed admiringly.

Myself: He had to do it! (I meant have the presence of mind to.)

We saw civil conflict and guerrilla fighting spread in the South, the English prisons turn into concentration camps, pillaging increase, Tories hanging Patriots and Patriots hanging Tories with the same degree of hatred, and the English generals incapable of following up their advantages. The extent of the atrocities surprised me less when Luronne told me that the English army was recruited from the dregs of society. It is a known fact. The English took all that their prisons contained in the way of hardened criminals and sent them into their regiments and thus to America. Maybe the Americans had not too much room to talk? Forty thousand convicts had been transported to America in the eighteenth century. As the population increased from two hundred thousand to two million, this meant that one American out of fifty had done time in prison.

And I, overwhelmed: The poor Indians!

And Luronne: Just wait—We watched the temperamental, somewhat crazy Burgoyne at Saratoga, surrendering his army to the Americans, who on the other hand lost Charleston, the greatest of their defeats. Lafayette, whom the Americans worshipped, charmed me too. I loved his saying, "When you are twenty-three, when you have an army to command, and Lord Cornwallis to deal with, you do not have time for much sleep." The English behaved very basely to the blacks, whom they won over, promising them their freedom, and whom they abandoned without troubling about their fate. When the English ran short of food in besieged Yorktown, they thrust the blacks out of their entrenched positions and forced them to march between the English and Franco-American lines, in no-man's-land—a term that renders their state exactly—and in March 1781 we saw the coming of the Frenchmen under Rochambeau and de Grasse.

Luronne, dreamily: The Soissonais regiment, white coats with pink facings; the Bourbonnais, white and black; the Saintonge, white and green; the Royal Deux Ponts, the best manned of all the regiments, in blue coats with yellow sleeves and facings.

At Yorktown Cornwallis surrendered to the six thousand allies, thus setting the seal on American independence. There we watched America receive its true baptism, and then Luronne and I had a rest. She was out of breath: my head, stuffed with battles and generals, was aching, but I was about to say something when she began again.

Myself: Wait: I was thinking.

Luronne: Listen: Chateaubriand.

So I listened.

Luronne: Believe it or not, but when he left France for America in 1791, what do you think filled his mind? The Northwest Passage. Neither more nor less. He took it into his head that he would find it. In 1790 he was a stocking merchant, to which base occupation he demeaned himself and earned the money for his . . . .

Myself, interrupting her, amazed: Chateaubriand, stockings?

Luronne: Yes—the money for his voyage. He had made thorough preparations. Listen to him: "After these conversations with Malesherbes, I looked through Tournefort, Duhamel, Bernard de Jussieu, Grew, Jacquin, Rousseau's *Dictionnaire* and the elementary Floras; I hurried off to the Jardin du Roi, and already I thought myself a second Linnaeus."

Myself: How splendid!

(I liked Chateaubriand's having plunged into books before his journey to America, just as I had done for twenty-five years on end before mine.)

Luronne: Listen to him and his delight in his "balsams, shad-berries, palms, huckleberries and atocas."

It seemed to me that I could almost hear him.

We watched him doggedly traveling west for a while, looking for the passage, and I was pleased that Chateaubriand, on leaving for America, should have had a wild dream in his head, I listened to him listening to the barn owl, I saw him seeing the snow finch, I followed him as he shot the muskrat and the lynx, and I longed for him to come into contact with Indians.

Iroquois: dancers who seemed to him "all daubed and smeared." He was disappointed, just as Tocqueville was disappointed forty-one years later.

Irritated and grieved, I asked Luronne to come to *Le Voyage en Amérique* and as she hesitated . . .

Myself: "I traveled across a prairie scattered with yellow-flowering ragwort, pink-plumed mallows, and those purple sprays of lobelia," perhaps the loveliest sentence in the world: and we heard Chateaubriand speak of the Seminoles and the Creeks; we followed him along the Iroquois Trail, which goes from Albany to Niagara; and we saw him lying, inventing a journey to the Mississippi and to Florida, and doing it badly. René in *Les Natchez*, was happier among the Indians than among the whites.

Myself: Bravo!

And I suffered because Chateaubriand, speaking of the Indians, spoke as a prophet: "I believe that I, the last historian of these peoples, am opening the record of their death"; but for some time Luronne had not left me with them for long. Yet now, in connection with the Iroquois, she had found a passage that in fact was worth its weight in gold.

Chateaubriand: "In the event of an extremely difficult childbirth, it is still the custom to give the woman who is in labor a great fright: a band of young men silently creep up to the purification hut and suddenly utter a war cry. These shrieks fail with brave women, and there are many of them." A ridiculous custom that neither Luronne nor I had seen mentioned by any traveler or ethnologist or Iroquois specialist and we flew into a rage with Chateaubriand here guilty of inventing such tawdry nonsense. And to punish him I chased Luronne, under whose skirt I had fastened a big bag which she held in both hands while screaming, "Scare me! Scare me!" This went on until we were both out of breath. I did feel regretful about Chateaubriand; I should have preferred having Luronne beginning with that farce of the bag and winding up with the yellow-flowering ragwort. She liked him less than I did.

That morning Chateaubriand had led us on into the wee small hours, and I guessed that I should not see Luronne before evening—she had got up earlier than I. It was an absence that I found irritating today, even if she were going to give me ten wild minutes that night, telling me how she had spent her day. Things were not going well. To begin with, I was not proud of the horseplay in which we had indulged yesterday, the Chateaubriand-inspired nonsense with the bag and the chasing around. Maybe after the tension generated by the War of Independence, we were looking for an excuse to unwind. I had got over the exaltation and the hope that the Proclamation Act had aroused in me; its success seemed pretty dubious. All the more so in that the king who had issued the proclamation was the shifty George III. A discovery that had given me a bad shock. And lastly, wasn't Luronne avoiding any prolonged stay with the Indians? Whereas our game, hers and mine, was to be played out between the Alleghenies and the Mississippi, where, thanks to the Proclamation Act, they lived by themselves! There Luronne had an excellent chance of winning. Happier circumstances could not have been dreamed of, and all at once I felt much better. History had never been more humane, more concerned with the humble, the despoiled, and with the justice of their cause. Tomorrow the injustice born of Christopher Columbus's discovery would be undone. The crimes put right. If the white men obeyed and did not invade America beyond the Alleghenies, all was saved. If the white men obeyed.

Luronne came back at about nine o'clock, long after the winter night had fallen: she hurried into the bedroom, came out ritually dressed in a nightgown, and uttered some strange words, speaking so fast that I could not catch them. The words: We are coming to the end today. Then she put out the light. I sat opposite her, five yards away, and I said:

Myself: The Indians.

Luronne, cutting me short: Wait: Jefferson.

And as it had been with Chateaubriand, I was bathed in happiness right away.

One of the white men who really went along with the Indians inside me. They and I had plenty of evidence: Jefferson loved them, maybe even understood them. Even though his love may not have been much good to them. Because of an agrarian myth running from St. John de Crèvecoeur to Turner, with Thomas Jefferson at the heart of it, I had grown used to his weaknesses and imperfections. To be sure, I was not taken in. Myth: that is to say the opposite of reality. In the correspondence of Lafayette, who one day in 1784 rode to Mount Vernon, where George Washington was expecting him, we read: "We traveled through one of the last vestiges of that enormous forest which covered America in primeval days. Everything around us had an air of grandeur and sadness, of antiquity and decline, that I cannot describe, but that stirred the soul to its depths." As early as 1784! Apart from one noun and adjective that make it sound old-fashioned, this observation still holds. Lafayette speaks regretfully of the forest, destroyed by farming. Who has not despised agriculture in his dreams and myths, longing rather for the forest to be reborn? Luronne agreed, and she told me that Jefferson, the same Jefferson who had included that fine short piece about happiness in the Declaration of Independence which had pleased us so, had for forty years been the lover of a mulatto slave who bore him seven children and whom he did not emancipate because according to Virginian law she would have had to leave for another state.

Myself: Surely not!

And we saw Jefferson experience the reality and not the myth of love, and we liked him too because, although he was so concerned with happiness, he had a rough time of it—one in which I recognized myself.

(And, said I within, who would not recognize himself in that?)

Then in Santo Domingo, where they were trying to put down Toussaint L'Ouverture's black uprising, we saw General Leclerc's thirty-five thousand men die of yellow fever—the same troops that Napoleon had intended for the occupation of Louisiana, five hundred and forty thousand square miles running from Texas to Canada and from the Mississippi to the Rockies which he now renounced and from which the Americans were to make twelve states.

Myself: What year was that? (forcibly tearing myself away from memories of the savannahs and bayous that take possession of my mind every time I heard the word Louisiana).

Luronne: It was 1803, when Jefferson, intensely curious about unknown America, chose Meriwether Lewis for a great journey into the West. Curious not only about the Indians but also about the flora, the fauna, the hydrography, orology, and climatology; and he had his dream. We saw the dream form in his mind, following the line of a river from the upper Missouri, a stream which would prove navigable as far as that other river, the Columbia, which, since 1804, was known to come out into the sea.

Myself: But this river he's looking for, Luronne, it's the Northwest Passage all over again!

Luronne: If you like—and Jefferson took to hating the English, the masters of trade with the Orient. He saw the merchandise of those countries spreading freely in America, now that, thanks to this imaginary river, there was a route from the Pacific coast to the Atlantic. Lewis felt that he needed a second-in-command—Roger Clark, whom he placed on an equal footing with himself: and we watched the expedition get under way on May 14, 1804—forty-five men, including several smiths and carpenters. They left from St. Louis, Luronne's town; and as the flotilla weighed anchor we thought of her mother—thought of her with much emotion, for she was still sick.

Luronne spoke in short sentences often broken by long pauses, which was her way when she wished to share her feelings; and in the darkness her silences lengthened. I kept my eyes firmly shut so as to be able to concentrate successfully and to favor the birth of fleeting visions—images that I ran down faster than a dog hunting its prey, if they resisted me: but from time to time I also opened them. They were so used to the darkness that they appeared to me to be seeing. At this moment they were inspecting York, a member of the expedition and a black into the bargain. Easy to imagine that, like Estebanico two hundred and fifty years earlier, he astonished the Indians, who knew no races other than themselves and the whites. Some two hundred miles above St. Louis we saw the Osages, the friendly Osages. On the left, the Kansas prairies, admired by the men of the expedition. In May, they were at La Charrette.

Myself: You would think we were in Poitou!

Luronne: La Charrette, the last white settlement. Beyond that, Indian country. (Which I gazed at, looking above and beyond La Charrette.)

Luronne: Day after day they rowed when the breeze failed, or when there were rapids, they carried their boats over a portage.

(I beat the drum of love for America; and the painters of Indians, George Catlin, Karl Bodmer, Charles Russell, Alfred Jacob Miller and Frederic Remington lent me their wild scenes of buffalo hunting or their calm landscapes of rounded hills rolling away into infinity: I was happy when Luronne was talking, happy when she fell silent.)

We reached the country of the Ottoes, the Missouris, and the Pawnees, who complained of the Shoshonis. An old story. Then an unpleasant incident—the desertion of Moses Reed, who had had enough of it. He was caught, and stripped to the waist he had to pass between two ranks of men drawn up face to face while they lashed him right and left. Horrifying. His sentence obliged him to go through this twice again, and the Indian chiefs stepped in, deeply shocked by such barbarity.

Myself: moved, delighted: No!

Luronne: Yes: but Lewis and Clark disregarded them. The expedition traveled on into Sioux country, and Lewis set fire to the prairie.

Myself: No!

Luronne, irritated: It's the custom when you want to invite

Indians to a council. The Sioux were Yonktans. The great chief Shake Hand was there, and his three lieutenants, White Crane, Struck by Pawnees, and Half Man. For the first time Lewis and Clark went through the performance that they were to repeat throughout their journey: they hoisted the American flag, made speeches, and handed out medals. Smoking a pipe meanwhile.

I watched, suspicious.

And, for a long while, I gazed at the buffaloes, one herd of which the two captains judged at five hundred head.

Now we were among the Teton Sioux, with their chief Black Buffalo and his second-in-command, Partisan. Impressive: and I was impressed. Black Buffalo's scalp was clean-shaved, all but a little round patch from which there hung a pony-tail with feathers and porcupine quills stuck into it, while in front of it he wore a great headdress of eagle's feathers, and they gilded. Need I say that he was totally unlike the phony Sioux of Caughnawagha?

I was struck by the number of French traders the expedition came across. They made wonderful interpreters, of course. Then Lewis and Clark reached this village of Arikaras: York was a great success, and I watched the Indians come up to him and scratch his skin, supposing that they could remove the blackness. And here were the Arikaras refusing the whiskey the white men offered them.

Myself: Bravo!

Luronne: Exceptional, alas. Among the Arikaras, the women all wanted York rather than the white men.

I was amused—and I noticed that in speaking of these Indian women, Luronne did not say *squaws*, as ignorant people do: she knew that *squaw* was an Algonquin word, comprehensible to Algonquins alone.

Luronne: Once again a man committed some crime. He was punished with a flogging, and look—an Arikara chief, watching the scene, bursts into tears.

Myself: The too-human savages.

275

We uttered a wry laugh and it began to grow cold. Lewis and Clark had to think of winter quarters, and these they set up in the neighborhood of the Mandans, the Annahaways, and the Gros Ventres. The expedition had traveled nearly fifteen hundred miles, and now the Missouri tended away to the west. The white men fraternized chiefly with the Mandans, who had recently suffered much from smallpox.

It was at this point that she made her appearance, together with her bigamous French-Canadian husband, and joined the band—Sacajawea, the bird woman, the boat woman, a Shoshoni whom the Hidatsas had kidnapped as a child and who had never returned to her own country.

Myself, happily: We've already spoken about her. (I was very fond of her.)

Luronne: She was pregnant, and Lewis and Clark were doubtful about taking her on. But she spoke Shoshoni and they could see that she was remarkably intelligent. From that time on the two captains never made a move without consulting her.

(And in so doing they increased my happiness.)

I saw the men build a fort, go hunting, and suffer from the winter to such an extent that the sentries had to be relieved every half hour—one night the temperature fell to forty degrees below zero.

I clung to the Mandans, who danced the buffalo dance, and another night the cold reached minus sixty-five degrees.

Myself: No!

Luronne: Yes. The buffalo were hunted on snowshoes, and on February 11, 1805, Sacajawea had her baby, a strong healthy boy, the birth being helped, it seems, by a potion made from water in which a piece of rattlesnake's tail had been pounded. Sacajawea's labor lasted less than ten minutes.

I saw Baptiste being born among the Gros Ventres in the bitter cold. My mind was full of Catlin's pictures. At four in the morning of April 7 the expedition set off again to make its way into a country that no white man had ever yet seen.

A country that I urged Luronne to reach.

This she did, and we saw Lewis and Clark discover the grizzly bear, and come to the meeting of the Yellowstone and the Missouri, a place sometimes swept by sandstorms, sometimes blanketed with fog. For the first time they beheld the Rockies.

Myself: Wait . . . I looked at them from far, far away and my heart beat as though I were actually there. In fact they were the Little Rockies. This was the time to look for the Shoshonis and borrow horses from them to cross the mountains. The men dug holes to cache food, instruments, records . . . A column of vapor rose into the air—the great roaring falls of the Missouri, and they, the first white men to reach the spot, gazed at them in fascination.

I gazed and listened with them.

Luronne: The expedition found its progress toward the Three Forks of the Missouri very hard going indeed. Men were so worn out they fainted. Now Sacajawea recognized her own country, that of the Shoshonis. With a small body of men, Clark scouted out ahead and nearly reached the Columbia; but it was impossible to find the Indians, who were hiding. On August 11, 1805, Lewis saw two of them with his field glasses: about two miles from the expedition and they were moving toward it. Lewis was sure of it—they were Shoshonis.

(Looking through Lewis's field-glasses, I watched them coming toward me. He was right: Shoshonis.)

Luronne: One of them never dismounted, on principle. He was Cameahwait, that is to say, He Who Never Walks. On this exceptional occasion, however, he consented to jump down from his horse, and putting his left hand over Lewis's right shoulder he rubbed his Indian chief's cheeks against those of the white leader. Marvelous welcome. Sacajawea, alas, was away on a scouting trip with Clark. The Shoshoni and the American conversed by signs. At last she arrived and surprise! Miracle! She was He Who Never Walks' own sister.

Myself: No, no. I don't believe you.

277

Luronne: You're wrong. It's absolutely true. Lewis and Clark, who had always had their doubts, now admitted it— Sacajawea was of the royal blood of He Who Never Walks.

(Happiness stifling me, and this knowledge that Sacajawea was finding her country and her people once again.)

Luronne: To reach the Columbia, they had to cross the Bitter Root Mountains, a difficult range. Clark had come back full of tales about the Indians he had met and in a way discovered. They had never seen a white man, and they gave him a splendid welcome.

Myself: Of course.

Now the expedition was crossing the Rockies and I saw them climb, zigzagging, pause for breath and start again, the men slipping, recovering their balance and going on, enduring rain, hail, hunger. They reached the Kooskooskee.

Myself: The what?

Luronne: The river Clearwater, in the Nez Percé language. For here, at the beginning of 1806, we are with the Nez Percés.

Myself: Stop.

These were the "noble Indians," if I may put it like that. The antithesis of the Comanches. My respectful, admiring eyes settled on the greatest among them, Chief Joseph, then upon those other chiefs, Looking Glass the Elder, White Bird, Toohulhulsote, Lean Elk, and Poker Joe.

Then in a whisper: Go ahead.

Luronne: They entrusted their horses to Twisted Hair, a Nez Percé chief. The expedition's carpenters built canoes, and then the men went down the Snake, a serpentine river that leads to the Columbia. For the first time since they left St. Louis, they were running with the current. Twisted Hair's confidential remark to Lewis and Clark: when I first saw you from far off, I was afraid; but then I said that evil-intentioned men would never have brought a woman with them.

Myself: Admirable!

And I commended Sacajawea.

Luronne: On October 16 they reached the Columbia at last, and Lewis solemnly drank its waters.

Myself: Wait—let me drink with him.

Well, go ahead.

Luronne: They still had to cross those mountains that are so aptly called the Cascades, and the expedition chanced upon some Chinooks, great salmon-eaters, and as friendly as the Nez Percés.

Myself: I follow you.

So we crossed over the Cascades, and now the Pacific Ocean heaved in sight. I had never seen it, yet I had been dreaming about the Pacific ever since 1513, when Balboa discovered it.

Sea otters swam around the canoes and the men explored the Columbia estuary. When they landed they carved their names on trees, like children or people in love. They had got there.

Myself: They've got there.

Luronne: America has been discovered.

And, my mind wholly taken up with Lewis and Clark, I repeated Luronne's words: America has been discovered.

Then: Go ahead.

Luronne: It's finished. America has been discovered. There's nothing unknown left in America, apart from a few remote parts of Alaska, the inner plateaus of the Rocky Mountains, and the Arctic islands. Nothing that's worth telling about: and in any case I've not read further than Lewis and Clark.

(So those words of hers at the beginning which I had understood more or less as "we are coming to the end today" must have meant that she was not going to talk about America anymore.)

Myself: It's not possible.

Luronne: But America's been discovered, I tell you.

Myself: What about the Indians on the other side of the Appalachians, after the Proclamation Act?

Of course I had been quite right to be afraid of the unbalanced George III and the weakness of an England so far away—and to dread the disobedience of the American whites. A revolting story, and one that Luronne had tried to suppress so as not to disappoint nor wound nor grieve me, and also because she was tired of it and wanted to be done. As though I could ever have forgotten that great hope of an Indian nation!

Now I understood why she had been avoiding the Indians these last days, avoiding them as far as she could without falsifying History too blatantly. Fear of going back to the tragic tribes. If she hadn't interrupted and prevented my speaking on two occasions when I wanted to ask how things were going on in the country beyond the Appalachians promised to the Indians, I might have learned the truth earlier. I had been cheated, the first time with Chateaubriand, with Jefferson the second. Knowing me, she was sure that with these two white men she could turn my attention from the Indians.

They had not just sat there, watching the English and Americans fighting in the distance! They too had been obliged to fly to arms and attack the settlers to save their land, thus bringing about the army's retaliation. An abominable tale, but one that I wanted to hear and that Luronne agreed to tell me, including everything this time—the coup de grace, as it were.

In the first place, and to begin at the beginning as you might say, it was doubtful that the number of Indians in North America when Columbus arrived was only a million, as people have always thought. Very recent studies lead one to believe that the population of the continent from north to south amounted to a hundred million, and that North America was inhabited by ten or even twelve million five hundred thousand: this means that mumps, smallpox, syphilis, white men, and alcohol, to say nothing of humiliation and despair, must have killed ten or twelve times more Indians than had been supposed. A demographic disaster unparalleled in time or space.

Then the lies by omission: Luronne concealing a smallpox epidemic in 1780 that carried off half the Indians of Canada. Luronne, during the War of Independence, in which the whites were historically more important, concealing the fact that the Indians also took part. Choosing, alas, the English side, the losing side, against the land-hungry Americans. In 1779 Sullivan led an expedition against Thayendanegea, otherwise Joseph Brant, and his British allies; and this expedition set about a systematic Indian hunt, destroying forty towns and villages in the Six Nations country, without distinction of friend or foe. In 1794 Anthony Wayne launched his devilish column against the Six Nations once more, and reduced the Iroquois, lately so proud and beautiful, this time forever. That witless remark of Fenimore Cooper: "The white invasion of the United States was accomplished without those shocking injustices and brutality which have characterized other invasions elsewhere."

And all at once History paused, as though ashamed of the horrors it was piling up. For a few moments it grew calm and happy with Audubon, the greatest ornithologist in the history of men or birds, who reached America in 1803, and I listen to the twittering, the fluttering of wings and cooing murmurs of the lesser egret, the ruddy duck, the gray sea eagle, the marbled godwit, the Anna hummingbird, the flicker, the red-headed woodpecker, the eastern bluebird, the cedar waxwing, the yellow warbler; and I do not know which I like more, the birds or their names; but you can do nothing against men with birds, and after this interlude History carried on with the record of their crimes.

Even so, Luronne found it hard to come to the Proclamation Act. I had to remind her of her promise to tell me everything. I remembered my enthusiasm, my hope, when Luronne told me about the royal decision, and, the one in the other, I had believed in it. At this point History was, if possible, even more abominable than before.

It possessed the ferocity of thousands of settlers who, in spite of the prohibition, were waiting in West Virginia for a chance to get to Kentucky, from which hunters were perpetually returning with tales of paradise. In October 1772, that is to say nine years after the Proclamation Act, the Pennsylvania

281

and Virginia papers brought out notices inviting those who wished to acquire land in Kentucky to gather next spring at the mouth of the Great Kanawha. The Indians and the settlers were to fight with such ferocity that both sides, in agreement for once, adopted an Indian expression and called Kentucky the Dark and Bloody Land.

And now a memory came back to me: as a child, deep in Daniel Boone's autobiography, I had felt all his own enthusiasm that morning when he discovered the plateau of Kentucky, which he called Kentucke—Boone, who never suspected that in his flight from civilization he created it wherever he saw fit to stop and to kill Indians in order to make a settlement. His account is so full of killed and wounded that it is less a book than a hospital. He lost a brother and two sons at the hands of the Indians. As in the finest hours of Luronne's enthusiasm, I took a last look at the Shawnees, the Cherokees, the Hurons, the Delawares, the scalp hunters, the greedy landgrabbers, and the country that is so much praised for its bluegrass, although for my part I saw it red.

We were reaching the dénouement. John Adams had lied: this eighteenth century was the worst of them all. In 1783 the whites in the absurdly protected country of Kentucky numbered twenty-five thousand, and more were pouring in every day. In 1801, with the dead century's corpse still warm, the whites in America amounted to five million. As opposed to three hundred thousand in 1701! Too many, too many by far. A terrifying increase, and panic seized upon Tecumseh, a Shawnee, the greatest of that handful of Indians who tried to bring about a union of their own people, from the Seminoles of Florida to the Osages of Missouri. When I saw him beginning his tour of the wigwams and tepees I wanted to cry out to him that I'd already seen it all, that I no longer believed in it, that it was too late, and that I advised him to submit to fate, to drink, and to let himself be deported. It was all over. I didn't want to know anymore. I didn't want to hear anymore. I no longer listened. I did not want to see my dream die with Tecumseh's downfall, the great dream of a happy America, of the driving back, the expulsion of the whites, the dream I lived through with Philip, Popé, and Pontiac. Luronne was right: America had been discovered.

The next day Luronne went out. She was going to buy Christmas presents for her family—she meant to take me to see them—and for me. I had spent a sleepless night, rarely dropping off for more than five minutes at a time, my mind harrowed by incessant fugitive visions of Indians and of Luronne. So she had failed. And lied, because even with the Proclamation Act she had felt herself powerless to change the course of History. I had hoped that the great statesmen of American Independence, who were full of reservations about westward expansion, would have given her the extra help she may have felt she needed in spite of the British support. Why and how she had failed when I loved her so and expected so much from her, I shall never know. No doubt you asked too much of her, and no doubt she lacked a certain quality. I had some reason to believe that this was the case, since I knew that the Indians were despoiled, the great animals slaughtered, the American forest destroyed. When she had closed the door behind her, I got out of bed.

I brought down my two suitcases with the same lightness of heart I should have felt had I been leaving for a happy journey. The difficulties began the moment I set about packing. All at once I was so much alone that I could not bear it. I absolutely had to have someone beside me, next to me, shoulder to shoulder, someone to warm you because your teeth are chattering, someone to hold you if you fall, because you're staggering.

Talking to myself, instinctively splitting myself in two, I found this companion. First you put your shoes in the suitcase. At the bottom. Then all your underclothes. Shirts. Ties. Don't forget your electric shaver. The cord. Books in the other case. Fine. Now shut them. Put them down on the floor. There. It's done.

Then you ring for the elevator. You go down to the doorman on the ground floor. Stand up straight. Smile at him. You ask him to call a cab. You slip him a tip. He hurries out into the street to flag one down. You go up again. Take your baggage. This sudden tearing of your heart. Nothing serious. Don't be afraid. All right, so you're gasping. Breathe deep—there—take it easy. Sit down. The cab will wait: pull yourself together. Don't hurry, walk naturally: you're doing nothing that's not perfectly usual—everybody's left a woman sometime or another—nobody dies of it.

The driver gives you a look, then another, then another. Now he's happy: you're not drunk. You just tripped over a suitcase. The doorman opens the door for you. You collapse, recover, sit up. Brother, the worst is over.

Maybe. Through the open glass partition the friendly driver talks to me. We go down Riverside Drive and I look at the little private residences I'm so fond of, with their carvings and moldings. On my right, the Hudson. Verrazano's river, Hudson's, Luronne's, and mine. I feel sick. The cab has taken Forty-sixth Street; we've already passed Columbus Circle, and here is Central Park, where we so often came to take a walk, to see the gorilla in its cage. I feel very sick. I recognize the theater district: Times Square already and Forty-second Street, where we used to hurry when crazy fits inflamed us. I'm so very sick. Good-bye to the stone lions forever guarding the New York Public Library, the biggest in the United States and therefore one of the places that smells more of books than anywhere else in the world: yet a place we never came to, Luronne and I. I'm so ill we'll have to stop. But where are we? We've already crossed Park Avenue and Third; we're on Second and I can see the Queens-Midtown tunnel. You can't stop in a tunnel. This one goes under the East River, which ranks only third in our love for rivers of New York, coming after the Hudson and the Harlem for Luronne and me. I'm going to die, it hurts me so. We're out of Manhattan: here is Queens Expressway. People have stayed at home for the holidays. The end of the

Van Wyck Expressway. Here's the airport: maybe we're reaching it just as Luronne walks into the apartment. Open, open—the pain's killing me.

When the driver leaves, the Other takes me over again. You pick up your bags. Fine. Easy. Toward the counter. You ask whether there's a seat in the plane for Paris this evening. Splendid. Hold your ticket tight. Go around this way—they take your luggage. Fine. You've plenty of time. Go and sit down over there. It's comfortable. Read. No, sleep. Yes, sure you can—well anyhow, doze. There. Because it'll hurt less if you sleep.

When the voice on the loudspeaker asked the passengers to go to the departure gate, night had fallen. I hadn't the strength to get up: the Other appeared—come along. Be strong. See where they're milling about, down at the far end by the barrier—that's where you must show your ticket. Right. It's all in order. Yes, I know: you're sick: a few yards more, go through the barrier, it's done.

I'd not walked twenty yards, with him talking to me, bearing me up, before I heard her. Perhaps she'd just arrived or perhaps she'd been at the airport some time, looking for me in vain. A cry that stopped me dead. I turned and saw her there the other side of the barrier, her face all ravaged. Mine couldn't have looked much better. She called again, and her words, rising above the noise of the crowd, struck me head on: "Why are you going?" and in the huge quivering silence that had just fallen I scarcely had to raise my voice to answer, "America has been discovered."

She bowed her head and I walked on. Alone forever, because from this time forward, I should no longer need anyone at all.